The Winter Bride

Katie Flynn is the pen name of the much-loved writer Judy Turner, who published over ninety novels in her lifetime. Judy's unique stories were inspired by hearing family recollections of life in Liverpool during the early twentieth century, and her books went on to sell more than eight million copies. Judy passed away in January 2019, aged eighty-two.

The legacy of Katie Flynn lives on through her daughter, Holly Flynn, who continues to write under the Katie Flynn name. Holly worked as an assistant to her mother for many years and together they co-authored a number of Katie Flynn novels.

Holly lives in the north east of Wales with her husband Simon and their two children. When she's not writing she enjoys walking her two dogs, Osiris and Tara, in the surrounding countryside, and cooking forbidden foods such as pies, cakes and puddings! She looks forward to sharing many more Katie Flynn stories, which she and her mother devised together, with readers in the years to come.

Also available by Katie Flynn

A Liverpool Lass
The Girl from Penny Lane
Liverpool Taffy
The Mersey Girls
Strawberry Fields
Rainbow's End
Rose of Tralee
No Silver Spoon
Polly's Angel
The Girl from Seaforth Sands
The Liverpool Rose
Poor Little Rich Girl
The Bad Penny
Down Daisy Street
A Kiss and a Promise
Two Penn'orth of Sky
A Long and Lonely Road
The Cuckoo Child
Darkest Before Dawn
Orphans of the Storm
Little Girl Lost
Beyond the Blue Hills
Forgotten Dreams
Sunshine and Shadows
Such Sweet Sorrow
A Mother's Hope
In Time for Christmas
Heading Home
A Mistletoe Kiss
The Lost Days of Summer
Christmas Wishes
The Runaway
A Sixpenny Christmas
The Forget-Me-Not Summer
A Christmas to Remember
Time to Say Goodbye
A Family Christmas
A Summer Promise
When Christmas Bells Ring
An Orphan's Christmas
A Christmas Candle
Christmas at Tuppenny Corner
A Mother's Love
A Christmas Gift
Liverpool Daughter
Under the Mistletoe
Over the Rainbow
White Christmas
The Rose Queen
The Winter Rose
A Rose and a Promise
Winter's Orphan
A Mother's Secret
The Winter Runaway
Forgotten Child

Available by Katie Flynn writing as Judith Saxton

You Are My Sunshine
First Love, Last Love
Someone Special
Still Waters
A Family Affair
Jenny Alone
Chasing Rainbows
All My Fortunes
Sophie
We'll Meet Again
Harbour Hill
The Arcade
The Pride
The Glory
The Splendour
Full Circle

Katie Flynn

The Winter Bride

PENGUIN BOOKS

PENGUIN BOOKS

UK | USA | Canada | Ireland | Australia
India | New Zealand | South Africa

Penguin Books is part of the Penguin Random House group of companies whose addresses can be found at global.penguinrandomhouse.com

First published by Century 2025
Published in Penguin Books 2025
001

Copyright © Katie Flynn, 2025

The moral right of the author has been asserted

Penguin Random House values and supports copyright. Copyright fuels creativity, encourages diverse voices, promotes freedom of expression and supports a vibrant culture. Thank you for purchasing an authorised edition of this book and for respecting intellectual property laws by not reproducing, scanning or distributing any part of it by any means without permission. You are supporting authors and enabling Penguin Random House to continue to publish books for everyone. No part of this book may be used or reproduced in any manner for the purpose of training artificial intelligence technologies or systems. In accordance with Article 4(3) of the DSM Directive 2019/790, Penguin Random House expressly reserves this work from the text and data mining exception.

Typeset in 11.18/14.2pt Palatino LT Pro by Six Red Marbles UK, Thetford, Norfolk
Printed and bound in Great Britain by Clays Ltd, Elcograf S.p.A.

The authorised representative in the EEA is Penguin Random House Ireland, Morrison Chambers, 32 Nassau Street, Dublin D02 YH68

A CIP catalogue record for this book is available from the British Library

ISBN: 978–1–80495–385–3

 Penguin Random House is committed to a sustainable future for our business, our readers and our planet. This book is made from Forest Stewardship Council® certified paper.

To Jasmine and Adrian, with all my love

Prologue

1ST MARCH 1942

Isla Donahue could barely contain her excitement as she gazed at her reflection in the mirror which stood on top of the dressing table. Lifting a hand to her auburn curls, which had been pinned neatly into place, her attention was drawn to the intricate stitching of the pearls which buttoned the cuffs of her wedding dress.

She had long dreamed of marrying her Prince Charming. Tall, dark and handsome, he would dote on her just as her father had worshipped her mother. They would have a fairytale wedding that would make Cinderella herself green with envy, and their idyllic marriage would be matched only by her own parents'. In short, they would live happily ever after.

But of course dreams don't always come true, and Isla's had been well and truly shattered the day her mother died giving birth to her baby brother, who had also perished. The devastating loss had brought both Isla and her father to their knees. Unable to cope, her father had done the unthinkable and abandoned his daughter to Coxhill poorhouse whilst he sailed the ocean waves.

Isla knew all too well that the only people who got out of Coxhill did so in a wooden box. Determined not to be one of them, Isla had come up with a plan of escape along with the help of Sophie and Meg, two of the girls whom she had befriended whilst in the poorhouse. As far as they were aware they had been the first inmates to make it out of Coxhill alive, something which they had first put down to good fortune, but when things continued to go their way, they began to suspect that they might have had help from a guardian angel in the form of Isla's mother, Agnes, for the series of events which had taken them from Clydebank to Liverpool had seemed too fortuitous to be down to coincidence alone.

Now, as Isla used a finger to smooth down an eyebrow, she recalled the string of incidents that had led them to this conclusion. It had all started when Miss Harman, the woman who ran Coxhill, was in the middle of dishing out a dose of corporal punishment to Sophie. Until that point they had no idea that one of the staff, Harvey Ellis, was a private detective who was secretly working undercover in order to expose Harman's cruel regime. Had he not walked into the dining hall when he had, Miss Harman would've undoubtedly burned Sophie's hand, which she was holding over a naked flame, with disastrous consequences. A faint smile touched Isla's lips now as she remembered how Harvey had helped them to escape. *We thought all our Christmases had come at once when we left Coxhill – until the air raid sounded. I remember thinkin' then it was typical of our luck, but had we not been down that shelter I'd never have known who Rory was, and whilst we never actually spoke to one another then it did mean that I heard all about his girlfriend Tammy Blackwell and her rotten father Dennis.* When the all clear had sounded, Isla and her friends had hurried off to the train station leaving Rory to look for his girlfriend in the hope that she wasn't amongst the dead. *I never expected to see or hear from Rory again,* Isla remembered now, *and when Theo came to my rescue after my havin' boarded the wrong train, I thought that it was he and I who were destined to be together. It was only as time progressed that I realised we weren't meant to be.* Isla had been the one to call their relationship off much to the disappointment of Theo, but the two had remained friends despite her discovering his dark past. Whilst she had long suspected that he'd been hiding something from her she hadn't thought for one minute that he'd been widowed whilst having an affair with his wife's best friend. The unwelcome news had been relayed to Isla whilst she was waiting for Theo at a bus stop. When he had finally arrived her first reaction had been to tear a strip off him, but he quickly explained that the war was the reason behind their hasty decision to marry and, even though they had thoroughly regretted their decision to wed so young, their inability to divorce had seen them stuck in a loveless marriage. She still hadn't agreed with his infidelity but neither did she think he should be punished for something he did at such a young age for the rest of his life.

It wasn't long after this that she had met Rory in the Grafton ballroom, something which had come as a complete surprise considering she had no idea that he was stationed in RAF Woodbury not far from her base in Fazakerley. *From the moment we started to talk I just knew that we were meant to be together,* Isla reminded herself as she applied her lipstick sparingly, *and when he told me that he felt the same way, I thought I couldn't be any happier until the day he proposed that is . . .*

A frown creased her brow. How odd! She knew that Rory had proposed, but for the life of her she couldn't remember just how he'd done it. She hesitated. *Had* he proposed? She tutted irritably: of course he had, or she'd not be getting married today. But even so, why couldn't she remember it? Thinking that the excitement of the day was clouding her memories, her attention was drawn to the mirrored reflection of the door as someone knocked. 'Hello?' she said expectantly.

When the caller failed to reply she turned in her seat, thinking that they hadn't heard her. 'Hello?' she repeated, but instead of answering the caller slowly opened the door, and to her delight, shock and surprise Isla's father, Patrick, entered the room.

Leaping to her feet, Isla lifted her skirts as she rushed across the room to fall into his arms, tears streaming down her cheeks as she sobbed uncontrollably. 'You said you'd be back for me in a couple of months, but that was eighteen months ago! Where've you *been*?'

Hugging her close, Patrick spoke soothingly. 'I know, and I meant to come back, but you know what it's like. Life just gets in the way sometimes.'

Isla lifted her chin. 'Life gets in the way?' she repeated, her voice rising. 'I've been goin' out of my mind with worry, not knowin' whether you were dead or alive, and that's your reply? *Life gets in the way?*'

He tousled her hair, as though she were a child. 'Look on the bright side – better late than never, eh?'

She wriggled out of his arms. 'You walk in here, after leavin' me in that godforsaken place, as though you've not a care in the world! For God's sake, Dad, you haven't even bothered to apologise!'

He held up his hands in mock surrender. 'All right, so I apologise. Happy? Now if you're ready we'd best be gettin' you to the church.'

Isla couldn't believe what she was hearing. 'How can you act as if nothin's happened? You come in here—' She stopped in her tracks. How had he known where she was? She stared at him accusingly; something wasn't right. 'How did you know that I was gettin' married? Come to that, how did you know to find me in Liverpool when you last saw me in Clydebank?'

'A father knows these things,' he said, tapping the side of his nose in a conspiratorial fashion. He then eyed her accusingly. 'I take it you *do* want me to walk you down the aisle?'

'Well of course I do,' she snapped irritably. Her frown returned. 'But—'

He wagged a chiding finger. 'But me no buts, as your mammy used to say. If we don't leave now you'll miss your own weddin', and that would never do! I know he wasn't exactly your first choice, but even Theo deserves to have his betrothed turn up on time.'

Her lips parted slowly. 'What on earth makes you think I'm marryin' Theo?'

Her father eyed her sceptically. 'Who else would you be marryin'?'

'Rory!' she said brusquely. 'I don't know where you got the idea that I'm marryin' Theo from but you couldn't have got it more wrong if you tried!'

Patrick eyed her sympathetically. 'Sorry, lass, but it seems you're the one that's got hold of the wrong end of the stick. Rory's marryin' Tammy. Remember? His childhood sweetheart?'

Isla swayed as her father's words washed over her. How could he have got it so wrong? 'But Tammy's dead! She died in the air raid . . .'

He raised his brow in the most irritating manner. 'How can you say that when you've seen her with your own eyes?'

Isla's mouth hung open. 'How can I possibly have seen her? Tammy died the night we ran away from Coxhill. I should know – I saw the tenement where she lived, and there was nothin' left of it.'

'Then who was it that turned up at your base all that time later? Wasn't her name Tammy?'

Isla stamped her foot irritably. 'No! That was Mary – one of Harman's favourites from Coxhill. They only thought she was Tammy because she nicked Tammy's documents! Good God, she was even arrested for it.'

His brow rose slowly. 'That's *Miss* Harman to you, and as for Tammy, how do you explain the documents? When and where could she have stolen them?' He eyed her in what Isla considered to be feigned sympathy. 'I know you desperately want Rory to be your husband because you believe him to be your soulmate, but Tammy's his soulmate, not you.'

Isla spoke softly, her voice barely above a whisper. 'Why would you say that?'

'Because it's true, and what's more you know it.'

She was shaking her head fervently, new tears beginning to cascade down her cheeks. 'Why would you come back here after all this time just to be cruel?'

'I'm not bein' cruel,' said her father matter-of-factly. 'It's not my fault Tammy's still alive.'

'She's not!' Isla protested. But deep down she feared her father might be correct. Why else would Dennis Blackwell have marched into the police station claiming that his wife, Grace, and his daughter, Tammy, had struck him over the head before leaving him for dead? When Rory had told Isla of the rumours, he had dismissed them without question, claiming that the woman who'd started them had only done so because she hated Tammy. Isla, however, hadn't found the rumours so easy to bury. After all, why would Dennis have made the accusation of them running away if he really had killed them? Surely, he'd have realised the truth would out as soon as their bodies were discovered? She gave herself a mental shake. Even if Tammy had returned from the dead, there's no way that Isla would be marrying Theo.

She stood up. 'I haven't needed you for the last year, and I don't need you now,' she snapped as she headed for the door. 'I'm marrying Rory, and I'll prove it to you.'

Sweeping out of the room, she hurried down the steps of the hotel and ran outside, where she found herself inexplicably at the door of the church where she was due to be wed. Confused, she was about to storm down the aisle when she realised there was a wedding already taking place. Her cheeks reddening, she had turned to head back when Rory's voice called out from behind her, and she slowly rotated to see her beau walking towards her.

'Where are you goin'?' he asked, his kind brown eyes gazing at her with deep affection.

Isla glanced to the bride, who still had her back to them. 'Why didn't you tell me that Tammy was still alive? Why did you let me believe we had a chance of makin' a life together?'

He shrugged. 'I only found out myself that she was alive the other day. You must've realised I'd choose my childhood sweetheart over you, even if you are my soulmate.'

'But she left you thinkin' she was dead!' cried Isla. 'And after everythin' you'd done to help her and her mammy escape from her father, too.'

'No sense in cryin' over spilt milk . . .' Rory began, but Isla's outrage drowned his next words.

'*Spilt milk*? Is that what you'd call this? Because I

don't! You knew how scared I was that she'd come back for you, yet you swore you wouldn't go back to her, even if she did!'

'I'm entitled to change my mind,' said Rory simply.

She eyed him incredulously. '*Change your mind?*'

The bride, who was still standing before the altar, turned to face them, and Isla's heart plummeted. 'That's *not* Tammy!' she squealed, her voice rising several pitches. 'That's *Mary*, the woman who stole Tammy's documents!'

Rory slid his arm round Mary's waist as she arrived at his side. A wicked grin splitting her cheeks, she wagged a reproving finger as she eyed Isla evilly. 'Now, now, there's no point in bein' jealous. Rory's made his choice.'

Isla hid her face in her hands. How the hell could this be happening?

'Isla?' A soft voice cut across her thoughts.

She lowered her hands from her face to see who was saying her name, but Rory was the only one there. Looking around her, she heard the voice again, speaking more earnestly this time. 'Isla!'

Isla blinked as Rory's face morphed into that of her father, who was smiling at her. 'Aren't you goin' to answer her?'

'Who?' asked Isla, her voice barely above a whisper.

'My fiancée, Kate,' he replied simply, adding for clarity, 'you know the one, or you should do seein' as how the two of you are pals.'

'You cannae be talkin' about Kate Cunniff . . .'

He gave her a chiding smile. 'You're not *jealous*, are you?'

'Jealous?' Isla cried. 'She's the same age as me, which makes you old enough to be her *father*!'

His brow rose swiftly. 'So, you *are* jealous!'

Kate's voice cut across the two of them. 'Isla!'

'Don't shout at me!' snapped Isla, 'I'm not the one—'

'Isla, for goodness' sake wake up!'

Isla's eyes snapped open to see Kate looking down at her, her face masked with concern. 'That must've been one humdinger of a nightmare, cos you've been tossin' and turnin' in your sleep somethin' terrible.' She glanced at some of the other girls, who were peering over from their beds at Isla's blankets which were laying in a heap on the floor. 'You were shoutin' a fair bit, too.'

Relieved to learn that it had just been a nightmare but embarrassed to hear that she'd been shouting in her sleep, Isla pulled an apologetic grimace. 'I'm so sorry, I didn't realise ... I hope I didn't disturb anyone?'

'Don't worry. Reveille will be . . .' Kate's words were drowned out by the sound of the bugle, and she smiled kindly at Isla. 'Do you want to talk about it? The nightmare, I mean? Only you were ever so upset, and I know how realistic some dreams can be.'

Isla waved a dismissive hand. 'Thanks, Kate, but there's no need to worry. It was just my imagination gettin' the better of me. Besides, I'm off to see my pals in Worcester today, and a chat with them normally sorts me out.'

'If you're sure?'

Isla nodded as she swung her legs out of bed. 'Positive, but thanks for the offer.' She donned her greatcoat and picked up her wash bag. 'I'd best get a wriggle on if I'm to call in at Peggy's first!'

Chapter One

1ST MARCH 1942

With Isla stationed in Liverpool, Meg in Portsmouth, and Sophie in Scarborough, they had decided that it would be easier all round if they were to rendezvous midway between the three, which was why they had chosen Worcester.

'It might be a little longer for me,' Sophie had admitted to Isla when discussing their options over the telephone, 'but as I've been asked to drive some documents down that neck of the woods anyway, it's too good an opportunity to pass up.'

Now, as the train drew into Worcester station, Isla's face lit up when she saw Sophie and Meg waving to her from the platform. The very thought of spending the next forty-eight hours with them was already proving to be a real tonic, and she very much hoped that a little time with her pals would soon lay her worries to rest. She collected her bag from the rack above her head and made her way to the door of her carriage, where she waited patiently for the guard to open it.

Stepping down on to the frosty platform, she was immediately engulfed by her two best friends, who'd rushed to greet her with cries of delight.

'I know it's only been a little over a month since we saw you last, but it feels so much longer!' said Sophie, her breath clouding the air as she rocked Isla from side to side.

'I second that,' agreed Meg, who was currently squashed between the other two. 'I really miss bein' with the pair of you.'

'Same here,' said Isla. 'Hardly surprisin' considerin' we were practically livin' in each other's pockets when we were in Coxhill. Can you believe it's been a year since we escaped, give or take a couple of weeks?'

'A year!' breathed Meg. 'Has it really been that long?'

Sophie nodded. 'It probably doesn't feel like it for you and Isla because you were stationed together for a few months, but I was sent to Plymouth not long after we arrived in Liverpool.'

'I hate not havin' the two of you close to hand,' Isla told them, 'and whilst I'd like to think I'm copin' well without my bezzies – as they say in Liverpool – I had the rottenest nightmare last night!'

Sophie eyed her sympathetically. 'About Coxhill?'

'You'd think so, but no,' Isla said, before heaving a rueful sigh. 'Kate's a dear, but I had to decline her offer to talk it through, given she was a part of it.'

Meg looked surprised. 'She was?'

'Aye, but not the worst part. That was when Rory married Mary, believin' her to be Tammy!'

Sophie rubbed Isla's arm. 'Oh, Isla sweetheart, I

didn't realise you were still havin' nightmares. But no matter how realistic, you do know that's all they are, not some sort of premonition? Because that would be impossible, what with Tammy no longer bein' with us – may she rest in peace.'

'Only we don't know that for certain, do we?' Isla pointed out. 'Not if the rumours are to be believed, and as I've always said, there's no smoke without fire.'

'That might be true a lot of the time,' said Meg, 'but I wouldn't listen to a word that Mary said. She's nothin' but a spiteful gossip whose words should be taken with a pinch of salt, and a large one at that.'

Isla grimaced. 'I know, but—'

Sophie wagged a chiding finger. 'But nothing – Meg's right.'

Meg took Isla's bag whilst hooking her free hand through the crook of her friend's arm. 'You know what your trouble is?'

Isla shrugged. 'I'm paranoid?'

'Aye. Cos you cannae believe that you and Rory finally got together after your moonin' after him for the longest time, and it's playin' out in your dreams.'

Isla gave her a guilty grimace. 'That's *exactly* what Peggy said when I nipped in to see her this mornin'.'

'That's because she knows her onions,' said Sophie, adding wistfully, 'You're ever so lucky havin' Peggy so close to hand; not only is she wise, but she's the closest thing to a mother any of us have.'

Isla envisaged Peggy as she had appeared with her smiling blue eyes and soft features when they had first arrived in Liverpool. They had met her through

Harvey Ellis, and as soon as they'd explained their plight she'd taken the three of them under her wing, and had continued to be there for them ever since.

'She's one in a million,' agreed Isla as they stepped out of the station.

Steering Isla in the direction of the B&B where she and Sophie had checked in earlier that morning, Meg spoke the thought uppermost in her mind. 'I'm guessin' you haven't told Rory about your nightmares?'

Isla looked stunned. 'No I have not! And nor will I. The last thing I want is for him to think that I'm obsessed with his ex.'

'Even though you are,' Sophie pointed out, quickly adding, 'which is perfectly understandable given the circumstances behind your gettin' together. After all, you really didn't want to be the one to tell him about Mary stealin' Tammy's identity.'

'Too bloomin' right I didn't – talk about drawin' the short straw! I'm just lucky he took it as well as he did.' Isla heaved a sigh. 'I'm so grateful that I've got the two of you and Peggy to talk to. You're the only ones who will ever understand why I am the way I am. Anybody else would think me mad if I told them I was jealous of a ghost.'

'For a start you're not jealous of a ghost, you're worried the rumours might be true, and no one can blame you for that,' said Meg. 'Havin' said that, we all saw the tenement buildin' where Tammy and her mammy lived, and there's no way anyone could've come out of there alive, and the sooner you accept that the sooner you can lay her ghost to rest.'

Taking up the baton from Meg, Sophie added, 'Plus, if you don't put the past behind you, you're in real danger of pushin' away the love of your life.'

'A bit like what you did with Theo,' said Meg.

'I think you'll find that Theo's failin' to tell Isla the truth about his bein' a widower put an end to that relationship...' Sophie began, only to have Isla step in.

'You're both wrong. I decided to call it a day *before* I discovered the truth about his past.'

'Aye, you did that,' said Meg, adding with a wry smile, 'and all because you were in love with Rory, a man you'd never so much as spoken to.'

'But as we agreed at the time, the fact that I felt more for a man I didn't know than I did for Theo was proof enough that Theo and I didn't have a future together.'

'It's no wonder you've been havin' nightmares,' said Meg as they waited to cross the road. 'You've had an awful lot happen in a very short time.'

'You're tellin' me!' Isla said wholeheartedly as she began to tick off her run of bad luck. 'In the past two years I've lost not only my mammy but my baby brother too, on top of which I was dumped in the poorhouse by my own father who then buggered off to sea. And when I finally manage to escape, the man I thought to be my knight in shinin' armour turns out to have more hang-ups than the two of us put together!' She rolled her eyes. 'Is it any wonder I have trouble trustin' men when the two who've meant most to me have let me down in one form or another?

With my luck, it's only a matter of time before Rory does the same!'

'He won't, though, because they're totally different circumstances!' cried Meg as they walked alongside the perimeter of the park. 'Your father and Theo ran away because they couldn't cope with the death of their wives. Rory's never done anythin' remotely like that.'

'But Rory left Scotland for the RAF when he believed the love of his life to be dead, and if the rumours *are* true, and she *is* still alive, then there's every possibility that they might meet again, and where would that leave me? We've only been together for a couple of months, which is no time at all when you look at how long he and Tammy were together.'

'Rory's already told you that there'd be no future for him and Tammy even if she were alive!' said Meg in exasperated tones. 'And who can blame him? No matter the reason, you don't run out on someone who's put everythin' on the line for you. Good God, Isla! He'd never be able to trust her again.'

'That may well be, but I cannae afford to get lulled into a false sense of security just to have it go wrong at the last minute,' Isla said as they entered the B&B. 'It would be more than I could bear!'

'So what, then? Cos you cannae keep your guard up for ever,' said Sophie as she followed them inside. 'Or is it more a case of forewarned is forearmed? Are you hopin' that by preparin' for the worst you'll be able to cope better should it come to fruition? You must know that's not true. Even if you'd had advance warning of your mother's death, it wouldn't have made you feel any better when she did pass.'

'I don't know!' wailed Isla. 'I just know that I cannae help feelin' the way I do no matter how much I try to rationalise things.'

They paused their conversation as they entered a room at the back of the B&B where they found their hostess, a portly woman who was busy knitting what looked like the start of a jumper.

'Aha!' she said, her rosy cheeks breaking into a cheery smile as she stood up to greet her new arrival. 'Am I right in guessin' that you must be Isla?'

Isla smiled, grateful for the distraction. 'You are indeed.'

The woman placed her knitting down on her seat. 'Pleased to meet you, Isla. I'm Mrs Stebbins, but I insist you call me Dora.' As she spoke she took a key from a board of hooks and handed it to Sophie, who was nearest. 'The girls will show you what's what. I only ask that you leave the key with me before you go out so that it doesn't get lost, and that you're home before ten thirty else you'll find yourself locked out. Breakfast will be served between seven and nine a. m.'

'Sounds good to me,' said Isla. 'Shall I pay you now, or . . .'

Dora beamed. 'If you don't mind, dear. That'll be nine shillings.'

After a quick rummage in her purse, Isla handed over the money, which was swiftly pushed into Dora's apron pocket as she gave her thanks. 'Just give me a knock should you need anythin'; other than that

I shall look forward to seein' you at breakfast.' The girls bade their hostess goodbye, and trooped up the steep staircase which led to the third floor.

'Not bad, eh?' said Sophie as she opened the door to their room.

Isla was nodding with approval at the neat room. With its wooden floors and warmly papered walls, it put her very much in mind of the room they'd shared whilst living with Peggy. She glanced to the metal-framed beds. 'Have any of these been bagsied?'

'Feel free to take your pick,' said Sophie, before reverting to their earlier conversation. 'Gettin' back to your paranoia, you're simply goin' to have to learn to let things go.'

'But how do I do that?' said Isla, walking over to look out of the bedroom window.

'Time,' said Meg. 'It makes everythin' easier – better, if you like. It would be wonderful if we could give you some sort of advice that would fix every-thin' in the blink of an eye, but I'm afraid it's not as simple as that.'

Sophie joined Isla at the window. 'Even if your father had turned round on the doorstep of the poorhouse and taken you back home, do you really think you would ever have completely trusted him again, knowin' what his intention had been?'

Isla watched the people hurrying about their business on the street below. 'Possibly not.'

Meg gave her a shrewd glance. 'I don't think there's any "possibly" about it; there's no way you'd be able to trust him after that. You'd have been like a cat on a hot tin roof, constantly worried that he might decide to take you back to Coxhill at the drop of a hat.'

'I guess we'll never know, will we, considerin' he didn't bother to come for me when he said he would,' said Isla, her tone slightly sullen.

'Because sailors cannae jump ship at will,' Sophie chided. 'Be fair – you know as well as I do that he couldn't have done that no matter how much he wanted to.'

'He could've written,' Isla pouted. 'Peggy's hubby Clive writes and he's been at sea a lot longer than my dad.'

Sophie was about to speak when she appeared to have an epiphany. 'How do we know that he *didn't* write to you?'

'The absence of letters?' said Isla cynically.

'You truly believe Harman would've handed them over out of the goodness of her heart?'

'Of course not,' retorted Isla, somewhat petulantly, 'but surely he'd have wondered why I hadn't written back?'

'Maybe he did,' said Sophie reasonably, 'but unfortunately we'll never know for sure, what with Harman doin' time for fraud and Coxhill now a military hospital.'

'He could've gone to the polis and asked them to investigate. I could have been dead for all he knew!'

Uncertain whether it would be wise to put up another obstacle to Isla's theories when it seemed that's all she and Sophie were doing, Meg spoke slowly but deliberately. 'You're a balloon operator in the WAAF, so you know as well as I that the polis haven't the time or the resources to go chasin' after mail what's gone missin'.'

'Touché,' Isla conceded reluctantly.

'We're not tryin' to battle with you,' Sophie added, 'we just want to be fair to your father as well as to you.'

Isla relented. 'I know you do. I just feel guilty for blamin' him for doin' what he did, despite knowin' he only acted out of desperation – love, even.'

Sophie placed her arm around Isla's shoulders. 'Blamin' your father is easier than facin' the truth.'

'I'm overthinkin' everythin' again, aren't I?'

'Yes, but no one's blamin' you!'

Isla rested her head against the window frame. 'Why does life have to be so complicated?'

'Because we're all different, and a good job too. Imagine what the world would be like if everyone thought the same way as Hitler, for example.'

'Most likely be the end of the human race,' Isla grimaced.

'Exactly! So stop bein' so hard on yourself. We each muddle our way through as best we can. As long as you've a good heart – which you have – and you can look yourself in the mirror each mornin', then you're not doin' a bad job as far as I'm concerned.'

Isla mulled Sophie's words over as her thoughts drifted back to her father. Could Patrick look himself in the mirror after dumping his one and only child at Coxhill? *He might have thought it was his only choice, but he'll have struggled to live with his decision even so,* thought Isla, and said as much to Meg and Sophie, who both agreed.

'A tough row to hoe,' said Meg.

'A terrible burden to bear,' added Sophie sympathetically.

'I just hope I get to see him again some day, so that I can tell him that I understand why he did what he did and that I forgive him,' said Isla.

'You will,' said Sophie, 'cos your mammy will make sure of it.'

'And if I can rely on anyone it's her,' said Isla, 'cos she's done a crackin' job of lookin' out for me so far. In fact, everyone who's come into my life since she passed has helped me in one way or another, and I've learned something from each and every one of them.'

Meg eyed her curiously. 'What did you learn from me and Sophie?'

'That real friendship can get you through anything and everything,' said Isla, 'no matter what. It's why Theo and I remained close in spite of everything.'

Meg smiled. 'Cheers to that. Which reminds me – did you tell him there was no chance of the two of you rekindlin' your relationship? I know you were meanin' to.'

Isla pulled a sidelong grimace. 'I did, and what's more I felt a real heel havin' to break it to him when he's all the way out there in Africa.'

'What did he say?'

Isla shrugged. 'I don't know, cos I've not heard anythin' back and it's been a couple of months since I wrote.'

Sophie frowned. 'That doesn't sound like Theo. Do you think everything's all right?'

'That's what's been worryin' me. Theo's not the sort to give someone the cold shoulder or get the hump because they don't like what they've been told.'

'Maybe he's holdin' on to the hope that things might change,' said Meg. 'You did say that his parents were pretty keen for the two of you to keep in touch.'

'It's a possibility, but I'd be surprised if he chose to behave like a petulant child if that were the case.'

'You're forgettin' that he's only young,' said Meg. 'Eighteen's hardly any age, especially for a boy.'

'Granted, but Theo's the same age as you and me,' Isla said, 'and like us he's been through more than most for his age.'

'That's as may be, but war can have a funny effect on people, especially when they've been torn away from everythin' and everyone they know and love,' Sophie told them. 'There might be an eleven-year age gap between myself and the two of you, but you'd never know it, and that's down to everythin' we went through together in Coxhill. Hard times make people grow up faster than they should.'

'Which is why I hope that he's all right,' said Isla. 'I'd hate to think of him bein' miserable – or worse.'

'Why don't you write to him again?' Meg suggested.

'But what if I do and I just end up rubbin' more salt into the wound?'

'What about his mammy? You're still in touch with her, aren't you?'

'But what would I say?' Isla put on a sarcastic voice. 'Hello, Mrs Stratham. Have you heard from Theo? Only I broke his heart a while back and he hasn't replied to my letter.'

Meg rolled her eyes. 'Obviously not. You simply say you're concerned because you've not heard from Theo in some time. When all's said and done, it's not your fault that the two of you didn't work out, or that you're in love with someone else. Theo wanted to remain friends, and rather than tell him to sling his hook – as most women would've – you agreed, which he was bloomin' grateful for.'

'And so was I. Theo's a smashin' lad who doesn't deserve to have me turn my back on him because of something he did before we even met.'

'There you go, then,' said Meg. 'As far as I can see there's no harm in askin' after someone you genuinely care for.'

'I'll write to her as soon as I get back to base.' Relieved that they appeared to have come to the end of that conversation, Isla brightened. 'How's Kenny?'

'Devoted.' Meg smiled. 'And missin' me terribly already, I hope.'

'And are you still equally smitten?'

'Of course,' said Meg. 'Kenny and me go together like fish and chips.'

Isla looked to Sophie inquisitively. 'Not a dickie bird, and I'm happy that way,' said Sophie primly.

'No sign of that feller you quite liked?'

Meg's brow rose. 'Oh aye? And what feller's this?'

'His name's Blackbeard,' Isla chuckled, 'or at least that's what I call him.'

'And?' Meg wriggled her eyebrows at Sophie in a suggestive manner.

'And nothin',' said Sophie firmly. 'I saw him once and that was only fleetingly, when I was stationed in Plymouth. The closest I've come to chattin' to a feller was last September when Madson threatened me.'

Meg's face dropped in an instant. 'That pig! They should've slung him in the clink along with Harman...' She paused before asking with bated breath, 'You haven't seen him again, have you?'

No,' said Sophie, 'and I don't expect to either. He spouts nothin' but hot air. If he really wanted he could've lamped me one right there and then.'

'He wasn't blowin' hot air when he threatened Isla with the poker,' cried Meg, 'and had you not hit him in the head with the coal shovel I dread to think what the outcome would've been.'

'He *had* just caught us red-handed with the ledgers that he and Harman had made to defraud the government,' said Sophie reasonably.

'Aye, which is probably why he wants to get his own back,' said Meg quietly, 'hence his saying if he ever saw any of us again it would be for the last time. We all know what he meant by *that*.'

'He's not that stupid. He might hate the ground we walk on, but I don't think he'd willingly swing for us,' Sophie told her. 'And besides, he knows we're not afraid to strike back when threatened. He just wanted to put the frighteners on us because he believes that we're responsible for ruinin' his life, nothin' more, nothin' less.'

Isla's eyes were practically out on stalks. '*Us* ruin *his* life? Is he insane?'

'As far as he's concerned, if we'd not uncovered his and Harman's fraudulent dealings he'd still be sittin' pretty.'

'Yeah, but at the price of everyone else's misery,' muttered Isla.

'Men like Madson will never learn. They just blame everyone else for their mistakes. Well, if I ever see *him* again he'll be gettin' a piece of my mind,' said Meg firmly, adding, 'a large piece, because he needs to know that he cannae go round threatenin' innocent people just for the hell of it.'

'Madson's a bully who'll only confront someone when he thinks he has the upper hand,' said Sophie. 'That's why he made sure to keep a good distance between the two of us when he was shoutin' his mouth off.' She looked to Isla. 'He only tried to attack you because he had a weapon and he thought you'd not fight back.'

Isla grinned. 'Until I bit his wrist and kicked him in the shins!'

Sophie began to giggle. 'When you think about it, he'd have to be bonkers to attack either of us again!'

'I wish I'd arrived in time to see you in action, Sophie,' said Meg. 'That must be one crackin' aim you've got!'

'Aim had nothin' to do with it,' Sophie told her. 'I just grabbed the nearest thing to hand and threw it.

The fact that it connected with his head was pure luck. I don't know what would have happened if I'd missed.'

'He doesn't know that, though, does he?'

'He sure doesn't; as far as he's concerned I'm a psychotic woman with a fantastic aim,' said Sophie with a wry smile, 'and that's the way I'd like to keep it.'

'If I ever run into him, I'm goin' to do the same as Meg,' said Isla, 'cos you're right, Soph: men like him are only tough when they've a weapon to hand. Now, what's the plan for the rest of the day?'

'A stroll around the town?' suggested Sophie. 'Meg and I had a quick gander on the way to meet you at the station and there are some lovely little caffs on the high street.'

'Real food!' Isla said hungrily. 'Sounds good to me!'

Ian Madson stormed into the ablutions and headed straight for the nearest sink to throw cold water over his face, which was still burning from the dressing down he'd just received from the sergeant in charge of his platoon. With the water evaporating from his heated skin, he kicked out viciously at the sink. Never in his life had he been spoken to in such a manner, and especially not by someone whom he guessed to be a good ten years younger than himself. How the man had risen to the rank of sergeant was beyond him, and whilst he believed that the role didn't require a great deal of intelligence, he thought it did call for a modicum of common sense. *The man's an imbecile who cannae string a proper sentence together, yet he has the nerve to look down his nose at me?* Madson seethed as he glowered at his mirrored reflection.

As far as Madson was concerned it only stood to reason that a man of forty years plus couldn't be expected to do the same level of exercise as a man half his age, but the sergeant had thought otherwise and had decided to prove his point by bawling derogatory remarks at him as though that would suddenly give him the strength of the younger men. *I dare say he joined the army straight from school because he was too thick to do anythin' else, and he sees me as a threat because he knows I can run circles round him intellectually*, Madson thought now. *So he uses his physicality to belittle me because that makes him feel superior somehow.* The door to the ablutions had just opened, and he turned to see who had come in.

'Why, if it isn't Madson the moron,' chuckled the newcomer, a private named Bill who'd been on the parade ground when the sergeant had started to hurl insults.

'Don't you start,' growled Madson.

Holding his hands up in mock surrender, Bill walked over to join him at the line of sinks that flanked one side of the multi-cubicled room. 'I'm not havin' a go, just a laugh is all. You've got to learn to roll with the punches. I reckon there's not one man in this entire platoon that Sarge hasn't had a go at some time or other, so you needn't think he's singled you out.'

'How the hell that man expects me to keep up with the youngsters is beyond me,' snarled Madson. 'It's bloody obvious that I'm just too old for that type of crap! Before I came here I was dealing with the top dogs in the government, makin' important decisions that affected the lives of hundreds, not runnin' round in soddin' circles like a bleedin' hamster!'

Bill slowly arched an eyebrow. 'Are you sayin' that you think the services do less important work than what you used to do?'

Madson replied without thinking. 'A bloody monkey could do this job.'

Bill stiffened. 'I thought you were meant to be intelligent, but you'd have to be a complete idiot to think it safe for a monkey to handle a gun.'

Madson replied through thin lips. 'I'm sayin' that brain-dead jobs require brain-dead people, who are used to the mundane.'

Up until this point Bill had remained calm, but this was an insult too far. 'Are you callin' me brain dead?'

A short, balding man exited one of the cubicles. 'Ignore him, Bill. He's not worth the aggravation.'

But Bill wasn't going to let Madson's comment pass him by. 'If you were that bloody important, how come you're servin' as a private in His Majesty's army? Surely your government pals would've objected to you givin' up such a vital role? So why didn't they?' Seeing Madson evade his gaze, Bill nodded slowly to himself. 'You're either full of crap or you weren't as high up as you claim to have been. Which is it?'

'There is another alternative,' said the balding man. 'He could've signed up to do his bit.'

Madson nodded, but kept his gaze lowered. 'Nail on the head.'

Bill wasn't having any of it. 'Nah. Someone who signs up to do their bit doesn't care what job they're given as long as they're part of the war effort. From what I've heard you've whinged and whined from the moment you left basic training – probably before that too, I shouldn't wonder.'

Madson shook his head as he pushed past them. 'I don't have to explain myself to the likes of you.'

'The likes of *me*?' hissed Bill. 'What the hell do you mean by that?'

But Madson didn't reply; instead he strode out of the ablutions before the argument could escalate. After all, if it came to blows Bill would be the clear winner, something which would just add physical injury to Madson's already bruised ego. Striding towards his hut, he pushed his hands deep into his pockets. Ever since being drafted some eleven months previously he had found life in the services almost unbearable, and even though some people thought being in the ack-acks an enviable role, he hated performing what he saw as the same remedial tasks week in week out. In fact, the only way he could get through the days was to plan for his future once peace was declared. Ruling out a return to Clydebank on the basis that the locals would undoubtedly still bear a grudge for his involvement in Coxhill – something Madson found laughable, considering that they were the ones who'd surrendered their nearest and dearest to the system in the first place – he had been forced to turn his attention elsewhere. But exactly what he would do when he got to wherever it was he ended up was anybody's guess. Paperwork of some description was the obvious choice, but starting off in a new town or city wouldn't come cheap, and with all his earnings prior to losing his job gone on rent and food he only had his army wages to see him through. And they wouldn't be enough to give him a decent start. He turned his thoughts to the day Sophie and her pals had discovered the two sets of accounting books at the poorhouse. He had warned Harman time and again to leave the books to him, because he knew what he was doing. But she had refused, accusing him of trying to pull the wool over her eyes.

'How will I be able to keep track of everythin' if I don't even get to see the books?' she had asked, her eyes narrowing. 'If we're to do this then it's on my terms, which means both books stay with me.'

'And what if someone gets suspicious!' Madson had cried. 'If someone sees—'

'Well they won't, will they?' Harman had replied, ending the conversation.

Now he shook his head angrily as he continued on his way. 'I should've insisted,' he muttered to himself. 'If I had, I wouldn't be here and we'd still be on to a nice little earner!' He rolled his tongue around the inside of his mouth. He was good at fixing books, and he knew from some of his contacts that there were plenty of people who required a dodgy accountant. And even though he wasn't strictly an accountant, he knew the taxation system – and how to get around it – like the back of his hand. But starting up a business cost money, money he didn't have because Harman had insisted on keeping their misbegotten earnings under lock and key in her office where she believed them to be safe.

He hesitated. He'd automatically assumed the money would have been found along with the books, but what if it hadn't? Harman couldn't possibly have had time to move it elsewhere. But with the poorhouse now being used as a hospital for wounded soldiers, what *had* happened to it? His brow furrowed. If the authorities hadn't found it, then there was every chance it was still there. But where? He screwed his lips to one side. Would Harman be willing to tell him where the money was hidden if he were to go and visit her? On one hand it would be better than someone else coming across it by accident, because if that were to happen they'd both be out of pocket when she finally got out of jail. But on the other hand it might look suspicious if he visited her with the sole purpose of asking where the money was hidden, ergo he would have to assure her that it was as much for her benefit as his own. A malicious grin slowly made its way across his cheeks. He would suggest that he used her half of the money to hire a lawyer good enough to reduce her sentence. If that didn't appeal to her, then nothing would. His mind was made up: he would visit Harman at the first opportunity.

Chapter Two

3ʳᴰ MARCH 1942

It was their final day in Worcester and the girls were visiting their favourite café, the Cadena. 'Forty-eight hours goes by far too quickly,' Meg said as she hungrily eyed the plated scones which the waitress was setting down before them.

'Doesn't it just?' said Isla, taking a scone and slicing it in readiness for the jam and cream. 'It seems we've barely had a chance to say hello before we're havin' to say goodbye.'

'It might help if we weren't at opposite ends of the country.' Sophie licked jam from her thumb. 'I've been badgerin' them to send me to Liverpool ever since they posted me to Scarborough, but it's like talkin' to a brick wall. They nod and smile but nothin' ever happens.'

'It would be the icin' on the cake if you could both get posted to Liverpool. Peggy misses you like crazy, and so do I,' Isla said thickly through her mouthful of scone.

Meg began to pour the tea through the strainer into the cups. 'It's a shame she couldn't join us here.'

'I know, but she hardly gets to see Clive as it is, and what with his ship comin' into port . . . ' Isla raised her hands in a gesture of 'What can you do?'

'I guess that's the downside of bein' married to a sailor,' said Meg.

'I did suggest that both of them might like to come to Worcester, but with him only havin' one night's shore leave it would've been impossible.'

'It makes you realise how unfeasible it would have been for your father to come and see you in Coxhill,' said Meg. 'One night doesn't give you time to do much more than change your knickers, never mind anythin' else!'

Isla chuckled softly. 'I very much hope my father isn't wearin' knickers, but I suppose you're right.'

Sophie, who had been sent to the WRNS rather than the WAAF like her friends, spoke knowledgeably. 'Remember, the merchant ships tend to dock here there and everywhere because they're deliverin' goods all over Britain. That's probably why Clive hardly ever gets to see Peggy – not because he's in the West Indies or somewhere, but because he's trawling the coast of Britain with supplies.' Realising that she might have inadvertently suggested that Isla's father could've called in to see her, she quickly added, 'Although that doesn't mean to say your father docked in Clydebank at any stage.'

Isla smiled. 'I know.'

'Talkin' of your father,' Meg put in, 'I didn't hear a

peep from you last night. Am I to take it you slept well?'

Realising that she had indeed had a peaceful night's sleep, Isla smiled again. 'Like a baby! Which makes it the first night in a long time that I've not been disturbed by some awful nightmare.'

'That's wonderful!' Sophie exclaimed. 'Do you think it's because you were with us?'

'Definitely,' said Isla. 'I always sleep better when the three of us are together; talkin' things through with you helps massively because it enables me to see things from a different perspective.'

'Well, I sincerely hope that's the end of your nightmares, cos I know what it's like to have dreams that seem so realistic you have to wonder if there's some hidden meanin' behind them. I had some rotten ones when we first escaped Coxhill.'

Isla paused, her scone poised before her lips. 'Now I come to think of it I do remember you sayin' somethin' about havin' nightmares.'

Sophie stirred her tea. 'I didn't say too much; I didn't want to worry either of you unnecessarily, or put ideas into your heads.'

'So, what happened? In your dreams, I mean,' Meg asked.

Sophie's cheeks coloured as her eyes met Isla's. 'Don't read anythin' into this, but I dreamt that Madson came after us.'

Isla put her scone back down onto her plate. Keeping her eyes fixed on Sophie's, 'And he did!' she breathed.

'No,' Sophie said sharply, 'he was forced to join up and our paths just happened to cross, which is quite common when you're in the forces, as you both well know. And that's all it was, nothin' more, nothin' less.'

Meg locked eyes with Isla. 'Did you have any dreams about Mary before she turned up at your station?'

'Not a single one,' said Isla. 'In fact Mary was the furthest thing from my mind until she actually appeared.'

Meg visibly relaxed. 'Thank God for that!'

'Which just goes to prove my point!' cried Sophie with an air of satisfaction. 'You never dreamed about Mary because she wasn't in your thoughts. I dreamed about Madson, because I was worried that he might come after us. After all, it only stood to reason that he might, after me lampin' him one.'

'Which makes perfect sense,' agreed Meg.

'Aye. It didn't come true just because I had a dream about him, and neither will Isla's dreams about Tammy – or anyone else for that matter.' Sophie gave a cynical laugh. 'I mean, can you honestly see your father gettin' engaged to Kate?'

Isla's eyes widened. 'God no.'

'There you go then!' said Meg happily. 'Dreams are definitely not crystal balls!'

'Exactly!' said Sophie, adding, 'I mean, as if Rory would marry Mary!'

Meg was gazing out of the café window in a thoughtful manner. 'Talkin' of Mary, I wonder what happened after the polis caught up with her.'

Isla rolled her eyes. 'I should imagine she walked

free; people like Mary always get away with stuff like that.'

'But she *lied* . . .' Meg began, only to have Sophie talk over her.

'So did you and Isla, along with countless others.'

Meg was looking perplexed. 'No, we didn't.'

Isla took a sip of her tea. 'Well, we did, Meg, cos we weren't eighteen when we signed up.'

'A white lie, which is hardly the same,' Meg protested.

'A lie's a lie,' said Sophie reasonably, adding, 'Even so, they'll probably not keep a skilled balloon operator under lock and key when she could be helpin' to save her country.'

Meg tutted beneath her breath. 'Isla's right. People like Mary always come up trumps.'

'Apart from when she broke her toe in the laundry room,' Isla reminded her with a chuckle. 'There was only one winner that day and it was the mangle.'

'Serves her right for tryin' to kick me in the face – had she not been tryin' to earn brownie points with Harman in the first place her toe would've been just fine,' said Sophie. 'But it does feel good to know that people like her do get their comeuppance from time to time.'

'Do you honestly think they'll let her back into the services, though?' asked Meg, who was clearly aghast at the thought. 'Cos you've got to be able to trust the women you work with, especially on the balloons, and whilst Isla and I lied about our age we didn't half-inch the documents of a dead woman to get in.'

Isla agreed with Meg in theory, but she also knew

that the WAAF needed every woman they could get. 'I'd hope not,' she said after some thought, 'but could they really afford to turn her away when she already knows the ropes?'

'Possibly not,' sighed Meg. She looked to Sophie. 'At least you don't have to worry about bumpin' into her in the Wrens.'

'I won't deny that I'm less likely to come across her than either of you two,' conceded Sophie, 'but I do visit RAF and army bases as part of my job, so you never know.'

'Do any of us know how Mary came to be in Coxhill?' asked Meg, although she was really directing the question at Sophie, who had been at the poorhouse years longer than either herself or Isla.

'Not a clue,' said Sophie. 'You know what Mary was like! Hardly the sort to tell you her life story.'

Isla rested her chin in the palm of her hand. 'Surely she didn't have the same lousy attitude when she first arrived?'

Sophie's eyes rounded. 'She most certainly did! I remember the day she came in. She might have had a face like thunder, but it was obvious from the get-go that she was one of Harman's favourites. She wasted no time at all in gettin' her feet under the table.'

'I thought you had to earn Harman's favours?' said Isla, somewhat confused as to how Mary had managed to skip that part of the process.

'You're right, most people do, but not Mary,' said Sophie. 'No idea how or why, but it was crystal clear that they were on the same side from the word go.'

'That still doesn't answer the question as to how she came to be in Coxhill,' said Meg.

Isla pulled a downward smile. 'What difference does it make?'

'None, I suppose,' said Meg, 'but I'm a firm believer in people bein' shaped by their environment, which must be why Mary made sure that she was one of Harman's favourites from the off.'

Isla was nodding slowly. 'I've heard as how weak people pair up with those stronger than themselves in order to survive. Perhaps that's what Mary did.'

'If that was the case, I suppose I can understand why she was the way she was in Coxhill,' said Sophie, 'but what about when she landed at Isla's balloon base and told everyone that Isla was the one who did all those awful things in Coxhill when really it was her!'

'Force of habit?' suggested Meg.

'Or bein' the first to get your oar in,' said Isla. 'I'd sworn I wouldn't say anything, but she might have thought it better to hedge her bets by gettin' her version of events in first.'

'I suppose I can see that,' said Sophie, 'but then why did she go AWOL?'

'She must have realised that the truth would out sooner or later – especially when I told them that she wasn't Tammy Blackwell but Mary—' Isla stopped short. 'What *was* her surname? Does anyone know?'

'Not the foggiest,' said Sophie. 'Mary's nothin' but a nasty piece of work. Why else would she blacken your reputation when she didn't even intend to stick around?'

Isla blew out her cheeks. 'Unless she wanted to create a huge fuss so she could slip below the radar?'

'As good a strategy as any,' Meg said. 'After all, it did work, if only a little bit.'

Sophie wrinkled her brow. 'How do you mean?'

'The RAF were so busy unravellin' fact from fiction they didn't look into Mary's disappearance until it was too late,' said Isla.

'Method in her madness, then,' said Sophie, 'but even so it just goes to show that she's still out for herself.'

'Maybe she's never had a choice,' said Isla softly. 'If she came into Coxhill as a fighter, it could mean that she was used to having to fight.'

'Bad parents?' said Meg.

'If any at all.'

'She certainly didn't turn to her family once she got out,' said Meg, 'or if she did they must have turned their backs on her.'

Sophie wiped the jam from her plate with her forefinger. 'How do you make that out?'

'She's still on her own,' said Meg matter-of-factly. She emitted a small gasp as she glanced at the clock above the counter. 'You'd best shake a leg, Isla.'

Isla followed her gaze. 'Cripes! What a good job you noticed!'

'That's the beauty of bein' a driver,' said Sophie, standing up to join her friends, 'I'm the mistress of my own destiny!'

'Mistress of your own destiny,' said Meg as she opened the door of the café. 'Doesn't that sound good!'

'Bein' a driver certainly makes meetin' up a lot easier,' said Sophie as she wound her scarf around her neck. 'All I have to do is wait until I get a job that takes me roughly halfway between Liverpool and Portsmouth and Bob's your uncle!'

Worried that her train might be early for once, Isla picked up the pace whilst taking care not to slip on the wet pavements. 'I wish I could take you both back with me. I know I'm lucky to have Peggy in Liverpool, but it's not the same as havin' the two of you around. We'll have to meet up again as soon as we can. Next time you both get a decent amount of leave you must come to Liverpool.'

Sophie brightened at the very thought. 'And see Peggy. Sounds like a plan to me!'

Hastening into the station, Isla glanced at the clock which hung above the platform. 'I hope it's not runnin' too late. I've got a date with Rory when I get back.'

'Makin' the most of every minute, eh?' said Sophie, with a cheeky wink.

'Too right!' said Isla. 'You'll be the same when you meet the man of your dreams.'

Sophie rolled her eyes. 'I think that boat's well and truly sailed.'

Isla's brow shot towards her hairline. 'Don't be daft! You're a real catch!'

Sophie eyed her sceptically. 'Really? How many thirty-year-old women do you know who've never been kissed?'

'Just makes you even more special,' said Meg loyally.

'Or somethin' that nobody else wanted!' said Sophie.

Isla snorted. 'Poppycock! Any man would be lucky to have a woman like you as his wife!'

'And you'd make a brilliant mammy,' added Meg.

'I've not even met anyone yet!' cried Sophie.

Realising that the last time she'd asked Sophie about the man they'd christened Blackbeard they'd ended up discussing Madson, Isla put it to her again. 'You never did say whether Blackbeard had put in another appearance,' she said, arching a hopeful eyebrow.

Sophie paused before answering, giving Isla the impression that there was more to her reply than she was letting on. 'Didn't I?'

'No you didn't,' said Isla. 'You changed the subject to Madson, if I remember rightly.'

'Perhaps you're like ships passin' in the night,' said Meg, striking a theatrical pose, 'doomed never to meet!'

'You've been readin' too many romances,' Sophie began, but their conversation was interrupted by the sound of an approaching train.

'Is this yours, Isla?' Meg craned her neck in order to see better.

'I'll check with the guard,' said Isla, already hurrying towards him with ticket in hand. After a brief conversation and much nodding, she returned to her friends.

'It is! What a good job we left the caff when we did.' Taking them both in a tight embrace, she blinked back the tears. 'I ain't half goin' to miss the two of you.'

'Not as much as we'll miss you!' sniffed Meg.

'I'll drop you a line when I finish my shift tomorrow,' said Isla as she released herself from the embrace.

'Make sure you do!' said an emotionally hoarse Sophie. 'And don't forget to give our best to Rory as well as our love to Peggy.'

Having waved their friend off until she was lost from sight, Meg and Sophie walked slowly back along the platform towards the waiting room. 'How come you never answered Isla's question just now?' asked Meg.

Sophie pulled a nonchalant face. 'Didn't I?'

Meg shot her a sidelong glance. 'You know full well you didn't, which leads me to believe that you have seen him. Am I right?'

Sophie answered her slowly. 'Ye-es, but if I'd told Isla that she'd only have got her hopes up.'

'And shouldn't she?'

Sophie shook her head ruefully. 'He's not in the market for a relationship.'

Meg whipped her head round to face Sophie. 'You *asked* him?'

'Of course not!' cried Sophie, genuinely shocked.

'Then how do you know?'

Sophie sighed heavily. 'I was sent to the docks where his ship was berthed to pick up some papers, and our paths crossed. Havin' seen me in passin' whilst I was in Plymouth, he stopped to speak.' She envisaged the brief encounter she'd had with the relative stranger, who was tall and dark as well as handsome.

He'd stepped past her before turning on his heel, a

frown creasing the laughter lines on his handsome face. 'Didn't I see you in Plymouth a while back?' he'd asked.

She had nodded, then cursed herself inwardly. Acknowledging that she recognised him was as good as saying she was keen. 'Or at least I think it might have been you,' she had said lamely.

He looked up at the clouds which were racing across the sky. 'Looks as though we're in for another storm,' he said, and hesitated. 'Is that a Glaswegian accent I detect?'

'Aye.' Eager to keep the conversation going, Sophie added, 'Am I right in thinkin' that's an Irish accent I can hear?'

He gave her a silent round of applause. 'Spot on. Born and raised in the Emerald Isle but lived and worked . . .' he paused before adding, 'well, all over really.'

She looked at the berthed ships. 'I suppose the same can be said for most seafarers.'

'Part and parcel of the job.' He cast an eye over her uniform. 'Do you get to go to sea much?'

She shook her head fervently. 'Never. I'm a driver, so the road's my ocean.' She felt herself cringe inside as the words left her lips, but he didn't seem to notice.

'I've never thought of it like that before, but I suppose you're right – the roads take you all over the country much as the rivers take the boats.'

Pleased that he hadn't thought her remark silly, she smiled. 'It's not as free as being at sea, though, or at least I should imagine not.'

He was stroking his beard between his finger and thumb in a thoughtful manner. 'Part of the attraction, is that.'

She smiled. 'It must be wonderful to just jump on a ship and leave your worries behind.'

The twinkle left his deep brown eyes as he replied. 'If only that were possible.'

Sophie had felt herself melt under the huskiness of his voice, which made everything he said sound intriguingly full of meaning and mystery. She stepped forward, her hand outstretched. 'I'm Sophie.'

He took her hand in his and she could feel the rough calluses against the softness of her skin. 'They call me Donny,' he replied simply.

They call me Donny, Sophie reiterated in her private thoughts. *It makes it sound as though there's more to him than just a name.* She felt her cheeks warm as his fingers slipped through hers. She couldn't explain why, but she had never felt attracted to a man the way she was to him, and it wasn't just down to his looks. Gazing into the depths of his eyes, she asked, 'And should I call you Donny too?'

He nodded. 'If you like.'

She tried to swallow her smile. 'Are you based in Scarborough?'

A smile twitched his lips. 'The *Tamora* – that's our vessel – has no permanent dock, which is just how I like it.'

His reply had told Sophie he either wasn't the type to settle down, or was giving her a hint that he wasn't interested. Either way, it didn't bode well.

A man with flaming red hair had clapped a hand on Donny's shoulder as he walked by. 'C'mon, Donny. Skipper's callin' for all hands on deck.'

Donny had touched the peak of his Breton cap.

'Comin' now, Pat,' he said.

Sophie had raised her brow. 'Another Glaswegian?'

He'd nodded. 'Aye. Mind, that goes for half of the crew.'

Now, as they headed out of the station, Meg's words brought Sophie back to the present. 'What did he say exactly?'

Sophie smiled briefly. 'That his ship has no permanent berth, and that's just the way he likes it.'

Meg grimaced. 'I see.'

'Exactly.'

Determined to lighten the mood, Meg brightened. 'His loss, cos there're plenty more fish in the sea! Now, how about a stroll around the town? I've got a couple of hours before my train leaves.'

Sophie smiled. She knew she could rely on Meg to cheer her up.

*

Mary sighed happily as she kneaded the dough. When she had been arrested some seven months previously she had thought her goose was cooked, but the authorities had been far more understanding than she would have dreamed possible.

'I panicked,' she told the policeman who had taken her in. 'I knew I didn't have any identification but I was desperate to do my bit, so when I saw the papers lyin' on the ground I grabbed them without thinkin'. Is that really a crime?' She crossed her fingers, hoping that this version sounded better than the truth, which was that she had in fact been handed the documents by a stranger who thought she'd dropped them in the street.

The policeman had exchanged glances with the officer in charge of the station, who had heaved a sigh. 'Plenty of folk enter the services without any documentation. Why couldn't you have done that?'

She tried to look incredulous. 'Because I didn't know that's what people did. Livin' in the poorhouse is like livin' under a rock – you don't have a clue what's goin' on in the outside world. Why, if it weren't for the sirens, we wouldn't even have known we were at war!'

He grimaced. It had been a long day, and as far as he was concerned the RAF should've been dealing with Mary, not the police, whose resources were already stretched to their limit. He appeared to reach a decision.

'You've done a very silly thing, but for the right reasons. I dare say the WAAF aren't keen to have you back what with your history an' all, but I personally see no gain in keepin' you under arrest when at the end of the day there was no harm done. As far as I'm concerned, you're free to go.'

Mary had felt a wave of relief engulf her. The last place she wanted to be was prison – especially if they sent her to the same prison as Harman. *The very idea of bein' anywhere near that woman makes my blood boil,* she thought now as she began to cut the dough into rounds. *All those years of havin' everyone look down their noses at me cos they thought I was her favourite little snitch. If only they knew the truth!*

Mary heaved a resigned sigh. It was all well and good for her to think that way, but deep down she knew she couldn't really blame them when it was true she'd gone running to Harman with every bit of information that came her way. However, being taken on by the NAAFI at RAF Coningsby had been a second chance to prove that she was nothing like the person she used to be, and she was determined that from now on everyone should know the real Mary and the truth about who she was. Warts and all. As such she had been upfront and honest when she had applied for the job as assistant cook.

The head cook, Angela, had listened with patience as Mary told her tale of woe. 'You've had a rotten time of it and I honestly don't know what I'd have done in your position,' she had said sincerely. 'From what you've told me I think it's fair to say that could you turn back the hands of time you'd have done things differently when you joined the WAAF.'

'One hundred per cent,' confirmed Mary. 'I really loved workin' on the balloon sites and I'd do anythin' to go back, but the RAF don't deem me trustworthy – which is completely understandable given the circumstances – and so cannae give me such a responsible role.'

'Their loss is our gain,' said Angela, much to Mary's delight.

'You mean I've got the job?'

The cook had nodded. 'When can you start?'

Mary was beaming. 'Now?'

Angela had taken her on there and then, and Mary thought she had never been happier – or certainly not that she could remember, at any rate. For the first time in a long time she'd been shown respect by people she respected. Angela had proved to be a real tonic for the soul by not judging Mary for her past misdemeanours, and it was with her guidance that Mary had come to believe that she was a victim of her own circumstance, and that many others would've reacted in the same way if they'd walked her path.

If I ever see Isla, Sophie or Meg again, I shall tell them the truth, thought Mary as she continued to cut the dough into rounds ready for shaping. *I deserve to have people know that I'm not the person they believe me to be!*

Chapter Three

Rory eyed his reflection in the mirror as he shaved the stubble from his chin. He was very much looking forward to seeing Isla, but at the same time he couldn't help but feel slightly apprehensive about their date. He knew that she had been hesitant when they had first got together, believing that he wasn't over the loss of Tammy, and he could understand why she would think that way, even though he had tried to reassure her that he was well and truly ready to move on. However, it seemed as though he faced an even bigger hill than the death of his ex alone; there were also Isla's insecurities surrounding abandonment. Having been abandoned himself, first when he'd been orphaned by his parents and then when Tammy died, he could understand why she would be anxious that it might happen again. But how on earth was he supposed to prove to her that she had nothing to worry about? He supposed under normal circumstances he too might be anxious if he thought she might walk away from him. But that would never happen . . . he hesitated. Would it? After all, what would Isla do if her father were to come back on the scene? Was she only drawn to Rory because she recognised him to be a stand-up feller who wouldn't dream of turning his back on someone? Was she idealising him in order to stick it to her father, as it were? He shook his head. He was overthinking things, purely because he was so desperate to prove himself. It wouldn't help matters to cast doubts on their relationship when there was no need to do so. Isla was as potty about him as he was about her, and they were only questioning their happiness because they'd both experienced grief and were finding it hard to believe that their luck had finally changed for the better. But how could he make her see that he was true blue and would never up and leave when the fancy took him?

By always being there for her, thought Rory as he rinsed the shaving soap from his razor, *because only then will she know that I would* never *walk out on her, no matter what.*

Having arrived back in Liverpool earlier in the day, Isla was currently waiting outside Lyons café for Rory to join her. She had spent the entire train journey thinking over their relationship and the promising future they now had together, thanks to her friends, who had helped her to see that her dreams were just that. Seeing him alight from the tram that had pulled up a little further down the road, she felt her tummy flutter with excitement as she waved to gain his attention.

Jogging over to greet her, Rory lifted her from the

ground as he wrapped his arms around her. 'How was Worcester?'

'Wonderful,' breathed Isla. 'Seein' my pals was just what the doctor ordered.'

'You certainly seem more chipper,' said Rory as he gazed down at her. 'Or is that because you're delighted to see yours truly?'

She tapped him playfully on the lapel of his jacket. 'Cheeky! Although I suppose you could say it was a bit of both,' she said, adding truthfully, 'Let's just say the girls helped me lay a few demons to rest.'

He arched an eyebrow. 'Oh?'

'Mainly the stuff with my dad, but it's all sorted now, so nothin' for you to worry about.'

'You do know that I meant every word when I said I'd do everythin' I could to help you find him,' said Rory earnestly.

'I do, but it isn't so much not knowin' where he is that has weighed on my mind so heavily, but more the circumstances behind his leavin' me at Coxhill in the first place.'

'Understandably.'

'And now, thanks to my pals, I can look myself in the mirror and say truthfully that I understand why he did what he did, and that I don't blame him for it – not any more.'

'Forgiveness is a big step forward,' said Rory, as he hooked his arm through hers.

'Isn't it just? And I feel so much better for it,' said Isla. 'I can even forgive Mary for tellin' a pile of porkies about me before she did a runner.'

Rory was clearly impressed. 'By all that's holy! I can see that your break did you the world of good.'

'It certainly did. Life's a lot easier when you try to put yourself into the shoes of others.' By this time they had reached the café, and Rory opened the door to let Isla through. She thanked him as she continued, 'Before talkin' to the girls, all I wanted to do was find someone to take the blame for everythin' that had gone wrong in my life.'

'You didn't really blame your father for the loss of your mammy, though, did you?'

Isla pulled her mittens off and pushed them into the pockets of her jacket. 'No, but I was angry that she'd died long before her time, and that I'd lost my little brother in the process. I was also angry because I wasn't there when she passed, so didn't get a chance to say a proper goodbye.'

Rory pulled out a chair for her to be seated. 'Only because you didn't know that she was goin' to die,' he pointed out.

'True, and even though I hate myself for sayin' it, Mammy passin' so unexpectedly was the first time I experienced what it was like to be abandoned. Daddy leavin' me at Coxhill was the second. I could hardly shout at Mammy for goin' the way she did, but I could sure as heck be angry with my dad.'

'Anger is part of the grievin' process,' said Rory. 'It's easier to cope with the grief if you can focus your anger on somethin' or someone else. In my case I was furious with Tammy's father, because he was the reason why Tammy died. But it's different for you, because you're not dealin' with horrible people you've never liked but with people who meant the world to you.'

'You're right,' said Isla. 'I dare say a lot of people would say the Luftwaffe were ultimately to blame, but Tammy and her mammy would've been safe as houses had Dennis not been holdin' them against their will.' Her words took her thoughts to Theo and what he'd said about his sending his wife off on a wild goose chase minutes before the Luftwaffe bombed their base. *But it was different for Theo, because he wasn't holdin' his wife against her will. She was just in the wrong place at the wrong time, and even if he hadn't sent her off there was no guarantee that she wouldn't have been in the line of fire*, she thought, and said as much to Rory.

'Whilst I don't approve of him havin' an affair behind his wife's back, you're right,' said Rory. 'He couldn't have predicted where she would be whether he intervened or not.'

'I hope the truth catches up with Tammy's father,' said Isla, 'cos if he's still alive he deserves to be punished for what he did.'

Rory eyed her thoughtfully. 'Do you believe in karma?'

'What goes around comes around?' said Isla. 'I'd like to. Why?'

'Because if it's true, Dennis Blackwell will get his comeuppance one of these days.'

'But people like that always seem to get away with the worst, don't you think? We were only sayin' the other day that Mary would probably escape punishment because people like her always seem to land on their feet.'

He furrowed his brow. 'Then what was that about you forgivin' Mary?'

'Ah! I've now realised that she might have had a tough upbringin' that could have caused her to be the self-centred person she was in Coxhill.'

The waitress approached, her pencil poised above her pad. 'Are you ready to order?'

Despite having not so much as glanced at the menu, Isla ordered without hesitation. 'Fish and chips for me and a pot of tea for two?' she said, looking at Rory for his approval.

'Sounds good to me. I'll have fish and chips too, please, along with a couple of rounds of bread and butter.'

'I know I always have fish and chips when I come here,' said Isla as the waitress left them to pass on the order, 'but they make such lovely batter!'

'They do that,' Rory agreed, before harking back to their previous conversation. 'You certainly managed to do a lot of soul-searchin' whilst you were with your pals. Was there anythin' in particular that prompted your discussion?'

Isla grimaced. 'I dreamt that you were marryin' Mary, because you believed her to be Tammy.' She then went on to tell him of her nightmare in its entirety.

He tried to hide the smile which was forming on his lips. 'You do know that was just a dream, right?'

She rolled her eyes. 'Of course I do, but it seemed *so* real, so much so I couldn't help but wonder why I would dream something so outlandish. Especially the bit where my father was engaged to Kate.'

'Everyone likes to know where their future is headed,' said Rory; 'you and I know that more than most.'

She eyed him shyly. 'Do you have bad dreams too?'

'I used to,' Rory admitted. 'You see, in the beginnin' I blamed myself for Tammy's death because I knew somethin' was wrong and I should've fought harder to leave the shelter – well, you know I tried, because you were there.'

'I was indeed, which is how I know it would have been complete and utter madness for you to have gone outside with the Luftwaffe droppin' bombs left right and centre.'

'But if I'd gone and checked *before* goin' into the shelter—' Rory began, only to have Isla cut across him.

'Don't forget, you had no reason to believe she wasn't down the shelter until you got there yourself, and even then you couldn't be sure she hadn't headed for one of the other shelters nearby.'

'I know, and you're right. Still hard to deal with, though, isn't it?'

She was about to reply when the waitress arrived with their tea and put it down on the table.

'Shall I be mother?' asked Isla, picking up the pot.

'Please do,' said Rory, his eyes twinkling as he gazed affectionately at her.

'What?' Isla chuckled, noticing his expression as she poured the tea through the strainer.

'Just wonderin' what I did to deserve you,' he said. 'Cos I've not exactly been on my best behaviour since losin' Tammy – much to my regret.'

'You handled it badly because you're a man, and men are notorious for not bein' able to deal with their emotions,' said Isla frankly, picking up the small pottery milk jug.

'I feel as though I should protest, but actually I think you've hit the nail on the head,' said Rory ruefully. 'Men do run away from their troubles, and there's no point in my pretendin' otherwise when you've me, Theo and your father as prime examples.'

'I wonder why, though, when men are typically thought of as being the stronger sex,' Isla mused, her head on one side as she eyed him thoughtfully. 'Surely they should be able to handle anythin' that's thrown at them?'

He pulled a rueful smile. 'Well, women like to talk things through, whereas men prefer to fight it out – possibly because punchin' someone on the nose is a quicker and easier way to solve our problems.'

She stirred her tea. 'I don't think I'll ever understand the male mind if I live to be a hundred!'

Rory coughed on a chuckle. 'If it's any consolation, I think most men feel the same about women.'

She gently blew on the surface of her tea. 'When you look at it from a logical point of view, men are instinctively hunter-gatherers, whereas women are natural nurturers – or at least they are in most cases.

It clearly wasn't the case with Harman, though! I've never encountered a woman so cold, not to mention heartless.'

'Probably why she never had any kiddies of her own,' said Rory. 'Just as well, when you think about it.'

'Well, I'm just glad my past is no longer gettin' in the way of the present,' said Isla, cradling her teacup in her hands, 'because that would've been the greatest shame of all.'

'Hear, hear!' said Rory. Holding his cup up, he indicated Isla do the same and they chinked them together. 'Live for today, cos none of us are guaranteed a tomorrow!'

'Absolutely!' said Isla. She took a quick sip of her tea before adding, 'So, what shall we do after we've had our meal? Dancin'? The flicks? Or a stroll around one of the parks . . . or do you fancy the docks?'

'As you're the lady, I shall let you decide,' said Rory.

'In that case, a stroll round the docks it is. You never know – I might bump into my father whilst I'm there.'

Rory raised his brow. 'Wouldn't that be something!'

The waitress appeared with their meals, and he eyed the food with hungry approval, rubbing his stomach in anticipatory delight. 'No wonder it's your favourite dish,' he said, as the waitress left them to enjoy their meals.

'I love everythin' about it, from the smell of the fish to the crunch of the crispy batter,' said Isla, sprinkling salt over her meal before handing the cellar to Rory.

Rory paused mid-sprinkle. 'Talkin' of batter, I wonder who came up with the idea of coverin' a fish in it before fryin' it in the first place?'

'Whoever they were, they deserve a medal,' said Isla as she sliced through the crispy coating with her knife.

Rory placed the cellar back on the table. 'I don't know about you, but I seem to talk about food a lot more since rationin' came in.'

'Constantly!' said Isla, her words muffled by the fingers which were hiding her mouthful of food. 'But I suppose that's only natural, cos the more you cannae have somethin' the more you want it, don't you think?'

'Oh aye, but on the other hand I wouldn't be bendin' over backwards to get my hands on a plateful of tripe if they put that on ration.'

Isla pulled a face as though she were about to gag. 'You couldn't get me to eat that godawful stuff for all the tea in China!'

'Food aside, what else do you like to do?'

Isla held a forkful of fish before her lips as she mulled this over. 'Spend time with my loved ones, whether that be seein' a good film, dancin' the evenin' away, or even simple things such as playin' a game of rummy. How about you?'

He grinned impishly. 'I really don't mind what I'm doin' as long as I'm doin' it with you.'

She tutted good-humouredly. 'Smooth talker!'

He held his hands up in mock surrender. 'I was bein' serious!' Avoiding the half-hearted swipe she'd made from across the table, he chuckled softly. 'All right, so when you're not available, I like to tinker with engines, which you already know. Other than that?' He shrugged. 'The usual stuff: trips to the cinema, a spot of dancin' and of course a good meal.'

Isla eyed him with interest. 'What is it about fixin' engines that you like so much?'

He looked thoughtful. 'The knowledge that I can take somethin' that's broken and make it work again. It gives me a real sense of accomplishment – I find it quite therapeutic.'

She gave him a look of recognition. 'I used to feel the same way when I was workin' as a seamstress.'

'There you are,' said Rory approvingly. 'Yet more things that we have in common.'

Isla gazed at him across the table. She had felt an instant, inexplicable attraction to Rory from the first moment she'd set eyes on him. So convinced was she that he was the man of her dreams, she had sometimes worried that he might not live up to her expectations. However, the more time she spent with him, the more she realised that her initial reaction was correct and that he truly was the man for her.

Speaking in soft tones, he cut across her thoughts. 'Penny for them?'

'Just thinkin' how lucky I am – despite everythin'.'

He slapped the table with the palm of his hand. 'I've been feelin' the exact same way since the day we met!'

'And do you feel equally strongly that somethin's goin' to come along and blow everythin' out of the water?'

He drew a deep breath. 'I sincerely hope not,

because I truly think that would be the last straw for me. As you know, it's taken a lot for me to lay my cards on the table, and I couldn't imagine myself doing that for anyone but you.'

Isla felt her cheeks begin to warm. The more Rory spoke the more she felt her heart melting under his words. But she had been through too much emotionally to lay herself open to any more pain, and despite all her words about being ready to move on she knew that it might be some time before she was able to drop her guard completely. 'One day at a time,' she said. 'Just until I feel secure in myself.'

He nodded sympathetically. 'Don't worry. We'll go at your pace, and no faster.'

They ate the rest of their meal in relative silence, only pausing to comment on the size of the portions despite rationing, and to wonder how the cook got the batter so crispy. And before long, having cleared his own plate as well as polishing off the remainder of Isla's chips, Rory was leaning back in his chair, puffing out his cheeks. 'I think I'd pop if I took another bite!'

Isla grinned as he stood to fetch their coats from the hat stand nearby. 'You're just like my father. He never could turn down my or Mammy's leftovers!'

Helping her into her jacket, he pulled a guilty grimace. 'I've always had a healthy appetite. It's just as well we're goin' down the docks, cos I could really do with walkin' this lot off!'

He settled the bill, and they left the warmth of the café. As the cold bit the nape of her neck, Isla lifted her collar. 'Golly, it's cold!' she said, watching her breath crystallise in the frosty night air, and Rory immediately placed his arm around her shoulders, pulling her close.

'Not to worry, I'll keep you warm. We can snuggle whilst we walk.'

Grateful for an excuse to get close as they strolled towards the docks, Isla slipped her arm round his waist and breathed in the scent of his aftershave. Not only did he look good, she reflected with satisfaction, he smelled it too.

Rory was gazing up at the star-speckled sky. 'I don't know which is the more beautiful, the glistening pavements or the stars shinin' like diamonds in the sky.'

'"Diamonds in the sky",' breathed Isla as she followed his gaze. 'That's *exactly* what they're like, only brighter.'

'That's the one good thing about blackouts,' Rory remarked. 'We get to see the heavens in all their glory.'

'They truly are beautiful,' said Isla, still looking to the skies.

'They are indeed, but all the stars in heaven cannae beat the ones we have right here on earth', said Rory, and Isla could tell by the pitch of his voice that he was no longer looking at the stars but directly at her. Grateful that he couldn't see her blush, she lowered her gaze.

'Charmer.'

Bringing her to a halt, Rory turned to face her. 'I cannae help myself when I'm with you.' His eyes dazzled as they met hers. 'From your fiery hair to your sea-green eyes, you bring out the poet in me, Isla Donahue.'

The blush burning brighter than ever, Isla tried to avert her gaze by lowering her head, but Rory was gently chucking her under the chin, guiding her back to face him. 'I'm not used to compliments,' she murmured.

'Well, I'm afraid you're goin' to have to get used to them if you're to be with me,' said Rory.

'Have you always had such a silver tongue?'

He eyed her reassuringly. 'If you're askin' whether I spoke to Tammy in this manner, then the answer is no.'

Isla felt her cheeks grow even hotter, something which she hadn't thought possible a few moments ago. 'How come?' she said, quickly adding, 'Only I know how much you loved her.'

He rubbed the nape of his neck with the palm of his hand. 'You're right, I did love Tammy. But even so, she and I were just a couple of kids when we first met on the playground. In fact, when I joined the RAF I used to describe Tammy as my childhood sweetheart, and that's exactly what she was. The trouble is, we never really progressed from that. And the more I'm with you, the more I see my feelin's for Tammy as bein' puppy love – not that I saw it that way at the time.'

Isla very much wanted this to be true, but she still had her reservations. 'In that case I think you went to remarkable lengths to get her away from her father.'

'Your pals, Meg and Sophie?'

'What of them?'

'Would you do anythin' to keep them safe from harm?'

She nodded fervently. 'Of course I would!'

'And would you say you were in love with them?'

Isla opened her mouth to respond, then closed it. Even in the platonic sense of the word, she wouldn't say she was *in* love with them, but she did love them as a sister would love her siblings, and said as much to Rory.

'Well, it was like that for me and Tammy,' he told her. Seeing the doubtful look on her face, he did his best to help her understand his point of view. 'I'm not sayin' that I didn't believe things would work out for us then, because I very much did, but feelin' the way I do about you now I doubt that mine and Tammy's love would have stood the test of time.'

'But if you and I hadn't met, you'd have been none the wiser,' Isla pointed out.

'Granted, but even so I still think our relationship would have come to a natural end.'

'And do you think you would have described her love for you as puppy love?'

'Not at the time,' said Rory, 'but neither would I have called my love for her puppy love, back then.'

Isla lowered her gaze. She was badgering him for answers that were unnecessary. 'I'm sorry. I shouldn't be askin' all these questions, it's unfair of me . . .'

He gave her a one-armed squeeze. 'Don't be daft! It's only natural that you should be curious, and it's important that we're open about the past if we're to have a future together.'

She grimaced. 'Talkin' of bein' open about the past, I still haven't heard back from Theo.'

He faltered mid-step. 'I thought you wrote to him some time back?'

'I did, which is why I'm a tad concerned,' Isla confessed.

'Do you think he's taken the news badly?'

'Even if he has, the last thing I thought he'd do was send me to Coventry – not after everythin' we'd been through.'

'So what do you propose to do about it?'

'The girls suggested I should write to his mother, just to make sure he's all right, and hasn't been hurt in action. I'm goin' to do just that when I get back tonight.'

'Good idea,' said Rory. 'At least it'll put your mind at rest.'

'That's what I thought,' said Isla and indeed she very much hoped this would be the case, because she didn't think she could live with herself if she were to learn that he'd died not long after receiving her news.

Theo reread Isla's letter for what felt like the hundredth time. In the depth of his heart he'd known there could be no chance of rekindling their romance – that much had been obvious the night Isla had learned the truth of his past – but that hadn't stopped him from hoping she might change her mind given the fullness of time. He'd fully intended to wait a good six months before even hinting at trying again, but Africa had proved to be a large dose of reality and quite frankly he didn't know whether time was on his side, given the number of men his unit had lost already. Had he blown his chances altogether by bringing the matter up? He hoped not, but only time would tell.

Isla's been to hell and back since her mother passed, and I didn't exactly help matters by lyin' to her, Theo thought. *She says that our splittin' up had nothin' to do with my past, but she also said that my actions reminded her of her father – hardly a feather in my cap! If only I'd been truthful with her straight off the bat we might have stood a chance, cos I reckon it was the nigglin' doubts that caused her to question her feelin's for me in the first place, and those doubts would never have existed if I'd been honest with her. What Isla needs is space to get over everythin' that's happened to her in the last two years. I can prove to her that I can be trusted by keepin' my cool until the time is right, and the best way to do that is with actions not words. I shall keep my distance until she can see I really do respect her wishes. Given time, the feelin's she had for me at the start might just reignite.*

His mind made up, Theo took a pencil and paper from his locker. He knew that he should've written sooner, but he'd needed to make sure that he would be able to speak from his head and not his heart.

MAY 1942

A couple of months had passed since the girls' weekend in Worcester, and Isla was currently enjoying a

Spam and tomato sandwich whilst on her lunch break in the NAAFI with Kate.

Seeing one of the Waafs enter the NAAFI with a clutch of mail, Kate jerked her head in the woman's direction. 'Here comes the mail – best part of the day as far as I'm concerned.'

'Me too,' said Isla. As the Waaf headed over to their table, she crossed her fingers in the hope that at least one of the letters might be for her.

'Three for you, Isla,' said the Waaf as Isla held out an eager hand, 'and two for you, Kate.'

Thumbing through her mail, Isla's heart skipped a beat as her eyes fell to one envelope in particular. 'It's from Theo,' she told Kate, who looked up with interest.

'That's good!' she said, before reading the expression on Isla's face. 'Isn't it?'

Isla nodded uncertainly. 'I'm glad he's safe. I'm just a bit apprehensive, that's all.' She glanced up from the envelope. 'What if I've hurt his feelings?'

Kate pulled a sympathetic grimace. 'He needs to know where he stands, and you mustn't pretend to have romantic feelings for him when you haven't. He might be lickin' his wounds right now, but he'll thank you for your honesty in the long run, cos you're freein' him to move on, which is only right.'

Isla slid a knife along the envelope flap and pulled out the letter within. Casting an anxious eye over Theo's words, she grimaced, and quickly put the paper down.

'Oh dear. That doesn't look as though it bodes well,' said Kate.

Isla looked up. 'He says he doesn't blame me for not wantin' to rush into another relationship so soon after we broke up, and that that was his fault for tryin' to push me into somethin' I wasn't ready for and he should've been more sensitive.'

'Oh dear. So what now?'

'I honestly cannae say. I know I should write and tell him the truth about me and Rory, but it'd feel as though I was addin' insult to injury and that's the last thing I want to do. When all's said and done, I really did have feelings for him – still do to a certain degree – but it might not look that way when I break the news.'

'To be fair, it's Theo's own fault for jumpin' to conclusions,' said Kate, 'and even though it's goin' to be painful for him, sometimes you have to be cruel to be kind. It's better he learn the truth now than build his hopes up even higher than they already are.'

'You're right. Only problem is, I don't know what to say or how to say it without hurtin' his feelings.'

'You tell him the truth,' said Kate, simply. 'That's all you can do.'

Isla took a bite of her sandwich and chewed thoughtfully before responding. 'There's the truth, and then there's the cold hard truth. I'm sure there must be a way to let him down without breakin' his heart.' She gazed off into the distance. 'I haven't seen Peggy in a while. She's always good with these sorts of things. I'll nip and see her after my shift this evenin'.'

Like her friends, Isla wasn't expected to knock on Peggy's door but to enter the house as if it were her own, because as far as Peggy was concerned it was just that. Calling out 'It's only me' as she opened the front door, she wiped her feet on the mat and walked straight into the kitchen, where Peggy greeted her with a cheery hello before her face dropped when she saw Isla's expression.

'What's happened? It's not Rory, is it?'

Isla wrinkled her brow as she took the letter out of her handbag. 'Why would you assume it was Rory and not one of the girls?'

Peggy raised a knowing eyebrow. 'Cos only a man could make you wear a face like that.' She glanced to the letter in Isla's hand. 'And I see that I was right!'

'That's why I came to you for advice – you always seem to know about these things', said Isla, handing the letter over before filling the kettle with water and popping it on to boil.

After what seemed an age to Isla, Peggy eventually folded the letter back into the envelope. 'Oh, dear,' she said. 'I can see your dilemma.'

'So what do I do?' Isla asked. 'I want to let him down gently, but I don't want to give him false hope.'

'First off, you have to tell him the truth. That you've met someone else, and even though you care deeply for Theo you don't feel the same about him as he does about you.'

'Ouch!'

Peggy smiled softly. 'You should also tell him that he'll find someone who'll love him just as much as he loves them, and they won't share a past like you and he.'

Isla smiled. 'I knew you'd know what to say.'

'Theo just needs to bite the bullet,' said Peggy. 'At the moment he's stuck in a rut and you're that rut.' She laughed as Isla pulled a disgruntled face. 'Of course I use the word rut in the nicest possible way.'

Isla's expression turned thoughtful as she scooped the tea leaves into the pot. 'When I saw the girls in Worcester we talked of how Theo, Rory and I have all been livin' in the past at one time or other. Now I come to think about it, Theo still is, and I reckon that might be why he's hangin' on to the hope of a relationship with me.'

'Go on.'

'I'm the easy option,' said Isla, 'because I know everythin' there is to know about him. Whereas he'll have to explain his infidelity to someone else, which will not be easy to say the least!'

'Very true,' Peggy agreed, 'but he needs to see that he can't hang on to you just because it's easier than facing rejection. And besides, Theo's a lovely lad. I'm sure the right girl will be as understanding as you were – more so, if he's upfront from the start.'

'If he explains it to them as he did to me, I'd be shocked if they turned him down.' Isla sighed deeply. 'I really hope he finds someone, Peggy, cos he deserves to be loved.'

Peggy took the cup of tea Isla was holding towards her. 'And he will be. We all have pasts and we all have faults – it's how we move forward that counts. And if Theo is truthful from the off, it will show any potential belle that he's learned from his mistakes, and that can only be a good thing.'

JULY 1942

Having acquired a visiting order, Madson was waiting for Harman to join him in the room the prison officer had escorted him to. As he shifted his position on the hard wooden seat, he wondered – not for the first time – whether he'd made a mistake in coming to see her. After all, his hands had been just as dirty as hers when it came to swindling the government, and when push had come to shove he had well and truly landed her in it by laying the blame at her door. If he didn't play his cards right this meeting could end in disaster. But to stand any chance of a decent future he'd have to bite the bullet and hope she was in the right frame of mind to grasp the benefits they both stood to gain. He pulled a sidelong grimace. If the shoe were on the other foot, he'd have told her to sling her hook and refused to see her, which begged the question why she had agreed to see him.

He started as the warden opened the door and led Harman in. Once a smartly dressed woman, she now wore a drab grey linen dress which hung from her bony frame just as the smocks had hung on the women in Coxhill. Her hair, which used to be scraped back into a tight bun, was a lot greyer than he remembered, and it looked as though it hadn't been properly combed in days. Aware that he was staring, he smiled briefly as he half rose in his seat to greet her.

'You've got a nerve!' she spat as she stood beside the vacant chair.

He gestured for her to be seated. 'Just hear me out. I know I threw you under the bus.'

'You didn't just throw me under the bus, you bloody well reversed it back over me!' she hissed, her eyes spitting fire.

He grimaced ruefully. 'I know, but I promise you that I can make up for it.'

Locking her eyes with his, she remained standing for a few seconds before tutting beneath her breath and sitting down opposite him. Leaning forward so that they could speak in relative privacy, her eyes narrowed as she spoke in warning tones. 'You'd better have a good reason for coming here, cos the way I feel at the moment, I'm just seconds away from singin' like a canary!'

His throat bobbed nervously as he tried to calm the situation. 'I'm here because I owe you one, and no other reason than that.'

She gave a short sarcastic laugh. 'Oh aye? Got a file in your pocket, have you?'

'I can do one better. But you're goin' to have to trust me.' Seeing the look of incredulity on her face, he held up his hands placatingly. 'I know I shouldn't have ratted you out like that, but it was pretty obvious that they'd got you bang to rights already.'

She cast him a cynical glance. 'Just say what you came here to say and go.'

'It's about the money.'

She furrowed her brow. 'What money?'

Leaning forward, he took care to lower his voice so that the guard couldn't hear what he had to say. 'The money we earned—' He reeled back as the look of anger on her face hit him like a tidal wave.

'I bloody well knew it!' She seethed. 'The only person you're here for is you! I don't know why I thought it could be anythin' else. Same old Madson – me, myself and bloody I!'

As if to diffuse her wrath, he waved his hands in front of him. 'Not at all! I'm here because I know I did wrong that night, and that's why I'm goin' to hire a good lawyer so that we can get you out of here.'

Choking her disbelief, she eyed him cynically. 'And just how do you intend on payin' for a decent lawyer?'

Madson swallowed. This was it. She'd either hear him out or send him packing. 'If you could tell me where the money is . . .'

She shook her head slowly. 'What? So that you can take it and scarper? I don't think so!'

'No!' he cried, a little too loudly for the liking of the guard, who snapped at him to be quiet. Hastily apologising, Madson continued. 'I know I should've fessed up and taken half the blame, and I'm grateful that you didn't turn me in – you still could, in fact, which is why I wouldn't dream of double-crossin' you. If you tell me where the money is, I swear I'll get you the best lawyer money can buy.'

She gazed at him steely eyed. 'And why in God's name should I tell where the money's hidden when I can easily get it for myself once I'm out of here?'

'How can you be sure you can, though? If someone gets to the money before you, we'll have lost the lot.' He hesitated. 'You do know that Coxhill's been turned into a military hospital?'

'Oh aye, the guards keep me abreast of all the latest news,' she said sarcastically, but he could tell by the hunted look on her face that she was just as worried as he was that the money would be discovered, and he played on that fear.

'How long do you think it will be before some nurse, doctor or patient happens upon the hiding place?' he said. 'And then not only will you never see it again, but you won't get out of here any time soon either.'

Harman envisaged a nurse finding the secret panel in the window seat of her office and discovering a fair amount of money in an old tin box. 'What's to stop you from runnin' off with it leavin' me high and dry?'

'As I've already said, you can easily spill the beans on my involvement if I do. As for the money, half of it's mine by rights, so as long as I have enough to start a little business when I get out of the services I'm happy enough with that.'

For the first time, she acknowledged his uniform. 'I must admit, I didn't think you'd be the sort to sign up.'

'And you'd be right, but thanks to those snoopin' bitches I lost my job – in a reserved occupation, too! It wasn't long after that I received my call-up papers.'

He smiled evilly as the memory of the day he confronted Sophie came to mind. 'I got my own back on that Sophie, though; I dare say she's had a few sleepless nights since I told her what's what.' Appearing to realise that he'd digressed, he pulled the collar of his army shirt. 'I *hate* bein' in the army, and I've tried just about every trick in the book to get myself discharged, but it looks as though I'm in it for the long haul. Whilst I cannae do anything about that, I can at least have a decent future to look forward to when I get out!' He heaved a weary sigh. 'Look, you don't have to tell me where the money is if you don't want to. But surely it's got to be worth a shot, and certainly better than watchin' some bleedin' nurse walk off into the sunset with it?'

Harman's jaw twitched. 'I swear, if you double-cross me . . .'

A slow smile made its way across Madson's cheeks as he saw her resolve start to crack. 'On my life.'

'Good. Because if you even think about doin' a runner, I'll tell the polis how it wasn't just me that defrauded the government, but you too – and that's a promise!'

He eyed her thoughtfully. 'Given that you could've done that at any time, why didn't you?'

'Because I'm not a bleedin' snitch, and never have been!' she said, her tone filled with disgust. 'But put one toe out of line and I'll break my golden rule!'

He nodded. 'I believe you.'

'You best had. Now, just how do you intend on gainin' entry to a military hospital?'

He shrugged. 'I've not thought that far ahead, but there's bound to be a way.'

She eyed him shrewdly. 'You said somethin' earlier about Sophie. Where did you see her exactly?'

'Scarborough. Why?'

'Just curious.' She glanced meaningfully at his uniform. 'Is that where you're based?'

'It is, aye. And I reckon Sophie must be too, because I've seen her out and about in the staff cars a few times now.'

Harman raised her brow. 'She's a driver?'

'Aye.'

'Do you think those pals of hers have also joined the services?'

He looked momentarily blank until Harman elaborated. 'Isla Donahue and Meg Daniels?'

He shrugged. 'Possibly, although I cannae be sure of their names – they were just inmates as far as I was concerned.'

'You knew Sophie's name, though.'

He rubbed his head where the coal shovel had connected. 'I think you'd remember her name too if she'd tried to kill you!'

She envisaged Madson the last time she'd seen him, and the enormous lump on his head. 'So it was Sophie that gave you that bloomin' great lump?'

His jaw flinched. 'Aye. She threw a coal shovel at my head, which is why I've told her to watch her back.'

Harman's eyes narrowed as she gazed thoughtfully at him. 'I've an idea how you could show her who's boss once and for all! It just depends on how badly you want to see her suffer for what she did.'

He leaned forward. 'Keen as mustard.'

'In which case, I think I have a plan that could see Sophie behind bars, as well as gettin' you out of the services and leavin' the two of us quids in.'

He rubbed his hands together hungrily. 'Tell me more!'

Chapter Four

AUGUST 1942

Isla basked in the afternoon sunshine as she waited outside the cinema on Stanley Road for Rory to arrive. Glancing at the poster advertising the dreaded movie, she chided herself for ever agreeing to see *The Hound of the Baskervilles* with him.

'Are you *sure*?' Rory had asked as they left the same cinema a few days prior.

'Positive!' said Isla, with forced confidence. 'We're always seein' films that I want to watch and it's high time that you got to choose somethin' you like.'

Rory had rubbed his cleanly shaved chin whilst he mulled over his choices. 'I do enjoy a good detective story, but the only one that's on at the moment might be a wee bit scary for you.'

'How so?'

He had indicated the poster behind her. '*The Hound of the Baskervilles*?' he ventured. 'I know you draw the line at horror films, and whilst it's not a horror film per se, it's probably scarier than any other detective film you might have seen . . . if the book's anythin' to go by, that is.'

Thinking that she would hardly describe any of the Sherlock Holmes films as being scary, Isla had agreed without hesitation. It was only when she'd been talking to the girls in her hut that she realised it might not be the film for her.

'It's not as bad as *Dracula*. I saw that with my Pete a couple of weeks back, and whilst I spent most of the film peepin' through my fingers it was still better than hearin' that godawful thing emit that gut-wrenching howl in *The Hound of the Baskervilles*.' Kate had shivered as though an icy sensation had entered her spine. 'Damn thing made my blood run cold.'

'It did that to me too!' cried another girl. 'Mind, I was put off as soon as I seen that spooky house in the openin' credits.'

'The ghostly fog on the moors,' agreed another girl. 'There's no chance you'll find me wanderin' the moors at night after that!'

'Me neither!' said Kate. 'That feller in the beginnin' put the willies up me good and proper, the way he was—'

The first girl held a finger to her lips, indicating that Kate should say no more. 'You don't want to go givin' the game away.'

Isla was staring at them both round-eyed. 'Is he a werewolf?'

Kate was about to speak again when the same girl wagged a reproving finger. 'Don't say a word! It's nowhere near as much fun if you know what's goin' to happen!'

Standing outside the cinema now, Isla wished she'd pushed Kate for an answer. Not being able to guess the ins and outs of the film was already giving her the heebie-jeebies. So engrossed was she in her thoughts that she never noticed Rory arrive behind her, and when he laid his hand on her shoulder she practically jumped out of her skin.

'Rory! You shouldn't sneak up on folk like that!' she gasped.

'Sorry, but I did call out to you twice,' said Rory. 'Didn't you hear me?'

'I was too busy tryin' to second-guess what happens in the film,' said Isla. 'Kate's been to see it, and she said it made her blood run cold!'

He smiled kindly. 'Would you rather we saw somethin' else?'

She shook her head fervently. 'I said we'd watch a film that you wanted to see, and I stand by that.'

Taking her by the hand, he led her into the cinema and paid for two tickets. 'You can always close your eyes and cover your ears should it get too scary,' whispered Rory as the usherette showed them to their seats.

Sitting down in the seat next to his, Isla stared as the curtains slowly pulled away from the screen. 'I don't want to know the endin', but is it about werewolves? Only Kate said somethin' about a gut-wrenchin' howl...'

Rory's teeth glinted as the lights danced across the silver screen. 'Shall I just tell you?'

She held up a hand. 'Ignore me! I'm bein' silly.'

As the music began to play, Isla gripped hold of Rory's bicep, causing him to smile. 'Nothin's happened yet!' he whispered quietly.

'It looks spooky!' Isla hissed. 'And someone said somethin' about fog on the moors, and—' She broke off as a man, obviously terrified out of his wits, ran across the screen, accompanied by the sound of howling. Burying her face in Rory's arm, Isla gave a frightened squeak. 'I cannae look.'

By the time the film ended, Rory reckoned that Isla had probably only watched around fifteen minutes of the action, choosing to spend the rest of the time with her face hidden in his coat. 'I would ask if it was as bad as you imagined,' he said as they left the cinema, 'but seein' as you hardly saw any of it, I don't see how you can really judge.'

'Never again!' said Isla, her eyes still round with fear. 'It might not have been a werewolf, but by God it was just as scary! If Dracula's worse than that then I don't see how anyone could remain in their seat. If it weren't for you, I'd have left before the opening credits stopped rolling.'

'So, it's a no to scary films,' said Rory. He looked down at his arm, which Isla still held in a vice-like grip. 'Don't tell me that you're still scared?'

'I've never been bothered by the blackout before,' she told him, as she peered into the darkness ahead of them, 'but after that film I don't think I'll ever feel safe walkin' through the streets of Liverpool again!'

He frowned. 'If we were walkin' across moors or fields I could understand your reasonin', but Liverpool streets are a tad different from Dartmoor!'

'Aye, but the dark's the dark,' Isla pointed out unanswerably.

Wrapping his arm around her shoulders, he kissed her on the cheek. 'Well, don't you worry. Nothin's goin' to get you whilst I'm around.'

She smiled. 'My knight in shining armour!'

It was a good twenty minutes before they finally ducked through the doorway of the Pig and Whistle. Slipping his arm from around her shoulders, he held on to her hand as he led her to the bar. 'What would you like to drink?'

'Ginger beer, please.'

Ordering their drinks, Rory looked to the chalk board which listed the menu. 'Shepherd's pie! Don't mind if I do! Isla?'

'Sausage and mash for me, please,' said Isla promptly. '*Shepherd's* sounds a little too countryfied for me just at the moment!'

An amused smile creased Rory's cheeks as he gave the barmaid their order. Taking their drinks, he looked round for a suitable table and chose one close to the coal fire which was burning merrily in its grate. Placing the glasses down on the table, he pulled Isla's chair out for her as a deep chuckle rose in his throat. 'Does that mean you're swearin' off anythin' and everythin' to do with the countryside?'

'You might find it amusin', but yes,' said Isla. 'That film really gave me the collywobbles!'

He ripped off a mock salute. 'Message received and understood!'

She smiled. 'Thank you!'

'It would be nice to own a house like the one in the film, though, don't you think?'

'No it would not!' Isla was clearly horrified that he should think otherwise.

'Oh, I don't know. I think it would be fun to see how the other half live even if only for a little while.'

'I'm happy where I am, thank you very much,' she said primly.

'That's a shame. I thought we could have a house like that when we're demobbed.'

Isla lowered her gaze. 'I know you're only teasin', but do you mind awfully if we don't talk about life after the war?'

His face fell. 'Sorry. I didn't mean to offend you.'

She pulled an apologetic grimace. 'You didn't. Ignore me – it's just that I worry somethin' bad will happen if I start gettin' excited about the future, cos that's what happened the last time I got really excited about somethin'. One minute I couldn't wait to meet my new siblin', an' the next I was standin' over his and Mammy's grave.' She shuddered. 'Talk about don't count your chickens.'

Rory took her hand across the table. 'I'd love to sit here and promise you that everythin's goin' to be all right, but that wouldn't be fair.' Lifting her hand to his lips, he kissed the backs of her knuckles. 'On the other hand, there has to come a time when you look to the future. Everybody has to at some point.'

'I know, but I don't think I'm quite ready to face up to it yet.'

He kissed her knuckles again. 'That's fine, but just for the record, I'm not goin' anywhere, so you'd better get used to havin' me around.'

The barmaid arrived with their plates, and after establishing whose was which she put them down on the table along with their cutlery and condiments. Isla waited for her to leave before speaking her thoughts.

'You really shouldn't make promises you might not be able to keep.'

He drew a deep breath. 'The Luftwaffe would have to take me out in order to stop me from bein' by your side.'

Her eyelids dropped. 'That's what I'm afraid of.'

'But you cannae think like that, or you'll be livin' in fear for the rest of your life.' Rory sprinkled his pie with salt. 'Cos if it's not the Luftwaffe, it'll be somethin' else.'

'I know I'm bein' silly, but I just don't want to risk gettin' hurt all over again,' Isla told him.

'None of us do,' said Rory, 'but you cannae control those around you, so you just have to sit tight and hope for the best. The only thing I *can* promise you is that I'll never leave you of my own free will.'

She smiled, and deftly changed the subject by indicating his food with her knife. 'Eat up, else it'll get cold.'

Rather than push the issue, Rory sliced through the mashed potato of his shepherd's pie. Isla had been through an awful lot for someone of her age, but he was going to make it his mission to ensure that she never felt insecure again, because he knew what it was like to feel that way. Although just how he'd do that when she seemed determined to keep him at arm's length he hadn't the foggiest. Blowing on his forkful of pie, he eyed his belle thoughtfully. They hadn't been courting for very long, but he knew without doubt that she was the one for him, and he was certain that she felt the same. He also knew that she thought marrying in wartime was an act of desperation, and of course learning about Theo's past had only gone to reinforce this belief. *Only I'm not Theo,* Rory thought now, *and I wouldn't dream of askin' her to marry me because I thought the proverbial might hit the fan! When I ask Isla to marry me it'll be because I'm totally and utterly in love with her. Quite frankly I'd marry her tomorrow, but given her current frame of mind I rather fear I know what her answer would be.* With that being said, when would be a good time? There was only one person he could ask for their opinion, and that was Jimmy, his oldest pal in the RAF, and the wisest man that Rory knew.

SEPTEMBER 1942

Dennis Blackwell had spat at the feet of the prison guard as he left his cell. 'Nigh on a bleedin' year you've kept me under lock and key, and for what? I said you shouldn't detain me for somethin' I hadn't done, and I was right. Bleedin' pigs, you're all the same: too thick to see what's under your nose.' He gave a snort of cynical laughter. 'I bet you've not so much as raised a finger to track down the lyin' bitch that stitched me up like a kipper, have you? No, far easier to blame an innocent man who happened to be in the wrong place at the wrong time!'

'Spit at me like that again, and I'll have you arrested for assault,' snarled the guard. 'And as for bein' in the wrong place at the wrong time, I highly doubt that!'

Dennis had muttered what sounded like a threat as he walked to his freedom. He had no idea how Tammy had got her hands on that money, and nor did he care. The only thing that concerned him now was how he was going to make her pay for trying to get him sent down for a murder he didn't commit.

She must've been laughin' fit to burst knowin' the polis would be sat in wait for me, Dennis told himself as he stole an apple from outside a grocer's store, *but it's not who laughs longest but who laughs last what counts, and that's goin' to be me, cos I dare say she hasn't the foggiest I've been released. What with the bloodied knife an' all she'll have assumed I'd be banged up for the rest of me natural.* A wicked grin twitched his lips. *Well, isn't she just in for the shock of her life when she learns the truth? I made the mistake of threatenin' her mammy the last time we met, but I shan't make the same mistake twice. This time I shall cut the head off the snake by sendin' Tammy on a one-way trip to the bottom of the Clyde . . . or in her case the Mersey.*

He gave this some thought. He knew from Tammy's uniform the last time he saw her that she was in the WAAF, which could mean that she was no longer in

Liverpool. Only how could he find out where she was based? He couldn't exactly ask her mother, because not only would she refuse to tell him, she'd also forewarn Tammy that he was no longer incarcerated. But he had to start his search somewhere. And seeing as the last time he saw his wife and daughter had been at the safehouse in Liverpool it would only make sense for him to begin there. *I can stow away on a train like I did the first time,* thought Dennis, *but I'll have to rely on my wits once I'm there, cos I haven't a ha'penny to my name.*

With that thought uppermost in his mind, Dennis headed for the train station.

OCTOBER 1942

Madson stared at his sergeant as though he'd grown two heads. 'Why do I have to go? Couldn't it be one of the others?'

The beefy sergeant frowned down at him. 'Yours not to wonder why, yours but to do or die – and for the record I wouldn't mind if you chose the latter, cos it's not as if you're any use to man nor beast!' he growled nastily.

'But . . .' Madson began before giving up under the sergeant's steely glare. It had been a good month since his visit to Harman, and despite his intention to put their plan into action as soon as he'd left the prison he'd not so much as caught a glimpse of the wretched Wren. *And I'm not likely to, either, down in London*, he thought miserably as he watched the sergeant walk away. The burly man had told him he would only be displaced for a short while, but time was ticking on, and Madson was beginning to worry there might never be an ideal opportunity. *Just my rotten luck*, he told himself as he made his way towards the Nissen hut. *There's no way I'll have time to do anythin' before I leave, and God only knows when I'll be back, but as soon as I am, Sophie's downfall will be my top priority!*

NOVEMBER 1942

Rory hailed the passing bus and jumped on board. Getting hold of his pal Jimmy had been harder than he had imagined it would be, but he had finally got to speak to his friend on the phone the previous evening.

'It'd be easier to track down the Scarlet Pimpernel than it is you!' he had chuckled. 'What's been goin' on?'

'Can't say, cos it's all a tad hush-hush, but they've had us up and down the country more times than a bloomin' yo-yo!' Jimmy had paused. 'Is everythin' all right? Only it's not like you to call. Write yes, telephone no.'

'It's Isla—'

'Ah! The newest love of your life!' Jimmy interrupted, adding a tad pessimistically, 'Or at least she was ... don't tell me you've gone back to your old ways?'

'No I have not! And yes, she still is,' Rory said, sounding slightly affronted. 'I told you when I left Syerston that I wasn't goin' to flit from one woman to the next, and I meant it. So I'm pleased to report that everythin's goin' swimmingly.'

'Glad to hear it, but if that's the case, what's the problem?'

'Well, I'm not goin' to rake over her past, cos you already know the ins and outs, but in short, that's the problem.'

'Eh?'

'She thinks I'm goin' to leave her, because everyone she cares about has done just that.'

'Ah! I guess I can see why she'd think that. Except in the case of her ex, though, because it was her that pulled the plug on that relationship, wasn't it?'

'Aye, but . . .' Rory hesitated briefly before pressing on, 'well, supposin' they hadn't split up, he still would have left her when he got shipped off to Africa. Not that I've said that to her, you understand.'

'Yeah, probably best you don't mention that,' Jimmy agreed. 'But I'm not altogether sure I see your dilemma.'

'I want to ask her to marry me. However, I rather fear that askin' her to be my wife will make her go weak at the knees for all the wrong reasons.'

Jimmy laughed. 'You're just goin' to have to learn to be patient.'

'I understand that, but for how long?'

'Why? What's the rush?'

'I want to show Isla that I mean it when I say I'm not goin' anywhere, and what better way to prove it than by askin' her to marry me? Surely a proposal would put her mind at rest!'

'You obviously don't believe it would, else you'd have done it by now,' said Jimmy frankly.

Rory thought this through. 'You're right. So how can I prove to her that I'm goin' nowhere?'

'By bein' a constant in her life,' said Jimmy simply. 'You don't need to be married to do that.'

'For how long?' said Rory. 'Only I love the bones of her, and I want the whole world to know!'

'You'll know when the time's right.'

'How?'

'You just will.'

Now, as the bus neared the stop where he'd agreed to meet Isla, he switched his thoughts from the conversation with Jimmy to the last time he'd seen Isla. Having sworn off anything even slightly scary, they had been to see *Tom, Dick and Harry*, only this time it was Rory who saw little of the film. Not because he didn't find it amusing, but because he couldn't take his eyes off Isla and the way her face lit up every time she laughed.

So deep was Rory in his thoughts of that night, he had to do a double take when he saw a face he never expected to see again. Unable to believe his eyes, he leapt across the aisle to a vacant seat in the hope that he might get a better view but, with the man walking in the opposite direction to the bus, he could now only see him from the back. Determined to catch him before he rounded the corner, he ran down the aisle of the bus. He knew that if he didn't act soon the man would be lost from sight, and with that thought uppermost in his mind, Rory leapt from the bus whilst it was still in motion. Taking a tumble as he fell, he quickly scrambled to his feet, but to his dismay the man was nowhere to be seen.

Having witnessed Rory's desperate act, Isla was hurrying over. 'Rory! Are you all right? What happened?'

Continuing to walk in the direction of where he'd last seen the man, Rory spoke whilst craning his neck in search of the warden. 'Did you see him?'

Isla looked at him with alarm whilst hurrying in his wake. 'Who?'

'Do you remember Archie, the ARP warden who was down the shelter durin' the Blitz?'

Isla went to shake her head, before nodding. 'Vaguely. What about him?'

'I *swear* I just saw him,' said Rory.

She stared at him in disbelief. 'Is that why you jumped from a movin' vehicle? Because you thought you'd seen someone from Clydebank?'

Rory tutted his disappointment as he drew to a halt. The man had gone. Turning to look at her he wrinkled his brow. 'Don't you think it a bit odd? Him bein' in Liverpool, I mean?'

'Not as odd as jumpin' off the bloomin' bus!' snapped Isla. 'An' even if it was him, then so what? He's allowed to be here, isn't he?'

'Of course he is,' said Rory, a tad irritably, 'but why would he be in Liverpool of all places?'

Isla, who could see nothing remarkable in the warden's presence, shrugged. 'Same as us?'

He eyed her doubtfully. 'For a start, he's too old to be in the services, and I'd also have thought him too old to have upped sticks and moved hundreds of miles away from his home, as well.'

She eyed him sceptically. 'Are you thinkin' his presence might have somethin' to do with Tammy?'

'No.' But Rory hesitated as he weighed the idea up. 'Or at least I wouldn't have thought so. Why? Do you?'

'How could it have?'

'My thoughts exactly,' said Rory, but deep down he was beginning to wonder.

'So why did you jump from the bus?' Isla was watching him with an air of concern. 'What could possibly be so important that you'd risk your neck like that?'

'Gut reaction,' said Rory, 'but I guess I wanted to know whether he'd heard anythin' about Tammy supposedly leavin' her father for dead before leggin' it.'

'And what if he had?'

Rory sagged. 'I suppose I hoped he'd say that it was a pile of stuff and nonsense.'

'But what if he hadn't? What if he'd said that Dennis was alive and kickin' and as far he knew so were Tammy and Grace?'

Rory sighed. 'Then I would know that Tammy had acted selfishly, and perhaps I wouldn't feel so guilty about bein' in—' He stopped speaking abruptly, a bloom colouring his cheeks as he faltered mid-step.

Aware that she was staring at him, Isla quickly averted her gaze. Had Rory been about to say that he was in love with *her*? Trying to look unconscious of any awkwardness, she said, 'I didn't realise you did. Feel guilty, I mean.'

'I don't, but I would if I found out she was still alive, if that makes sense.'

'I think it does. So what will you do if you see him again – assuming you were right and it was Archie you saw, of course?'

'I wouldn't be able to let sleepin' dogs lie. I'd have to ask him, just to put my mind at rest either way.'

'When you put it like that, I suppose I'd agree with you,' said Isla. 'No one likes bein' left in the dark.

Rory looked visibly relieved. 'Thanks, Isla.'

'What for?'

'For bein' so understandin'.'

'When it comes down to it, I'd probably like to know the answer as much as you would,' she said, 'but seein' as we don't even know for sure it was him this is all pie in the sky.'

He opened the door of the Kardomah coffee house for her. 'Very true, which is why I intend to put it to the back of my mind – unless I see him again, of course.'

Stepping into the café, Isla found that she had crossed her fingers. Even though she hadn't seen him herself, she couldn't help but think that it must have been Archie Rory had seen, because he'd not have jumped from the bus if he hadn't been sure. *Some people might say it's just a coincidence*, she thought, following the waitress over to a table, *but from what I've learned there's no such thing!*

Later that day, Isla had just finished giving her rendition of Rory's near encounter with the warden and was waiting anxiously for Sophie's response, but all she heard was a long 'Hmmmm.' 'So, what do you think?' she prompted. 'Was his reaction normal? Or should I be worried?'

'Jumpin' off a bus before it's stopped isn't normal by anyone's standards,' said Sophie. 'On the other hand, would I have done the same as Rory, in the circumstances?' There was a slight pause before she provided the answer to her own question. 'Well, yes, I think I would. Only I'd have shouted for the driver to stop the bus first.'

'I'm blowin' it out of proportion, aren't I?' sighed Isla ruefully. 'I even admitted that I'd be as curious as him to know the truth, given the opportunity. So why can't I dismiss the thought that he only did what he did in the hope of reunitin' with Tammy somehow?'

'Because you still cannae believe how lucky you are to have a man like Rory on your arm,' said Sophie plainly.

Isla tutted beneath her breath. 'I honestly thought I was over all that.'

Sophie shrugged. 'And you probably were until your beau went on a kamikaze mission.'

'So do you think I'll ever be able to lay Tammy's ghost to rest?'

Sophie's voice was soft with sympathy as she replied. 'Yes – but it will take time.'

'Whoever said that patience was a virtue was speaking the truth – I really need to take a leaf out of their book.' Isla paused before continuing, 'All that aside, what do you think of the warden bein' in

Liverpool when he should be in Clydebank, if it *was* him? Rory thinks it's a big coincidence, but I don't believe in them, as well you know.'

'He must've got it wrong,' said Sophie confidently. 'Let's face it – all ARP wardens look the same once they're in uniform, so I'm pretty sure this is purely a case of mistaken identity.'

'I suppose so,' said Isla, who wasn't as convinced as her friend, 'but he did seem quite certain.'

'Trust me, that man's no more in Liverpool than I am,' Sophie concluded. 'Rory's just lettin' his imagination get the better of him, and I'd guess that's because he came within an inch of sayin' that he loved you, and that's makin' him feel guilty. Didn't he almost say as much?'

Isla brightened. 'Oh my goodness, you're right, he did! Do you really think that's the case?'

'Certainly more probable than an ARP warden from Clydebank bein' seen in Liverpool!'

Rory pummelled his pillow in an attempt to fluff it up. He had no idea what the time was, but he'd not been to sleep since rolling into bed some time ago. Laying his head back on the hard pillow he closed his eyes, only to see the face of the warden appear before him yet again.

I can see why Isla would think I'd made a mistake, he thought, *but I'm absolutely positive it was him, in fact I'd lay my life on it. I just wish I'd been a bit quicker off the mark, so I wouldn't be lyin' here wonderin' 'what if'!* Annoyed by the thought that he had been too slow, he asked himself why he hadn't acted sooner than he did.

Maybe I'm scared of hearin' the answer, he thought. After all, for the first time in a long while he had been feeling truly happy, and the last time he'd felt that way was when he was waiting in the van to take Tammy and Grace to their new life far away from Dennis. If he were to find now that Tammy was still alive it would certainly put a spanner in the works. Though . . . *would* seeing Tammy complicate things so much? He had no doubts as to how he felt about Isla, so why would Tammy's being alive create turbulent waters? He heaved a sigh. It was the not knowing that was causing him to doubt himself. He'd told Isla that he and Tammy were over whether she was alive or not, but how would he really feel if he spotted her walking through the streets of Liverpool? Would he jump from a moving bus to speak to her? He felt his cheeks bloom – he knew the answer to that. *I would* have *to know why she ran off without tellin' me what was goin' on*, he thought. *I deserve the answer to that much at least*. On the other hand, what if Tammy leapt into his arms? What if she had a jolly good reason for running off the way she did? What then? He gave himself a mental shake. There was only one person putting a spanner in the works and that was Rory himself, by conjuring up all kinds of scenarios that couldn't exist because Tammy was no longer alive. *This whole incident happened because you've been wondering whether to ask Isla to marry you, and you think that would be drawing a line under your relationship with Tammy when in fact that happened the moment you asked Isla to be your belle.* He nodded to himself thoughtfully. He was letting the past get in the way of his future, and he'd be damned if he would allow it to stuff everything up when he'd finally found happiness.

Chapter Five

DECEMBER 1942

Madson could've crowed with delight when he learned that he was being posted back to Scarborough. *Talk about the best Christmas present I could ask for,* he thought as he hurried down the lane to his billet. *With any luck I'll be startin' the new year as a wealthy man and Sophie will be behind bars where she belongs.* But how to do it? He'd been waiting for an opportunity to present itself before leaving Scarborough and that had got him nowhere. Lifting the collar of his jacket against the sharp wind, he pressed on. *I need to think this through and set a proper trap,* he told himself now, *cos if there's one thing that's certain, you have to make your own luck in this world!*

Mary hadn't been this happy since her days in the WAAF, but despite her new start she was finding it difficult to move on from the past. Lightly buttering slices of bread ready for sandwiches, she looked up as Angela's voice cut across her thoughts.

'You do realise you've already buttered that slice?'

Snapping out of her trance, Mary murmured an apology before passing it over and starting on the next, but Angela left the ham resting on the meat slicer and walked over to join her. 'Are you all right, luvvy? Only you look as though you've got the weight of the world on your shoulders. Don't you like it here?'

Mary whipped round. 'I love it here! It's not that, it's . . .' she hesitated, 'just stuff from my past.'

'Oh?'

'I thought that by leavin' Clydebank I'd be leavin' my past behind, but it seems to follow me wherever I go. I'm not talkin' about the time when I bumped into Isla, but up here.' She tapped her right temple. 'I just don't seem able to escape it.'

'That's because you need to clear your head, and you can't do that until you've made peace with your past.'

Mary stared at her. 'How on earth can I do that?'

'Have it out with whoever's makin' you feel the way you do.'

Mary rolled her eyes. 'Believe you me, she won't give a rat's behind how I'm feelin'.'

Angela smiled sympathetically. 'Not that I wish to pry, but I take it we're talkin' about someone from Coxhill?'

Mary nodded. 'The woman who ran it.'

'Isn't she in jail?'

'Aye, for defraudin' the government,' said Mary. 'She was literally stealin' from the mouths of those who were too poor to feed themselves, an' if that doesn't tell you what kind of woman she is, I don't know what will!'

'She certainly doesn't sound as though she has a conscience,' agreed Angela, 'but you're goin' to have to forgive her in order to move on.'

Mary's eyes nearly popped out of her skull. 'How can I possibly forgive her after all she's done to me?'

Angela rested her chin on her hand. 'I don't know, but you won't find true happiness until you do.'

'I think there's a better chance of hell freezin' over,' Mary said sullenly.

'Well, you're goin' to have to find a way, because it's not just her you have to forgive, but yourself as well.'

'*Me*?' asked Mary incredulously. 'What do I have to forgive myself for?'

'For allowin' her to make you feel the way you do about yourself.'

Mary hadn't thought of it that way before, but now that she came to think about it, Angela was right. 'So if I forgive her, I'm also forgivin' myself?'

'That's about the size of it,' said Angela. 'And strictly speakin' you don't need her to say that she's sorry, just to know how she made you feel. Whether she apologises or not is kind of irrelevant, although it would be nice.'

'So get it off my chest type of thing.'

'With her bein' in jail you'll certainly have a captive audience. All you have to do is apply for a visitin' order.'

Mary laughed. 'She'd either refuse to see me, or walk out as soon as I told her the truth.'

Angela smiled. 'You won't know that unless you try, though.'

'I'm not sure I want to give her the satisfaction.'

'I don't know how long she's banged up for, but from what I've heard, prison is a lonely place. I should imagine she'll agree to see you, if not for the company then certainly out of curiosity.'

Mary frowned. 'And do you honestly think I should tell her that I forgive her?'

'If you want to be rid of her, then yes.'

Mary fell into silent contemplation. 'It would be good to let her know that I wasn't the waste of space that she believed me to be,' she said at last. 'I know I might have screwed the whole balloon thing up, but I soon bounced back when I came to the NAAFI.'

Angela smiled. 'Success is the best form of revenge. I learned that through my ex.'

Mary furrowed her brow. 'I don't follow.'

'My last boyfriend was forever puttin' me down, sayin' that I needed to stop eatin' like a pig and go on a diet.'

Mary's face clouded. 'I hope you told him to sling his hook!'

'Not at first,' said Angela ruefully. 'I thought he had a point so I did my best to slim down, but I just wasn't happy.' Her cheeks coloured. 'He used to call me his little piggy, makin' it sound like it was a term of endearment, but I knew it was his way of twistin' the knife. I told him to find a woman who was more his type, but he said he couldn't do that, because no other man would have me so I'd spend the rest of my life on my own and he'd never forgive himself.'

Mary gaped at her. 'But you're not even fat!'

'Not now I'm not,' admitted Angela, 'but I was when I was with him. It was only after I left that the weight began to fall off me. It turns out I was eatin' my emotions.'

'What gave you the courage to leave?'

'One of my friends heard the way he was speakin' to me, and she asked me why I stayed with him. I told her he was better than nothin' and she said I'd never find the right man until I felt good about myself, but I could only do that by leavin' him.' She shrugged. 'So I told him the relationship was over, and he got really nasty. He laughed at me and said I was mad for lettin' him go and he should've written me off a long time back, and the only reason he'd not done so was because he felt sorry for me. He also told me I'd never find a man who'd stick with me the way he had, and that I'd be dead from obesity before I hit forty if I didn't have someone like him by my side tellin' me to lose weight.'

'Good grief. What did you say?'

'I told him the truth. That it wasn't me that had the problem but him, because people who are happy in themselves don't need to put others down in order to make themselves feel better. You should've seen the look on his face!'

'You said that success was the best form of revenge!' Mary chuckled.

Angela beamed. 'It was even better when he saw me after I lost the weight.'

'Gobsmacked?'

'At first, but when he saw how happy I was he looked like he'd swallowed a lemon. I must admit, I wanted him to know how well I'd done since we broke up, so I went over to tell him I was a cook in the NAAFI and that despite his concerns I now had a very nice boyfriend who treated me like a queen.'

Mary gave a small whoop of joy. 'What did he say?'

Angela chuckled to herself. 'That I looked like a floozy.'

'The man's an imbecile!'

'I know! And to think I thought I couldn't live without him!'

'What happened next? I hope you put him in his place!'

'I did,' said Angela with a smug smile. 'By tellin' him that I forgave him and wished him all the best for the future.'

Mary looked sorely disappointed. 'Why didn't you tear a strip off him?'

'I honestly think that would have made him feel better, because he'd know that he'd got under my skin. By tellin' him I forgave him and wished him the best, he knew he'd had no lasting effect on me, and that was as good as any form of revenge.'

'Why? What did he say?'

'He was furious. He said that if anyone should forgive anyone, it should be him forgivin' me. I told him that I accepted his forgiveness, and smiled.'

'But you didn't do anythin'!'

'I know that, and so did he. Which is why he spat at my feet before storming off.' She gave a sigh of satisfaction. 'It still feels good to this day to know that I got the upper hand and that he really was the one in the wrong, not me.'

'But how could you ever have doubted that?'

'Because he made me think that I'd be nothin' without him. Quite frankly when somebody tells you somethin' over and over again, you begin to think it's true – especially when you believe they love you.'

'And you think that Harman will feel the same when I forgive her?'

'It doesn't really matter – it's how it makes *you* feel. If she accepts your forgiveness, she's admitting she did wrong, and if she doesn't she's in denial, but you'll have moved on regardless, because forgiveness is the key to healing.'

'That's where I've been goin' wrong,' said Mary, with a hint of amusement. 'I always thought that holdin' a grudge was best because she'd know how much she'd affected me.'

'But if she truly doesn't care, that won't make any odds to her. It will, however, stay with you.'

Mary heaved a sigh. 'How do I go about gettin' a visitin' order?'

Sophie was on her way to the office when she saw a face she'd hoped she'd never see again.

'Don't be scared,' said Madson, walking towards

her from the camp gate. 'I'm here on business – nothin' to do with you.'

She gave a derisive snort. 'You think I'm scared of you?'

'Nah, but Isla Donahue should be.'

Sophie felt her heart drop. As far as she was aware Madson hadn't known Isla's name – especially not her surname. She wanted to ask where he'd come by the information, but also didn't want to show she was concerned. 'You really are a vile toad of a man, aren't you?'

'Sticks and stones,' said Madson. 'A poker, on the other hand . . .'

Sophie stormed towards him. 'You harm a hair on her head—'

He backed off, hands raised in mock surrender. 'Steady on. I was only sayin'.'

'Well don't!' snapped Sophie. 'If I hear that you've been anywhere near Isla . . .'

'You'll what?' he sneered. 'Beg me not to do it again?'

'I'll make you rue the day you were born!'

Still backing away, Madson smiled. 'Don't worry. I don't need to go after your little pal, not now.'

Having no idea what he meant by that, Sophie shook her head. She was letting him get under her skin, and she could see he was revelling in the fact that he'd managed to upset her. Rather than get drawn into a pointless argument, she yelled at him to 'go to hell' before storming off.

Grinning fit to bust, Madson hurried to the office,

where he handed over the instructions he'd been given. As he neared the gate again, the guard stepped out to speak to him. 'What did you say to ruffle *her* feathers?'

Madson looked fearfully in the direction where Sophie had gone. 'Nothing! She's had it in for me for years.'

The guard furrowed his brow. 'I don't know her awfully well, but she's always seemed nice enough to me.'

'Let's see if you still think that after she's clocked you one with a coal shovel,' said Madson darkly.

The guard stared at him in astonishment. 'Are you *sure* we're talkin' about the same woman?'

'You seen the way she reacted to me! I never said nothin'.' Madson pointed a trembling finger to where they'd argued. 'I was in the wrong place at the wrong time once, and I caught her and her mates up to no good. They've never forgiven me, and that's why she clocked me one.'

'Blimey!'

'Exactly. Believe me, you cannae trust the quiet ones,' said Madson, who was delighted that his plan was working out as he had intended. 'You won't tell anyone what I told you, though, will you?'

The guard frowned. 'Why don't you want me to tell anyone? Surely people deserve to know what she's really like?'

'Didn't you hear what she said about makin' me rue the day I was born?'

A look of realisation dawned on the guard's face. 'So *that's* what she meant.'

He nodded. 'She doesn't want anyone to know what she's really like, and that's why she threatened me. I tell you now, if any other woman were to say that to me I'd laugh at them, but not her. She'll clack you with whatever comes to hand.' He rubbed his head where the shovel had connected all that time ago. 'I'm just lucky it weren't an inch or two to the left, or I'd've been pushin' up daisies.'

The guard nodded solemnly. 'I won't say anything, but I will keep an eye out.'

Madson thanked him before continuing on his way. As far as he was concerned, revenge was a dish best served cold. This was certainly going to be a Christmas to remember.

Isla had been on her way to meet Rory in town when she was waylaid by Kate. 'Isla! You've a phone call in the NAAFI. I think it's Sophie.'

Resigning herself to the fact that she would most likely miss the bus, Isla hurried back inside and picked up the receiver. 'Hello, Sophie! How's tricks?'

'Not good,' said Sophie, before going on to relay everything that had transpired between herself and Madson.

Her heart in her mouth, Isla looked over her shoulder to make sure that there was nobody nearby before speaking conspiratorially into the mouthpiece. 'How the heck did he find out my name?'

'I haven't the faintest idea. I would've asked him, but I didn't want him to think that he'd worried me any.'

'Well, he obviously has,' Isla pointed out, 'cos you'd not be phoning me otherwise.'

'True,' Sophie conceded. 'But it's what he said just before he left that bothers me most.'

'What? That he didn't need to go after me? Surely that's good news, isn't it?'

'It was more the way he said it,' said Sophie slowly, 'as though there was some sort of hidden meaning behind his words.'

'The man's bonkers,' said Isla. 'If you ask me he just wanted to put the wind up you, and it's worked.'

'No,' said Sophie decidedly. 'There was more to it than that. He was lookin' at me like he was pleased as punch with himself.'

'Probably because he could see that he'd managed to get under your skin,' said Isla. 'Just because you didn't say anythin' doesn't mean your face didn't give away how much he'd got to you.'

'I suppose you could be right . . .' Sophie hesitated. 'Unless . . .'

'Unless what?'

'I didn't deny that he was correct when he mentioned your name. Maybe that's what he wanted me to confirm?'

'Nah, he didn't need confirmation from you to know he'd got the right person – he didn't just pluck my name out of thin air. However, that does rather beg the question as to why he mentioned it at all, and as far as I can see there's only one answer to that. He wanted to put the willies up you.'

'Well, if that was it, it worked. I know he's unlikely

to come after me, or he'd have done somethin' as soon as he saw me, but I'm not so sure about you. I think it best if we both err on the side of caution.'

'How do we do that?'

'It wouldn't do any harm to tell Rory. Forewarned is forearmed, so it's only fair that he's aware, just in case you should bump into Madson whilst you're out and about.'

'Do you really think that's necessary? I don't want Rory thinkin' that bad news follows me round like some sort of horrid smell!'

'Given the circumstances—' Sophie stopped short.

'Sophie?'

'Oh, my good God.'

Isla's heart sank horribly. 'What?'

'Madson said that *he* didn't need to go after you.'

Isla inhaled sharply. 'Are you sayin' what I think you're sayin'?'

'I'm saying that maybe he's goin' to get someone else to do his dirty work.'

Isla felt her stomach drop as Sophie's words confirmed her thoughts. 'It would certainly make sense of what he said to you,' she agreed, 'and whilst I doubt that anyone would actually put their necks on the line for him, you never know. As it so happens, I was just on my way to meet Rory so I'll tell him what's happened and see what he thinks. I take it you'll telephone Meg, seein' as she had a part in us takin' him down?'

'I will, but I don't think she's in any danger of him turnin' up, because he didn't mention her, plus she didn't really do anythin' to him even though she was there at the time. Whereas you bit him on the wrist and kicked him in the shins, and I . . . well, we all know what I did.'

'Fair enough. And for the record I reckon you're right and Meg's safe enough – thank the Lord. I'm still certain that Madson's only blowin' hot air, but it's better to be safe than sorry. However, I really must dash now if I'm not to miss the bus. I'll let you know how it goes with Rory.'

'And I'll let you know if there're any developments on my side,' said Sophie, before adding. 'Mind how you go!'

'You too!' said Isla before bidding Sophie goodbye and running for the bus.

Even though Rory had seen Isla on several occasions since the supposed sighting of the ARP warden, the incident still weighed heavily on his mind.

If I don't see him again then that's fine by me, he thought as he waited for Isla at the bus stop, *cos even though I'd like to know the truth behind the rumours, I'd rather live in ignorance than risk messing things up with Isla.*

At that moment he saw Isla descend from the bus, only instead of the happy, bright expression he was used to seeing, her face as she hurried towards him was a mask of concern.

'What's up?' Rory asked, stepping forward to greet her.

'What makes you think somethin's up?' puffed Isla as she accepted his peck on the cheek.

'The expression on your face,' said Rory. 'You look like you did the night we watched *The Hound of the Baskervilles*!'

Isla sighed heavily. 'There's somethin' you should know.' As they made their way to the Grafton, she went on to tell him all about Madson's threats to Sophie, ending with their most recent confrontation.

He waited until she had finished before asking in exasperated tones, 'Why on earth didn't you tell me any of this sooner? The man's clearly unhinged – he'd not have threatened you with a poker otherwise! Good God, Isla. Most people in his position would rather leave sleepin' dogs lie than poke the bear, but not him. It seems he's hell bent on gettin' his revenge no matter the consequences to himself.'

'What consequences?'

'I'm assumin' Sophie's goin' to tell the authorities this time?' He sighed heavily. 'Talk about makin' matters worse for himself.'

'Tell them what?' said Isla, as she hooked her arm through his. 'That Madson said he wasn't a threat to me? Hardly the crime of the year.'

He mulled it over before eventually coming to a decision. 'All right, so maybe not go to the authorities,' he said slowly, 'but we do need to be on our guard, cos I reckon he's boxin' clever by makin' sure he's said enough to frighten you, but not enough to get himself into trouble. It means he's usin' his brain, and that makes him extremely dangerous.'

'That's what I think,' said Isla. 'I wonder how he found out my name?'

He held the door ajar so she could enter the dance hall ahead of him. 'Who knows Madson that would know you by name?'

Isla's blood ran cold. 'Oh hell, no!'

'Isla?'

'Harman. She's the only one I can think of who knows both of us.'

He waved a dismissive hand. 'She might've told him your name, but she's in prison! What could she possibly do to you from in there?'

Turning so that he could help her off with her jacket, she spoke over her shoulder. 'Nothin' personally, but bein' in prison means that she's rubbin' shoulders with the sort of lowlifes who'd do anythin' for a few quid.'

He checked their jackets in, looking worried. 'I don't like the sound of this at all. I know you think it's pointless for Sophie to say anythin', but to my mind this changes things somewhat. Even if the authorities don't take her seriously, they'd have a record of her concerns should somethin' happen further down the line.'

'Only they won't record them, because they'd just deem it a case of "he said, she said". We only take it seriously because we know what Madson and Harman are like.'

'In which case I don't think that either you or Sophie should leave camp unaccompanied. It's just too risky!'

'Bit hard for Sophie, with her job,' Isla pointed out.

'She should be safe enough in her car, though,' said Rory. 'It's your safety that worries me most.'

She leaned her head against his shoulder. 'I'm so sorry to have landed this at your door. I just seem to have one stroke of bad luck after another!'

'Don't be daft – it's hardly your fault. If anythin' I'm glad you told me; how else am I meant to protect my lass?'

'You're a good man, Rory Dougal, I hope you know that.'

'For sticking up for someone who's done nothin' wrong?'

She shook her head. 'For not runnin' a mile. Most men would've in your situation.'

'That's because most men don't feel the way I do about you.'

Isla walked over to the bar with him. 'I really am one lucky girl!'

Having reached Liverpool, Dennis had decided to try his hand at gaining work down the docks.

'You're a long way from home,' the supervisor pointed out. 'What brings you to this neck of the woods?'

'I'm tryin' to find my daughter,' said Dennis truthfully. 'We lost contact a while back, but I do know that she was in Liverpool around this time last year.'

The man eyed him thoughtfully. 'How can a father not know where his daughter is?'

'She's in the WAAF,' said Dennis, 'and whilst I'm the first to admit that I wouldn't exactly qualify for the father of the year award, I'm here now.' He certainly appeared rueful enough, so the man had nodded.

'You say you worked down the docks in Clydebank, so you shouldn't need anyone to tell you what's what.'

Dennis touched his fingers to the peak of his cap. 'Been down the docks all my life,' he said. 'And thanks, I appreciate it.'

He'd worked the rest of the day before going to a house share with some of the other dockers. When he'd last been in Liverpool he'd gone in all guns blazing, which had landed him in custody. This time he'd sit back, see what was what, and strike when the time was right. Tammy might be his daughter, but had he not woken when he had he'd have been buried under the rubble with the rest of the poor souls of Jellicoe House. *I'm goin' to make sure she rues the day she was born*, thought Dennis, *and when I'm finished with her, I'll see to her mother!*

Tammy Blackwell, or Tammy Lloyd as she had been known since leaving Clydebank, was knocking on the door of the women's shelter where her mother had been staying since first coming to Liverpool, thanks to a fortunate meeting with Annie – the woman who ran it – whilst looking for work as a seamstress.

Hearing the sound of approaching footsteps from the far side of the door, Tammy waited for whoever it was to look through the peephole before the door swung open. Smiling broadly at her mother, Tammy gave Grace a quick peck on the cheek as she slipped past her into the hall. 'I cannae stop for long because I'm in between jobs, but I've time for a cuppa if you have,' she said, going through to the kitchen.

'I have indeed. I'm not in work for a couple of hours yet,' said Grace. 'Would you like a sarnie?'

Tammy rubbed her hands together. 'Yes, please!'

'Cheese and onion, or Spam and pickle. What takes your fancy?'

'Surprise me,' said Tammy, putting the kettle on to boil. 'Have you seen Archie lately?'

Grace reappeared from the pantry balancing the ingredients in her arms. 'He's takin' me out for dinner and dancin' tomorrow night. I bet you're lookin' forward to spendin' Christmas with Cecil.'

Tammy sighed happily. 'I cannae wait! It's been a good few months since I saw him last, but it feels like much longer!'

Grace pouted. 'I wish he could come to Liverpool so that we could all spend Christmas together, but seein' as you were here last year I guess it's only fair you spend it with him this. I'd still like to meet him, though. Why do you have to be the one that goes there all the time?'

Tammy scooped tea leaves into the pot. 'You know why, Mammy.'

'Because he's an officer,' Grace sighed.

'That and the fact he cannae get more than a forty-eight, which doesn't give him much time. After all, it's a fair old trek from Faringdon to Liverpool. He's promised he'll come to Liverpool just as soon as he can, though.'

Grace handed a plate of cheese and onion sandwiches to her daughter. 'I know, and I don't mean to nag. It's just that I've heard so much about him.'

'I know,' soothed Tammy, 'and he'd be here if he could.'

'I just hope I get to meet him before your weddin'...'

Tammy choked on her mouthful of sandwich. 'Give him a chance to ask me first!'

'He's clearly dotty about you,' said Grace, pouring tea into the cups. 'It's only a matter of time, you mark my words.'

Tammy felt her heart rise in her chest. She had only come clean to Cecil about her past when the powers that be had taken it upon themselves to send her to Liverpool. She had known she would miss him at the time, but she had no idea she would miss him as much as this.

'If I did get married I wonder what that would mean in terms of where I'm based?' she mused out loud.

Grace shrugged. 'I suppose that depends on whether you marry durin' wartime.' She sat down next to her daughter. 'Will you be meetin' his parents this time?'

'Nope. Which is quite a relief, cos I'm not sure I'm ready to meet them yet.'

Grace rolled her eyes. 'Not this nonsense about you not bein' good enough for their son again? I thought he said that his parents weren't like that.'

'And he did,' said Tammy, 'but it's not so much what they think as how I feel, and the truth is I feel inferior.'

'Because they live in a big house and their sons are all officers? If it doesn't bother them why should it worry you?'

'Because my father's a no-good woman beater who tried to kill his own wife,' said Tammy, 'and I'm afraid they might think the apple doesn't fall far from the tree.'

'Only they won't, will they? They must know that Cecil wouldn't fall for a woman like that.'

'I clobbered my father across the head and left him for dead,' Tammy said evenly.

'You were defendin' me!' cried Grace. 'And a good job too, cos he'd have throttled me otherwise!'

'I know, and you're right, it's just . . .'

'Just nothin',' said Grace, annoyed now. 'It's about time you started seein' your worth, Tammy Lloyd, cos everyone else does, and so will Cecil's parents – his brothers, too!'

'I know *you* do,' said Tammy, 'and I hope I will too, in time.'

'Are you still worried about Rory?' Grace asked, cocking an eyebrow.

'Not consciously,' said Tammy, 'but I suppose it might be playin' on my mind, deep down.'

'As long as you're not beatin' yourself up over it,' said Grace. 'Cos we've trodden that path too many times already.'

'I know, and Rory made his feelings clear the day he sent my opened letter back to me. But surely it's natural to worry about someone you once loved?'

'Of course it is, and for the record I worry about him too.'

'I just hope he's found someone worthy of him, because he deserves to be happy.'

'He will be, cos he's a smashin' feller,' said Grace, sipping her tea thoughtfully. 'As far as I can see, everythin's where it should be.'

Tammy's brow furrowed. 'I'm not sure I'm with you.'

'You're with Cecil, I'm with Archie and I'm positive that Rory will soon be with someone too. As for your father, well, he'll never darken our doors again now he's got that money.'

Tammy gave a small harrumph. 'It really gets my goat to think of him livin' it up, though, when he doesn't deserve to.'

Grace wagged a reproving finger. 'You and Gina agreed that the money would only bring grief because of the way it was obtained.' She shuddered. 'I don't know whose blood it was on that knife, but I doubt they're still alive.'

A half-smile twitched the corner of Tammy's mouth. Tammy had met Gina when they were both fleeing Clydebank, though for very different reasons. In Gina's case, it was because she'd inadvertently grabbed the wrong bag when leaving the scene of a murder she had accidentally witnessed, and had discovered all too late that the bag was stuffed with money and a bloodstained knife. As it turned out, the man responsible for the murder was part of the infamous Billy Boys, a Glaswegian gang notorious for violent crimes. In desperation to separate themselves from the money the girls had hidden it in a hotel room hoping to never see it again. However, when Dennis turned up on Grace's doorstep demanding they pay him what he thought himself to be owed, the money became a perfect way to get both Dennis and the money off their backs – what they hadn't known was the money had already been discovered and the police were lying in wait after being tipped off by the hotel that the person who'd hidden the money was on their way back for it.

'I believe that you reap what you sow in this life,' said Tammy, 'and if there's any justice in this world, karma will catch up with dad as well as the Billy Boys.'

Grace smiled at her daughter over the top of her teacup. 'Amen to that!'

It was Christmas morning and Isla had arranged to meet Rory in Princes Park. Taking care not to lose her footing in the snow as she hurried towards him, she was breathless as he held his arms open to take her in a warm embrace. 'Merry Christmas!' she gasped, and slipped just before reaching him, resulting in a gentle collision.

'Steady on!' he chuckled.

'Sorry. And just when I was doin' so well!'

Brushing an escaped lock behind her ear, he kissed her softly. 'Merrry Christmas to you too, and no need for apologies. You can fall into my arms any day of the week!'

'Charmer!'

'I mean it! In fact I'd rather welcome it!' He jerked his head towards the people who were enjoying the slopes on their sledges. 'Fancy a go on this?' Stepping aside, he revealed a wooden sledge which looked as though it had seen better days.

Isla eyed the sledge uncertainly. 'Where on earth did you get that from?'

'It belongs to one of the lads on my base. He said that we were welcome to use it whilst he's at work.' Seeing the slightly dubious look on her face, he held the sledge up for examination. 'It's not as flimsy as it looks, see?' As the words left his lips, he thumped the sledge against the snow to prove its stability.

Reassured, Isla gave a small, excited round of applause. 'In that case, you can count me in!'

'Excellent!' Offering her the crook of his arm, he pulled the sleigh behind them as they walked somewhat unsteadily towards the slope. 'So, how's your Christmas been so far?'

Isla shrugged. 'Same old, only with tinsel and hats. You?'

'Much the same as yours,' said Rory, adding with a sloppy grin, 'although it's all the better for seein' you!'

'Ditto,' Isla chuckled, before giving a small gasp as her foot slid backwards.

Rory laughed. 'I don't reckon you need a sledge; you're doin' just fine without it!'

'I think you're right,' said Isla, keeping hold of his arm as they made their way to the top of the slope.

'Have you heard anything more about the Madson situation?'

She shook her head. 'It seems all's quiet on the western front, and long may it remain that way.'

'Any more thoughts on Harman's involvement?'

'I put it to Sophie, and whilst she agrees it was most likely Harman who told him who I was, she doesn't think she'd do anything else to get her hands dirty. Not when she's doing time already. If she were to be found out, they'd most likely lengthen the sentence.'

'So you don't think she'd be as keen on revenge as Madson, then?'

'I wouldn't have thought so. If she were goin' to blame anyone, I reckon it'd be Harvey, because she must know by now that he was workin' for the government. We might have been the ones to find the books, but in the end he'd have done it with or without our help.'

'At least that's one less worry on our minds.' Rory put the sledge down in front of him and sat astride it, patting the space between his legs as he looked up to her. 'Let's be havin' you.'

Taking a tight hold of his shoulder, Isla tucked her handbag out of the way and carefully lowered herself onto the sledge, where Rory hooked his legs up on either side of hers and clamped them close. 'Are you ready?'

Isla was beaming as she held on to the rope attached to the front of the sledge. 'As I'll ever be!'

He punched the air with his fist. 'Charge!'

By the time Rory and Isla were ready to leave the park, most of the snow had turned to slush.

'I cannae remember the last time I laughed so much,' Isla giggled as they headed for the bus stop. 'Those kids had a wonderful time, thanks to you.'

'Thanks to both of us,' said Rory. 'Cos you had as much fun with them as me.'

Isla was still smiling as she replied, 'Guilty as charged! I wish we could do that every day. I reckon it's taken years off me.'

'It's certainly good to have a bit of fun amongst the madness,' agreed Rory. He looked down at his sodden shoes and trouser hems. 'Even if we are a wee bit on the wet side.'

Isla rested her cheek against his arm. 'I wish we didn't have to go to work.'

He kissed the top of her head. 'Me too.' Walking her to the bus stop, he dug his free hand into the inside pocket of his greatcoat. 'Merry Christmas, Isla. I hope you like it.'

Isla eagerly took the small package from him, her eyes lighting up as she pulled out a small bottle of scent. A tiny gasp escaped her lips. 'Rory! It's wonderful! How on earth did you manage to get your hands on somethin' so precious? I've not seen scent in . . .' she blew out her cheeks, '. . . forever.'

He tapped the side of his nose conspiratorially. 'Let's just say I have my ways and means!'

Tucking the treasured gift into her handbag, she pulled out a brown paper bag. 'I'm afraid my gift's nowhere near as grand,' she said, handing it over.

Rory withdrew the book from the bag with a cry of delight. *'The Body in the Library*!'

'You haven't got it, have you?' she asked anxiously.

'Nope, but I have got some of her others, so I shall add this to my collection.'

'I'm glad you like it.' She groaned softly as the bus trundled towards them. 'This is me.'

Putting his arms round her shoulders, Rory leaned in for a kiss, which Isla shyly received. Aware that the people on the approaching bus would be able to see them, she felt her cheeks grow warm as she surrendered to his embrace, her heart thundering so hard in her chest she was certain that Rory must be able to feel it.

As the bus came to a halt just short of where they stood, Rory leaned back. 'When are you free to meet me next?'

Isla spoke quickly, aware that the driver was waiting. 'I'm off on Wednesday, if that suits you?'

'Dinner and dancing?'

'You bet! Eighteen hundred hours outside the Rialto?'

He touched his forelock with his fingers. 'I shall look forward to it!'

Harman had been in her cell when the warden came to deliver the news.

'You've received a request for a visiting order.'

She perked up. 'Is it a feller by the name of Madson?'

He handed her the paper. 'Not unless his first name's Mary.'

Harman stared at him in disbelief for a second or two before glancing down at the page before her. 'Well, I never,' she said softly, and looked back up. 'When did this come?'

'Couple of days ago. We hung fire because we

thought it might make a nice Christmas present for you,' he finished sarcastically.

Harman stared at the request before handing it back.

'Well? Do you want to see her? It's not until February—'

She shrugged. 'May as well.'

Rolling his eyes at her lack of enthusiasm, the warden wished her a cynical Merry Christmas and left her to her thoughts.

What the heck does Mary want to see me for? Harman wondered as she heard the key turn in the lock. *I'd have thought she'd have been long gone by now.* An image of her only other visitor sprang to mind. Had Madson got something to do with this? It was quite possible; she knew he was never keen to carry out his own dirty work. She nodded: it was the only plausible answer. He must've tracked Mary down and told her that he'd give her a slice of the action if she agreed to help. She supposed she could understand why he'd chosen Mary, but could she really trust the girl any more than she could trust him? There was only one way to find out, and that was to hear what Mary had to say and take it from there.

Chapter Six

FEBRUARY 1943

With the snow falling thickly, Sophie cracked the window of her car just enough to show the guard her pass. 'Hello, Martin! Long time no see.'

Martin gave her a fleeting, uncertain smile before averting his gaze and waving her through. Confused by his odd look, she assumed there must be something wrong with the pass itself and turned it round for a quick inspection, but as far as she could see it appeared to be fine.

Her brow furrowing, she pulled on to the main road. There was no doubt in her mind that Martin had looked uncomfortable when she saw him, but what could she possibly have done to upset him when she hadn't seen him in months? In fact, now that she thought about it, just when *had* she seen him last? As she tried to remember anything she might have said or done which would make Martin react in such a fashion, an imagine of Madson entered her mind's eye. She would be the first to admit that she hadn't handled the situation well that day. Instead of walking away and leaving him to it, she'd stood in the middle of the road shouting like a fishwife and making all kinds of threats. Had Martin been the guard on duty that day? She cringed. He had. *What must I have looked like to someone who didn't know the ins and outs of it?*

The snow was falling steadily, and Sophie turned the wipers on to clear the windscreen. Madson had deliberately kept his cool, leaving Sophie to lose her rag as she responded to his threats. *Martin must have thought I'd lost my mind, cos I don't think I'd ever so much as raised my voice the whole time I'd been on base.* She felt herself shrinking in her seat. Had Martin told anyone else of her behaviour that day? If he had, none of them had let on. She remembered walking away from Madson, but where had he gone? Had he spoken to Martin? And, if so, what had he said? *Whatever he said it wouldn't have been the truth*, thought Sophie, *but by the look on Martin's face he fell for it!* Grinding the gears in her frustration, she speeded up. She needed to get her chores done so that she could get back to base and find out exactly what Madson had said.

Mary was fidgeting with the hem of her skirt as she sat in the prison waiting room. Glancing from the bars on the windows to the grey walls, she felt as though she had been transported back to Coxhill, except that the prison was cleaner; cheerier, even.

A man in guard's uniform opened the door. 'Mary—'

Answering. 'Yes' before he'd managed another word, she was already on her feet.

He jerked his head in the direction of the corridor. 'Come with me.'

She followed him a short distance down the long corridor and through to another room, as depressing as the first. 'In here, please, miss,' he said, standing to one side of the door.

Mary entered the room, noting the single table with two chairs either side. She heard the door bang shut behind her and whipped round. The guard had only closed the door whilst he went to get Harman, but even so, the thought of being locked in such a foreboding place was enough to make her hair stand on end. *The sooner I get out of here the better*, she thought. Had she made the right decision in coming to say her piece at all? She'd told Angela that she half hoped Harman would refuse to see her, just so she wouldn't have to go through with the visit.

'You never know, she might surprise you,' Angela had said. 'Prison gives folk time to think, to mull over the past and see things from a different point of view. For all you know she might want to apologise, say that she's seen the error of her ways—' Angela had broken off as she waited for Mary to stop laughing.

'And pigs might fly!' chortled Mary cynically. 'I'm sorry, Angela, truly I am, but you have no idea what she's like. Hell would freeze over before she admitted she'd made a mistake. There's only one thing she respects and that's money; nothing else is of any interest to her. She couldn't have run Coxhill the way she did otherwise. I saw that woman work the old and the sick until they could do no more, after which they'd be left to die because they weren't earning the money to cover their keep.'

Angela's face fell in horror. 'Flippin' Nora! I know you said she was stealin' food from your mouths, but I didn't realise she was as bad as that!'

Mary eyed her woodenly. 'Put it this way. Anyone who did stand in her way didn't do so for long, but at least they got out of Coxhill.'

'She let them out?' said Angela, her brow rising.

Mary laughed without mirth. 'In a manner of speakin'.' She held Angela's gaze. 'They went out toes up.'

'Don't visit!' Angela said hurriedly. 'She doesn't deserve forgiveness.'

Mary raised her eyebrows. 'I thought you said it was the only way I could move on?'

'I did,' admitted Angela wretchedly. 'But there must be another way.' After a moment she snapped her fingers. 'I know! You could write your feelin's down in a letter! That way she'll know what you think, but you won't have to actually speak to her.'

'If you'd suggested that a few weeks ago I'd have jumped at the idea, but the more I talk the more I realise I have to get it off my chest, face to face, so that I can see her reaction.'

'But she won't care! You said so yourself,' wailed Angela, who was fervently wishing she'd never persuaded Mary to ask for a visitation order in the first place.

'I dare say she won't, but it'll be good to let her know exactly what I think of her, and see her fret.'

Angela's brow creased. 'Why would she fret?'

'Because I know every bit of her business, and if the polis know the half of what I do Harman would never see the light of day again!'

Angela eyed her cautiously. 'What exactly *do* you know?'

Mary tapped the side of her nose. 'The less I tell you the better. Suffice to say Harman had dealin's with a lot of bad people, some of whom make the Billy Boys look like small fry.'

Angela's frown deepened. 'Who the heck are the Billy Boys when they're at home? They sound like some sort of musical duet.'

Mary's eyes widened. 'I forgot you wouldn't know, what with you bein' from Norwich an' all. The Billy Boys are a Glaswegian gang who'll do anythin' for money, and I mean anything!'

This conversation had taken place a few days before Mary's visit to the prison, and whilst she might have felt brave and defiant in the warmth of the NAAFI kitchen, she felt anything but that sitting in a dreary room waiting for Harman to arrive. She was so lost in her thoughts she never heard the sound of approaching footsteps. Jumping as the door opened, her eyes met Harman's before falling to the woman's cuffed hands.

Prison's aged her, she thought as the warden locked the door. Harman was viewing her through narrowed eyes. *Although I see it's done nothin' for her demeanour, which is still as icy as ever.* The warden stood with his back to the door and indicated for both women to be seated.

Mary must have imagined this moment a hundred times or more on her way to the prison, but now she was actually sitting in front of Harman she couldn't remember a single word she'd rehearsed, not that it mattered, as the older woman was already speaking.

'Let me guess. You've spoken to him.' She shook her head. 'I knew I couldn't trust that man.'

Mary knitted her brows. 'Who's *him* when he's at home?'

'Don't come all innocent with me. You know damned well that I'm referrin' to Madson. Let's face it, you'd not be here otherwise.'

'*Madson!*' exclaimed Mary. Her eyes widening, she continued in disbelief, 'What on earth makes you think I've spoken to him?'

'Oh, pull the other one, it's got bells on!' Harman snapped. She had fixed her visitor with a cynical glare, but seeing the look of total incomprehension on Mary's face she relented slightly. 'Well, if you're not here because of him, why are you here?'

'Good question,' said Mary somewhat sarcastically. Folding her arms across her chest, she tutted beneath her breath. 'And to think I thought it might do me some good to come and see you.'

Harman gave a short mirthless laugh. 'Of course you did! Full of heart, you are!'

'Oh, I'm not goin' to pretend that I'm doin' any of this for you, or that I've missed your company. Far from it. I've only come because try as I might I cannae get you out of *here*.' Mary tapped the side of her skull as she spoke.

Still determined that Mary was hiding the real reason for her visit, Harman rolled her eyes. 'And you thought comin' to see me would . . . what? Make me go away?'

Mary shrugged. 'I suppose that depends on what you have to say, but from what I've seen so far I'm not holdin' out much hope.'

Harman raised her hands into the air before dropping them by her sides. 'What the hell do you expect me to say? I've not seen you for the best part of three years, which quite frankly suited me just fine.'

'I knew it was a mistake comin' here. I don't know what made me think you might actually apologise, but—'

Harman coughed incredulously. 'Apologise? Me? What the hell have I got to apologise for?'

Mary's jaw dropped. 'Are you kidding me?'

Leaning back in her chair, Harman gave her a brief downward smile. 'Do I look like I'm laughin'?'

Mary continued to stare at her. 'You really cannae see it, can you? As far as you're concerned you did nothin' wrong.'

Harman looked around her with exaggerated sarcasm as if looking for a clue. 'Cannae see what?'

'That how you treated me was wrong! I bent over

backwards to please you, but nothin' I said or did was ever good enough, was it?'

Harman leaned forward in her seat, her eyes growing ever wider with disbelief. 'Seriously? You're bringin' this up now?'

'Because I've only just found the courage to speak my mind!'

Harman shook her head. 'Don't give me that! You've got the hide of a rhino!'

'Only I haven't,' said Mary softly. 'Not really. It was you that made me appear that way.'

Harman's jaw flinched. 'Don't go blamin' me! It's not as if I had a choice. It was either lie or throw you to the wolves, and I *told* you what would happen if the others knew the truth. Come to think, the way I remember it, you were in full agreement, so if anythin' you should be blamin' yourself, not me. That bein' said, I still reckon you should be grateful, cos I only did it to protect you—'

'No, you didn't. You just say that to excuse your behaviour. In truth you were only bothered about yourself and how it would look for *you*.'

Harman leaned forward. 'You put me in an impossible position.'

'Me? Are you actually bein' serious?' cried Mary, tears pricking her eyes. 'My daddy *died*! How the hell could that possibly be seen as bein' my fault?'

Harman's jaw twitched. Her eyes darting towards the guard, who was watching with interest, she tried to encourage Mary to lower her voice by lowering her own. 'I didn't say it was.'

'Yes, you did!' seethed Mary, although she did so quietly. 'I bet you even think that it was my fault that Mammy died whilst givin' birth to me!'

Harman opened her mouth, then quickly shut it again. Mary stared at her in horror. 'Oh my God, you actually do, don't you?'

Rather than answer, Harman changed the subject. 'I took you in, didn't I?'

Mary gave her a slow, sarcastic round of applause. 'Well done! How very kind . . . I *don't* think.'

'So what? Are you sayin' you'd have preferred the orphanage – or the streets?'

Mary banished the tears which were trying to form. 'I'd have preferred to be treated like your niece, cos that's who I am!'

Harman rolled her eyes. 'You make it sound so easy, but in reality it would've been far from that. I might add that you seem to be forgettin' that I lost my brother in all of this.'

Mary gave a mirthless chuckle. 'So, you do remember him then? Only you never spent any time with us. In fact, I didn't even know I had an auntie until after he passed.'

'It takes two to tango!' she snapped, before continuing in calmer tones. 'However, I suggest we leave it at that, as I have no desire to speak ill of the dead.'

Mary met her gaze. 'Now I know you're jokin'. I've heard you speak ill of the dead on many occasions.'

Harman leaned forward. 'So, what do you want me

to apologise for exactly? Takin' you in? Only I need to be clear on this, as I'm strugglin' to see what I'm supposed to have done wrong.'

'For treatin' me like one of the inmates instead of your niece,' said Mary, 'and for not showin' an ounce of compassion when you must've realised how tough it was for me.'

'And if I had everyone would have known something was amiss,' said Harman. 'I was keepin' our relationship quiet for your own good, though whether you believe that or not is up to you. But I remind you again that you thought it was a good idea when I put it to you.'

'Because I didn't know any better, and because you didn't make it clear that you expected me to snitch on them!' said Mary sullenly. 'And when I refused you threatened to tell them who I really was, and by that time even *I* knew that my goose would've been well and truly cooked!'

Harman heaved a weary sigh. 'In order to give you special treatment I had to make out that you were one of my favourites. I could hardly have done that without a reason, which is why I asked you to keep an eye out for rumours and gossip!'

'That may be so, but why couldn't I have lived with you in your quarters? Why did I have to be in the poorhouse at all?'

For the first time, Mary had silenced her aunt, and it was some time before Harman spoke again. 'Because I thought I was doin' the right thing. Apparently, I was wrong.'

Mary gave a disbelieving cough. 'Was that meant to be an apology?'

Harman finally gave in, if for no other reason than to get Mary off her back. 'If I didn't do right by you, then I'm sorry.'

Mary could've crowed with delight. It wasn't the most heartfelt apology in the world, and maybe not even the most sincere, but it was more than she had hoped for, and as such it would do. 'Thank you.'

Harman glanced towards the door. 'Is that it?'

Mary was about to say yes when something Harman had said earlier in the conversation came back to her. 'When I first came in you were convinced that I'd spoken to Madson. Why?'

Harman, who had not seen or heard from Madson for six months, pulled a disgruntled face. 'Cos he always did like gettin' others to do his dirty work for him, the lily-livered coward that he is.'

'But what would make him think that I would do anythin' for him?'

Harman spoke in undertones, whilst still appearing disinterested. 'He knows the two of us are related, so he probably figured that you'd do it for me if not for him.'

Mary was still confused. 'Do what, exactly?'

Harman was about to say that it was no concern of Mary's, but it had been too long since she'd seen Madson and she was more convinced than ever that he'd done the dirty on her. Feeling she had nothing to lose, she gestured for her niece to lean forward. 'When I left Coxhill there was a substantial amount of money hidden in a tin box under the window seat of my office. Madson knew about the money, but he didn't know where it was until he came to visit me.'

'What on earth would make you tell him where it was hidden?'

Harman glanced meaningfully around her. 'Because I wanted to get out of this hellhole and he said he'd use half the money to pay for a good lawyer.'

Mary's brow rose swiftly. 'And you believed him?'

Harman shrugged sullenly. 'I didn't see that I had much choice!'

Mary appeared thoughtful. 'But just knowin' where the money is won't do him any good. He cannae simply walk into a military hospital without a good reason for his presence. And they sure as hell wouldn't let him go into your office without being challenged.'

'Exactly! Which is why we came up with a plan,' said Harman. She went on to explain the conversation in great detail, much to the alarm of Mary, who struggled to keep the look of horror from her face.

'You couldn't have seriously thought you'd get away with it?'

Harman shrugged. 'Worth a shot.'

'But what if it went wrong?' said Mary, before adding, 'In fact, how do you know it hasn't? For all you know he might've been stupid enough to carry it out only to have things go drastically wrong, in which case he might well be dead!'

It seemed that this was something her aunt hadn't thought of, not that she showed any signs of remorse.

'If he is, then the money's still there . . .' she began excitedly.

Mary stared at her in disbelief. Uncertain how to respond, she turned the conversation back to the part of the plan that bothered her the most.

'Why Sophie?'

'Because she clacked him over the head with the coal shovel,' said Harman simply. 'Madson's always been one to bear a grudge, and it just so happened that Sophie's occupation meant he could get his revenge on her whilst also gettin' his hands on the money – two birds with one stone.'

'If he's gone ahead with the plan without you, then . . .'

Harman nodded, a disgruntled look on her face. 'Not that it's of any comfort to me.'

Mary remembered the day she had broken her toe hunting for Sophie whilst following her aunt's orders. *It was my own fault that I broke my toe*, she told herself now. *Sophie didn't deserve any of what my aunt had planned for her. And she sure as hell doesn't deserve what Madson has in store for her either – that's if he hasn't carried it out already. At best she could be dismissed from her job, at worst thrown in jail, and for what?*

Unable to keep her emotions under control, Mary stared at her aunt aghast. 'You don't care about anyone other than yourself, do you? Why would you do that to Sophie?'

'Because it was her fault that Madson didn't manage to destroy the evidence!' Harman hissed. 'Besides, why would you be bothered when she broke your toe?'

'She didn't! I broke my own toe by bein' vicious, because deep down I was jealous of Sophie and her pals because, unlike yours truly, they didn't have to dance to your tune!' She laughed at herself, incredulous. 'Jealous of people who had no livin' relatives, because it was better than having you as an aunt!'

Harman's eyes were spitting fire. 'You ungrateful little bitch!' Getting to her feet, she brought her cuffed hands back to take a swing at Mary, but the guard was too quick for her. Grasping her wrists in a vice-like grip, he spoke through gritted teeth.

'Now, now, we'll have none of that.' He glanced at Mary. 'I think it best if you take your leave, miss.'

Mary stood up. 'It'll be my pleasure.' She shot her aunt a withering look as she walked to the door. 'I hope to God he doesn't do anything before I manage to speak to Sophie.'

'Once a grass, always a grass. I should've known better!'

'Aye,' said Mary, a smile tweaking her lips. 'You should, considerin' you taught me everythin' I know.'

She could hear her aunt shouting profanities after her as she strode out of the room. *I must tell Sophie what Madson's planning*, thought Mary as she stepped through the outer door of the prison, but how could she do that when she had no idea where the other girl was? An image of Isla entered her mind, and she drew a deep breath. Isla was her only hope of getting her message to Sophie, so she had better start apologising, and fast!

*

Sophie was on her way back from her rounds, eager to quiz Martin on whether Madson had said anything to him. She knew it shouldn't matter what sort of nonsense the ghastly man might have been spouting, but if Martin had taken heed of any of his words it wouldn't be long before the rumours spread, which could have been Madson's intention all along. *It was probably the perfect form of revenge in his eyes*, Sophie thought as she pulled off the main road into the base. *All he had to do was light the touch paper and walk away. Well, not on my watch!* Seeing that Martin was still on duty, she leaned out of the window to flash her pass. 'Can you stay where you are? Only I'd like to have a word with you after I've called in at the office, if that's all right with you?'

He nodded, but she noticed that he did so grudgingly, as if he'd rather not talk to her given the choice. His expression left her in no doubt that Madson had indeed been bad-mouthing her to Martin. Worse still, it looked as though he believed what Madson had had to say.

Parking neatly, she popped into the office to report her return, before trotting back to the gate, where Martin was waiting for her with a look of anticipatory dread. Hoping to alleviate his worries, she gave him a cheery wave. 'Thanks for waiting.'

He stepped back into his kiosk. 'Is everythin' all right?'

'That depends on what that feller had to say about me, you know? The one I was havin' a heated discussion with a while back.'

Martin considered feigning innocence by saying he didn't know which feller Sophie was referring to, but he could see by the look on her face that he would be fooling no one. He sighed heavily, and told her everything that Madson had to say. Sophie listened without interruption, her cheeks growing pink as he described how Madson had told him of the incident with the coal shovel.

'He's not lyin' to you, exactly,' she admitted, trusting honesty to be the best policy if Martin were to believe her word over Madson's.

'So you did attack him, then?' Martin swallowed.

'Only because he was goin' to thrash my pal with an iron poker. And it wasn't us bein' up to no good – we were only exposing his part in defrauding the poorhouse. In short, he was stealin' the food from the inmates' mouths by creamin' money off the top and pocketin' it for himself.'

Martin's cheeks coloured slightly. 'He didn't mention any of that.'

'Well, he wouldn't, would he?' Sophie could hear her tone rising, and took a deep breath before continuing. 'Sorry, I didn't mean to snap, but it's frustrating to think you believed him over me when you don't even know him!'

'I wouldn't have done ordinarily, but from where I stood it looked as though you were the one having a go at him.'

Sophie thought back to the argument, and how Madson had lowered his voice while keeping his back to the gate the whole time. 'He set it up deliberately. He made sure it looked as though I were the aggressor by sayin' stuff he knew would rile me, and I fell for it.' For Martin's benefit she went on to elaborate. 'He made a stupid comment about a poker, knowin' that it would get my goat because it was obvious he was referring to the time he'd threatened to hit Isla.'

She could tell by the look on Martin's face that the penny had dropped. 'The devious sod! He made out he was scared of you because you'd nigh on killed him.'

'To be fair, he is scared of me, but only because he doesn't realise that it was a lucky shot. I wasn't aiming – I threw the shovel in desperation and it was sheer chance that it connected with his head!'

Martin smiled. 'The only bit I don't get is why he asked me to keep shtum. Surely he'd want that sort of thing spreading in order to create problems for you?'

Sophie thought for a moment. 'He probably wanted you to think that he was being noble by keeping quiet, while hoping, of course, that *you* would tell everyone what a horrible person I was, so I'd be hated and my life would be miserable as a result.'

Martin clapped a hand to his forehead. 'When he asked me not to say owt, I said that people had a right to know what you were really like. But he made out that he was worried about what you'd do to him if that were to happen, saying that you'd already threatened to make him rue the day he was born. Which is why I kept it to myself.'

'Thank goodness you did, cos I'd have had an awful job trying to prove my innocence with him no longer on the scene for people to question.'

'Which is why he did it,' said Martin.

'Well, let's hope he's got it out of his system,' Sophie sighed. 'And thanks again, Martin. You're a gem.'

'I'm just sorry I took any notice of him,' said Martin with a guilty grimace. 'What will you do if you see him again?'

She shrugged. 'There's no point in havin' it out with him because he'd be delighted to see that he'd got under my skin. If I do see him I shall just ignore him, pretend he doesn't exist. In the meantime, however, I will give Isla a call to let her know that we can lay our worries to rest.'

'You did have your doubts, then?'

'We weren't a hundred per cent certain. You see, Madson may have escaped jail due to lack of proof, but his partner in crime is currently servin' time, and she makes Madson look like an angel in comparison.'

'Good job she's the one inside, if that's the case,' said Martin.

'Exactly! The only trouble is, she knows all the right people from the wrong side of the tracks. So even if she cannae do anythin' herself, she could get someone to do her dirty work for her.'

He eyed her curiously. 'I hope you don't mind my askin', but where on earth did you meet these people?'

She grimaced. 'I was one of the inmates in the poorhouse.'

His face flushed. 'Sorry, I didn't realise – it must've been awful havin' people like that in charge!'

'Believe you me, I could tell you stories that would make your hair curl!'

'Well, should he ever call back, I shall make it clear that I'm not interested in what he has to say,' said Martin. 'But I shan't let on that I've been talkin' to you, just in case he decides to spread his poison elsewhere.'

She gave him a thumbs-up. 'Thanks, although I very much doubt he'll be back. He probably thinks he's done enough to get the ball rollin'. The last thing he'll want is to provide me with an opportunity to show him up as a liar.'

A car approached the gate, cueing them to part ways. 'Thanks again, Martin. I'm sorry you got dragged into this.'

'Not to worry; no harm done.'

Hoping the telephone in the NAAFI would be free, Sophie was glad to see the person using it was about to hang up the receiver. Hurrying over, she picked up the handset, and was relieved when Isla's voice came down the line a few moments later. 'I'm pleased to report that I've managed to get to the bottom of the whole Madson business,' Sophie told her, and described her conversation with Martin.

'So no need to worry, then. That's a relief!' said Isla once Sophie had finished.

'Isn't it just! I'm sure Meg will be happy to know it's all over and done with, so I'll drop her a line as soon as we're through. I'd wager it'll come as a relief to Rory, too.'

'Very much so. I know he meant well when he insisted I should never go out on my own, but that's not always easy when everyone's workin' different shifts, and I didn't much fancy explainin' why I wanted company in the first place, so I only went into town when I knew for certain that someone else was goin'.'

'He cares about you, which is very sweet,' said Sophie, adding as an afterthought, 'How are things on that front? Any more cases of mistaken identity?'

'Not a single one, thank goodness,' said Isla, 'and as for everythin' else, I'd say we're goin' from strength to strength.'

'Sounds as though you've turned a corner.'

'I hope so,' Isla sighed, adding, 'Madson might actually have done me a favour, cos focusin' on him made me realise there were bigger and more immediate things to worry about.'

'Which brings me to my next question. Have you heard from Theo?'

'Not since I told him about Rory.' Isla grimaced. 'I wish I could've told him face to face, but an opportunity like that could be months away – if not years!'

'You did the right thing,' said Sophie. 'This way he has a chance to start anew, rather than holdin' on to somethin' that was never goin' to come to fruition.'

'Exactly.'

The operator cut across, letting them know their time was up.

'I'll give you a call at the weekend,' said Sophie. 'Take care, Isla.'

'You, too! T.t.f.n.'

Sophie replaced the handset with the satisfied air of a job well done. *No more Madson or Harman*, she told herself. *There's nothin' they can do to touch me now!*

Chapter Seven

It had been several weeks since Sophie's phone call, and Isla was sitting on the end of her bed reading a copy of *Vogue* magazine when Kate came in with the mail.

'It's rainin' cats and dogs out there,' she said as she sifted through the envelopes. 'Better that than the hail they promised, though.'

Isla shivered. 'Anythin's better than hail!' She glanced to the wad of envelopes in Kate's hands. 'Anythin' for me?'

'There is indeed!' Kate said as she gathered Isla's post together. 'Not that I'm bein' nosy or owt like that, but you've five letters today, one of which you've been waitin' on for quite some time.'

Isla put the magazine to one side. 'Theo?' she enquired, with anxious hope.

Kate nodded with a grim smile as she handed them over. 'On the bright side, there's no smudged ink.'

Isla frowned as she glanced at the envelopes one by one. 'Why would there be smudged ink?'

'From his tears,' teased Kate, before holding up her hands in mock surrender. 'Sorry, I couldn't resist.'

'I feel bad enough as it is, without you addin' to it,' Isla mumbled.

'I know, and it was wrong of me to tease you, but I'm sure Theo's big enough to take it on the chin. He has written back, after all!'

'Let's hope you're right.' Selecting Theo's letter, Isla slit it open. Crossing her fingers, she was about to begin reading when her eyes fell to the date at the top.

'He wrote this months back!' she cried. 'All this time I've been worryin' over what he might be thinkin' just because his letter got lost in the bloomin' mail!'

Kate shrugged. 'At least it got here in the end.'

Isla gave a resigned sigh. 'There is that.' Her eyes fell to the rest of the letter and she began to read.

My darling Isla,

I'm so sorry it's taken me so long to reply, but things have been heating up over here and I'm not referring to the constant sunshine!

I won't deny that I was sorry to hear that you've found someone else, but I mean it sincerely when I say that I hope he's the right man for you, because you deserve someone special who will treat you like the queen you are.

You've done so much for me by just being there and I hope you know how important you are to me. A part of my heart will always belong to you, because you were the first woman who treated me like a decent human being after learning the truth about my past. The fact that you were gracious enough to remain my friend just proves what a beautiful soul you are both inside and out. I truly hope that you will remain a part of my life, as you're very dear to me, and I'd hate to lose you as a friend.

That being said, life over here . . .

Having read the rest of his epistle, which was short but sweet, Isla looked up at Kate who was eyeing her apprehensively. 'Well?'

'He's taken it like a true champ, and I was silly to ever doubt him. He's always been upbeat, even when the chips are down, and I count myself lucky to have him as a friend, no matter his past.' Elated that all her worries seemed to be dissipating, she sifted through the rest of the envelopes until she came across one with handwriting she didn't recognise. She pulled a downward smile. 'Odd.'

'What is?'

Isla picked up the envelope and looked at the back. 'This has been forwarded from my last station, RAF Immingham, but I don't recognise the writing at all.'

Kate wriggled her eyebrows. 'A secret admirer?'

Isla shook her head fervently. 'I very much hope not! Havin' the attention of two men at once was more than enough, thank you very much!' She slit the envelope open and cursed softly beneath her breath as her eyes fell to the signature at the bottom.

'Not good news?' hazarded Kate with a grimace.

'It's that bloomin' Mary, the one I told you about,' said Isla sullenly.

'*Her*?' Abandoning her mail mission, Kate sat down on the opposite bed. 'What the heck is she writin' to you for?'

Clearing her throat, Isla read the letter out loud. '"Dear Isla, I realise that I'm probably the last person you'd want to hear from, and I could understand if you threw this letter straight into the bin, but please believe me when I tell you that Sophie's in real danger."' Isla's sarcastic tone wavered, but she continued, '"I won't write everything down in this letter because I can't take the risk that the censors might blot out important pieces of information. I know that I've done some terrible things in the past and I'm truly sorry for that, but I've learned something lately that made my blood run cold, and it involves Madson."' Isla's eyes flicked to Kate before looking back at the letter. '"I really hope I'm not too late, because despite what any of you may think, I would hate to see Sophie behind bars. So please, please, please, if you do anything today, either contact me at RAF Coningsby, or if you can't bear the thought of talking to me, then at least tell Sophie to take extra care when she's out in her car, because she's heading for disaster."'

Kate stared. 'Bloody hell, Isla, what on earth has been goin' on?'

'God only knows. We have had a spot of bother with this Madson chap, but we thought it had all been laid to rest. However, if I'm to believe Mary, and I'm rather inclined to say that I am, then it would appear that things are far from over after all.'

'But what could this person possibly do that would land Sophie behind bars?' She hesitated. 'I know from what you've said that this Mary character can be a right piece of work – you don't suppose this is her idea of some sort of sick joke, do you?'

'Before the business in Immingham I'd have said yes, without doubt, but there's somethin' in the urgency of her words which makes me think this might be genuine.'

'Then why didn't she telephone Sophie herself?'

'She wouldn't know where Sophie was based. She didn't know I'd moved, either; it was just lucky for her that they sent the letter on.'

'Hmmmm ... you might be right. After all, it sounds as though this Madson bloke knows where Sophie's based, so he'd have told Mary if they were on some sort of wind-up mission.'

'Good point,' said Isla, 'but why would she warn us? I'd have thought she'd have revelled in the fact that we were goin' to get our comeuppance.'

Kate cast her a shrewd glance. 'Depends on how bad his idea of revenge is. Were he and Mary close?'

Isla pulled a revolted face. 'No! He was old enough to be her father. As far as I'm aware they never so much as spoke to one another, and I certainly wouldn't have thought even she'd have done his dirty work for him.'

'All you can do is give her a ring and see what's

what, and the sooner the better if that letter's anythin' to go by!'

Isla was in full agreement. 'Shan't be a mo,' she said, and headed for the NAAFI.

Mary wiped her floury hands on her apron as she took the phone from the Waaf who was holding it out for her. 'Someone by the name of Isla Donahue?' said the Waaf.

Nodding, Mary felt her tummy flutter as she held the handset to her ear. 'Hello?'

'It's me,' said Isla, somewhat stiffly.

'Is Sophie all right?'

'As far as I know.' Isla paused. 'What's this about, Mary?'

Mary gave an audible sigh of relief. 'Thank goodness for that. As for what it's about, safe to say that Madson is plannin' to get his own back on Sophie . . . and I'm talkin' big time.'

'How do you know?'

It was the question that Mary had been dreading. 'I know how this is goin' to sound, so please hear me out.' She went on to explain her reason for the prison order, and the conversation thereafter.

Isla listened carefully, only interrupting once to say, 'Harman's your *aunt*?'

'I'm afraid so, but we've more important things to worry about right now,' said Mary, before continuing her tale.

Having listened in stunned silence, Isla found it difficult to believe that Madson would take such an idiotic risk, and said as much. 'Are you certain that Madson and your aunt aren't sayin' all this just to have a bit of fun at your expense, or to cause more beef between us?'

'Positive. She actually got excited when she thought the money might still be there if Madson was dead!'

Isla was convinced. 'That sounds like her. But are you sure he intends to throw himself in front of her car?' she said, her tone incredulous. 'I mean, what if it goes wrong?'

'That's what I said. Although I don't suppose he's plannin' on steppin' into the road when she's goin' hell for leather. And he'll want as many witnesses as possible, so he'll do it in a populated area where there's a speed limit.'

'Actually, on reflection I think it's exactly the sort of dumb thing he would do,' said Isla. 'You said in your letter that you were servin' in the NAAFI at RAF Coningsby, correct?'

'Yes. Unsurprisingly, they wouldn't have me back on the balloon sites after I lied about my identity. Why d'you ask?'

'So that we can keep in touch. I'm goin' to give Sophie a quick call now to let her know what's afoot, but I'll keep you in the loop so that we can work together to stop Madson from doin' the unthinkable.'

Mary felt herself begin to well up. 'Thanks, Isla,' she said, her voice heavy with relief.

'What for?'

'For believin' me when you didn't have to, and for

not tearin' a couple of strips off me, cos it would have been no more than I deserve.'

'We all make mistakes,' said Isla. 'It's how you deal with them that counts, and it sounds to me as though you're sorry for your past behaviour.'

'Very much so,' said Mary with verve. 'Good luck with Sophie, and please tell her that I'm truly sorry for everythin' I did in Coxhill, and that I hope she gets Madson bang to rights for even thinkin' about this.'

'Will do.' Isla briefly replaced the receiver before asking the operator to put her through to Sophie's base in Scarborough.

'Sorry, but she's left for the day,' said the Wren who had come back from trying to find Sophie. 'Can I take a message?'

'Yes. Please tell her that Isla Donahue called, and that it's imperative she call me as soon as she gets back.'

'I'll make sure to pass it on.'

Isla bade her goodbye, and had a swift conversation with the telephone operator. 'I know I've already made more calls than I should, but this could be a matter of life and death!'

Grudgingly, the operator put her through, and Isla almost wept with relief when Meg's voice came down the line.

'Isla! How's tricks?'

Isla explained.

'The sneaky, connivin' rat!' hissed Meg. 'I knew he must be up to somethin', cos men like Madson don't stop until there's bloodshed, and this just goes to prove it. Only how is Sophie meant to stop him from jumpin' out in front of her?'

'That's the trouble, cos she cannae. All she can do is be extra vigilant,' said Isla. 'Forewarned is forearmed, which is something at least, although what happens next I really cannae say, other than that she should report him to his superiors, so they've at least been told of his intentions. That way, if he ever goes ahead with it, she's got some sort of proof that he'd planned to do it in advance, and if they have a word with him it might be enough to make him leave her alone once and for all!'

'Do you really think it will, though? He's like a dog with a bone, is that one.'

Isla heaved a sigh. 'I'd like to think so, but he does seem to be hell bent on revenge; add the money to that and I don't think there's an awful lot that will stand in his way. In the meantime, we're goin' to have to get our thinkin' caps on and come up with a plan that will get that rotten man out of our lives once and for all!'

'I'll run it past my Kenny,' said Meg. 'He's normally good with this sort of stuff.'

'The more heads the better,' agreed Isla, before adding, 'I bet Rory will have an idea or two, as well.'

Blissfully unaware of the plan that Madson had in store for her, Sophie was on her way to the docks to hand over several boxes of paperwork before receiving fresh instructions.

Waiting in the stationary traffic for the lights to change, she kept a keen eye out for the handsome seaman whom she sometimes saw in the area of the docks. *I know Isla would think me soft for pinnin' my hopes on someone who is married to the sea, but I cannae help the way I feel. No other man has drawn my interest the way he has, and even though I know I should give up the idea, I just don't seem able to.* The cars in front began to edge forward slowly as the lights changed, and Sophie turned her attention to the road ahead. Gathering speed, she was changing up to third gear when from out of nowhere someone shot across the road in front of the car, closely followed by another man, who pushed the first out of the way only to go flying over the bonnet himself. Ramming her foot hard on the brake, Sophie ripped the handbrake into position before leaping out of the car and running to where the man who'd been hit was lying face down on the road. Throwing herself onto her knees, she yelled out to the gathering onlookers, 'For God's sake, don't just stand their gawpin'! Call for a bloody ambulance!'

A man in docker's clothing hurried off, shouting 'I'll go' over his shoulder as he went.

'I'm so, so sorry,' said Sophie, panicked tears streaming down her face, her lip quivering as she continued to talk to the prone man in apologetic tones whilst praying that she hadn't actually killed him. 'I swear I didn't see you!'

The man grunted, but whatever it was he said was unintelligible.

Thankful that he was at least still breathing, Sophie

felt relief flood through her. 'Don't worry. Someone's called for an ambulance.'

The man turned his head ever so slightly, and Sophie recognised him instantly. 'You!' she cried.

His white teeth flashed as he attempted to smile. 'We really have to stop meetin' like this.'

Sophie was beside herself with apologies. 'Oh, Donny! I really am sorry. Are you all right?'

Donny peered at her through a bleary eye, a weak smile forming on his lips. 'I am now.'

Relieved beyond measure that he was able to make light of the situation, she asked the question uppermost in her thoughts. 'What on earth possessed you to run out into the road the way you did?' She stroked his hair away from the blood which was seeping across his forehead.

'It was that feller in front of me,' said Donny. 'I can't imagine what made him jump out in front of you the way he did, cos we could all see that the lights had changed, but he just ran into the road as though he hadn't a care in the world.'

Sophie looked round at the curious onlookers. 'Is the other man all right? Did anyone see where he went?'

'He legged it,' said one of the women. 'He probably realised what he'd done and didn't want to hang around to face the music.'

However, a policeman who'd witnessed the whole incident had managed to apprehend the man who'd been the cause of it all, and had escorted him back to the scene of the accident. 'Here he is. I caught him tryin' to run off,' he said, before addressing his captive directly. 'You owe this man – and the driver here – an apology as well as a huge thank you, not to mention a couple of drinks. What the hell were you thinkin' of?'

Sophie looked at the man, who was doing his best to tear himself from the policeman's grip. '*Madson?*'

The policeman looked from Sophie to Madson and back again. 'Are you tellin' me you know him?'

'Unfortunately, yes,' said Sophie.

Madson pointed a trembling finger at her. 'She tried to kill me! You all saw it! If it weren't for this feller I'd be pushin' up daisies.'

Grimacing in pain, Donny shook his head, whilst others in the crowd expressed their disbelief. 'Rubbish! The whole thing was your fault! Only a madman would have tried to cross the road after the lights had turned green.'

'Complete and utter codswallop,' the policeman agreed. 'I saw the whole thing with my own eyes. You were lookin' her square in the face when you jumped out, so you must've realised she hadn't seen you.'

Sophie stared at Madson, who was refusing to look at her. 'Did you know it was me?'

'Don't talk rubbish!' Madson shouted at the policeman, although his cheeks were beginning to ruddy. 'Why the hell would I do somethin' like that?'

The constable looked from Sophie to Madson and back again. 'I don't know what's goin' on here, but if the two of you have got beef I suggest you sort it out some other way, before someone gets seriously hurt!'

'It's a bit late for that!' Sophie objected as the

policeman released his grip on Madson. 'Surely you can arrest him for the harm he's caused?'

The policeman shook his head. 'Unfortunately, being stupid isn't a crime. The cells would be full to the rafters if it were.'

Sophie cried out in frustration as Madson scurried into the crowd and disappeared. 'Maybe not, but that was no accident: he did it on purpose. Surely there has to be somethin' you can do?'

But the policeman pulled an apologetic grimace. 'I'm afraid not, unless you've proof he intended to do it all along?'

Sophie shook her head miserably.

Turning his attention to Donny, the constable got down on his haunches to speak to him. 'Do you reckon you'd be able to stand up?'

'Tough as old boots, me,' said Donny, but even the smallest movement caused him to cry out in pain. Speaking through gritted teeth, he stared down at his motionless limb. 'I think my leg might be broken.'

Sophie covered her eyes with her hand. Any hope she had that she and the sailor might one day become an item had died the moment he hit the ground.

It was much later the same day that Isla got the message that Sophie was on the phone, wanting to speak to her. Hurrying to the NAAFI, she thanked the Waaf who passed her the handset and gabbled into it without waiting for Sophie to speak. 'Am I glad to hear from you! What I'm about to say is goin' to sound bonkers as well as outlandish, but here goes:

Madson's plannin' on gettin' you done for attempted murder by jumpin' out in front of your car.'

There was a brief pause before Sophie said: 'How the hell did you know that?'

Isla stood in shocked silence before eventually finding her tongue. 'You mean to say you already know?'

'I didn't until he jumped out in front of my car this morning,' said Sophie. 'But you've not answered my question.'

Keen to hear the rest of Sophie's tale, Isla spoke quickly. 'It was Mary,' she said, and went on to tell Sophie everything Mary had told her, adding at the end, 'So did he achieve his goal? Please tell me he didn't.'

'He would have,' said Sophie grimly, 'only that feller I told you about, the one you call Blackbeard? Well, he pushed Madson out of the way just in the nick of time. Trouble is, he took the full force, and now it's him who's in hospital with a fractured leg and pelvis, not Madson.'

Isla clapped a hand to her mouth. 'No!'

'I'm afraid so, and I feel absolutely terrible about the whole thing. Madson tried to leg it, but a policeman managed to catch him before he got away.'

Isla brightened. 'That's good! Am I to take it he's been arrested?'

'No! In fact he was blethering on sayin' that I'd tried to run him over intentionally, but luckily for me Donny said that Madson had waited for the lights to change before stepping into the road on purpose and if anyone was to blame it was him not me.' She sighed.

'I asked the policeman if he could arrest him for causin' the accident, but he said no.'

'So where's Madson now?'

'Probably back on his base,' said Sophie. She hesitated. 'There was one thing the policeman did say . . .'

'Oh?'

'He said he couldn't arrest Madson unless we had proof that he'd intended to jump out in front of me. Of course, I didn't think we had at the time, but do you think Mary would be willing to tell the police that he'd planned the whole thing?'

'Without a doubt,' said Isla. 'She's eager to make amends for everythin' she did in Coxhill, and to prove that she's no longer the person she was under Harman's rule.'

Sophie began to sound more chipper. 'If she did, then surely they'd have to arrest him, given what the policeman said?'

'I'd have thought so. I'm not sure what the charge would be, but I hope they'd take Donny's injuries into account.'

'Trouble is, Mary telephoned you, so there's no actual proof of the content of the call. It would be different if you'd got somethin' in writing.'

Isla gave a strangled cry of triumph. 'But I have! She wrote to tell me that Madson was going to try and get you arrested – she didn't go into much detail, but I'm sure it'd be enough to prove that we're tellin' the truth! Not only that, but Mary knows where the money is that Madson was after, and if it's still there it will go to show that he had motive as well as reason.

Surely all that would be too big a coincidence for the police to ignore?'

'Along with Donny's account of the facts, plus Mary's chat with Harman, I reckon we could have him bang to rights! Even the policeman said that Madson was looking me square in the face before walking out in front of me.'

'Leave it with me!' cried Isla. 'Oh, and tell Blackbeard I hope he gets better soon – I take it you will be goin' back to visit him?'

'Of course I will. I could hardly turn my back on him when it's my fault he's in hospital in the first place.' Hearing Isla begin to protest, Sophie continued quickly, 'I know that what Madson did wasn't my fault, but if it had been any other driver behind the wheel of that car Madson wouldn't have done it and Donny would still have two workin' legs.'

'Still not your fault,' said Isla, 'but I suppose I can see where you're comin' from, an' I'd probably feel the same in your shoes. Anyhow, I'd best say goodbye and call Mary; strike while the iron's hot, as they say.'

'Be sure to keep me in the loop.'

'Of course! Keep your fingers crossed.'

'Will do!'

Isla had a brief conversation with the operator, ending, 'I know it's my second call in a row, and I'm also very much aware that I've been usin' the telephone a lot of late, but this is really important, and I promise you there's no one else waitin' to use the phone.'

'As long as you don't make a habit of it,' warned the operator. 'And please keep it brief.'

Isla promised she would, and was relieved when Mary was the one who answered the phone in her NAAFI.

'I was too late to warn Sophie,' Isla paused as Mary groaned wearily on the other end of the line, 'but the good news is she hit someone else.'

Mary gasped. 'My God! Are they all right?'

'Yes. And I didn't mean it was good news, exactly, but better than hittin' Madson, who did jump out in front of her. What's more, she kind of knows the feller that she hit . . .' She went on to tell Mary everything that Sophie had told her, asking when she had finished, 'So what do you reckon? Are you willin' to tell the polis your side of the story?' She waited with bated breath to see if Mary would agree, and wasn't disappointed with her reaction.

'Consider it done! Only who do I tell, the police here in Coningsby or the police in Scarborough?'

'Scarborough,' said Isla promptly. 'We don't know where Madson's based, but we do know that he's in khaki uniform, so he's got to be in the army.'

'I'll make sure to pass on the information,' said Mary, adding, 'Do I tell them about the money, or should we leave that to the polis in Clydebank?'

'I'd say Scarborough again, and they can take it from there. And in the meantime I'll have a word with Harvey Ellis—'

'The feller that used to be in Coxhill?'

'Aye. It was him that helped us escape, and we've kept in touch with him ever since.'

'If he'd be willin' to tell the polis everythin' he

knows about Madson and my aunt's schemes, it would be further proof as to Madson's character, and I reckon they'd soon have him behind bars then.'

'I'll make him my top priority,' said Isla. 'The operator here hasn't exactly been pleased with all the calls I've been makin' of late, but this is important.' She heard a small hurrumph, which she didn't think came from Mary.

'And I'll call the polis station in Scarborough,' said Mary. 'In the meantime, if it's any use to Mr Ellis, you can tell him the money's hidden in a tin box under the window seat of Harman's old office.'

'Will do. And thanks, Mary. You wanted us to know how sorry you were, and you've certainly proved it. In fact, you've really come up trumps!'

'Least I can do, all things considered.'

Hearing the operator clearing her throat, Isla said 'Speak soon' before replacing the receiver and waiting for all of thirty seconds before picking it back up. To her immense relief it was a different voice that came down the line, and she asked to be put through to Harvey Ellis.

'Isla! How's tricks?'

Isla told him as quickly as she could, then waited for his response.

'I don't know where to begin,' he breathed. 'I suppose I should start with Mary, cos she had us all fooled, didn't she?'

'And for good reason,' said Isla, 'but she's doin' her best to make up for it now. Regarding Madson, what do you think? Can you do anythin' to help?'

'Yes, I can! Mr Armitage has turned the place upside down looking for the undeclared money. He'll be delighted to know we can finally lay our hands on it.'

'Brilliant! I just hope it's still there, and someone hasn't pinched it in the meantime cos it'll give real weight to Mary's story.'

'The more evidence you have against them the better, and by the sound of things you've got quite a lot already. But Madson aside, how're things otherwise? Do you see much of the girls?'

'Not as much as I'd like,' confessed Isla, 'but we write to each other a lot, and we're always on the phone. But it's not the same as seein' someone in person.'

'And what about your father? Are you any closer to findin' him?'

Isla shook her head. 'I'm datin' a lovely chap by the name of Rory, who's promised to help me find him, but I'm not goin' to get my hopes up just to have them dashed all over again.'

'I'm sure he wouldn't do that,' said Harvey. 'As for your father, I'll make sure to keep my ear to the ground, cos I get to do a fair bit of travellin' in my line of work.'

'Thanks, Harvey. You're a gem, you truly are. In the meantime, I'll let you know how things progress.'

'No need!' said Harvey jovially. 'I fully intend to speak to Scarborough police before the day is through to bring them up to speed with everythin' that's happened.'

Isla beamed. 'Harvey, you're one in a million!'

*

Convinced that no real harm had come from his encounter with Sophie, Madson was about to go for his lunch when his sergeant entered the Nissen hut.

'Madson? You'd better come with me.'

Madson wrinkled his brow. 'I was just about to go on me lunch.'

The sergeant's face clouded. 'It wasn't a request.'

Madson stuffed his hands into his trouser pockets as he followed the sergeant over to the office. Seeing the parked police car he groaned inwardly. *No prizes for guessin' what this is over*, he thought bitterly. *That cow must've put in a complaint, which is ruddy ridiculous considerin' they've already told her I wasn't breakin' the law. Still, I suppose they have to check these things out.*

Entering the office he glanced towards the uniformed policemen who were standing next to a man in a pinstriped suit. Sighing wearily, Madson folded his arms across his chest. 'If this has anythin' to do with that Sophie, then it should be her you're talkin' to and not me. After all, she was the one that tried to run me over, no matter what she might say.'

The suited man stepped forward. 'I thought you might say that, so it's just as well that we have evidence to the contrary.'

Madson laughed in his face. 'You must be off your bloomin' rocker! How can you possibly have evidence when there isn't any?'

'Would you be surprised if I were to tell you that we are in possession of a letter that proves you'd intended to frame her for attempted murder?'

'Surprised!' Madson guffawed. 'I'd be bleedin' flabbergasted!'

'So it wasn't your intention to get Miss Garvey arrested for attempted murder, whilst you were taken to Coxhill Military Hospital with the intention of retrieving the money which Miss Harman had hidden below the window seat in her office?'

Madson stared at him open-mouthed, his eyes narrowing. 'Who the bloody hell have you been talkin' to? Cos they're lyin'.'

The inspector tapped the side of his nose. 'You must know that I'm not at liberty to divulge that sort of information, but what I can say is we know all about your shenanigans, including your visit to Miss Harman at Duke Street Prison.'

Madson paled. If they knew about the visit it must have been her that spilled the beans, but why would she do that? His eyes narrowed as he remembered her words. 'Put one toe out of line and I'll break my golden rule . . .' *It's been so long since I saw her, she must have thought I'd double-crossed her and taken the money for myself,* he thought. *Only rather than dob me in for my part in Coxhill she decided to tell them about the plan to put Sophie behind bars.* He shrugged inwardly. Throwing Harman under the bus had worked for him once: what was there to say that it wouldn't work for him again? 'It was all Harman's idea!' One of the policeman had slapped him in handcuffs before he could finish his sentence. Crying out for the policeman to remove the handcuffs he ploughed on, 'I told you! It weren't my idea. Harman set me up cos she's still bitter about Coxhill.' He stopped speaking as his words caught up with him.

The inspector frowned. 'Why would she be bitter about Coxhill?'

Madson refused to answer.

'Not to worry – we'll get Miss Harman's side of events in due course,' said the inspector.

Madson frowned. 'But you've already spoken to her.'

The inspector gave a fleeting downward smile. 'What makes you think that?'

'You said . . .'

He shook his head. 'I think you'll find I didn't say a word. You *assumed* we'd spoken to Miss Harman, whereas in actual fact we haven't.'

Madson's face dropped. 'You're lyin'.'

'I'm afraid not. We got our information from a totally different source.'

Madson was racking his brains. The only people who knew about the plan were him and Harman. He sure as hell hadn't breathed a word, which meant that she must have, but why or who would she have spoken to? It would have to be someone she trusted, someone who knew the girls as well as her . . . His face dropped. 'It was that bloody niece of hers, wasn't it?'

Once again the inspector shook his head. 'As I've already said, I'm not at liberty to divulge—'

'You don't have to,' said Madson, 'but I'm surprised you'd take her niece's word for anything considerin' it's obvious whose side she'd be on.

Which brings me to another matter. All this is hearsay. You've still got no actual proof.'

'Only we have, in the form of the letter, remember?'

'What letter?'

'The one warnin' of your intent.'

'But . . . ' Madson broke off as he lowered his gaze. If he were to stand a chance of getting out of this unscathed, he'd best wait until he'd spoken to a solicitor. *I was right to think that visitin' Harman in prison might end in disaster*, he thought as they led him away, *but I didn't think for a minute it would end as badly as this!*

Isla put her shoes to one side as Kate handed over the mail. 'Oooh, one from Theo I see,' she said as she slit the first envelope open.

'I'm glad that the two of you are still in touch,' Kate told her. 'Too many people *say* they'll remain friends when they don't really mean it.'

'Not Theo,' said Isla, 'he's one of the good ones.' Glancing down at the letter a slow smile split her cheeks.

My dearest darling Isla,

I'm pleased to say that since writing to you last I've had a really good think about my life in general and I'm finally beginning to see the man that you always saw in me! As such I no longer blame myself for things I did when I was still an adolescent. No longer do I hide behind the truth, instead I'm upfront and honest from the start, and it's already paying off! I've met the most wonderful woman by the name of Clara. She's not in the services, being native to South Africa. She reminds me a lot of you in that she has a good head on her shoulders, and she doesn't judge a person by their past. Whilst I'll always regret lying to you the way I did, I'm not sorry that our paths crossed because you've been the making of me, and I'll be forever grateful for that. I truly and genuinely wish you and Rory the best for the future and I'd love to meet up when I come back to Blighty!

He went on to tell her how he'd met Clara and how she'd put a smile back on his face. *Everyone deserves happiness*, thought Isla as she folded the letter and replaced it in the envelope, *and I couldn't be more pleased to hear that he's finally turned a corner!*

Chapter Eight

MARCH 1943

'Accordin' to what the inspector told Harvey, Harman was spitting feathers when she heard how Madson had tried to lay the blame on her doorstep!' cried Isla joyously as she and Rory walked through Princes Park. 'He said that she well and truly blew a fuse when she heard how Madson had tried to pin the whole thing on her, just as he had the last time, and that she had demanded to make a fresh statement concerning the night of her arrest where she confessed his involvement in defrauding the government. She cited dates, times and places, and when they found the money they also found a handwritten note from Madson giving clear instruction on how to fix the books.'

Rory gave her a one-armed hug. 'Sophie must've been cock-a-hoop when she heard the news.'

'And then some,' agreed Isla. 'Cos even though *we* all knew the truth, she did worry that the polis might believe Madson over her, because he was once in a position of importance.'

'Position of importance my arse!' said Rory, much to Isla's amusement. 'He's lower than a rat in my opinion – Harman too, come to that – and that's why they're both behind bars where they belong. Has Sophie done anything to celebrate?'

'Not as such, but I believe she intends to take Blackbeard out for a meal just as soon as he's up and walking.'

'He's damned lucky to get away with a fractured pelvis,' said Rory. 'What on earth possessed Madson to take such a risk is beyond me. For an intelligent man, he can't half be stupid!'

'My thoughts exactly,' Isla agreed.

'And what about Mary? I know Harman was the aunt from hell, but I believe she's the only livin' relative Mary has left?'

'Mary's just happy she could do her bit. She only went to visit Harman in the first place so that she could tell her what she thinks of her, and she's done that all right and then some!' said Isla. She shook her head. 'If you'd told me this time last year that I'd be talkin' favourably about Mary I'd have thought you were barmy!'

'The world is full of surprises. Just look at me. I swore off women for the rest of my life, and then I met you!'

She smiled. 'Did I tell you that I'd had another letter from Theo?'

'After the one where he said he hoped to keep you as a friend?'

'Aye. It seems that he's started datin' again. She's not in the services, but she does live in Africa, so what that will mean when the war's over, who knows? But he certainly seems smitten. His whole letter was Clara this and Clara that.'

'It just goes to show.'

'What does?'

'That good friends can get you through just about anythin',' said Rory plainly. 'You told Theo that he'd find the right girl for him in the fullness of time, and by the sound of it he's done just that.'

'He does appear to be very much in love,' said Isla. 'And she's in for no nasty surprises, because he says he's already told her everythin'.'

'She knows about him bein' married before?'

'The whole shebang,' said Isla. 'I must admit I'm really proud of him. It's taken a lot for him to forgive himself, but now he's done that he can finally move on.'

'Time certainly is a great healer, but as I said, havin' good friends helps a great deal too.'

'Are you referrin' to Jimmy?'

Rory nodded. 'I dread to think where I'd be without him.'

'I've said it before and I'll say it again: I hope my father has a good bunch of pals he can turn to, even if it's just to have a good old-fashioned whinge!'

'Men don't whinge!' Rory chuckled, tongue-in-cheek.

Isla laughed. 'They're worse than the women half the time!'

'They certainly are when it comes to gossip,' confessed Rory, 'but don't tell anyone I said that.'

'It's strange how we always try to pigeonhole people into certain categories, don't you think? For example, women making the best cooks! Why do people think that when I cannae cook to save my life? Apart from egg and chips, of course!'

'I think they're the roles society expects us to play. But the war's changed all that, don't you think?'

'I'd certainly like to think so, but I reckon women's part in the war is for convenience only. I mean, can you really see anyone hirin' Sophie to drive a car when the war's over? It's the same for the female mechanics. They're every bit as good as the men, yet they'll be thin on the ground when we're at peace.'

'I guess that depends on how many men make it back,' Rory said without thinking.

Isla's face fell. 'Please don't say that.'

He shrugged. 'It's true, though, and you and I both know it.'

'That's as maybe, but hearin' the words come out of your mouth makes it more real somehow.'

They walked into the Grafton, and checked in their jackets before heading to the bar. 'Lemonade for me, please,' said Isla as the barmaid came to take their order.

'And a half of bitter for me,' said Rory, fishing his wallet out of his trouser pocket.

'What do you think the world will look like when the war *is* over?' Isla said as she took her drink from the barmaid. 'Our parents have been through this once before and I dare say they never thought anything like it could happen again – in fact I know they didn't, because mine told me so when Chamberlain made his speech. But Dad knew we'd go to war the moment Hitler invaded Czechoslovakia.'

'I'd like to think that this will be the war to end all wars,' said Rory dolefully, 'but history proves otherwise.'

'Why do they do it? Why is there always one man who thinks he can rule the world?'

Rory took a drink from his glass and wiped the froth from his lip. 'Greed,' he said flatly. 'Nothin' more and nothin' less.'

'But history proves that dictators never win. Are they stupid as well as greedy?'

'Probably, but you have to remember that they most likely don't see themselves as dictators,' said Rory, putting his glass down on a table near the dance floor. 'They probably think they're far more intelligent than anyone else and their country would fall without their guidance.'

'So do you think that the Germans *want* to do what Hitler's tellin' them to, or are they only doin' so because they're as frightened of him as we are?' She lowered her lashes, her hands in her lap. 'Well, as I certainly am.'

He took her hand in his. 'I think they're just as scared as us. You only have to see what he did to his own party to know what he's capable of.'

She nodded. 'The night of the long knives.'

'Which is why we won't let him beat us,' said Rory, adding simply, 'We just cannae.'

'Do you think it will deter other dictators from doin' the same in future years?'

He gave her what he hoped was a reassuring smile. 'Certainly for some time to come.'

'Good. I wouldn't want my kids to go through somethin' like this.'

He raised his brow. 'Kids?'

She nodded. 'People always ask if losin' my mammy the way I did has put me off havin' kiddies of my own, and whilst I'll admit it did at first, I now realise you cannae go through the rest of your life too frightened to put one foot in front of the other on account of what happened to somebody else. If you do that you're not really living.'

'Very true!'

'What about you?'

'Two of each,' said Rory promptly. 'I'm – or rather I *think* I'm an only child, and I want my kids to have siblings, like a normal family.'

'Define normal.'

He rubbed his hand across his mouth to hide his smile. 'A large one, where everyone gets on like a house on fire and there's always meat on the table and a loaf in the oven – and a white picket fence, of course, because surely that's a must?'

Isla laughed. 'How very British! But not for me.'

He was intrigued. 'Oh aye? And what's your idea of perfection?'

The band had struck up a waltz, and she kept her eyes on them as she spoke. 'A croft, with sheep, and hens, and whitewashed walls. There'd be a cottage garden with heather, and harebells, and we'd have a vegetable garden with potatoes, carrots and runner beans.' She turned, to see Rory grinning at her. 'What?'

'Would you not be scared of things that go woof in the night?'

Isla shrieked with laughter. 'If you're referrin' to the hound of the Baskervilles, then no! I'm past that now. As I said, you cannae go through life bein' scared, and that includes films . . . although I won't be goin' to see *Dracula* any time soon!'

'And what about becomin' a seamstress? I thought that was your plan?'

'It still is, but everyone likes to dream, and that's just what runnin' a croft is to me – a dream which will never come to fruition because it's out of my reach financially, as well as bein' beyond my capabilities. I know nothin' about farmin', be it animals or crops.' She sighed heavily. 'It would be lovely, but in reality I'll either be cleanin' or workin' as a seamstress.'

'That's a shame. The idea of runnin' a croft paints an idyllic picture,' said Rory, stroking his chin. 'It certainly beats the pants off my white picket fence.'

Isla eyed him with surprise. 'You'd like the idea of runnin' your own croft?'

He nodded. 'I'd never thought of it until now, but yes, I rather think I would. I'd need lessons on how to care for the animals, and I haven't a clue what to sow and when, but other than that?' He gave her a thumbs-up. 'Why not? Especially if you're doin' it as a married couple.'

Isla felt her cheeks warm. She knew it was only a pipe dream, but even hearing him suggest that it might be possible made her heart sing. 'Lovely in theory, but not on paper.'

'Why not?'

'Because that sort of thing doesn't happen to folks like us, or certainly not to people like me.'

He patted her hand. 'If you want a croft, then a croft you shall have!' Isla smiled, but she wished he wouldn't keep making promises he couldn't possibly keep.

He held out his hand as he stood up. 'May I?'

Allowing him to take her hand, Isla melted into his arms as they stepped onto the dance floor. *Madson and Harman are a thing of the past, Theo has finally moved on, and Rory hasn't mentioned Tammy or the warden since the day he thought he saw him. Things are finally looking up!*

Rory slid his arm round her waist. 'Penny for them?'

She smiled. 'Just thinkin' how good life is at the moment.' An image of Sophie entered her thoughts. 'And who knows? Blackbeard and Sophie might even get together after her runnin' him down.'

Rory grinned. 'You are *sure* it was an accident, aren't you?'

'Oh, ha ha!'

His grin broadened. 'I'm only teasin'. I dare say she'd want him in workin' order so the *last* thing she'd do is run him down.'

Isla gave a wry smile. 'Jokin' aside, I really hope the

accident might finally put them on the road to a relationship!'

'Thank goodness we met in the dance hall,' Rory chuckled.

'Honestly, Rory, you're incorrigible!'

'I try my best!' He laughed as she tapped him playfully on his bicep. 'Sorry. Please do go on.'

'As I was sayin', Sophie and Blackbeard—'

'Why do you call him that when Sophie told you his name was Donny?'

Isla rolled her eyes. 'I've been callin' him Blackbeard for so long I keep forgettin' to call him anythin' else! As I was sayin', I think the accident might've been just the thing they needed to break the ice.'

'You could be right. Spendin' a bit of time on dry land might've turned him into a landlubber. If so, he might just change his tune. And after all that time in hospital he might be singin' yo-ho-ho and a bottle of TCP!'

'Good job I know you're only teasin',' Isla giggled, 'but even so, I do hope you're right, because I hate the thought of Sophie bein' on her own.'

'Then let's hope *you're* right,' said Rory. 'But please don't get your hopes up too much. Mariners are notorious for wantin' to spend their lives at sea. I know Sophie's special and he might well agree, but from what I've heard the pull of the sea can prove too strong.'

'Well, if he doesn't ask her to be his belle before settin' sail again, then I shall make it my mission to find her a man!'

APRIL 1943

Sophie gave a small wave to Donny, who was sitting at the far end of the ward, his leg heavily encased in plaster of Paris. Waving back, he brightened as she walked towards him.

'Any news?' she asked.

'Not yet, although they did say that in order to give it the best possible chance to heal I'd be here for at least another three weeks.' She grimaced apologetically, causing him to wag a reproving finger. 'None of this was your fault, so don't be lookin' at me like that!' he said with a smile which made Sophie's heart melt.

'It would've been better if I *had* run the bugger over!' said Sophie quietly.

'Ah, but who knows how it would have turned out if that had happened?'

'I suppose.' Keen not to project an aura of bad news, Sophie had only told Donny the bare minimum regarding her involvement with Madson, saying that she'd upset his scheme to diddle the government out of a substantial amount of money, and that his plan to get her arrested for attempted murder was his form of revenge, but that's where it ended. *It's not that I'm ashamed of havin' lived in the poorhouse, but I don't want him to think that I'm the sort of girl who goes snoopin' through other people's things, like when I was searchin' Harman's office, because it just doesn't paint a pretty picture, no matter how necessary it was at the time.* When he had asked whereabouts in Scotland she hailed from,

Sophie had struck the poorhouse completely from her history.

'Glasgow.'

'A beautiful city,' said Donny. 'I've worked down Glasgow docks quite a bit over the years.'

'You've worked in an awful lot of places,' said Sophie, remembering his tales of life at sea.

'You have to follow the money,' said Donny in matter-of-fact tones.

'You make it sound exciting!'

He'd laughed. 'I don't know whether I'd call not knowin' where your next wage packet is comin' from excitin' per se.'

Now, as she realised they'd both fallen silent, Sophie spoke up. 'What will happen about your ship? Will you just hop back on next time she's berthed – no pun intended?'

He smiled. 'That's my intention, but it's up to the skipper if he'll have me on board.'

'I'm—'

He held up a finger. 'No more apologies, or I shall tell the nurse to turn you away next time!'

'But your whole life is the sea!'

He frowned a little. 'Whatever gave you that idea?'

'Somethin' you said when we first met,' said Sophie, and thought for a moment before nodding. 'When I said that you weren't for settling down, you said that you didn't know a sailor that was, so I sort of assumed . . .'

'I see. Well, I've been off and on ships as well as working down the docks more or less my whole life,' said Donny, 'and I'll admit I've been at sea more than I've been on dry land of late, but that doesn't mean to say I'd rule out workin' down the docks again.'

She shot him a shy glance. 'Are you just sayin' that to make me feel less guilty?'

He placed his hand over his heart. 'It's the truth, I swear it.'

She couldn't keep the smile from her lips. 'That makes me feel heaps better.'

'Good! Now how about you tell me how you're getting on? Have you been anywhere nice?'

Sophie told him of her various trips and the endless documents she had been asked to ferry from one destination to another. 'I'm like a postman but with a car not a bicycle,' she finished.

'I'd say that you were far more important than a postman,' said Donny, his eyes glittering approvingly. 'For a start, they don't handle classified information that could help win the war!'

'Gosh – I've never thought of it like that before,' said Sophie. 'To me they're just bits of paper, but I suppose you're right: they literally could help to win the war! Funny when you think about it.'

'How so?'

'Everyone thinks that wars are won by armies and guns, but they don't think of the planning and paperwork that goes into makin' all that happen – and goin' off the amount of deliveries I make, it's a lot!'

'There's plenty goin' on behind the scenes that the likes of you and me aren't privy to,' said Donny.

'From secret bunkers to enigma codes, they all play a part in defeatin' Hitler.'

'Enigma?'

He held a finger to his lips and winked.

Feeling her tummy flutter, she tried to banish the blush from her cheeks. Hoping that he hadn't realised the effect his wink had had on her, she continued shyly, 'I hope you're goin' to allow me to take you out for dinner as soon as you're able?'

His cheeks dimpled. 'Don't be daft. It'll be me that takes you out, and I won't hear a word to the contrary.'

Sophie very much wanted to ask how it was that a man as handsome as Donny was unattached, but she was pretty sure she wouldn't like the answer. *If he says it's because he prefers the single life then I'll know there's no chance for us*, Sophie told herself, *and I'd rather remain in blissful ignorance, at least for now!*

Chapter Nine

MAY 1943

It had been four months since she had last seen Cecil, and Tammy had been delighted when he'd announced that he had managed to obtain a week's leave which he intended to spend in Liverpool.

'That's fantastic!' she said, running her finger up and down the telephone cord. 'Mam will be over the moon when I tell her! How did you manage to wangle that?'

'I used my good looks and charisma,' he had teased, before adding, 'Actually, I think they were quite enthused by the prospect of not seeing me for a whole week!'

'When you speak so highly of them?' chuckled Tammy, remembering the day he had described his fellow officers as walruses.

'Exactly! I'm a treasure!'

This conversation had taken place a month before, and Tammy was currently awaiting Cecil's arrival at Lime Street Station. Glancing at the station clock for what felt like the hundredth time, she shaded her eyes from the bright spring sunshine which penetrated what was left of the glass roof after the May blitz. Why was it, she wondered, that minutes always felt like hours when you were waiting for someone special to arrive? Turning her attention to the guard, she fought the urge to ask whether he had any information about when Cecil's train would arrive, as doing so would only annoy him more than she had already.

'Your guess is as good as mine!' he had snapped irritably. 'Nothin' ever runs on time any more and quite frankly I'm sick of hearin' myself repeat the same old story.'

Now, as Tammy looked longingly down the line, she turned her thoughts to the conversation she'd had with her mother when she'd told her Cecil's news.

'At long last!' Grace had said as she poured the tea into their cups. 'I thought the day would never come. Have you started to plan for his arrival?'

'It's all I've thought of,' admitted Tammy. 'I'm goin' to take him to all the dance halls, obviously, as well as cinemas, parks, shops . . .'

Grace had eyed her daughter with affection. 'He'll need another week's leave to get over this one!'

'I want to make sure that we make the most of every single minute, just like we did when I went to see him at Christmas,' Tammy explained.

The sound of an approaching train cut across her thoughts, and Tammy felt her heart rise in her chest as what she hoped was Cecil's train came into view.

Peering through the windows as the carriages flashed by, she followed the train along the platform until it came to a stop. *Please let it be Cecil's*, Tammy thought. *We have precious little time together as it is, without—* Her thoughts were interrupted by a cloud of negativity. *What if Cecil's missed the train? Or what if he's had second thoughts for some reason? Maybe his parents have found out about us and they've made him see that he can do much better than me?* So deep in thought was she, she never saw the handsome young officer approaching her from the side.

'Looking for someone?'

With a cry of delight, Tammy leapt into his arms. 'I was beginnin' to think you might have had second thoughts!'

'And miss the chance to spend some time with my favourite girl? No chance!'

Tammy knew how Cecil felt about her, but it was always good to hear him say it out loud. 'My mammy's desperate to meet you,' she beamed as she threaded her arm through his. 'I said we'd call in as soon as we'd had a chance to settle you into your B&B.'

'Super,' said Cecil, looking at a line of taxis. 'Talking of the B&B, is it far from here?'

'Walkin' distance,' said Tammy. 'That's the beauty of livin' in a city – or it would be if I lived here.'

'How far out is your base?'

'A good five miles away, but I come into the city whenever I can, if just to say hello to Mammy.'

'That's handy. Will you be stayin' at the barracks whilst I'm here?'

She shook her head. 'I'm stoppin' with Mammy and the girls at the safehouse. That way I'll feel as though I've had a proper break.'

'And will I get to see Archie whilst I'm here? Only I'd like to shake that man by the hand for helpin' you and your mammy get away from your dad.'

'You will indeed,' Tammy confirmed. 'In fact he did say that you'd have been welcome to stay with him but for the fact he's only got the one bed.'

'That was nice of him. Does he live far from the shelter?'

'Not at all. The court where he rents a room is only a couple of streets away, which as you can imagine makes me feel a lot better. It was Archie that recommended the B&B where you'll be stayin': it's the same one he stopped in when he first came to Liverpool. Mrs Helsby – that's the landlady – is a real dear, as well as a wonderful cook, and he cannae recommend her highly enough!'

'It's been over a year since he and your mother got together. I'm surprised he's not popped the question yet.'

'It's complicated,' said Tammy. 'Mammy might not be married to my father on paper – or not the ones that Rory got for her, at any rate – but as far as she's concerned bigamy is bigamy no matter what your papers might say.'

He nodded thoughtfully. 'I keep forgetting about the whole false papers thing. I guess I can see where your mother's coming from, but it's still a shame.'

'Tell me about it!' sighed Tammy. 'She's never goin'

to get a divorce from my dad, which means they can never be married, and my mammy wouldn't dream of livin' in sin, so it seems they're destined to live apart.'

'I cannot believe that bloody man still controls your mother's life when he's not even in it!'

'He's like one of those parasites that you cannae get rid of,' Tammy agreed. She pointed to the sign which read *Viola House*. 'Here we are!'

Tammy used the doorknocker to announce their presence before stepping back from the neatly painted door which was opened by a cheery-faced woman whose rollers were partly hidden beneath a brightly coloured headscarf. Her eyes falling on Tammy then Cecil, she beamed. 'Tammy, love. And you must be Cecil!'

He smiled. 'Guilty as charged!' Taking her outstretched hand, he kissed the backs of her knuckles. 'And you must be the beautiful Mrs Helsby.'

Blushing to the roots of her curlers, Mrs Helsby giggled like a schoolgirl. 'Charmer!'

He shot her a dazzling smile. 'I speak as I find.'

Still chuckling, Mrs Helsby ushered them inside where she momentarily disappeared before reappearing with his room key. 'You're on the first floor, room four. Breakfast is served between seven and nine, dinner can be pre-booked, and for anything else just shout. You'll find either myself or my hubby Malcolm in the room down the back.' She pointed to a passage which led towards the rear of the house. 'Any questions?'

Cecil had began to shake his head before changing his mind. 'Cash up front?'

She arched a single eyebrow. 'If you don't mind. I believe you're booked in for a week?'

Nodding, Cecil took his wallet from his trouser pocket and counted the cash into the palm of her hand.

She tucked the money into her apron pocket. 'That'll do nicely. Don't be surprised if you find an extra slice of fried bread on your plate come breakfast time – mushrooms too if I've enough,' she said. 'I do like to spoil my special guests.'

Cecil patted his stomach. 'I've heard all about your wonderful cooking, and I must say I can't wait to sample it for myself.'

She glanced at Tammy. 'He could charm the birds out of the trees, could this one.'

'Couldn't he just?' said Tammy with a wry smile.

'What can I say? It comes naturally!' Cecil winked at Tammy. 'I'm just goin' to quickly pop my things into my room. Shan't be a mo.'

As Tammy waited, she reflected on the difference between Cecil and most of the other officers she had come into contact with, most of whom looked down their noses at anyone in a skirt. Whereas Cecil, on the other hand, respected women. *He's the only officer who's ever asked me for my Christian name*, she reflected now. And he'd gone out of his way to prove to her that he wasn't like the others, in order to win her round. Respecting her boundaries, he had taken her out on a friends-only basis until she felt comfortable in his presence. Not wanting to pry, he'd not asked too many questions about her past, and when she'd finally come clean he hadn't batted an eye, instead seeing everything from her point of view, and telling her that he'd never known anyone to pay such a high price for protecting the ones they loved. He'd even said that if things didn't work out between them he'd not breathe a word of her secret to anyone else. *Cecil is a prince amongst men*, she thought as she heard him coming back down the stairs, *and I'm lucky to have found him*.

He smiled at her, cutting through her thoughts. 'Shall we?'

Tammy gazed fondly at him. 'I haven't half missed you, Cecil Carter.'

'As I you! But what's brought this on?'

'Just thinkin' about how lucky I am to have you, and how special you are to me.'

He eyed her suspiciously. 'Are you about to break some bad news?'

Tammy slapped his arm in a playful manner. 'No I am not!'

'A bump on the head, then?'

She eyed him quizzically. 'Can I not say somethin' nice to you?'

'All day long,' chuckled Cecil. 'It's certainly a step up from the days when you didn't know whether you could trust me!'

She followed him out into the street, and they began walking towards the shelter arm in arm, Tammy guiding their way.

'I was being careful because I knew I wasn't bein' entirely honest with you,' she told him. 'That and the fact that I didn't think I deserved the attention of a man like you.'

'You don't feel that way any more, I hope?'

'No. Although I dare say I'll always feel guilty about the way I treated Rory.'

'Even though it wasn't your fault?'

'Yes, because I never got the chance to apologise to him face to face.' She smiled briefly, changing the subject. 'How d'you feel about meetin' my mammy?'

He ran his finger around the inside of his collar. 'Rather apprehensive.'

'What on earth have you got to feel nervous about? You're an officer in the army. What mother wouldn't be cock-a-hoop to have you as their daughter's beau?'

He chuckled softly. 'When you put it like that . . .'

She rolled her eyes. 'Are you just fishin' for compliments?'

'Not this time!'

She eyed him affectionately. 'I've never thought of you as gettin' nervous before.'

'I suppose I'm worried that your mother might prefer Rory to me.'

'My mammy wouldn't care if I were datin' a prince or a pauper as long as I'm happy.'

'My mother's the same,' said Cecil, 'yet you still feel uneasy about meeting her.'

Tammy wanted to point out that their circumstances were completely different, but he had a point. 'Touché!'

'So you won't feel so nervous when it comes to meeting my parents?'

Tammy grimaced. 'Probably not.'

He slid his arm around her waist. 'Good, because they're as keen to meet you as your mother is to meet me.'

'As soon as I get some decent leave—' said Tammy, but Cecil was looking guilty.

'You might get to see them a tad sooner than that. They're arriving in Liverpool in a few days' time.'

Tammy stared at him in horror, before her face broke into a smile. 'You're pullin' my leg.'

Cecil swallowed. 'I'm afraid not. You see, I've not seen them in an age, and when I told them I was coming to Liverpool they suggested we hit two birds with one stone.'

She stared at him, aghast. 'Why didn't you tell me?'

'Because I didn't want you to worry yourself sick!'

Tammy wanted to protest, but he was right. 'I cannae believe I'm sayin' this, but I think you've done the right thing. Left to my own devices I'd have kept on comin' up with excuses; this way I've got no choice other than to bite the bullet.'

Cecil laughed. 'Bite the bullet? I don't think they're as bad as all that, but I know what you mean, cos I feel the same way.'

'Will they want to meet my mammy?'

'Yes, and before you say anything they know that your mother lives in a women's shelter, and they also know that your father was a right so 'n' so, and no, they don't hold that against either of you.'

Tammy breathed out. 'Do they know that my dad's no longer on the scene?'

'Yes. I told them because my mother was worried for your mother.'

Tammy brightened. 'That was nice of her.'

'My mother is a lovely, kind-hearted, caring individual. If only she could cook, she'd be perfect!'

Tammy laughed. 'Does she know what you think of her cooking?'

'Of course she does! She's not colour blind, and she hasn't lost her sense of smell!'

'I don't follow . . . '

'When something's meant to be brown not black, and there's a perpetual smell of burnt food in the air, she doesn't need us to tell her that she can't cook – we just confirm it.'

Tammy smiled. 'Only you could insult someone in such a way that they'd find it impossible to take offence, because I bet she doesn't.'

'Nah, she's got a good sense of humour. She has to have with her cooking.'

Tammy pointed to a large house on the corner of two streets. 'Here we are!' Cecil made the sign of the cross over his left breast, and she chuckled. 'She's not that bad!'

Tammy had barely knocked on the door before it opened, and Grace ushered them inside with a broad grin.

'Hello, Cecil dear. I'm Grace, Tammy's mother.'

Cecil removed his cap and smoothed his hair down. 'Hello, Grace – may I call you Grace?'

'Of course you may! Come on through to the kitchen; I was just about to brew up.'

Tammy watched as Cecil followed her mother through to the kitchen. Whenever she'd introduced him to people like Gina, or Gina's boyfriend Harry, Cecil had come across as totally laid back, either cracking jokes or playing the goat. She'd always thought that he'd been trying to put them at their ease because he was an officer, but now that she saw him with her mother she realised it was more than that. Whilst he respected Tammy's friends, he wasn't desperate to impress them in the way he obviously was her mother. She'd often said to Gina that she'd only seen his serious side a couple of times, but she was certainly seeing it now.

'Do you take sugar, Cecil?'

'No, thank you. Is there anything I can do to help?'

Tammy rested her hand on his arm. 'Who are you? And what have you done with Cecil?'

A chuckle rose from deep within his throat. 'I'm being on my best behaviour!'

'Only I've told my mammy what you're really like – always jokin', never takin' anythin' seriously unless it absolutely warrants it – and basically bein' nothin' like what you'd expect from an officer.'

'I'm flattered that you think you have to be on your best behaviour for me,' Grace told him, 'but I'd far rather meet the Cecil that my Tammy knows.'

He pulled off a mock salute. 'Consider it done!' He glanced around the huge kitchen. 'I suppose coming to a house full of women who've been abused by men has made me feel . . . guilty by association, as it were.'

'Archie felt the exact same way when he first

came,' Grace assured him, 'but Annie does a brilliant job with the women who come here and soon they don't view *all* men as bein' bad just because they're men.'

'And you do your fair share when it comes to helpin' them to recuperate,' said Tammy.

Grace waved a dismissive hand. 'I help out where I can, but it's Annie who makes them see that not every man is a monster.'

Cecil ran his fingers round the seam of his cap. 'No easy task, what with Hitler and his lot.'

She rolled her eyes. 'True, but thanks to men such as you and Archie, they—' She was interrupted by someone knocking on the front door. Excusing herself, she disappeared, only to reappear a few moments later with a tall man in ARP uniform. 'Archie, meet Cecil.'

Removing his hat, Archie walked over to Cecil, his hand outstretched. 'Pleased to meet you, Cecil.'

Shaking Archie heartily by the hand, Cecil smiled. 'And I you. Can I just say thank you for everythin' you did to rescue Tammy and her mother from that vile man the Christmas before last?'

Archie waved a dismissive hand – 'No thanks necessary.'

Grace caught his attention by holding up an empty cup. 'Tea?'

Archie placed his cap on the table. 'You know me!'

Grace nodded towards the seat next to Archie's. 'Take a pew, Cecil.' She turned to Archie. 'We were just talkin' about men, and how thanks to ones such as yourself and Cecil the girls in here do get to see the better side of the male sex, which is just as well, because like it or not we live in a man's world.' She held up a hand to quell Tammy's protests. 'I know that you're all for equality, love, but I'm a cynical old boot who doesn't believe that it'll ever happen – or not in my lifetime, at any rate.'

'Well, I'm still holding out hope that things will change,' said Tammy determinedly. 'They cannae brush us aside like they used to, not after everything we've done to help with the war effort.'

'I jolly well hope not,' said Archie, taking the cup of tea from Grace, 'but a bit like your mammy, I tend to remain a cynical old so 'n' so.'

'And you'll certainly hear no argument from me,' agreed Cecil, 'although I'm afraid that I too agree with your mother. You only have to look at the last lot to realise that nothing ever changes. If it had they'd have started the WAAF up straight away this time around, but they waited until they absolutely had to. Which is ludicrous, especially as I firmly believe it put us on the back foot.'

'And all because of their stupid pride,' sniffed Tammy. 'And you know what they say about that!'

'That it comes before a fall,' said Grace. She turned to Cecil. 'Tammy's always said you're nothin' like the other officers, because your parents kept you well grounded, and from what I've seen she's absolutely right. You're a credit to them.'

He performed a small bow. 'Thank you, cos I really do try my best to remember my place, which is shoulder to shoulder with everyone else. Quite frankly, if my mother thought for a minute that I was getting ideas above my station she'd soon bring me down a peg or two.'

'Only don't you sort of have to be bossy? Given your rank, I mean?' Archie asked.

'You can be in charge without being an absolute pleb about it,' said Cecil. 'I like to think that I have the respect of my men without belittling them in order to get it.'

Grace gave an approving nod. 'Well said. I firmly believe you get more with a kiss than you do with a punch – not that my husband would agree with that.'

'No, cos he's an idiot,' Archie murmured.

'I've never understood men who hit women,' said Cecil. 'If you have to be physically violent with someone in order to make them stay with you, then you've already lost, as far as I'm concerned!'

Grace cupped her hands round Cecil's face. 'If only there were more men like you and Archie!'

'And to think that you were worried my mother wouldn't like you,' Tammy chuckled.

Grace's brow shot toward her hairline. 'I'll tell you straight. If I had to choose any man for my daughter, it would be you, Cecil Carter. Now who's ready for a slice of Victoria sponge?'

Rory was in the café on Duke Street, waiting for Isla to join him for lunch. His love for her was growing with every day that passed, and he was having to bite his tongue more and more just to keep himself from blurting out the words that he feared might send her running for the hills.

I know things were different between her and Theo, he thought as his eyes rested on the menu, *but I also know that the thought of bein' let down is more than she can bear.* Question was, how could he prove to her that he would never do that? He'd done the small things such as making sure he was always on time for their dates, if not a little before, and he'd telephoned her when he promised he would. *It's just goin' to take time*, he told himself now. *It would help if we knew where her father was, because I think she might feel differently if she had the chance to speak to him, but that could be years away, if ever!*

Seeing Isla through the window, he waved to gain her attention, and she waved back, breaking into a smile as she entered. 'Have you been waiting long?'

'All my life.'

She rolled her eyes. 'Is it too cynical for me to ask what it is you're after?'

He laughed, adding half-jokingly, 'Your love?'

'Someone's in a good mood,' she said with a chuckle.

'Of course I am. I'm here with you, aren't I?' He turned to the waitress who had arrived to take their order. 'We'll have a pot of tea for two, please, and I'll have a cheese and tomato sandwich.' He raised his brow at Isla, who chose corned beef and tomato.

'So how're things at Kirby?' she said as the waitress left to fetch their order.

'Pretty good. What about Fazakerley?'

She gave him a brief smile 'Same old same old.'

'Don't you think that's kind of nice, though? To have some normality at last, instead of the tumultuous lives we were leading?'

She considered this for a moment. 'Do you know, I rather think you're right. I'd not thought of it before, but things have really settled down of late. I don't have half the worries I used to.' Seeing the smile broaden on his cheeks, she went on, 'Is that why you were smiling? Because you feel more relaxed?'

He nodded slowly. 'It finally feels as if all the uncertainty has come to an end.'

She fixed him with an inquisitive gaze. 'What do you think's happened to make you feel that way?'

'Time. I don't know about you, but for the longest while I was livin' in perpetual fear that somethin' was goin' to go wrong. But everythin's stayed the same for a long time now, and I feel . . . settled, I suppose.'

She snapped her fingers. 'Same here!'

They stopped speaking as the waitress unloaded their order onto their table, but Isla picked up the conversation as she began to pour the tea into two cups. 'I know what you mean. For the first time in a long while, I feel normal!'

'I used to think that bein' normal was boring,' said Rory, 'but it's anything but!' He took a bite of his sandwich and chewed thoughtfully before swallowing. 'You know, I never had a proper relationship until I met you.'

Isla looked at him in amazement. 'Have you had a knock on the head or somethin'?'

He waved a dismissive hand. 'I take it you're thinkin' of Tammy?'

'Of course I am! Good God, Rory, you moved mountains for that girl!'

'Maybe, but it wasn't what I'd call a "normal" relationship. When you and I are together I don't spend my time lookin' over my shoulder for fear that someone might see us. Nor do you jump at the slightest sound, fearful that your drunken father might be on to you. In fact, the more I'm with you, the more I realise that my relationship with Tammy was anything *but* normal. Good God, I was scared to death of holdin' her hand, never mind givin' her a kiss. I didn't realise it at the time, of course, but we never spent much time talkin' about the ordinary stuff most couples talk about – instead our conversations were made up of where her father was and what he'd done to them that day. We certainly never went out to dinner or dancin'.'

Isla grimaced. 'That doesn't sound like much fun. Surely you must've gone to the flicks?'

He shook his head. 'Never went, for fear that someone might see us together in the queue.'

'But her father did know the two of you were together?'

'Well, yes, but he forbade her to see me, so we had to pretend we were through.'

'A lot of people might think that made the relationship more excitin', all the sneakin' round and what not.'

He shook his head fervently. 'Not when you know she'd get the hidin' of her life if anyone saw us.'

'Poor Tammy. I can see why she wanted to leave.'

'And I wish she had, but she never did manage to get free of him.' Determined to brighten the mood, he pressed on. 'So now that we've confirmed just how boring we are, what would you like to do after lunch?'

She thought for a moment before replying.

'How about a ride on the Overhead Railway?'

'Perfect!'

Blissfully unaware that her father was back in Liverpool – or that he had been spying on her and Cecil – Tammy bade goodbye to her mother and Archie. 'I'll try not to make too much noise when I come back,' she said.

'Don't worry your head none,' Grace told her. 'There's always someone up and about what with everyone workin' different shifts. Just you enjoy your meal, and do a turn on the floor for me!'

'Will do,' Tammy called back over her shoulder. Tucking her arm into Cecil's, she finally asked the question she was dying to hear the answer to. 'Well? What do you think?'

'About your mother?'

'Of course my mother! And Archie too, cos he's part of the family now.'

'Archie's solid as a rock, a true gent amongst men, but I knew that before I met him. As for your mother? She's exactly how I imagined she would be, cos the apple certainly didn't fall far from the tree when it comes to you two. I don't know why I was ever worried!'

'See? I told you she was the tops! And like me she's really looking forward to meeting your folks.'

'You've changed your tune!'

'I think it was seein' the way you were with my mammy, once you'd got over your nerves. If you're the same way with your own mother, I think I'm going to like her.'

He wrapped his arm around her shoulders. 'They're like peas in a pod when it comes to wanting their children to be happy. In fact, the only difference I can see is that your mammy can cook!' Kissing the tips of his fingers in a theatrical manner, he sighed. 'That sponge was as light as a feather!'

Tammy laughed. 'Mammy's always been good at makin' the most of her ingredients – she had to be with Dad around – but even she'll admit that her culinary skills have improved vastly since she set up home in a houseful of women.'

'The last time my mother made a cake we used it as a doorstop.'

She slapped the lapel of his jacket. 'No you did not!'

He chuckled softly. 'All right, so maybe that was a bit of an exaggeration, but I bet it would've worked just as well if we had. Talking of food, where are we going for dinner?'

'The Adelphi,' said Tammy. 'It's a tad grand, but seein' as how this is your first time in Liverpool I thought we could splash out on somethin' fancy!'

'I don't need an excuse to spoil my girl!' said Cecil, pulling her close. 'Besides, if you can't push the boat out once in a while what's the point of living?'

'My thoughts exactly! And what about after dinner? There're plenty of dance halls, as well as cinemas.'

'Being as you're the expert on all things Liverpudlian, I shall let you do the choosing.'

'They're all good choices,' said Tammy, before adding thoughtfully, 'Do your parents like to dance?'

He nodded. 'Very much so. Why?'

'I thought it might be nice to take them to the Rialto later in the week?'

'Smart thinking! Do you think your mother and Archie would be able to join us?'

'I hope so. They would've come out with us tonight, but Mammy felt it was only right that we had at least our first evenin' on our own.'

'I wouldn't have minded.'

'I know, but we've only got a week, and whilst I love my mother dearly I'd like to spend at least some of the time bein' just the two of us.'

Walking through the city, Tammy pointed out all her favourite shops, including the ones that had suffered the worst bomb damage. 'I wish I could've seen the city as it was before the Luftwaffe did their best to take Liverpool off the map, cos Mammy said the difference is like night and day.'

'It's pretty impressive now,' said Cecil. 'I can see why you like it here.'

As they approached the grand exterior of the Adelphi, Tammy began to get an uneasy feeling that something was wrong, but she couldn't put her finger on what it was until Cecil opened the hotel door. Stopping in her tracks, she turned round, her eyes searching the crowds of people going about their business, a frown creasing her brow.

'Is everything all right?' Cecil asked.

'Ever get the feelin' that you're bein' watched?' Tammy murmured, continuing to scan the area.

He shrugged. 'On occasion, but the streets are packed. How could you possibly sense one person watching you in particular?'

She caught his eye. 'Just a feelin'. But so strong, I can practically feel their eyes borin' into me.'

'Have you any reason to think someone might want to spy on you?'

'Maybe it's my old paranoia raising its ugly head.'

'Because I'm an officer, and you're worried someone might spill the beans? Look, I'm miles away from my base, so the chances of our bumping into someone who knows me are small to say the least.'

'I know, but it's the only thing I can come up with.'

Taking her hand, he kissed the backs of her knuckles. 'You said that the Adelphi was a tad fancy. Maybe you're expectin' it to be full of officers.'

She relaxed. 'You're right! I reckon this is *just* the sort of place the walruses would frequent.'

'Even if it is, I very much doubt they'd be interested in us. Anyway, we could be married for all they know.'

Tammy pointed to her ringless finger.

'All right, so not married, but either way they don't know me from Adam. However, if it's making you uncomfortable, we could always eat elsewhere.'

She shook her head. 'I'm bein' daft, and you're right. No one will care, not this far from Faringdon.'

They walked into the hotel and Dennis – who had thrown himself behind a police box – peered round the corner. *Devious cow's properly fallen on her feet* he thought as he slowly ventured across the road, *I bet he'd run a mile if he knew the truth because I'd wager a pound to a penny she's not told him how she left her own father for dead. It would serve her right if I were to march in there and tell him what's what, see how she likes them apples.* But would that satisfy his need for revenge? No. He wanted to ruin her and Grace's life the way they'd ruined his. *Bein' of the same blood made no difference when they tried to do me in,* thought Dennis, *so why should it bother me? The two of them would quite happily have seen me swing for a murder I didn't commit, so I shall repay them by sendin' them on a one way trip to the bottom of the Mersey!*

Rory and Isla had thoroughly enjoyed their trip on the overhead railway and were chatting away merrily as the train made its way back to the terminal. Gazing out of the window as they talked, Rory was idly watching the people strolling through the fading summer sun when he saw a face he had very much hoped he'd never see again. Staring in disbelief, he breathed 'It cannae be,' beneath his breath.

'Sorry? Did you say somethin'?'

His heart racing in his chest as the horror of what he was seeing caught up with him, Rory leapt to his feet. His fingers splayed on the carriage window, he stared down at the man who was walking away from the docks. 'It's him!' he cried. 'I'd lay my life on it!' He prodded the carriage window with his finger. 'See him there?' Not waiting for a response, he pressed on. 'That's Dennis Blackwell. There's not a doubt in my mind!'

Hastening to his side, Isla followed Rory's line of sight, but as there were several men milling around below them she couldn't be sure which one Rory was referring to. 'You really think so?'

'I'm positive!' said Rory, who was now standing at the carriage door in his eagerness to descend to the walkway below.

'But how can you possibly be sure when you can only see the tops of their heads?'

'Because it's him,' said Rory. 'I know it is. I'd recognise that man anywhere – and I was a crane driver, don't forget, which meant I was always higher than everyone else, so I'm used to identifying the tops of people's heads.'

Worried that Rory was getting himself het up about nothing, Isla laid a hand on his arm. 'What are you intendin' to do?'

'Ask him what the hell he's doin' in Liverpool, that's what,' said Rory. The guard had barely opened the door to the carriage before he was rushing off in the direction he'd seen the man he suspected to be Dennis.

Hurrying in his wake, Isla called out for him to slow down.

Apologising for practically abandoning his belle at the station, Rory stopped and waited for her. 'I cannae let him go without speakin' to him, I did that with Archie and I'm not goin' to do it again,' Rory explained as he took her by the hand.

'But what if you're wrong?'

'I'm not!' Rory insisted. 'I *know* I'm not.'

'But . . .' Isla stopped speaking as Rory came to an abrupt halt.

He was pointing to a man who was no more than twenty feet away from them. 'That's him,' hissed Rory, 'that's Dennis!' Not wanting to waste another second Rory called out to the man, who continued to walk away from them. Hurrying after him, he landed his hand on the man's shoulder. 'Gotcha . . .'

The man slapped Rory's hand away as he turned to face him. 'Get your hands off me!'

Rory gaped at the man whilst mumbling a frantic apology. 'I'm sorry, I thought, that is to say . . .'

'We're really sorry,' said Isla. 'We thought you were someone else.'

'You wanna be careful how you approach people, pal,' said the man, who was eyeing Rory furiously. 'You're damned lucky I never lamped you one.'

Rory bowed his head in shame. 'I'm terribly sorry; I honestly thought you were someone else. I wouldn't normally approach someone in such a fashion . . .'

'Just as well, cos some of the fellers round here carry knives,' warned the man, before turning on his heel and stalking away.

Eyeing Rory sympathetically, Isla cupped his chin in the palm of her hand. 'C'mon, let's get you back to your base.'

'I cannae apologise enough, Isla,' murmured Rory, 'I could've *sworn* . . .'

'Easy mistake to make, especially as they all looked

the same from above,' said Isla. 'Question is, why do you keep thinkin' you're seein' people from your past when you know darned well it cannae possibly be them?'

'I really don't know,' said Rory wretchedly.

'Has the past been on your mind a lot of late?'

'No. Or at least not especially so.'

'Have you experienced anything like this before?'

'Never,' said Rory, 'and whilst it might not look like it, I honestly don't think I'm mistaking people I don't know for those back home.'

Isla stared at him round-eyed. 'But you saw for yourself that it wasn't Dennis.'

He sighed irritably. 'I know, and I cannae understand how I could have got it so wrong, because from the carriage . . .'

Isla cut across him without apology. 'Which is goodness knows how many feet up in the air! You cannae seriously be tryin' to tell me that you could see him clearer from that high up than you could close to?'

'It certainly felt that way,' said Rory. Turning to face her, he took her hands in his. 'I'm so sorry, Isla. I shouldn't have gone harin' off like a headless chicken. Not only was it not a gentlemanly thing to do; it wasn't the way to treat the woman you love.'

Isla's expression froze. Had he just said what she thought he had? Not knowing what to say, she waited for him to speak first, but instead of talking Rory touched his lips to hers. Melting into his embrace, she banished the voice that warned her not to get too attached in case things went wrong to the back of her mind. He had confessed his love and right now that was all that mattered.

Slowly leaning back, he gazed affectionately at her. 'I seem to be makin' a right hash of things lately, because I've been wonderin' how I should tell you I loved you for some time now, and I never intended to say it in such a slapdash manner!'

'You're breakin' all my rules, Rory . . .' Isla began, but he cut her off short.

'I'm sorry, but I cannae help the way I feel, and I've tried my best to keep my feelin's hidden, but,' he flapped his arms down by his side in a helpless manner, 'I guess love took over.'

Isla's lids pricked with tears as she gazed adoringly at him. 'By breakin' all my rules, I meant *my* rules, as in not admittin' how I feel about you. Cos for the record, I love you too.'

Picking her up in his arms he cried out for joy. 'You don't know how long I've been wantin' to hear you say those words! I was worried when you didn't say it straight back to me.'

She grinned. 'Bit hard to do, seein' as you kissed me before I had a chance.'

'I guess I was worried you might not say it back, so I kissed you instead!' Rory confessed.

'Do you not remember my sayin' the other day that I wasn't afraid of the future any more?'

'I do, aye.'

'I meant every word.'

Beaming, Rory spoke his own thoughts. 'I would've confessed how I felt a heck of a lot sooner, but I knew you'd been through a lot already, with Theo – and your family – and I didn't want to scare you off.'

'Maybe at first you might have, but not now.'

He kissed her softly. His hand firm on the small of her back, his teeth glinted in the moonlight as he broke away. 'This was not how I thought the evenin' would end after my earlier behaviour, but boy, am I glad it is!'

Isla gazed at him thoughtfully. 'You said that you've been thinkin' about confessin' your love for me for a little while now?'

'It's just about all I've thought about,' said Rory. 'Why?'

'By tellin' me that you love me, you're admittin' that you and Tammy are over. Maybe that's why you keep thinkin' you're seein' people who remind you of the last time you saw her.'

Rory's eyes grew wide. 'You think my mind's playin' tricks on me?'

'It would seem more likely than not,' said Isla. 'After all, *thinkin'* you've seen the warden and Dennis is very different from actually seein' them. What would be the odds, do you suppose, of seein' two men from Clydebank when you know they've no reason to be this far south?'

Rory grimaced. 'I did think it seemed unlikely, but seein' is believin', right?'

'Most of the time, but obviously not in this instance.'

Rory frowned. 'I completely understand what you're

sayin', and I guess you could be right. It just seemed so real . . .'

She rested her cheek against his chest. 'Perhaps it will all stop now that you've spoken your thoughts.'

He kissed the top of her head. 'Perhaps.' But deep down, Rory couldn't shake the conviction that the people from his past weren't quite done with him yet.

Having followed Tammy and the officer back to the safehouse, Dennis was making his way back to his digs. Coming up with a plan to find out when the officer would be leaving was proving harder than he suspected. Whilst he didn't relish the idea of camping outside the B&B he didn't see that he had any other choice. *It would be helpful if I knew when he was leavin'*, thought Dennis as he continued on his way, *but how can I find that out without—* an idea sprang to mind. He could always approach the landlady pretending that he was looking for a vacancy. It was a long shot, he had to admit, but better than camping outside the B&B indefinitely.

So deep in thought was he, he didn't notice the set-to between the two men under the dockers' umbrella.

Chapter Ten

Cecil was currently on his way to see Tammy at the women's shelter. Having spent most of the previous night tossing and turning at the prospect of what he had planned for the following day, his nerves were still unsettled as he walked along. He knew that Tammy had been surprised when she'd heard that he was finally coming to Liverpool, but what she didn't know was his intention to ask her mother's permission to marry her. *Grace believes me to be the only man for her daughter, so I know she'll approve. I just have to hope that Tammy says yes*, he thought now, *because even though my parents truly are only coming to Liverpool to spend time with me, I did rather hope that Tammy and I might tie the knot whilst they're here.* Gently rapping his knuckles against the door to the safehouse, Cecil hoped fervently that it would be Grace who responded, because he wanted to have a word with her behind Tammy's back, and the sooner the better.

Hearing the sound of approaching footsteps on the other side of the door, he crossed his fingers in his trouser pocket, but to his disappointment it was Tammy who answered his knock.

'Blimey! Who stole your smile?' she said as she ushered him inside.

Realising that his disappointment must be showing on his face, he quickly drew his lips into a smile. 'Sorry, I didn't realise I was looking miserable. Is your mother about?'

Tammy closed the door behind him. 'Ye-es,' she said slowly. 'Do you want to see her for some reason in particular?'

He waved what he hoped looked like an airy hand, but he could feel the sweat pricking his brow, and knew it hadn't gone unnoticed by Tammy.

'Are you not feelin' well?' she asked in concern. 'Only you look like you might have a temperature.'

He ran his finger around the inside of his collar. 'Just a bit hot, that's all.'

Convinced that he might be coming down with something, Tammy called her mother through to the kitchen, and when she saw Cecil looking decidedly uncomfortable Grace quickly jumped to the same conclusion. 'You don't half look peaky, Cecil love. Let's get you a glass of water.'

Grateful for the distraction, Cecil gulped it down, and Tammy refilled the glass. 'Is that why you asked where my mammy was?' she asked.

Cecil nodded. 'Kind of.'

Grace looked closely at their visitor, who if anything looked as though he was getting warmer not cooler. Her head on one side, she said, 'Can you give us a minute, Tammy love?'

Tammy looked from her mother to Cecil before nodding and leaving the room. Heading for the parlour, she wondered what on earth could be wrong with Cecil that he didn't want her to overhear. If it were a woman she'd assume it was women's troubles, but she had no idea what might be afflicting a man like Cecil.

Back in the kitchen, Grace asked Cecil to take a seat before, in her words, he collapsed. 'I can only think of one reason for a man to get so hot under the collar – other than the obvious, of course – and that's the thought of proposing. Am I right?'

He nodded, relieved to find her so understanding. 'Not that I'm nervous at the thought of marrying Tammy, of course – quite the opposite.' Rising to his feet, he looked Grace square in the eye and said as calmly as he could, 'I'd like to ask your permission to marry your daughter, if I may.'

A slow smile swept Grace's cheeks as she eyed him affectionately. 'I might have guessed you'd want to do things as traditionally as possible.'

'I think the world of Tammy, and as such I want to do what's right not just by her, but by you too.'

She flicked him playfully with her tea towel. 'Of course you have my permission, you daft sausage!'

Smiling weakly, he glanced nervously back to the parlour. 'All I have to do now is ask Tammy herself.'

He was pulling a small box out of his pocket, and Grace smiled. 'You've got a ring?'

He nodded. 'What with rationing and all I couldn't get her the one I wanted, but I hope she likes it just the same.' He opened the lid to reveal a silver ring with a gemstone set in the centre.

'I think we need to get Tammy back in here,' said Grace, and went to the door to call her daughter through. Looking back at Cecil, she asked if he would prefer it if she left them alone.

He shook his head. 'I'd rather you stayed, if you don't mind?'

'Not at all.' When Tammy appeared, looking apprehensive, she closed the door so they wouldn't be disturbed by any of the other girls and gestured to Cecil. 'Over to you, maestro.'

Taking Tammy's hands in his, Cecil cleared his throat before sinking to one knee. 'I've known that you were the one for me from the moment I first saw your reflection in the rear-view mirror of the staff car, and I don't want to spend another minute without you as my wife, so what do you say? Will you do me the honour of becoming my wife?'

Of all the things she'd imagined him saying whilst she'd been sitting waiting in the parlour, this wasn't one of them. Happy tears pricking her eyes, she nodded. 'I most certainly will!'

Crowing with happiness as he stood up, Cecil picked her up and swung her round, before gently placing her back down. 'You've just made me the happiest man alive! I hope you know that?'

Grace cleared her throat and nodded purposefully at his jacket. 'Haven't you forgotten something?'

Realisation dawning, Cecil hastily withdrew the box from his pocket and nervously showed Tammy the ring. To his delight, her face broke into a beam of approval. 'It's beautiful!'

Thrilled – and considerably relieved – by her response, he slipped it on to her finger. It was a perfect fit, and Grace hastened over to embrace her daughter. 'You'll have to set a date.'

'I was rather hoping that we could get married before I went back,' said Cecil. 'It would have to be a registry office wedding though.'

Tammy waved a dismissive hand. 'I don't care where we marry, as long as it's soon.'

He grinned at her. 'You're going to be Mrs Cecil Carter!'

Tammy gazed admiringly at her ring again before looking to her mother. 'Can I use the telephone, please? Only I have to tell Gina. She'll never forgive me if she's not the first to know!'

Grace smiled. 'Of course you can. Just pop the money in the box.'

Tammy hurried off. Picking up the receiver, she asked the operator to put her through to Gina's base and it wasn't long before her friend's voice came trilling down the line.

'Tammy! How lovely to hear from you! Did Cecil get to Liverpool all right? I know the trains have been awful of late.'

'He did indeed, and you'll never guess what . . .'

When she heard what had happened, Gina squeaked with delight. 'Oh, Tammy, that's such wonderful news!

I'm so happy for you both. You must take plenty of photos!'

'We will!' promised Tammy. 'I just hope nothin' goes wrong.'

'What on earth makes you think that anythin' could go wrong – except the Luftwaffe, of course?'

Tammy was silent long enough for Gina to become suspicious. 'Tammy? What is it you aren't tellin' me?'

'It's nothin' really,' said Tammy, 'but do you ever get the feelin' you're bein' watched?'

'After spendin' the whole train journey from Clydebank to Carlisle believin' the Billy Boys to be on my tail, yes I do!'

'I don't mean like that though, cos you had good reason to think that you were bein' watched. This is different.'

'How?'

'Ever since Cecil came to Liverpool I've had the feelin' that I'm bein' followed – I even told Cecil about it, but he thinks I'm paranoid because of the whole officer datin' a driver thing.'

'And he's probably right,' Gina assured her. 'Especially if you didn't feel that way before he arrived.'

'I didn't,' admitted Tammy, 'but even so . . .'

Having been with Tammy since they fled Clydebank, Gina knew her friend all too well. 'You've always thought that Cecil was too good for you, and I reckon his comin' to Liverpool has made you wonder how others will view the two of you bein' a couple. Cos the only time I've ever known you *not* to be paranoid over somethin' was the day you found your father holdin' a knife to your mammy's throat! As far as I remember, he'd been watchin' out for you by the steps of the Liver buildin' when he saw your mammy. If you didn't realise you were bein' watched then, what makes you think that's the case now?'

Tammy thought for a moment. 'You're right. This is just my paranoia over Cecil bein' an officer gettin' the better of me!'

'It is that, so for goodness sake relax and enjoy your weddin' day!'

'I wish you could be with me,' said Tammy ruefully.

'Me too, but we both know that life's too short to dilly-dally. Besides, I'll be with you in spirit!'

Kate poked her head round the door of the Nissen hut and called out to Isla, who was darning her stockings. 'Phone call for you in the NAAFI.'

'Any idea who it is?' Isla called back, putting down the stocking she was holding.

'Meg.'

Isla hurried over to the NAAFI and picked up the receiver. 'Meg?'

'The one and only!' chirped Meg. 'Guess who's comin' to Liverpool this Friday?'

Isla gave an excited gasp. 'Really? How come?'

'All thanks to a mix-up with one of the other girls in my hut. She was meant to go on a week's leave, but there was a change of plan at the last minute and she had to cancel. I asked if I could go in her stead and they said yes!'

'Oh Meg, that's marvellous news! Are you goin' to be stoppin' at Peggy's?'

'I am indeed – although I haven't actually asked her yet.'

'It won't be a problem,' said Isla, with confidence. 'She'll be cock-a-hoop to hear that she's havin' a bit of company.'

'I don't suppose you've any leave comin' up?' asked Meg hopefully.

'I have, actually, but I've not booked it yet, so keep your fingers crossed!'

'Will do! I wish Sophie would come, but she's too busy nursin' Blackbeard.'

'There's a name that's stuck!' Isla paused. 'Does that mean you've already asked her?'

'Aye, but she doesn't want to leave him. She says it's because she feels guilty, but I reckon that's just an excuse to be near him.'

'She's smitten,' said Isla slowly. 'I just hope to goodness her feelings are reciprocated. I was certain they'd get together under the circumstances, but the last time I spoke to Sophie it sounded as though their relationship was going nowhere fast. He's more conservative than I first thought, or it certainly looks that way.'

'Bit odd, that, don't you think?'

'Not really. You are what you are. Why would you think it odd?'

'Well, he must be what? Thirty-five, if not older. Given his age, you'd think he'd have a bit of experience under his belt when it comes to the opposite sex.'

'But if he's away at sea a lot . . .'

'Then he's either one thing or the other,' said Meg decidedly. 'A girl in every port, or . . .'

'Or what?'

'He's battin' for the other side,' said Meg matter-of-factly.

Isla shrieked with laughter. 'Oh, Meg!' she gasped. 'You cannae make assumptions like that!'

'Can you think of another reason why he'd be so shy?'

'Maybe he just doesn't fancy her.'

'Don't be daft!' scoffed Meg. 'Sophie's gorgeous!'

'She is to us, and I dare say countless others,' said Isla, 'but maybe she's not his type. Maybe he prefers blondes.'

Meg started to protest, but the operator cut across, letting them know that their time was up.

'Quickly!' said Isla. 'What train are you on? I'll come and meet you whether I'm granted leave or not.'

'Lime Street Station at seventeen hundred hours.'

'I'll be there—' was all Isla managed before she heard the familiar click of the call being cut off by the operator.

Replacing the handset, she telephoned Rory's base to let him know the good news in the hope that he, too, could wangle some leave. 'Will you be able to meet her off the train with me?' she asked hopefully.

'That'd be cuttin' it a bit fine,' said Rory, 'but I could meet you both somewhere afterwards, say for dinner?'

'That would be lovely!'

'I take it she'll be stayin' with Peggy?'

'Goes without sayin',' said Isla. 'I think Peggy would have a fit if either of the girls even *thought* of stayin' somewhere else when visitin' Liverpool!' She broke off momentarily to wave to Kate, who had come to see whether she was finished on the phone yet. 'I'd best be off.'

'Snap!' said Rory. 'See you on Friday, say twenty hundred hours at Lyons café?'

'Perfect!' Isla replaced the receiver and hurried over to join her friend. 'Don't you just love it when everythin' fits into place?'

'In your case, I'd say it's about time,' said Kate. 'I take it you've had good news?'

'The best,' confirmed Isla. 'Meg's comin' up from Portsmouth on Friday, and she's finally goin' to get to meet Rory, only properly this time.'

'That's nice. What about your other pal . . . Sophie, was it?'

Isla rolled her eyes. 'Sophie's too busy fussin' over Blackbeard to come to Liverpool.'

'I thought he wasn't interested?' said Kate who, like most women in the WAAF, was usually privy to what was going on in her workmates' lives.

'That's what worries me,' said Isla. 'I don't want Sophie upset if it turns out she's barkin' up the wrong tree.'

Kate whipped her head round. 'You think he might be married?'

Isla stared at her open-mouthed. 'Not until you just suggested it I didn't.'

Kate waved a nonchalant hand. 'Don't listen to me. I was just throwin' ideas out.'

'Considerin' Meg had him down as battin' for the other side, I wouldn't say your thoughts were too outlandish!'

Kate pinched her nose to stifle a giggle. 'There're no hairs on *her* tongue!'

'You're right there! However, married or ... not married, it doesn't bode well for Sophie. Assumin' we're right, of course.'

'And that's a big assumption to make, cos there are plenty of reasons for not being interested. After all, if he was married surely he'd say something? Unless he was playin' away from home, that is.'

'Which would make Meg's thoughts far more viable,' said Isla. 'Trouble is, how would I put it to Sophie? Because I very much doubt it's even crossed her mind.'

'Well, I wouldn't let Meg be the one to run it by her,' said Kate. 'Perhaps just let nature take its course? She's bound to give up the idea sooner or later.'

'Aye, but in the meantime she's gettin' her hopes up for nought.'

'True, but better it fizzles into nothin' than put ideas into her head which might have no substance.'

'Maybe Sophie just isn't his type?'

'Could well be,' said Kate, 'but don't suggest it, cos it wouldn't do Sophie's confidence any good when it came to the male sex.'

'So leave sleepin' dogs lie?'

'If you value your friendship, yes.'

Isla was disappointed that she was unable to help her friend, but decided to take Kate's advice. *Hopefully he'll get on his ship and never go back to Scarborough*, she thought. *Sophie's bound to forget about him in the fullness of time, and who knows? Maybe someone better will come her way in the meantime.*

They were halfway through the week and Cecil and Tammy had just left the B&B to go and meet his parents at the train station. 'Darn these butterflies,' said Tammy, 'They've got me all of a dither!'

'You'll be fine!' Cecil assured her. 'I guarantee you'll be as right as rain within the first couple of minutes, just you wait and see.'

'What shall I call your mother?'

'Hannah,' said Cecil promptly. 'And you can call my dad Ronnie.'

'I'm fine with that, but don't you think it's a bit informal?'

His brow rose swiftly. 'I'd say it's a tad *too* formal given that we're going to be married in a few days. You'll be calling them mum and dad after that!'

Tammy felt her cheeks warm. 'It'll feel odd to be callin' someone mum or dad when I've only just met them. Do you think they'll mind?'

'Not in the slightest. Now stop your worrying!'

Tammy's brow wrinkled. 'Two days ago you were standing in my mammy's kitchen sweatin' cobs at the prospect of askin' her permission to marry me.'

Cecil grimaced a chuckle. 'Oh, yeah. I'd forgotten about that!'

'Exactly!' She looked towards the looming train station. 'I don't think I was this nervous the night I ran away from Clydebank!'

Cecil gave a low chuckle. 'Are you actually saying that you found it less nerve-racking being on the run for attempted murder than you do meeting my folks?'

'All right, so perhaps that's a bit of an exaggeration,' she conceded, 'but it's a close call!'

'Just you wait and see! Ten minutes from now you'll be wondering what all the fuss was about.' He jerked his head in the direction of the steps that led up to the station. 'Ah! I see their train was early!'

Tammy looked over and saw a neatly dressed woman with dark hair and kind blue eyes waving to them excitedly. She was accompanied by a fair-haired man, who was smiling at Cecil. Praying that they would take the news of their son's engagement and imminent marriage well, Tammy waved back. She was just wondering how Cecil would break it to them when his mother cried out in excitement and pointed at Tammy's left hand. 'You're engaged!' she squeaked. Before either Tammy or Cecil could say a word, she enveloped Tammy in a warm embrace. 'Didn't I say so, Ronnie? Didn't I say I thought they'd be engaged?'

Ronnie nodded. 'Most of the way here!' Taking his son's hand in his, he shook it firmly. 'Congratulations, son.'

Cecil stared at his mother, who was holding on to Tammy's fingers so that she might see the ring better. 'Good God, woman. You must have eyes like a hawk!'

Breaking away from Tammy, Hannah stepped over

to hug him. 'Not at all! I knew you'd ask her to marry you, because I knew how you felt about her.' She fished a handkerchief from her handbag and wiped away the lipstick she'd planted on her son's cheek. 'So when's the big day?' Before either of them could reply, she gasped, a hand to her mouth, her eyes rounding as she spoke through her fingers. 'You're getting married whilst we're here, aren't you?'

Cecil and Tammy exchanged shocked, disbelieving glances. 'So you're clairvoyant now as well?' said Cecil.

'I could tell by the way you looked at each other,' sighed Hannah happily, before adding for the benefit of her husband's ears, 'Do I know my son, or do I know my son?'

Ronnie shook his head as he stepped forward to greet Tammy. 'There's no arguing with you there!' Taking her in a warm embrace, he grinned. 'Welcome to the family, Isla. I promise she'll let you get a word in edgeways soon enough.'

Tammy giggled nervously. 'I'm just grateful you've both taken the news so well.'

'We couldn't be more thrilled,' Hannah said, hooking her hand through the crook of Tammy's elbow. 'We always knew that he'd find someone special, and from what he's told us you're that and then some.'

Tammy blushed. Uncertain how to respond, she murmured, 'I don't know about that.'

'Well I do!' said Hannah firmly. 'When it comes to your father the less said the better, whereas by all accounts your mother's a true star.'

'Very much so,' said Tammy, relieved to know that Cecil had been speaking the truth when he'd said that he'd told his mother everything.

'And she's a really good cook,' said Cecil.

Ronnie chuckled. 'Does she give lessons?'

Hannah, who had sharp ears, raised a single eyebrow. 'Some of us are naturally good at cooking, and some of us . . .'

'Shouldn't set foot in the kitchen,' Cecil chortled.

She rolled her eyes good-naturedly. 'I'm not *that* bad.'

'Of course you're not, Mother dear. After all, we're still alive!'

Ronnie smiled. 'I think luck has a lot to do with that.'

'All joking aside,' said Cecil, as he placed his arm around his mother's shoulders, 'you simply have to get Grace to teach you how to cook a Victoria sponge. I don't think I've ever tasted cake so good!'

'I'm game – if Grace doesn't mind?'

Tammy smiled. 'It would be her pleasure, and she'll be the first to admit that the recipe isn't actually hers but from one of the girls livin' in the shelter. They're a fantastic bunch of cooks, they truly are. They did us the most wonderful Christmas dinner the time we sent my father packing.'

'We women are a force to be reckoned with when we put our heads together,' said Hannah. 'And from what Cecil's told me, your mother and her friend Annie are living proof of that.'

Ronnie nodded. 'Our family have always been firm believers in credit where it's due.'

Tammy glanced at Cecil, who was beaming at her

with an air of 'I told you so'. *And he was right*, thought Tammy happily. *His parents are just as wonderful as he said they were. I truly am the luckiest girl in the world!*

Having turned up early to wait for the officer to leave, Dennis had only just ducked out of sight of Tammy, who had been walking up the road in his direction. Relieved that she hadn't seen him, he watched her eagerly, his fingers crossed in the hope that the officer would emerge from the B&B with kitbag in hand. However, it seemed he wasn't leaving the city quite yet. Waiting until he and Tammy had turned the corner, Dennis smoothed his hair back with one hand and hurried towards the house. Clearing his throat, he rapped a brief tattoo against the door, and smiled hopefully at the landlady who opened it.

'Good morning. I see that your sign says no vacancies, but I was wondering if you had any comin' up?' His heart was hammering in his chest as he waited for her reply, and he hoped his unkempt appearance wasn't deterring her from offering him a room.

But luckily for Dennis, Mrs Helsby took in all manner of visitors, and a docker's workwear wasn't enough to put her off. She smiled back. 'Sorry, luvvy, but I've nothin' 'til Saturday.'

He feigned disappointment. '*Saturday?* Are you sure you've nothin' at all before then? A sofa would do? I've got a room comin' up in a week's time an' I just need somewhere until then.'

She shrugged helplessly. 'Sorry, but most of my

guests are nigh on permanent residents, apart from the officer of course, he'll be leavin' on Friday.'

Dennis could have crowed with delight. It was more than he had hoped for. He smiled gratefully. 'Not to worry, I'm sure I'll find somewhere, but I'll come back should I not find somethin' suitable by Saturday.'

She was about to close the door when she appeared to have a change of heart. 'If you're desperate, you can come Friday evenin', but not until after five. That should give me time to change the sheets and have a quick sweep round.'

He beamed. 'Thank you. You really have been most helpful. I shall indeed call by if I haven't found somewhere by then.'

Smiling, she closed the door.

Hurrying away from the B&B before his luck ran out, Dennis couldn't keep the smile off his face as he made his way to the docks.

I'll make sure I'm outside the B&B from early Friday mornin',' he thought as he hurried on. *That way there's no chance of my missin' him*!

It was the morning before Cecil's parents were due to go home and Tammy was sitting in front of the dressing table, admiring her reflection in the mirror. Today was the day of her wedding, and she couldn't be happier if she tried. Smiling as Hannah came into the room, she turned to face her.

'You look simply beautiful, my dear,' Hannah told her.

Tammy held a hand to her stomach. 'Thanks, but I feel as nervous as a kitten. My tummy's been performin' somersaults all mornin'.'

'Perfectly natural,' said Grace, entering the room behind Hannah. 'Marriage is a big step.'

'I cannae help but wonder what they'll say when I go back to my barracks. Do you think they'll be cross? Only they don't approve of relationships . . .'

'Oh, don't they now? Well, they'll just have to grin and bear it, because what's done is done,' said Hannah somewhat stiffly.

'Too right!' agreed Grace.

There came a gentle knocking on the door to her room, and Ronnie's voice came from the other side. 'Is everyone ready?'

Tammy nodded as she met him at the door. 'As I'll ever be!'

'Good. Because I reckon our Cecil will be just as nervous as you are, Tammy – if not more, what with him bein' on his tod in the B&B.'

'Poor Cecil. I hate to think of him on his own,' said Tammy as they got into the waiting taxi.

'He'll not be that for much longer,' said Grace. 'He'll have you by his side.'

Hannah dabbed away her tears before they could fall. 'Have you got everything, dear?'

Tammy looked down to her posy of flowers, which were tied with blue ribbon she had borrowed from one of the girls. 'I've got somethin' borrowed and blue, and as long as Cecil's not forgotten his grandmother's weddin' ring I'll have got somethin' old too.' She eyed her future mother-in-law shyly. 'Are you *sure* about givin' me her ring?'

'Positive!' said Hannah decidedly, looking to where she'd worn her mother's wedding ring on her right hand. 'She doted on the boys, and with Cecil being the first to marry I think it only fitting that his wife should be the one to have it.'

'Wife!' murmured Tammy. 'It sounds so grown up!'

'You're goin' to be just fine,' said Grace, before gasping, 'Somethin' new! You haven't got—'

Tammy laughed. 'I thought I was meant to be the one panickin'!' she said, indicating her stockings. 'They're new on today!'

Sighing with relief, Grace settled back into her seat. 'I know it might be superstitious, but who can blame me after my dreadful marriage?'

'And did you follow the old, new, borrowed and blue rule?'

'No,' said Grace. 'I thought I had, but your father was lyin' when he said the flowers were new. I found out later that he'd pinched them from someone's grave!'

'No wonder your marriage was doomed,' said Hannah, shaking her head. 'What a thing to do!'

'Sums him up in one, does that,' said Tammy.

'Well, you needn't worry with our Cecil,' said Hannah, pointing to the register office. 'We're here!'

Stepping out from the register office some twenty minutes later, both Cecil and Tammy were beaming fit to bust.

'Mrs Cecil Carter,' sighed Tammy as she looked at her wedding ring. 'I guess everything will change now.'

'Have you spoken to Mrs Helsby?' Grace asked Cecil.

'Mrs Helsby?' echoed Tammy. 'Why would he need to speak to her . . .' She stopped as the penny dropped. 'Oh . . .'

Cecil smiled kindly. 'Where did you think you'd be spending your wedding night?'

'I hadn't thought about it at all,' she admitted.

He placed his arm round her shoulders. 'I promise I won't bite.'

Tammy smiled, but inside she was as nervous as it was possible to be. She had no idea what was expected of her, and wished she'd spoken to her mother about it before . . . but no. This wasn't something she'd feel comfortable discussing with her mother, and as she didn't have any friends who'd actually slept with anyone, she guessed she would have to hope that Cecil knew what went where. Gazing into his eyes, she felt a sense of reassurance. Cecil knew she was a virgin, and she was sure he'd never do anything to hurt her. *He won't expect me to do anythin' I'm not comfortable with*, thought Tammy as the taxi drew up outside the Adelphi. Leaning forward, Cecil kissed her softly on the lips, and as her body tingled under his touch she supposed that things might just come to her naturally!

It was the morning after their first night together as a married couple, and when Tammy woke it was to see Cecil smiling at her from his side of the bed.

'Good morning, Mrs Carter,' he said, and kissed her softly on the lips.

Shading her eyes from the morning sunshine filtering through the gap in the curtains, she smiled back. 'Good morning, Mr Carter.'

'Are you ready for some brekker? Only my parents' train leaves in an hour.'

Tammy shot upright, narrowly avoiding hitting her new husband under the chin. 'An hour! Why didn't you wake me sooner?'

'You looked so peaceful,' he said, as she hurried over to the sink.

'We'll have to skip brekker if we don't want to risk missin' them,' said Tammy, throwing warm water over her face.

Cecil's eyebrows shot heavenwards. 'Miss breakfast? Are you insane?'

'I'm not havin' your mother thinkin' I don't care about them just because I've got a ring on my finger!'

'She'd be far more hurt if she thought you'd denied her son the most important meal of the day,' Cecil pointed out as he began to dress. 'Besides, we've plenty of time. The station's not far from here.'

'I know, but I wanted to call in at the shelter first to get the recipes for your mammy.'

'Only didn't your mammy say that she'd bring them to the station?'

Tammy fastened her skirt. 'She did, you're right! Why did I think otherwise?'

'Because these last few days have been a whirlwind,' said Cecil, holding out her shoes.

Doing up the laces, she waved a hand towards the door. 'We might have more time than I thought, but I still don't want to be late.'

Having gulped down their breakfast, they arrived at the station to see Cecil's parents and Grace standing on the platform.

'See!' hissed Tammy as they hurried over, 'I told you we hadn't time for another pot of tea!'

Grinning disarmingly, Cecil apologised for their apparent tardiness. 'Blame me!' he said, holding up his hands in mock surrender. 'Tammy did point out that we were running short of time, but would I listen?'

'Nagging you already, is she?' said Ronnie teasingly, 'Welcome to married life, son.'

Hannah rolled her eyes. 'Ignore him! And don't worry about the time – the train's not gone without us.'

Tammy turned to her mother. 'Did you remember the recipes?'

'Of course!' Grace held up a sheaf of handwritten notes and handed it to Hannah. 'I hope you can read my writing!'

Hannah flicked through them, nodding. 'Easily. Thanks for these – I shall be sure to let you know how I get on.'

Peering over his wife's shoulder, Ronnie smacked his lips. 'I can't wait to try some of those!'

'I just hope I do them justice,' said Hannah, tucking them into her handbag.

Cecil nodded to the train which was just pulling in. 'I think this one's yours.'

As she turned to look at the train, Hannah's eyes began to fill with tears. 'I hate goodbyes,' she said, fishing a handkerchief from her pocket. 'It's the worst part about seeing your family.'

Cecil enveloped his mother in his arms. 'I promise we'll come and see you soon.'

Hannah's eyes glistened. 'We'll have to see if we can get your brothers back for a visit at the same time.'

Cecil pretended to pull a disgruntled face. 'Them? Why do they have to come?'

Hannah rolled her eyes. 'To meet their new sister-in-law, of course! And don't tease! You know how much I love having you all under the same roof.'

He kissed her on the cheek. 'I know, and we all love being home. It'll be even better now we won't be getting indigestion.'

Laughing, Ronnie stepped forward to hug him. 'Cheerio, son. Take care of yourself, and Tammy too.'

Cecil smiled grimly. 'Will do.'

He stepped back so that his parents could embrace first Tammy and then her mother. All of whom – apart from Ronnie – were wiping tears from their eyes.

Clearing his throat, Cecil put his arm round Tammy's shoulders as he watched Ronnie and Hannah board the train.

'I cannae imagine why I was dreadin' meetin' them.' Tammy stopped to blow her nose. 'They're the nicest, kindest, most—'

'Loving,' said Cecil.

She nodded. 'I wish my father had been like yours.'

Grace was about to speak when the train driver

blew his whistle, half scaring her to death. 'That bloomin' guard! I'll stick his whistle where the sun doesn't shine if he does that again!'

The comment was the tonic they all needed. Laughing through their tears, they waved goodbye as Hannah and Ronnie watched them quizzically from their seats.

'That'll be you in a couple of days,' Tammy told Cecil sadly. 'I wish you could get a transfer to Liverpool.'

'Maybe I can now that we're married. Who knows?'

She eyed him hopefully. 'Really?'

He shrugged. 'I can but ask!'

It was the day before Meg's arrival, and Isla and Rory were browsing the market looking for bargains.

'I do love a good old mooch,' said Isla as she picked up a purse and inspected its condition.

Rory was looking down the length of a snooker cue as he replied. 'So do I, even though I never actually buy anythin' that isn't edible.'

'I suppose I don't really need to buy anything either,' Isla admitted, 'but I do like to go out in a frock rather than my uniform from time to time.' She turned to look at Rory. 'Do you realise that I've never actually seen you out of uniform?'

He wiggled his eyebrows suggestively. 'Just say the word. I aim to please.'

Blushing to the roots of her hair, she hid her face from the stallholder, who was laughing fit to burst. 'I didn't mean it like that!'

Rory pulled her in to his chest in order to hide her blushes. 'I'm only teasin'. I know what you meant!'

Her cheeks fading slightly, Isla deftly moved the subject away from clothes. 'I do like to buy my soap from the market, as well. The stuff they sell in the NAAFI doesn't smell of anything.'

His arm still looped around her shoulders they strolled on to the next stall, where Rory spied a copy of *For Whom the Bell Tolls*. Picking it up, he thumbed through the pages. 'I get nearly all of my books from the markets. There's always somethin' you haven't read yet, and you can even bring your old ones back to trade in.'

'Exactly!' Isla agreed. 'Markets are great for all sorts of different things.' As she spoke she held up a compact mirror and examined it for cracks or blemishes before snapping it shut and putting it back on the stall. 'I dread to think what the war would have been like without the markets,' she said thoughtfully. 'They seem to be able to get hold of all the stuff that shops can't.'

Rory raised a fleeting brow. 'Are you referrin' to the black market?'

'No I am not!' she cried indignantly. 'I'd never put money into the pockets of those people!'

'But what about those who simply cannae afford stuff unless it's sold under the counter?' said Rory. 'It hardly seems fair that the rich can buy whatever they want while the poor go hungry because it's against the law to trade on the black market.'

Isla's cheeks bloomed. 'If you put it that way . . .'

The next stallholder along joined in their conversation. 'Half the time the rich are buyin' more from the black market than the poor. I'll never forget goin' into my corner shop at the beginnin' of the last lot. I couldn't believe my eyes. The shelves were bare, and not because everyone had descended before I had a chance to get there but because rich sods had bought the lot, leavin' the rest of us mere mortals to go hungry.'

Isla's jaw dropped. 'That's disgustin'.'

He shrugged. 'I agree, but it also happens to be human nature.'

'Not mine!' snapped Isla, adding in disbelief, 'How could they?'

'Survival of the fittest – or in this case the richest,' said Rory.

'And they buy from the spivs too?' said Isla.

'Probably their best customers,' said the trader. 'Ironic when you think about it. I bet they snub their noses at the criminal fraternity until it means they can get the stockings they want, or the joint of lamb for their Sunday roast. It's all right to rub shoulders with spivs then.'

'Talk about double standards,' said Isla bitterly.

'It's why the rich get richer and the poor get poorer,' Rory told her.

'I still wouldn't buy from the spivs,' said Isla. 'I've heard they sell stuff that's intended for the boys on the front line.'

The trader shrugged. 'It wouldn't surprise me.'

'At least we can be sure that everything on this

market is kosher,' said Isla, but much to her surprise the trader pulled a sidelong grimace.

'Some of the traders do sell under the counter,' he told her. 'I don't always blame them, cos it can be difficult to make ends meet when you've got the spivs undercuttin' you.'

'It'll be a miracle if we win this war, the way we're goin' about it.'

'Luckily it's only a small minority of folk that break the rules. So don't you go givin' up hope just yet, young lady.'

'Aye, we'll win the war all right,' Rory put in. 'We did last time, and the black market was as rife then as it is now – or so I'm guessin'?'

'It was indeed,' the trader confirmed.

A slight frown still creased Isla's brow. 'I've browsed the markets a lot since the war began. How do people know when someone's dealin' under the counter? It's not as if they could pin up a sign advertisin' the fact, so how do the customers know?'

'Regulars,' said the trader. 'It's as simple as that.'

'That way they know who they can trust to keep shtum,' said Rory.

Isla shook her head. 'Sometimes I think I must wander round with my eyes shut!'

Rory laughed. 'Best way if you don't want to get arrested!' He was about to ask the stallholder whether he had a shaving brush when he stopped dead in his tracks.

Seeing the way Rory's face dropped, Isla followed his gaze. 'Oh, no. Not this again.'

Rory shook his head with an apologetic smile. 'Sorry, mind wanderin'. But I did think for a minute that I saw— but no! Dennis was no oil paintin' when I saw him last, but he didn't have a soddin' great scar down the side of his face, and he didn't look like a tramp neither.' He smiled fleetingly. 'My mind's definitely playin' tricks on me.'

For some reason, Isla wasn't as certain. She looked over to the man Rory had clocked, who was arguing with another stallholder. If the rumours were true, if Tammy really had clobbered her father over the head, surely it could well have left a scar? She turned back to Rory, whose eyes were still flitting between the distant man and the shaving brush the stallholder had handed him. Taking a deep breath, she jerked her head in the scarred man's direction. 'Just go and take a closer look; put your mind at rest once and for all.'

'No, I'm just bein' silly.'

'What's silly is standin' here wonderin' whether you're right or not when you could easily go and see for yourself,' said Isla. 'Does he resemble the man you saw from the overhead railway that time?'

Rory took a deep breath before letting it go with a whoosh. 'I'd say so, but then again, I'd have sworn the man I grabbed hold of was Dennis, and look where that got me.'

'No need to grab hold of him now, though,' said Isla, 'he's right there. I can practically see the whites of his eyes.'

But Rory was adamant. 'Even if it is him, what interest is that to me?'

'Answers,' said Isla simply, adding, 'and peace of mind.'

'Unless he fills my head with the rubbish he's been spouting to the likes of the polis,' said Rory, 'that would leave me with more questions than answers, and quite frankly I wouldn't want to give him the satisfaction.'

Isla looked back to where the man had been standing, but was now nowhere to be seen. Shrugging, she turned back. 'As long as you're sure?'

Rory nodded. 'Positive. Like I said, Dennis wasn't that ugly, and what would be his reason for coming to Liverpool?'

'I dare say he'd say the same about you should your paths have crossed,' said Isla. 'Still, as long as you're happy, that's fine with me.'

Rory paid for the shaving brush and tucked it into his pocket. 'You're all I need, Isla Donahue; I couldn't give a monkey's if half of Clydebank turned up in Paddy's market.'

She threaded her arm through his. 'Put the past behind you and move on. I'm pleased that you've managed to do that – and envious as well.'

'Because of your father, you mean?'

'Aye. Even though I forgive him, I cannae stop wonderin' what's happened to him. Is he alive? Is he happy? Did he ever go back for me?'

Rory rubbed his chin thoughtfully. 'Have you thought about approachin' the ships down the docks to put word out that you're searching for your father?'

Isla looked doubtful. 'There must be hundreds – if

not thousands – of merchant ships out there. The chances of findin' even one mariner that knew my father must be slim, to say the least.'

'But better than nothin',' supposed Rory. 'You could spread the word amongst the dockers, too.'

She gazed up at him. 'You're right. I've done absolutely nothin' to find him because I thought it would be like searchin' for a needle in a haystack, but the truth of the matter is that if I *don't* do something I really will never find him.'

'So what are we waitin' for? Let's get down the docks and start spreadin' the word.'

Chapter Eleven

Dennis had been lying in wait across the road from the B&B when – much to his surprise – the officer emerged from the house with Tammy on his arm. A frown creasing his brow, Dennis stared after them. What on earth was Tammy doing there at this hour? *She definitely wasn't stoppin' at the B&B a few days ago, cos I followed her back to her mam's*, he thought. As far as he could see there were only two possibilities: Tammy was either pretending to be the officer's wife so they wouldn't raise brows, or she actually was. He emitted a small groan. If they had indeed tied the knot, then he could hardly follow them back to goodness knows where, and even if he did what would be the point? He cursed inwardly. He had come too far and gone through too much to give up now. *I'll follow her to the pits of hell if need be*, Dennis promised himself, *cos whether she's in Liverpool or Loch Ness, she's a goner either way!*

It was Cecil's last day and they had opted to go for a walk around the lake in Sefton Park.

'Fancy a boat ride?' he asked, indicating the moored boats.

Tammy eyed the boat uncertainly. 'Have you actually rowed a boat before?'

'No, but it can't be that hard, surely?'

'I think a certain amount of balance is probably involved,' said Tammy thoughtfully. 'How deep do you think the lake is?'

'Pretty deep. I doubt you'd be able to stand up in the middle.'

She grimaced. 'Let me put it to you another way. Do you think it would be sensible for someone who cannae swim to go for a ride in a boat?'

He grinned. 'Half the Navy can't swim.'

She started to laugh, but seeing the look of sincerity on his face she stopped abruptly. 'You cannae be serious?'

'Very. Daft when you think about it.'

Tammy shrugged. 'Well, if it's good enough for the Navy . . .'

He raised his brow. 'Are you sure?'

'How hard can it be?'

Cecil led her over to the man who was hiring out the boats, and paid the fee. Taking Tammy by the hand, he waited until she was seated before joining her. 'There!' he said as he half sat, half collapsed onto the wooden bench. 'That wasn't too bad, was it?'

Swiftly rescuing one of the oars as it slipped its hook, Tammy frowned. 'Are you sure this is a good idea?'

'Easy as pie,' said Cecil, attempting to take the oar

from Tammy whilst wrestling with the one which was still in its hook.

Trying not to grimace too much as Cecil clunked the oars clumsily against the side of the boat, she peered over the side. 'We'll have to keep an eye on the time,' she said conversationally, 'we've only got the boat for an hour and your train leaves in four hours.'

'Oh ye of little faith,' said Cecil as the oar handles banged together by accident.

'I suppose it takes a little getting used to,' said Tammy, keeping her fingers crossed out of Cecil's sight.

'It's just a matter of co-ordination,' said Cecil as the oar handles continued to bump together.

'Practice makes perfect,' said Tammy loyally. 'I'm sure you'll get the hang of it before we have to take it back.'

Cecil threw his head back and laughed. 'Why do I get the impression that I'm not impressing you much?'

'I don't need to be impressed,' said Tammy, keeping her eyes on the silky water, which sparkled under the gaze of the summer sunshine. 'I just need to stay as dry as I was when I got into the boat.' To her alarm, Cecil momentarily let go of one of the oars to rip off a mock salute.

'Yes ma'am!'

Hiding her eyes with her hands, Tammy eventually peeped through her fingers to check that Cecil had both oars back in his hands. 'No party tricks, please!' she chuckled. 'I don't think my heart can take it.'

He twinkled at her as he began to row successfully. 'God, I'm going to miss you!'

She gazed back at him with equal affection. 'And I you. I cannae believe this is our last day together.' She glanced around them. 'What do you think the punishment would be if we lost both the oars, and you missed your train as a result?'

He smiled at her sympathetically. 'Put it this way; more than it was worth.'

'We *have* to do something,' said Tammy determinedly. 'I'd ask to swap places with Gina, but that wouldn't be fair because I'd be takin' her away from her Kenny, somethin' I'd never do.'

Cecil looked over his shoulder to make sure there were no other boaters in his path. 'If either of us has to move, then it's me to you, not the other way round. I don't know whether our being married will sway them any, but I doubt it.'

'I thought that part of bein' an officer was gettin' to go wherever you pleased,' said Tammy miserably. 'Why isn't that the case with you?'

'Because I'm quite low down the peckin' order when it comes to rank. It might be different if I were a brigadier, but even then you have your duty to your men, and that comes above everything.'

'I know, and I shouldn't even ask,' said Tammy. 'It's just that it's horrible knowin' that I might not see you again for goodness knows how long.'

'If we're lucky the war will be over soon.'

'You and I both know that peace isn't comin' to our shores any time soon.'

He eyed her thoughtfully. 'What makes you say that?'

'Common sense. Everyone thought the war was as good as over when the Yanks came in, but that was nigh on a year ago and there's still no end in sight, or none that I can see.'

'There's not a doubt in my mind that we'll win in the end,' said Cecil, 'but I'm sorry to say that you're probably right and it's far from over yet, barring some sort of miracle, of course.'

'No wonder people pray,' said Tammy. 'I've questioned my beliefs in the past, but if faith brings this thing to an end sooner rather than later, then I'm all for it.'

Their time spent boating on the lake had been memorable to say the least, and for all the right reasons. Tammy had told Cecil that she couldn't remember the last time she'd laughed so hard, and that they'd have to make it a regular thing when they met up, in Liverpool or anywhere else. 'You looked like you were doin' some sort of tap-dancin' routine,' she chuckled as they headed over to say goodbye to Grace.

'But on rollerskates,' Cecil agreed. 'I still don't know how I managed not to fall in.'

'I think the feller hirin' the boats was relieved to see the back of us, and what's more I don't blame him. I think he thought you were either goin' to dance your way through the bottom of his boat or tip it over.'

'I'm just glad there weren't many spectators,' said Cecil. 'The last thing I needed was an audience!'

'It was good fun, though,' said Tammy. 'I'd love to do it again.'

He grinned. 'So you can have a good laugh at my expense?'

'Preferable to my own,' said Tammy, before adding, 'How about we go ice-skatin' this Christmas? I've never done it before, but I'm game if you are – providing we're in the same part of the country, of course.'

'I was rather hoping that you could come to my parents' this Christmas – your mam and Archie too, if possible. We could make it a real family affair.'

'Oh, that would be lovely!' said Tammy. 'As long as it's all right with your parents, of course.'

He cast her a cynical glance. 'Can you honestly see either of them objectin'? They'd be over the moon if they thought you could join us. Providin' we could both get Christmas off, of course.'

'There is that,' said Tammy, 'but there's no harm in askin'.' By this time they had arrived at the shelter, and Tammy announced their presence by rapping her knuckles against the front door.

Checking through the peephole before opening the door wide, Grace ushered them inside with a smile. 'Come on in out of the cold,' she cooed.

Tammy handed her mother her small overnight bag.

'Is it all right if I leave this here?'

Taking the bag, Grace put it to one side.

'Of course it is! Have you had a nice last day together?'

'Wonderful, but as ever it was over too soon,' said Tammy.

'Isn't it always the way?' Grace turned to Cecil. 'I do hope it won't be too long before we see you again.'

'I'm hopin' not,' said Cecil, and told her the idea about Christmas.

'That would be wonderful!' said Grace, her eyes shining with delight. 'I know that Archie would be up for it, and I'm sure Mrs Latimer won't mind me havin' a bit of time off, but what about the RAF and the WAAF? Do you think they'll say yes?'

'We can but try,' said Tammy, 'but remember I've had the last two Christmases off.'

Cecil grimaced. 'I'd forgotten that.'

Grace looked at the grandmother clock which stood in the hallway. 'Oh, heck. I'd best shake a leg if I'm not to be late for work.' Taking her coat from its peg, she hurried to the door.

'It's a shame you have to work on my last evenin' off,' said Tammy as they walked Grace down the street.

'I know, but we've had a good time, haven't we?'

'The best,' Tammy agreed.

'And besides, the bills won't pay themselves.'

'That's my father's favourite saying,' said Cecil; 'that and "I'm not paying to heat the street" if you hold the front door open for too long durin' the winter months.'

'At least you had heatin',' said Tammy waspishly. 'Dad was that tight, he'd rather we froze than spend money on coal.'

'We didn't even have much furniture,' said Grace, 'cos Dennis sold most of it for beer money. It wouldn't have been so bad, but it wasn't even ours to begin with!'

Cecil stared at Grace in disbelief. 'Surely you're joking!'

'Nope! We kept our cutlery and crockery – such as it was – in crates. I was surprised he hung on to the kitchen table and chairs, but I suppose he had to have somethin' to eat his supper off.'

'Didn't the landlord say anything?'

'Luckily for Dennis the whole tenement went up in flames before he found out.'

'Did he not do inspections?'

Grace shrugged. 'I don't think he was bothered as long as he was gettin' his rent on time, and Dennis always made sure he was up to date with that, probably because he didn't want him comin' round and findin' out what had happened to his furniture.'

'I cannot fathom why anyone would see their family go cold just so that they can drink themselves into a stupor,' said Cecil. 'The very thought is enough to put me off alcohol for life!'

Grace stopped walking as they reached her place of work. 'This is me.'

Cecil took her in a warm embrace. 'I'll keep you in the loop regarding Christmas, but even if we can't all get the same time off together I'm sure we can arrange something round abouts that time.'

'Good thinkin',' said Grace. 'If we cannae celebrate Christmas on the actual day then we'll do it the followin' day, or the week after! Whatever suits everyone best.'

'We've really got to kick Hitler into touch,' said Tammy sadly. 'I'm sick of havin' to march to the beat of someone else's drum because of him! We should be able to spend as much time as we want together, not have it dictated to us by some fascist across the sea.'

'And we will,' said Grace. 'Now off you trot, else Cecil will be late for his train!'

Bidding Grace a fond farewell, Cecil and Tammy headed for the B&B. 'It hardly feels like two minutes have passed since I met you off the train, and here I am comin' to wave you off already,' pouted Tammy. 'Why does time never go by this fast when you're at work?'

'Because work's no fun, but being with someone you love is!' said Cecil. 'It'll be the same waiting for us to be together again. Time always drags when you don't want it to and flashes past in an instant when you do.'

'I'm goin' to have a word with my sergeant as soon as I get back to base,' said Tammy. 'You never know, he might say yes, given my new title.'

Cecil was furrowing his brow before it clicked. 'Because you're Mrs now and not Miss?'

She shrugged. 'I might be clutchin' at straws, but you never know.'

At the B&B, they quickly retrieved Cecil's belongings and sought out the landlady, who was having a well-earned cup of tea in the room at the back.

'It's been lovely meetin' you, Cecil,' she said as he hefted his kitbag onto his shoulder.

'And you too, Mrs Helsby,' he said. 'I shan't half miss your breakfasts. Especially those succulent sausages! An excellent start to the day, they are.'

Mrs Helsby blushed. 'Only the best for my customers!'

'Which is why you have so many permanent residents,' said Cecil. 'I'm just lucky you had enough room for me!'

She beamed. 'You're welcome back any day of the week.'

Tammy glanced meaningfully to the clock which sat on the mantel. 'I know we've plenty of time, but I'd rather be early than late.'

Cecil thanked his host once again, and opened the front door for Tammy to pass through ahead of him. Joining her on the pavement outside the B&B, he took one last look at the house which had been his home for the past week. 'She certainly knows how to spoil a feller,' he said as he fell into step beside Tammy. 'No wonder she never has any vacancies.'

'I think it must be Scousers in general,' said Tammy. 'They really know how to make someone feel at home.'

'No airs and graces,' said Cecil. 'The officers in my platoon would hate it here!'

Tammy laughed. 'Snooty beggars.'

'Apt description, considering they're only happy when they're looking down their noses at someone. They think they're a cut above everyone else because they're rich, but money isn't everything.'

'It is when you haven't got any,' said Tammy. 'Take if from one who knows.'

'True, but it's more their attitude that gets my goat. I'm sure they actually think that people who haven't got money aren't worth anything. Which is bloomin' rich considering most of the lads at the front haven't got two pennies to rub together, yet they're the ones putting their necks on the line every day. In my opinion it's men like them who are the important ones, *not* men like me.'

'I've said it before, and I'll say it again,' said Tammy, 'I wish more officers were like you.' She hesitated. 'The only thing I don't understand is why they think that havin' more money makes them more important?'

'A good education costs money,' said Cecil simply.

'Well it shouldn't,' said Tammy. 'The whole class system belongs in the dark ages, if you ask me. Everybody deserves a decent education no matter their bank balance.'

'Couldn't agree more,' said Cecil. 'But I doubt those born into money would be willing to hand over their silver spoons just yet.'

'No, because they know how good they've got it.' Tammy stopped walking and looked over her shoulder. 'That's odd.'

'What?' said Cecil, following her gaze.

'I've got that feelin' again,' said Tammy, 'the one where I think I'm bein' watched.'

He looked around him. 'As far as I can see, no one's even looking in our direction.' He eyed her curiously. 'Maybe you're just feeling uneasy because we've been chatting about the officers, or because I'm going back to Faringdon, and you're worried that they'll object to our being married.'

'I suppose it could be either,' admitted Tammy. 'I know they cannae do much about our bein' married, but it doesn't mean to say they have to like it.'

'You need to forget about them,' said Cecil. 'That's what I intend to do.'

'You're right, and the sooner the better,' said Tammy. They started walking again, but despite her confident words, she just couldn't shake the feeling that someone was watching them.

Having waited an age for them to return to the B&B, Dennis couldn't have been more pleased when they emerged again shortly afterwards and he saw that the officer was the only one carrying a suitcase. Making sure he kept himself well hidden from their view, he had waited until they were a good way down the road before beginning to follow them at a distance. *For once the cards are in my favour*, he thought. *All I have to do now is keep my distance, then pounce when the time is right.*

So deep in thought was he that he almost didn't notice Tammy come to a sudden stop and look behind her. Diving out of sight just in time, he hoped he hadn't been spotted. His heart pounded in his chest as he waited a few seconds before gingerly poking his head around the corner. Had she seen him? If she had, it was all over. At first he thought he had lost sight of them altogether, but seeing movement as Tammy turned to go on, he breathed a sigh of relief. Taking great care to keep his eyes fixed on his quarry Dennis followed at a distance. *If she sees me then the game's up,* he reminded himself. *And I cannae afford for that to happen, not when everythin's goin' my way for once!*

Isla and Rory had spent the previous day trolling the docks, speaking to various dockers and sailors in the hope that someone might know her father's whereabouts, but despite their best efforts they had drawn a blank.

'At least we're gettin' the word out there,' Rory had comforted Isla as they made their way back to the bus stop. 'Everyone I spoke to seemed keen to help, and even if they don't come across your father themselves then someone they've spoken to might!'

'I really hope so, and I'll keep visitin' the docks in the meantime to keep the word alive, as it were,' Isla had agreed brightly. 'I know it might be a bit of a shot in the dark, but it feels good to be out there doin' somethin'.'

'Certainly better than sittin' on our laurels,' said Rory. 'Some of the fellers I spoke to were settin' sail for Africa, which just goes to show how far the word will spread.'

'And with Meg bein' in Portsmouth, I'll ask her to do the same,' said Isla; 'Sophie too. And if Peggy gets her Clive to help as well then I really think we might find him.'

Now, as Isla made her way to the train station, she hoped that Meg's train would be on time. *There's not much worse than standin' round a station for hours on end twiddlin' your thumbs,* she thought, sighing irritably. The government's insistence that names be removed from station signs for national security had been bad enough, and the least they could do was ensure the railway staff were kept abreast of any news. As she entered the station, she looked round to see if there were any seats available, but all the benches had been taken. Seeing a guard pacing the platform, she headed over to ask which platform the train from Portsmouth was due in at.

He rubbed his hands across his face, immediately indicating to Isla that he was not having a good day. 'They've had disruptions on some of the lines, so *everythin'* is comin' to this platform.'

Isla groaned inwardly. 'So that's why it's so busy.'

'It's a bleedin' nightmare,' said the guard, before hastily apologising for his language. 'It's bad enough at the best of times, but this is sheer carnage. I haven't a clue which train is which so I've no idea what's goin' out or when. Plus everythin's backed up because there's no room at the bloomin' inn!'

Not wishing to aggravate him further, but needing to ask the question uppermost in her thoughts, she spoke tentatively. 'I hate to ask, but how can I tell which train my friend's on?'

'Wait to see which one she gets off. And please don't ask me when her train's due in, because I won't have a clue,' he said miserably. 'Just be glad that you're not waitin' to get *on* a train, cos that's when the real fun begins.'

Grimacing to indicate that she recognised his problem, Isla thanked him for his help before walking along the platform to see if she could see Meg on one of the waiting trains. *It's like lookin' for a needle in a bloomin' haystack*, she thought as she weaved her way through the crowds. *It'll be a miracle if we don't miss each other!* For a moment she considered whether it would be better to wait at Peggy's, but she'd agreed to meet Meg off the train and that's what she intended to do.

'He said he had no idea when the train would arrive, because there's only one working line so *all* the trains are delayed.'

Tammy rolled her eyes. 'Absolutely bloomin' typical! I bet some spiv's half-inched the tracks to sell down the black market.'

Cecil chuckled. 'At least we get to spend a little more time together.'

She tucked her fingers through his. 'Aye, there is that. Only what will they say if you're late? I know how unforgivin' they can be.'

He pulled her hand to his lips and kissed the knuckles. 'As I'm not goin' to be the only one who's goin' to be late there won't be a lot they *can* say!' He glanced towards the service men and women jam-packed along the platform. 'If they want to reprimand me then they'll have to have a go at this lot an' all. At the end of the day we all got here in plenty of time, and it's not our fault the rail services can't get their act together.'

Tammy looked around to see if there were any vacant seats, but it looked as though they were all taken. She did, however, think that she saw a figure whisking out of sight as though trying not to be seen. She scolded herself. *You're lettin' your imagination get the better of you, Tammy Carter. All you saw was someone leavin' the station in a hurry, which is hardly surprisin' considerin' the circumstances.* Someone else was hurrying from the platform, their arm raised as they tried to gain the attention of someone waiting on the concourse. The man caught up to his friend and began pointing in an animated fashion to the taxi rank outside. *I wonder where they're going, she thought. It cannae be far if they're goin' by taxi . . .* A new idea occurred to her, and she looked at Cecil. 'I've just had a thought.'

'Oh?'

'Why don't you see if there's a train leavin' from Central Station? I reckon that's what some of the other passengers might be thinkin'.'

He looked doubtful. 'I suppose I might have to in the end,' he said, 'but I'm not goin' to rush off just yet.' He pointed out the swarm of people leaving the platform. 'If that's where this lot are going, it just means there won't be any trains from the other stations either.'

She pulled a disgruntled face. 'I wish we'd known before settin' off. We could've stopped somewhere for a cuppa.'

Cecil automatically glanced at the station café, but quickly dismissed the idea when he saw the queue stretching halfway down the platform. 'It's at times like this that I wish I'd joined my pals when they pooled together to buy a motor,' he said wistfully.

'Not that I imagine there's enough petrol available to get me from Faringdon to Liverpool and back!'

Tammy brightened as another idea came to mind. 'I could always give my station a quick call, see if there's any deliveries need takin' down your neck of the woods? Not only would we get to spend more time together, but I'd be able to say a quick hello to Gina whilst I was down there.'

He smiled at her affectionately. 'That's a crackin' idea, but I honestly don't think it will be necessary. It's not as if the trains aren't arrivin' – they're just havin' to take their turn. So with my train due in at this platform I think I'd be daft to walk away just yet.'

Tammy glanced at the queue, which didn't seem to her to have gone down at all. 'In that case we may as well grab a cup of tea whilst we're waitin'. If the train comes before we get to the head of the queue, all well and good, and if not at least we'll have wet our whistle!'

'What about some supper?' said Cecil. 'I know it's a bit early . . .'

She shook her head. 'I'll grab a bag of chips on my way home.'

He groaned softly. 'Not from the fried fish shop down by the docks?'

'Of course!'

'That's my favourite!' Cecil mock-whimpered, adding, 'Not fair!'

'Don't worry, I'll think of you with each and every crispy morsel!'

He pulled a disappointed face. 'And I'll think of

you when I'm tucking into my semi-stale railway sarnies!'

She grinned. 'Indigestion guaranteed with every bite!'

'Bit like my mum's cooking!'

Having nearly been discovered by his daughter for the third time in a row, Dennis did his best to remain out of sight. He hadn't a clue why this platform in particular was so busy when the others looked empty, but seeing the exasperation on people's faces he assumed they would all be there for some time to come. Leaning against the wall, he took his tobacco pouch from his pocket and rolled a cigarette. As long as they didn't cancel the officer's train he didn't care how long he had to wait.

Isla shifted from one foot to the other as she listened to the disgruntled passengers around her.

'It's a damned disgrace,' an older woman had been muttering as she and her friend made their way past Isla. 'You'd think they'd be better prepared, what with the war and all.'

'I was meant to be goin' to a pal's weddin' tomorrow mornin',' a man was complaining to the guard, 'but if the train doesn't arrive soon I'll miss my connection and then where will I be?'

Isla listened with half an ear as the guard and the prospective wedding guest continued to argue. Having stood in the same spot for the past thirty minutes or so, Isla had considered moving to a different area if just for a change of scenery, but had decided against it after determining that she probably had the best viewpoint on the platform. The guard had chosen to stand nearby too, so he was close at hand should she need to speak to him.

Sighing, she cast her eyes once again around those who had been there before her. There was the mother of three young boys, all of whom Isla guessed to be under the age of six. The smallest had fallen asleep on his mother's lap whilst the other two played a raucous game of tag. Next she turned her attention to an officer and his belle who, after reaching the head of the buffet queue, had emerged with a cup of tea each and a small packet of biscuits. Wishing fervently that she had a cup of tea herself, Isla knew she would only rue her decision if she missed Meg whilst in the café. She continued to scan the crowd, and her eyes fell on a man who was wearing a decidedly dog-eared donkey jacket, the elbows of which were peppered with holes, reminding Isla of the men she'd been speaking to down the docks the previous day. Propped up by one shoulder against the wall, he'd had his back to her the whole time she'd been on the platform so she had no idea what he looked like, but, from his build she guessed him to be middle-aged or older. She watched as he stubbed out a cigarette using the toe of his boot. As far as she was aware, everyone else had at least gone for a little stroll, or nipped to the lavvy, or bought some refreshments, but not him. He'd not moved the whole time she'd been there.

He must have a bladder like a camel, she thought, *and*

I'm surprised his legs haven't gone to sleep, given he's been rooted to the spot this whole time. In fact, if it hadn't been for the number of cigarettes he'd smoked she might well have assumed him to be sleeping on his feet. She couldn't explain why, but something was bugging her about his presence. It wasn't just that he hadn't moved; it was more than that. For a start, why was he there? Everyone else either had luggage, making them passengers, or they were watching for trains, meaning they were waiting for someone to arrive. But this man had no luggage, and he wasn't watching the trains. It was then that it hit her. He had to be watching something or someone. But what? Or who? Stepping over so that she was following his line of sight, she looked to see what could be holding his attention. Nearest was the mother with three children; with the officer and his belle the only others clearly within his field of vision.

She glanced to the woman with the three children. It was possible that the man was with them, but if so why wasn't he standing with them? True, the children could be considered annoying, but if he had been a friend or relation surely they would have run over to him occasionally, or at least looked in his direction? No. He wasn't with the family. This left her with the officer and his belle, both of whom had their backs to the man. She was about to dismiss this thought for its sheer improbability, when the woman in ATS uniform started to walk towards the conveniences. Isla sharpened her attention. He was *definitely* watching the officer and his companion – it was the first time Isla had seen him move his head, and it was to follow the path of the young woman to the Ladies. But why? *He could always be her father*, supposed Isla. *Perhaps he doesn't like his daughter datin' and has come to see who she's with?* She watched as the young woman came back to her beau, noting as she did so that the eyes of the man in the donkey jacket followed her again. Isla knitted her brow as her attention was drawn to the train pulling into the platform. She prayed for Meg to be on board the train, or on the one that was pulling in directly behind it. *Double the chances*, thought Isla. *She simply has to be on one of them.* As she moved forward, she noticed that the couple followed suit. The only person who didn't move was the man in the donkey jacket.

Cecil took Tammy in a brief embrace. 'I'd better be off,' he whispered. 'The guard said none of the drivers are hanging on for anyone, as they're running late enough as it is.'

'I know,' sniffed Tammy. 'I'm just glad you're goin' to be back before your leave's over. I don't want to give those stuffy old walruses an excuse to have a go at you, especially if we've to have a hope of spendin' Christmas together.'

The guard blew his whistle impatiently, and Cecil pecked Tammy on the lips before hurrying towards the train. 'Ring me as soon as you can,' cried Tammy and Cecil came to a sudden stop. Turning on the spot, he dropped his bag and rushed back to take her in his arms, lift her off her feet, and press his lips to hers before setting her back down on the ground and running back to the train.

Tears lining her cheeks, Tammy waved goodbye, mouthing the words *I love you* as his train pulled slowly out of the station.

Chapter Twelve

Meg waved a hand in front of Isla's face. 'Oi! Deaf adder!'

Breaking out of her trance, Isla smiled apologetically as Meg took her in a warm embrace. 'Sorry, Meg, I never saw you there. I was miles away.'

'So I can see!' said Meg, following Isla's gaze. 'I'll forgive you, but what's so interestin' it caused you to be oblivious of everythin' else?'

Isla was still watching the couple as they said their goodbyes. Nodding in their direction, she said: 'See those two over there?'

Meg followed her line of sight, eventually nodding. 'Aww, sweet! Do you know them?'

'Not from Adam.' Isla indicated the man in the black donkey jacket, who had moved slightly in order to get a better view of the couple. 'See that feller?'

'Aye.'

'He's been watchin' them for ages,' said Isla, as though this was the news of the century.

'All right,' said Meg slowly, 'which means you

must also have been watchin' them for ages. Question is, why?'

'I've been people-watchin' whilst waitin' for your train to arrive, but I don't think that's what he's doin'.'

Meg wrinkled her nose. 'You think he might be some kind of pervert, or a peepin' Tom?'

'Bit too public to be the latter, but he could certainly be the first.'

'Are you goin' to say somethin'?'

'Not yet; I want to see what he does first. After all, it'll be pretty embarrassin' if I go in all guns blazin' just to find that there's a perfectly reasonable explanation for his behaviour.'

'Whoever they are, they seem to be very much in love,' said Meg, her tone heavy with awe as she watched the man run back to the woman and sweep her off her feet.

'I did think he might be an over-protective father at one stage,' said Isla, 'but even so I think his behaviour's a bit creepy.'

'Me too,' Meg agreed. 'Plus he doesn't exactly look like he's related to her. I know they say you shouldn't judge a book by its cover, but those two look poles apart.'

'They do, don't they! So not family members, in which case it's back to square one.'

'Bein'?'

'Who is he and why is he watchin' them?'

Meg looked pointedly at the officer's train, which was pulling out of the station. 'Looks as though we're about to find out.'

265

Ushering Meg back a pace or two, Isla half hid behind the pillar as she watched the woman go past the man, who much to Isla's alarm had also slunk out of sight. But he emerged from his hiding place and hurried after her, while clearly taking care to keep his distance as they left the station. Meg and Isla's exchanged glances said the exact same thing. Whoever he was, and whatever he was up to, it didn't look good.

'Shouldn't we tell one of the guards?' Meg hissed as the girls followed the man at a distance.

'Not yet,' Isla whispered. 'If we do he'd probably scarper, which might seem good right now, but what's to stop him from followin' her again?'

'Good thinkin',' said Meg, adding, 'What'll we do if she jumps into a taxi?'

Isla shrugged. 'I guess we'll have to cross that bridge when we come to it.' Seeing the woman walk past the line of taxis, she breathed a sigh of relief. She couldn't explain why it was so important, but she knew she had to keep this man in her sights.

'Where do you suppose she's headed?' Meg asked.

'It could be anywhere,' said Isla, 'but if I were to guess, I'd say she's headin' in the direction of the docks.'

'He looks like a docker,' said Meg. 'Unless he's in disguise, of course.'

Isla faltered mid-step. 'Disguise? Who on earth disguises themselves as a docker?'

Meg shrugged. 'Private dicks?'

'But what on earth could she have done to warrant bein' spied upon by a private detective?'

'We all know that the services frown on relationships of any kind,' said Meg. 'I should imagine they really wouldn't approve of an officer datin' a private – even if it's every private's dream!'

Isla wrinkled her nose. 'But would they really go to these lengths? Surely they'd just tell him to end the relationship?'

'They'd have to prove the relationship first,' said Meg, 'or . . .' Her eyes rounded as she turned to Isla. 'Maybe she's havin' an affair!'

Isla's brow rose in disbelief. 'You saw the man she was with! Would *you* want to stray if you had a man like him on your arm?'

Meg shook her head. 'Good point.'

'I reckon he *has* to be a private detective,' said Isla, 'it's the only plausible explanation. If he was a disgruntled father, he'd have accosted her before she'd left the station, not follow her back to goodness knows where. No, whoever this woman is, the man must have some sort of vested interest in her, cos there were loads of unescorted women in the station, an' if he were a pervert he could easily have followed any of them.'

Meg nudged Isla as the woman slowed down and the man followed suit. 'I know you don't want to do anythin' rash, but it's gettin' awfully dark, and I don't like the way this is pannin' out.'

'Why on earth is she headin' towards the docks?' wondered Isla, who was too engrossed in the situation to have heard what Meg said.

'I don't know, but the docks aren't the safest place to be under normal circumstances, let alone . . .' Meg breathed a sigh of relief as the young woman headed into the fried fish shop. 'Thank goodness for that. I was beginnin' to think she'd lost the plot for a moment there. I mean, who goes for a wander down the docks in the dark?'

Isla nudged Meg into silence, pointing. 'He's waitin' for her!'

Meg was shaking her head. 'I reckon we find a policeman and tell him what's goin' on. I don't care if he is a private dick, he shouldn't be followin' her the way he is.'

Isla agreed. 'One of us will have to wait here whilst the other looks for a scuffer, just in case they move on.'

Meg smiled briefly. 'I see you're already talkin' like a native,' she quipped, in an effort to dilute the tension they were both feeling. 'I'll look for a scuffer whilst you keep an eye out here – unless you'd rather go?'

'No, you go,' said Isla, thinking, as Meg hurried away. *I hope she takes her chips and eats them somewhere crowded, cos I don't much fancy followin' her any further down the docks.*

Tammy was trying to take her mind off of Cecil and how much she was missing him already, but was finding it impossible to do so.

He should be here with me, not on a train to Faringdon, she thought as she handed over the money for her chips. *Life can be so unfair!* Blissfully oblivious of being watched, she decided to eat her chips down by the water, where it was quiet. Peeling back the paper, she briefly savoured the scent of salt and vinegar that reached her nostrils before breaking a chip in half and popping it into her mouth.

Cecil wouldn't be disappointed, that's for sure. She was so deep in thought that she didn't notice the lorry that whisked behind her, although she did think that she heard someone shout out a warning. Turning to thank them, all she saw was a fist coming towards her.

Meg was so desperate to find a policeman, she was running around like a headless chicken. Only when she collided with a woman, knocking her shopping to the floor did she take a moment to breathe. 'I'm so sorry,' gasped Meg as she helped the woman to pick up her belongings. 'I'm tryin' to find a policeman.'

The woman's annoyed frown dissipated in an instant, to be replaced with one of worry. 'Why? What's up?'

Meg quickly explained, finishing with, 'We don't know what he's up to, but it cannae be anythin' good.'

The woman held up a reassuring hand. 'Don't worry. I'll find a policeman while you get back to your pal. Where was she again?'

'Down the docks next to the fried fish shop. Only I cannae remember its name,' she wailed, wringing her hands in earnest.

The woman nodded. 'Not to worry, I know the one. I'll be as quick as I can.'

Thanking the woman profusely for her help, Meg was about to hurry back to Isla when she realised she hadn't a clue how to get there.

Isla had been keeping a keen eye on the man, whilst also watching the queue in the fried fish shop. *Who are you, and why are you bein' followed?* she thought as she watched the woman pay for her chips.

Quickly glancing back to where Meg had left her to go for help, Isla hoped her friend would return before the woman left the shop. *We won't be able to prove he was up to anythin' untoward*, she thought, *but at least she'd be safe with two of us watching her, because there's not a doubt in my mind that he's up to somethin' sinister!*

Wishing fervently that she had alerted the woman to his presence sooner, Isla watched as she left the shop. Crossing her fingers in the hope that she would head back to civilisation, Isla was dismayed when the woman turned to walk down to the dockside. Whilst she was wondering whether she should jog over to join her and explain what was going on, her attention was drawn to the man in the donkey jacket. When he turned his head away from the woman in what Isla suspected was an attempt to hide his face from view Isla gasped as she saw him clearly for the first time.

It's Dennis! Or rather, it's the man that Rory was convinced was Dennis. But what the hell is he doin' here? And why is he followin' that poor girl? I know from what Rory's said that he's a nasty piece of work. She thought about it. Following a lone woman down to the dock was just the sort of cowardly thing she'd expect from the man Rory had described. *He's a nasty, violent brute, and while I know it would be more sensible to wait for Meg to come back with the polis, I cannae take the chance he won't do somethin' awful to her in the meantime.* In desperation, Isla shouted out his name just as a convoy of lorries went past.

Cursing softly beneath her breath, she waited for the procession to pass, but when the last lorry swept by she was horrified to see that both Dennis and the woman had seemingly vanished into thin air. Rushing forward, Isla felt her foot slip on something, and looking down she saw a mess of chips, complete with wrapper, scattered across the ground.

'No, no, no!' she cried in quick succession. Where had they gone? Surely to goodness he hadn't bundled her into one of the lorries? She quickly dismissed the idea as impossible. The convoy hadn't even slowed as it left the docks with its cargo. On the other hand, neither Dennis nor the girl were to be seen. *If I were him, where would I take her? Somewhere far from pryin' eyes, that's for sure.* There was only one place that Isla could think of, and that was the waterside at the far end of the dock. Running as fast as her feet would carry her, she could only pray that she could get there before Dennis did the unthinkable.

When Tammy came to, it was to find the ground bobbing about below her. Thoroughly confused, she attempted to move, but she was instantly hefted further forward, bringing the ground closer to her face. It was then that she realised she was being carried over someone's shoulder. But what had happened to bring her to this point? Still groggy, she did her best to cast her mind back over recent events, starting with her goodbye to Cecil, followed by her visit to their favourite fried fish shop. She could remember leaving the shop, and someone calling out to warn her about the lorries as they rolled past, but nothing else. Had one of the lorries hit her? Was she now being carried to safety by the driver, or one of the dockers?

Feeling sick, she mumbled, 'Please put me down,' but rather than do as she asked the man carrying her laughed gruffly.

'I don't think so.'

Hearing that all too familiar voice caused her blood to run cold. Swallowing, she desperately tried to remember how she'd come to be in such a predicament, and after a few moments she envisaged the fist as it connected with her face. But what were Dennis's intentions now? Frightened tears welled in her eyes. It didn't take a genius to work out what they were. She'd told Cecil that she thought they were being watched, and she'd been right. Dennis must have followed them from the B&B to the train station and waited until he could get her on her own. *He must've decided to come back for his revenge*, thought Tammy as she swung helplessly over his shoulder. *I should've known he'd not be satisfied with the money. Why on earth did I take him at his word?*

Another, more miserable thought entered her mind. No one bar Cecil knew where she was, and he was on a train going back to his base. *He's goin' to throw me into the dock knowin' that I cannae swim. I'm goin' to drown and no one will know where I went, or what happened to me.* Her thoughts turned to her mother, who would be confused and devastated by her daughter's disappearance. *And just when things were finally lookin' good for her*, she thought miserably. She envisaged Cecil, who would be spending Christmas Day alone, wondering what on earth had happened to his wife. *They'll know I'm dead*, she thought, *because they know I'd never just up and leave like that.* She tried to wriggle, to escape her father's clutches, but he just dug his fingers deeper into her legs. She thought of Grace again. *He won't stop at me, he'll want to see her dead too, and she hasn't a clue that he's even in Liverpool.* Galvanised by the thought, Tammy began to thrash wildly, causing Dennis to stumble.

'Steady on,' he growled. 'Any more of that and you'll have us both in the drink, and there's only one person goin' in there tonight.'

Isla's heart hammered in her chest when she saw Dennis by the dockside with the woman over his shoulder. Seeing that his captive was putting up a fight, Isla did the only thing she could think of in the circumstances. Yelling out his name, she ploughed towards him.

'The polis are on their way, Dennis Blackwell, an' they know what you're doin', so if you even think about killin' either of us you'll swing for murder.'

Turning with a look of complete surprise and incomprehension on his face, Dennis stared at her. 'Who the hell are you?'

Isla's heart was beating so loudly she could actually hear it. 'Your worst nightmare, that's who!' She pointed to Tammy with a quivering finger. 'Now, either let her go, or face the consequences.'

Dennis's lip curled. 'You must think I was born yesterday! If you'd told the polis they'd be here with you!'

'No – my friend went to get them while I followed you.'

Thoughts raced through Dennis's mind, the first one he uttered being 'How do you know who I am?'

'Never you mind,' said Isla, keen to keep him talking, but Dennis laughed.

'You know nothin'.' Turning back to the dock, he was about to heave Tammy into the water when Isla grabbed hold of his jacket and started pulling. Sliding from his shoulder as he battled with Isla, Tammy fell just short of the water's edge. Horrified that the woman might accidentally fall into the water, Isla let go of Dennis's jacket as he continued to pull and he staggered backwards; tripping over Tammy's legs, he disappeared over the edge of the dock.

Rushing to Tammy's aid, Isla pulled her out of harm's way, then peered over the edge to see Dennis flailing in the water. 'Serves you bloomin' right!' she shouted. 'Just you wait until the polis get here!'

But Tammy was shaking her head. 'He cannae swim! He'll drown before they arrive, and whilst I'd like to see the back of him I'm no murderer, no matter what he might tell folk.'

Isla tried to ignore Tammy's words as the truth washed over her. There were only two women that Isla knew of who had been accused of attempting to murder Dennis, and to her dismay one of them was standing in front of her. Trying to banish the thought from her mind, she looked round for a lifebelt, spotted one, and quickly threw it into the water. 'Grab a hold of that if you don't want to drown,' she yelled, just as Meg arrived with two policemen and the woman Meg had knocked down.

'Isla!' cried Meg, and rushed forward. 'What happened?'

'He tried to drown her,' murmured Isla somewhat distractedly. 'Only he tripped and fell, thank goodness, cos it nearly went the other way.' As she spoke, the police dragged Dennis out of the water and locked a pair of handcuffs over his wrists.

'What the bloody hell are you cuffin' me for!' he roared. 'It was them what tried to do me in. They know I cannae swim—'

The constable who had cuffed him instructed him to shut up; the other asked Isla and Tammy if they'd come to the station to make a statement.

'Of course,' mumbled Isla. She remembered that Rory would be waiting for her in the café, and much as she wished she wasn't in this position, he deserved to know the truth. She turned to Meg. 'I told Rory that we'd meet him in Lyons café at eight o'clock. Please will you explain to him exactly what's happened?'

Meg pulled off a mock salute. 'Will do! I'll bring him to the station,' she said, and hurried off.

Tammy, who'd been wondering how this stranger knew who Dennis was, wondered no more. 'You know Rory?' she asked in soft tones.

'Aye,' said Isla. Unable to turn her back on the glaringly obvious, her heart skipped a beat as she uttered the words she'd hoped she'd never have to speak. 'You're Tammy, aren't you?'

'I am. But how do you come to be here?'

Following the police as they took Dennis to the station, Isla explained how she'd been waiting for Meg to arrive when she'd noticed him watching Tammy and the officer. 'I didn't have a clue who you were – nor Dennis, come to that; it was only when he turned to face me that I recognised him. You see, Rory was convinced he'd seen Dennis down the market a couple of days ago, but he thought it was his imagination playin' tricks on him, because he'd also thought he'd seen the warden from the night of the blitz whilst he was travelling on a tram a couple of weeks prior.'

'Archie! Yes, he could well have, because Archie lives in Liverpool now.' Tammy was frowning. 'How long have you known Rory?'

Isla explained everything, from the moment she'd first seen Rory down the shelter to the present day. It was only when she'd finished that she spoke the thought uppermost in her mind. 'You know everything there is to know about me now, but I haven't got a clue as to how you got here or what happened the night of the blitz. However, I shouldn't be the one askin' those questions, cos they're not really mine to ask.'

Tammy nodded. 'I've got some explainin' to do, but we'd best get this over and done with first.' She slapped a hand to her forehead. 'I cannae believe I haven't even thanked you yet!'

Isla smiled. 'Don't worry. A lot's happened in an awfully short amount of time.'

'You're tellin' me! I feel as though I've lived a lifetime in the past ten minutes!'

Rory looked to Meg who was out of breath as she burst through the door to the café. Thoroughly alarmed at the way in which she'd entered, he sprang to his feet.

'Where's Isla?'

'Long story,' panted Meg, 'but she's safe.' As she continued to catch her breath, she urged Rory to follow her. 'She's at the polis station.'

'What happened?'

'Your belle is a flippin' heroine,' puffed Meg. 'She only went and saved some girl from bein' murdered.'

Rory stared at her open-mouthed. 'I only saw her yesterday!'

Taking no notice, Meg rushed back out of the café with Rory in hot pursuit. Stopping abruptly, she turned to face him. 'I don't know where the polis station is!'

Rory tried not to roll his eyes. 'Where were you when you saw her last?'

'Down by the docks,' said Meg promptly.

He nodded. 'I know the one. Follow me.'

As they hurried to the police station, Meg explained how her train had been late, and all that had happened as a result.

'Thank goodness Isla kept her wits about her,' said Rory. 'And just think, if it *hadn't* been late, Isla would never have seen any of this, and that poor woman would be dead. Do you have any idea what it was all about?'

'Not a clue,' said Meg. 'I very much doubt that Isla knows either; all she said was for me to come and tell you what was goin' on.'

'Isla is a force unto herself,' said Rory, 'and whilst I very much admire her tenacity she's ever so lucky, because it could so easily have gone wrong, and Isla could be at the bottom of the Mersey along with that poor girl.'

'I know,' breathed Meg. 'I nearly had kittens when I realised she'd left the fish shop, cos I hadn't a clue where she was until I heard the splash.' She shuddered. 'For one horrible minute I thought the worst had happened.'

Rory pointed to the police station before them. 'Time to find out what's what.'

Chapter Thirteen

To Rory it felt as though he and Meg had been waiting for hours before a policeman finally came from round the back, followed closely by Isla. Jumping up from his seat, he hurried over to her, his face a mask of concern. 'Are you all right? He didn't hurt you, did he?'

Isla shook her head, but it was clear from the look on her face that things weren't at all right. Meg jammed her hands onto her hips. 'Please don't tell me they actually believed the drivel he was spouting about the two of you tryin' to do him in?'

Isla shook her head, her eyes never leaving Rory's. They became glassy with unshed tears as she spoke in quavering tones. 'You were right.'

Rory blinked. 'Sorry?'

'It *was* Dennis you saw down the market that day, and it was probably Archie you saw too.'

Rory was looking thoroughly confused. 'What on earth makes you think that?'

Without saying a word, Isla looked behind her to Tammy who had just walked out of another room.

He stared open-mouthed as Tammy appeared behind her. 'Hello, Rory.'

Stunned, he turned disbelieving eyes to Isla. 'Am I seein' things again?' She shook her head, and tears left her lashes. Rory glanced back at Tammy, before turning on his heel and walking wordlessly out of the police station.

Isla tore her gaze away from Rory's retreating back and turned to Tammy, who was looking as if all her nightmares had just come true. 'I'll wait here whilst you go after him.'

Tammy was shaking her head. 'I don't think Rory wants to see me, and what's more I don't blame him.'

'He's hurt, as well as confused,' said Isla softly, 'but no matter how he feels he needs to talk to you as much as you need to talk to him. If nothin' else, the least you owe him is an explanation.'

'But I already did that when I wrote to him, and he made it clear how he felt by sending my letter back opened.'

Isla remained resolute. 'Maybe, but you still need to talk to him.'

'I know.' Tammy heaved a sigh before walking out of the station, where she found Rory standing with his back to the wall, his head in his hands.

'I know you don't want to speak to me right now, but Isla's right; we need to talk. For the record, I'm truly sorry about what happened—'

Rory's head snapped up, a look of incredulity on his face. He gave a short, cynical laugh. '*Sorry*? Do you think that even *begins* to cover what you put me through?'

'Of course not,' said Tammy miserably, her eyes glassing over as she saw the pain within Rory's. 'But you have to believe me when I tell you that I didn't want to leave you in Clydebank, not for one second!'

'Then why did you?' He ran his tongue over his bottom lip as he tried to contain his emotions. 'You knew full well that I was waitin' for you.'

She nodded wretchedly. 'I know, but Dad came home early to find me and Mammy in the parlour with our bags. He went ballistic, Rory, and if I hadn't done somethin' quickly he'd have strangled Mammy to death. I tried to pull him off her, but he was too strong, so I hit him with the first thing that came to hand – which turned out to be the iron.' The tears cascaded down her cheeks as she recalled the moment her father had fallen unconscious to the floor. 'We thought he was dead, and you *know* what would've happened had that been the case. Me and mammy would've been hanged for murder.' She looked back up as the tears continued to stream down her cheeks. 'I begged Mammy to let me tell you, but she said they'd hang you too if they caught up with us and I couldn't let that happen.'

Rory rubbed the back of his neck. 'So why not wait until the heat had died down and send me a note to let me know where you were?'

'I did!' cried Tammy. 'You sent it back!'

Rory crinkled his brow. 'No I didn't!'

'Well, someone did!'

'When?'

'After I found out that Dad was still alive and I knew it was safe to write, so probably a couple of months after the blitz.'

Rory rubbed his hands up and down his face before resting his chin on steepled fingers. 'I left Clydebank within weeks of the blitz. I'm guessin' the new tenant must've opened it by accident and sent it back once they realised their mistake.'

She shrugged helplessly. 'When the letter came back open, I assumed it was your way of tellin' me to go to hell.'

Rory stared at her. 'I would *never* have done that, which is somethin' you should've known.'

'I admit I was surprised, but I thought it was no more than I deserved.'

His anger beginning to wane, he softened. 'You did what you thought was right at the time, an' I cannae blame you for that.' He sighed heavily. 'What a flippin' mess!'

Tammy looked back to the police station. 'Isla seems lovely.'

'She is.' His eyes fell to her wedding band. 'I see you're married?'

Tammy looked at the ring on her finger. 'Aye, we got wed a couple of days ago in Brougham Terrace.'

He rubbed his hand across the nape of his neck. 'In which case I suppose congratulations are in order.'

Her bottom lip quivered. 'Never in my life did I think this would happen to us.'

'But it has,' said Rory simply. He looked over to the police station. 'I need to get back to Isla.'

Tammy followed his gaze. 'Does she make you happy?'

His eyes were glistening with tears. 'Very much so.'

She gave him a wavering smile. 'She's one heck of a woman! She didn't think twice before layin' her life on the line to save mine, an' she doesn't even know me.'

He blinked away a tear. 'That's my Isla, always puttin' others first.' He paused. 'I'm sorry. I didn't mean to be petulant earlier.'

'I know.' She paused. 'If there could have been any other way . . .'

He pulled a brief smile. 'There's no point in rakin' over the past. I'm with Isla, and you're with . . .?'

'Cecil.'

He glanced at her before looking away. 'Do you love him?'

'Very much.'

He appeared to hesitate before speaking again. 'I want to say things like *This wasn't how it was meant to be*, but that would be denying Isla, and despite everything I wouldn't have it any other way.'

'I'm glad you're happy, Rory, truly I am.'

He smiled at her for longer this time. 'And I you.' He paused. 'How did Dennis know where to find you?'

Tammy grimaced, before quickly relaying how she'd met Gina, the bag of the money, and the terrible moment when Dennis had her mother at knifepoint.

'All that trouble to change your name and he found you anyway,' he said in disbelief.

'Ironic, when you think about it,' said Tammy. 'But at least we can finally put him behind us.'

Rory rocked on his heels, aware that their conversation was coming to an end. 'So where do we go from here?'

She shrugged. 'If it's all right with you I'd like to stay in touch, but I'd understand if you'd rather not.'

He looked at his shoes briefly before looking back up. 'We've got too much history just to sweep it under the rug.'

Tammy smiled. 'I can be reached at Seaforth Barracks. You?'

'RAF West Kirby.'

Nodding, she stepped forward and kissed him softly on the cheek. 'Good luck, Rory. I hope it all goes well for you.'

'You too.'

Tammy looked back at the police station. 'I'm just goin' to nip in and say goodbye to Isla and her friend.' Rory followed her back, and Isla and Meg stood up to greet them.

'Thanks for everythin', Isla. You're a bloomin' star, I hope you know that.' Tammy took Isla in a friendly embrace.

'You'd have done the same in my position,' said Isla, but she was looking at Rory.

Tammy smiled. 'Still took guts.' She smiled at Meg. 'Thanks for gettin' the help we needed. I wouldn't have fancied fishin' him out of the dock myself!'

Meg pulled a sympathetic grimace. 'Does that mean you're off, then?'

'It certainly does.' She glanced at Rory before looking back to Isla. 'He's lucky to have you.' Isla smiled but said nothing as Tammy left the station.

Rory was approaching her, and she gave him a quizzical look. 'I take it everythin' went as well as could be expected?'

Enveloping her in his arms, Rory smiled at her affectionately. 'It did. We've agreed to stay in touch; too much history to just walk away.' He paused. 'Do you mind?'

She shook her head. 'Not in the least,' she said, and was surprised to find she meant every word.

Cecil listened with bated breath as Tammy relayed her near miss.

'I should've listened when you said you had a funny feelin' you were being watched,' he said, his tone leaden. 'If I had, I might've kept a keener eye out at the station.'

'Don't you go blamin' yourself,' Tammy chided. 'I might have thought I was bein' followed, but I didn't notice anythin' out of place in the train station.'

'What did your mum say?'

Tammy's eyes fluttered as she recalled the moment her mother had broken down in tears. 'How *could* he?' Grace had sobbed. 'His own *daughter*!'

'Because he's the devil incarnate,' Archie had growled, adding, 'Thank God Isla had her wits about her!'

'I owe her my life,' Tammy had said softly.

'Well, at least he's behind bars now, which is where he belonged all along,' Archie had said.

Coming back to the present, Tammy answered him simply. 'She was in bits at first, but elated to hear he's now behind bars, and of course she's eternally grateful to Isla for savin' my life.'

'Aren't we all?' said Cecil. 'I know there's no point in cryin' over spilt milk, but I can't help wondering what would've happened had Isla not been there.'

'I'd not be here, it's as simple as that,' said Tammy.

'I'm so sorry, Tammy,' said Cecil quietly.

'What've you got to be sorry for?'

'For not bein' there when you needed me the most for the second time in your life.'

'Hardly your fault,' said Tammy, adding in an attempt to change the subject, 'What did they say when you told them you were married?'

He gave a short, mirthless chuckle. 'Not much, although they did huff and puff quite a bit.'

The operator cut across, letting them know their time was up.

'I'd best dash,' said Tammy. 'I need to give Gina a quick call, let her know the latest.'

'Fair enough. Give her my best, won't you?'

'I will.'

Hearing the click of the call being terminated before they could say goodbye properly, Tammy assured the operator that there was no one waiting to use the telephone and asked to be put through to Gina's base in Woodbury. Crossing her fingers, she was delighted to hear her friend's voice come down the line.

'Tammy!'

'And you thought I was bein' paranoid,' was

Tammy's response, before quickly going on to describe everything that had happened since Cecil's departure.

'I'm so sorry, Tammy, I didn't think for a minute—' Gina began, before being cut short by Tammy.

'Don't you start blamin' yourself! I've had enough of that from Cecil and Mammy. No one's to blame for what happened but Dennis himself!'

'I guess the lesson we can learn from this is to trust your instincts,' said Gina. 'You thought you were bein' followed and you were right!'

'I didn't have an inklin' when he was followin' me from the train station, though,' Tammy admitted. 'I cannae express enough how lucky it was for me that Isla was on the ball.'

'Talk about a turn-up for the books! Of all the people to come to your rescue it was Rory's new belle. If that isn't fate playin' a hand in events then I don't know what is.' Gina hesitated. 'What's she like? Apart from bein' a heroine, of course.'

'She's lovely, just the sort of woman I'd have wanted him to end up with. A lot of women wouldn't have been best pleased had their beau's ex come back from the dead, but she couldn't have been nicer if she'd tried – even insistin' on my followin' Rory out of the polis station so that we could talk things through.'

'A rare gem indeed.' Gina changed the subject. 'We were right about the money, though.'

Tammy frowned. 'In what way?'

'We always said that it would only bring misery,

and we were right. If Dennis hadn't taken it he'd never have wound up in jail.'

'So we did! You even said we should've burned it!'

'Good job we didn't, though,' said Gina, 'because I dread to think what your father might've done to you and your mammy if we had.'

'Everythin' happens for a reason,' said Tammy softly.

'Amen to that!'

Hardly able to believe what she was hearing, Sophie listened to Isla's tale with bated breath as the girls caught up on the telephone.

'You couldn't make it up!' she breathed when Isla had finished. 'How's Rory feelin' about it all now it's had time to sink in?'

'Like a weight's been lifted from his shoulders, because he finally knows the truth.'

'And what about you? Only I know you were worried about what would happen if he and Tammy met up?'

'I was nervous at first, because who knows what sort of emotions might have resurfaced, especially with Dennis bein' involved, but I knew everythin' was goin' to be all right as soon as I saw the two of them together in the polis station. Rory didn't look at her the way he looks at me.'

'I'm so glad it's all worked out for you, Isla. You deserve to be happy.'

'Talkin' of things workin' out, how're things goin' with Blackbeard?'

'He's much better, thank goodness. I did worry he might blame me when his ship sailed without him, but he said he'd half expected it, and that he'd easily get a place on another one.'

'And what about the two of you?' said Isla. 'Are you any nearer to goin' out on a date, or is he still bein' moody and mysterious?'

'No nearer, I'm afraid, but all good things come to those who wait,' said Sophie. 'Or so I keep tellin' myself.'

'He's bloomin' lucky you're so patient,' said Isla, before changing tack. 'Have you told him of recent events on the western front?'

Sophie drew a deep breath. 'We don't really talk much about our personal lives, and if I'm honest that suits me just fine. I don't want him thinkin' I'm bad news.'

'Why would he possibly think that?'

Sophie's brow rose swiftly. 'He got run over because Madson was tryin' to get revenge on me, and my best friend just saved her boyfriend's ex from bein' drowned by her father, after she inadvertently framed him for murder.'

'Oh. Well, that's hardly your fault.'

'I know, but you can see how it might look? In fact you must be able to, seein' as you were reluctant to tell Rory about Madson for fear he'd think the same thing!'

Isla felt her cheeks warm. 'I'd forgotten about that, but you're right.'

'See? It's not me bein' daft.'

'I suppose not.'

The operator cut across them letting them know that their time was up.

'Do let me know when you've got some leave. It would be lovely to see you again.'

'Will do,' said Sophie. 'T.t.f.n.'

As Isla replaced the handset she mused over the fact that she hadn't seen Sophie since the business with Madson had blown up. *I'm always sayin' that I hate her bein' in Scarborough on her own, yet I've been so caught up in my own dramas I haven't even attempted to go and see her. Some friend I am!* Feeling ashamed, she picked the handset back up and in an attempt to disguise her voice from the operator she pinched her nose as she asked to be put through to Meg's base. When Meg's voice came down the line, Isla wasted no time in voicing her concerns.

'I'm goin' to go and see Sophie, cos I've not seen her in an absolute age. Would you like to come with me?'

'I'd love to,' said Meg, 'but I've not long had some leave, so unless you're prepared to wait . . .'

'How long?'

Meg gave a sharp intake of breath. 'Could be Christmas – if I'm lucky.'

Isla grimaced. 'I could really do with goin' before that.' She paused as an idea sprang to mind. 'Peggy's always sayin' she's not been away in ages. Do you think she'd like to come with me?'

'I think she'd jump at the chance! Will you go to Scarborough or meet halfway?'

'If I can get enough time and Peggy's in agreement,

I say we should go to her. It'll be nice to see where she lives and works.'

A few days had passed since Isla's phone calls to her pals, and she and Rory were in Peggy's kitchen enjoying a cup of tea.

'Just let me know when and I'll be there,' said Peggy. 'Poor old Sophie's not one to complain, but it must be ever so lonely bein' miles away from the rest of us.'

'My thoughts exactly,' said Isla. 'I'll drop her a line and find out when she's free and we'll go from there.'

Peggy clapped her hands together in an excited fashion. 'I'll have to dig my suitcase out from the bottom of my wardrobe. It's been a while since I've had a holiday, never mind a summer one!'

Sophie had just finished reading Isla's letter and she couldn't be more pleased to learn that she would soon be seeing her friends again. *It's lovely that Isla and Peggy want to come over, and I'm as eager to see them as they are to see me. I've missed them something awful this past six months or so. I know Isla's desperate for me to get together with Donny, but with him eager to set sail on the next ship that's in need of crew, I doubt he and I will ever be an item.* She thought of the letter Harvey had written her, and how Isla had once hoped that Sophie might get together with him one day. *I know she'd say that Harvey was a much better match for me than Donny, but she seems to forget that she gave Theo up for a man she'd only seen in passin'! Not that I blame her, because we cannae help who we fall for. Donny and I don't know each other awfully well, but I do know that he's the man for me, and even if he doesn't feel the same way I'm not goin' to settle for second best just to please my friends. I shall wait until another man comes along who makes my heart sing just as Donny does!*

Chapter Fourteen

AUGUST 1943

'I feel like a schoolgirl,' Peggy remarked as the train she and Isla were on pulled into a station. 'I can't remember the last time I was on a train, never mind left Liverpool!'

Isla smiled. 'Glad you agreed to come, then?'

'Very much so!' said Peggy, admiring the quaint little station on the other side of the carriage window. 'They say a change is as good as a rest, and I'm beginnin' to feel the benefit already!'

'Pleased to hear it,' said Isla, adding ruefully, 'It's a shame Meg couldn't wangle any time off, but hardly surprisin' considerin' she hadn't long had some leave.'

'And what a spot of leave that turned out to be from the very get-go!' said Peggy.

'Poor lass certainly hit the ground runnin'.' Isla chuckled. 'It just goes to show how much the three of us have been through when we can take stuff like that in our stride.'

'Like water off a duck's back,' said Peggy as the train pulled out of the station. 'Bein' in Coxhill made the three of you closer than sisters!'

'We're certainly a force to be reckoned with,' agreed Isla. 'Sophie was awfully disappointed that she wasn't part of the action when Dennis showed his ugly mug, or there as backup when I came face to face with Tammy, but in all honesty, just havin' her and Meg's support this past year or so has been enough to pull me through the darkest times.'

'A girl needs good friends to get by in life, which is why it's so important we see Sophie.'

'Aye; give her some reassurance,' said Isla. 'Show her things from both sides, as it were.'

'How'd you mean, "from both sides"?'

'Well, Sophie's worried Blackbeard might run for the hills should he hear all that's been goin' on, but you could easily say the same might apply vice versa. For all we know there might be a very good reason for him bein' single,' said Isla darkly, before Peggy stopped her with a wag of her finger.

'You shouldn't jump to conclusions. If we start judgin' books by their covers, where does that leave us?'

'I suppose you're right. It's wrong to judge.'

'I did hold out hope that she and Harvey might get together,' said Peggy sadly. 'I think they'd make a wonderful couple.'

'So did I,' sighed Isla, 'but it seems Sophie prefers pirates!'

Peggy laughed out loud. 'Is that how you think of my Clive?'

'No!' cried Isla hastily. 'Clive's completely different from Blackbeard—'

Peggy raised her brow. 'And how do you know that?'

Isla lowered her gaze. 'All right, so I don't, because I don't know anythin' about him save that he's a sailor with a black beard.'

Peggy glanced to the approaching platform as the train slowed down to a crawl. 'I hope this one's us. I really need the lavvy, and I hate usin' the one on the train.'

Isla smiled. Trust Peggy to tell it as it was. 'You certainly need a good sense of balance,' she chuckled, just as a guard walked past their compartment, announcing that they had arrived at Scarborough.

Peggy rolled her eyes to indicate her sense of relief. 'Thank goodness for that!' She peered out of the window at the people waiting on the platform. 'Can you see—'

'Sophie!' cried Isla, and pointed out their friend, who had just caught sight of them and was now waving frantically back.

'Ah, and she's standin' next to the lavvies,' said Peggy approvingly. 'Two birds with one stone!' Taking their belongings down from the rack above Isla's seat, they joined the queue of people who were all ready waiting to leave the train. 'I knew I should've gone at the last station,' Peggy hissed. 'It's always the same! I can hold on right up until I see the sign for the Ladies, an' then it's like tryin' to hold back Niagara Falls!'

Grateful that the other people in the queue were as eager to disembark as themselves, Peggy and Isla didn't have to wait too long before they were hurrying towards Sophie, who looked delighted to see them.

Being the first to take her in a one-armed hug, Peggy gabbled, 'Lovely to see you, Soph, but I'm dyin' for the loo!' Laughing, Sophie pointed out the facilities, but Peggy was way ahead of her. 'Shan't be a mo!'

'She doesn't like usin' the ones on the train,' Isla explained as she enveloped Sophie in a warm hug, 'and I can't say I blame her.' Holding on to Sophie's hands as she slid from her arms, she eyed her friend apologetically. 'I know things have been a bit hectic of late, but even so I should've made more of an effort to come over a lot sooner!' She brought Sophie back in for another hug. 'Gosh, how I've missed you!'

Sophie pulled a guilty grimace. 'And I you! As for not meetin' up more often, well, it takes two to tango, so the blame's not all on your side! I feel simply dreadful that I wasn't with you when Tammy turned up on the scene and at a time when you needed your pals the most, too! I cannae imagine what a horrible surprise that must have come as.'

'Put it this way: if I thought the whole Dennis ordeal was bad, it was nothin' compared to comin' face to face with Tammy!'

Sophie smiled back. 'I think it's safe to say that handlin' folk like Dennis is as easy as pie for the likes of us, but meetin' the former love of your beau?' Sophie shook her head. 'Not pleasant under normal circumstances, but certainly not when you believed her to be dead! Which brings me to another point. I cannae apologise enough for not listenin' to you when you voiced your fear that Tammy might still be alive . . .'

Isla held up a hand to quell her friend's words. 'Don't give it another thought. I had poor Rory thinkin' he was goin' bonkers when he'd actually seen not just Dennis, but Archie too.'

Sophie chuckled softly. 'What are we like, eh?'

'I believe more than ever now that everythin' happens for a reason,' said Isla. 'All those sightin's in a city full of strangers? There's no way that was down to coincidence; I reckon we were bein' given the heads up!'

Sophie eyed her friend with admiration. 'You've always been a strong lass, but you've matured into the most level-headed young lady I've ever had the pleasure to meet. Just when do you suppose that happened, exactly?'

Isla laughed. 'When I came face to face with my beau's ex-girlfriend's would-be murderer!'

Sophie shook her head, with a smile. 'We don't do things by halves, us lot, do we?'

Peggy came out of the Ladies looking a lot calmer than she had a few minutes ago. 'I take it you're talkin' about recent events?' she said as she joined them.

'Aye,' said Sophie, 'we are that. To say that trouble seems to follow some folk around is certainly true for us!' She glanced in the direction of the concourse. 'C'mon, I'll show you to your B&B.'

Following Sophie out into the crisp blue autumn afternoon, Isla decided to grab the bull by its horns. 'I don't suppose there's any chance of us meetin' Blackbeard whilst we're in Scarborough?'

'Sorry, but no,' said Sophie. 'His ship left a few days ago.'

Isla sighed. 'Typical! We were dyin' for a bit of a nose, weren't we, Peg?'

Sophie laughed. 'I thought you might be, somehow.' She pointed to a tearoom that stood across the road. 'Tell you what, how about we grab a cuppa before we go on to the B&B?'

'Good idea,' said Isla. 'I've a mouth like the Sahara.'

Crossing the somewhat busy road, the three women entered the café and were quickly seated by the waitress, who went off to fetch their order.

Eager to cut to the chase, Sophie started the ball rolling. 'I can understand why you're keen to see Donny, but I think there's somethin' you should know.'

Isla's face dropped. Whilst she very much wanted her friend to be free to date a man who had more enthusiasm for her than Blackbeard, she did not want to see her unhappy. 'Oh . . .'

Sophie leaned back so that the waitress could place the tea things down on the table, along with three toasted teacakes. 'As you know, I've been spendin' every spare minute visitin' him at the hospital, but when he said he intended to join the first ship lookin' for crew I took it as a sign that he didn't want anythin' more than friendship. Not that I hoped he'd give up his life at sea for me, you understand, but . . .' she sighed, 'there was just somethin' definite about the way he said it. Something his shipmate confirmed when he came to see him in hospital whilst I was there.'

'Oh?'

Sophie recalled the moment the sailor with flaming red hair whom Donny had referred to as Patrick, had walked onto the ward to tell Donny that he'd found places for them both on a new ship.

'It was the same feller who spoke to Donny when we first got chattin' down the docks,' she said, 'and a right miserable so'n'so he is. Looks like he hasn't cracked a smile in years.' Realising she had digressed, she resumed her tale. 'Anyhow, as soon as he told Donny that he'd found a place for them on a ship wanting new crew, I saw Donny's eyes light up, and that was enough for me to know that he and I would never become a couple. So I wished him well and walked away.'

'Oh, Soph, I am sorry,' said Isla sincerely. 'Sophie, however, was waving a dismissive hand.

'Don't be!'

'But I thought . . .'

'He came to see me at the base on the mornin' he was due to set sail,' said Sophie. 'I cannae tell you how surprised I was to see him wavin' to me from the gate. I went over to see what he wanted and he asked if he could take me out on a date when the ship came back to port.' She sighed happily. 'I was that surprised you could've knocked me down with a feather!'

Peggy lowered her teacup. 'I take it you said yes?'

'Of course I said yes!'

'Did he give you a clue as to why it took him so long to ask you out?'

'Just that he'd explain everythin' properly when his ship docks back in Scarborough in a couple of weeks' time.'

'Well, I for one couldn't be happier for you, Sophie love,' said Peggy, and Isla echoed her sentiment.

'Me too. It's the best news ever, and even if he took his time about it at least he got there in the end. I must say, I'm intrigued to know what took him so long, though.'

'I've been givin' that some thought, and I'd bet a pound to a penny that he's divorced,' said Peggy.

'What would make you think that?' Sophie asked curiously.

'Unfortunately, a lot of sailors find themselves divorced after a couple of years of marriage because their wives couldn't cope with bein' home alone all the time.' Peggy fixed her eyes on Sophie. 'As I've said before, being a sailor's wife is a lonely business, and it most definitely isn't for everyone. I think a lot of women go into marriage believing their newly betrothed will miss them to the point where they give up their life at sea, but what they fail to understand is that the sea is *part* of some men: it's not just what they do, it's who they are. Quite frankly, askin' them to give up the sea is as good as askin' me or you to stop breathin'. It's in their blood!'

Isla nudged Sophie's hand across the table. 'Are you sure you're cut out for a life where you hardly see each other?'

Sophie nodded with certainty. 'Love conquers all, right?'

'I hope it does in your case, because I think Peggy's probably hit the nail on the head and I'll tell you why. When we first left Coxhill, you said that you weren't interested in men because you didn't think any of them would be interested in a woman who had reached the age of twenty-nine without ever been kissed. Well, it's probably the same for Blackbeard. Not only does he not want to tell you that he's divorced because his wife couldn't stand him bein' away at sea more than he was home, but because he probably thinks there's no point in startin' another relationship knowin' what happened the first time round.'

'So you think that we're as bad as each other when it comes to worrying what potential partners might think?' said Sophie. 'I guess that would make sense.'

'Only he's already fallen for you because he got to know you better after you ran him over.'

Seeing the surprised look on the face of another diner, who'd obviously been earwigging, Sophie rolled her eyes. 'Please don't say that out loud again. It sounds terrible if you don't know the circumstances.'

Isla giggled. 'Sorry, Soph. Tell you what, though.'

'What?'

'It just goes to prove that a good old natter with friends can sort out just about anythin'!'

Isla and Peggy had nearly come to the end of their four-night stay in Scarborough, and Sophie was taking them to the spot where Madson had chosen to dive out in front of her car.

'We've often talked of your mammy lookin' out for you ever since she passed,' Sophie reminded Isla as they walked along the pavement, 'but I have to wonder whether my mammy's been doin' the same for me. Only it seems a tad coincidental that Donny just happened to be the one who knocked Madson out of the way, don't you think?'

'It does a bit,' Isla agreed. 'I mean, what are the chances of him bein' in exactly the right place on the very day that Madson decided to execute his plan?'

'They do say that stranger things happen at sea,' said Peggy, 'but I agree, Soph, that for Black— sorry, I mean Donny to've been the one next to Madson as they waited to cross the road?' She shook her head. 'Too much of a coincidence for my liking!'

They reached the spot where the incident had taken place and waited at the lights to cross the road. 'If Donny hadn't stood up for me the polis might not have been so quick to believe my side of the story,' said Sophie. 'I'm jolly lucky he'd been watchin' Madson as well as the traffic.'

'Did he ever say what it was about Madson that caught his interest in particular?' Isla asked as they crossed.

'Only that there was something about him that struck him as odd,' said Sophie, with a shrug. She indicated the tearoom they'd visited before. 'Fancy a cup of tea and a slice of cake?'

'Yes, please!' said Peggy, rubbing her hands together enthusiastically. 'I cannot begin to tell you how wonderful it's been to have other people cook for me these past few days; a real luxury that I shall miss when I'm back home.'

'We definitely need to do this more often,' agreed Isla as she opened the door to the café, 'cos everyone deserves a bit of a treat now and then, although if I'm honest I reckon I have more treats now than I ever did before the war.'

'That's because you appreciate them more than you used to, and so you're makin' the most of every minute,' said Sophie. 'When you've experienced the blitz you realise how quickly it can all be taken away from you.'

Unbuttoning her coat, Peggy headed for a table next to the window. 'How d'you both fancy a scone with jam and cream?' she asked as she swung her coat over the back of one of the chairs. 'My treat!'

'That sounds wonderful,' said Isla, 'but we cannae ask you to pay.'

'You didn't!' Peggy pointed out. 'I offered, and in fact I think I rather insist! But for the two of you I'd be sitting back home in Liverpool, and I can't tell you how good it's been to have a change of scenery – a real tonic for the soul.'

'I agree with you there, Peggy,' Sophie told her.

'Bein' a driver means I'm always gettin' to see new places as well as different faces, and I'd far rather that than be stuck on the base.'

'I sometimes wish I'd been chosen as a driver instead of a balloon operator,' Isla confessed, adding hurriedly, 'Don't get me wrong, I love my job and I get immense satisfaction from knowin' we've forced the buggers to fly higher, but it's bloomin' hard work and I won't be able to put any of it into practice when the war's over, so I'll be stuck with being a seamstress – unless I run a smallholdin' with Rory, of course.'

'A smallholdin' sounds wonderful!' Sophie sighed. 'I haven't a clue what I'll do once peace is declared. I know you think drivin' is a skill I'll always be able to use, but can you really see them lettin' me drive a bus or a taxi?'

'Unfortunately not,' said Peggy. 'Another case of double standards!'

Isla gazed thoughtfully at her friend. 'So what do you think you'll do?'

Sophie shrugged. 'If they keep the WRNS goin' – which I'm rather hopin' they will – I'll probably see if I can stay on.'

Isla's heart dropped at hearing Sophie's unexpected desire. 'But wouldn't you prefer to live free from an institution if only for a little while? You were in Coxhill for years, then the WRNS, and whilst the livin' conditions are a lot better in the WRNS than Coxhill, it's still sleepin' in dorms and marchin' to the beat of someone else's drum.'

'I can see what you mean, but isn't that the case with every job you do?' She looked at Peggy. 'You have to do what they tell you in the tobacco factory just as much as I do in the WRNS, the only difference bein' you get to go home at the end of your work day whereas I live where I work.'

Peggy nodded. 'You're right, it really is no different, although if anythin' I have less security than you, because I have to pay rent and utilities whereas your keep is all in, as it were.'

'I've always assumed that we'd each head off to pastures new once the war was over,' said Isla, 'and until now it hadn't occurred to me for a moment to think otherwise, but now you've spoken your piece it makes me wonder what Meg will do.'

'I think a lot of that will depend on what Kenny does,' said Peggy. 'I'll be surprised if they aren't married before the war's out, and if that's the case then Meg's decision will very much depend on what Kenny decides to do.'

'*I'm* surprised they're not married already,' said Sophie.

'Me too,' agreed Isla. 'By the way, do any of us know what Kenny did before the war?'

Sophie looked blank. 'I haven't the foggiest.'

'He was a baker,' said Peggy matter-of-factly. Seeing the look of surprise on the others' faces, she added, 'It came up in conversation one day.' She motioned to the waitress that they were ready to order, but when the woman arrived at their table it became clear that she was more interested in looking out of the window than in noting their requests. 'Has it all died down out there now?' she asked.

'Has what died down?' said Sophie.

'The hullabaloo down the docks earlier,' said the waitress, her frown now matching Sophie's own. 'Surely you must have heard about the *Apollo*? I thought everyone knew.'

Sophie's eyes widened. 'Do you mean the ship that set sail from here a few days ago?'

'It sank,' said the waitress matter-of-factly. 'The survivors are making their way back to the docks in lifeboats, but as you can imagine, they can't let just anyone come to shore, so they had to call the police and goodness knows who else to verify that they were tellin' the truth and that they're not a bunch of German spies chancin' their arm.'

Scraping back her chair, Sophie collected her coat. Tears pricking her eyes, her bottom lip trembled as she fought to contain her emotions. 'That was Donny's ship. I need to make sure he's all right,' she told Peggy and Isla, who were already on their feet.

'Of course you do, and we'll come with you,' said Isla.

'*Apollo* is quite a common name when it comes to ships, so it might well not be his, but even if it is, then depending on how much warning they had prior to the ship sinking, they might all have survived,' said Peggy as they hurried down to the docks. 'And that's even if she got her facts right, cos I'm sure we'd have heard somethin' by now. After all, a ship going down is pretty big news; surely it would've been in the papers?'

'I reckon Peggy's right; we'd definitely have heard somethin' before now,' said Isla.

Sophie began to slow her pace. 'Only why on earth would she say somethin' like that if it wasn't true? It's not the sort of thing you make up, or misunderstand!'

'Chinese whispers?' Peggy suggested. 'All kinds of information gets misconstrued once it's been through the rumour mill.'

Sophie still remained doubtful. 'But where would she have got the idea that the ship had sunk?'

'Perhaps they lost some cargo and she heard the word sank and put two and two together only to come up with five?'

Sophie wrinkled her brow. 'Only why would they be turning up on lifeboats if that were the case?'

'Maybe some of them had to get off in order to make the ship lighter?' suggested Isla, although even she had to admit that this seemed unlikely.

As they neared the docks, Sophie pointed to a policeman. 'Let's ask him!'

Peggy nodded. 'Good idea,' she said, and they all hurried over to where the man was noting down the names of arriving survivors. Sophie was the first to speak. 'We've just been told about the *Apollo* sinkin'. Is it true?'

The policeman nodded ruefully. 'Did you know someone on board?'

With Sophie too choked up to answer him, Isla stepped in. 'Aye, a friend of hers.'

The policeman pointed towards the dock where the girls could see lifeboats being taken from the water. 'You're best askin' the fellers down there. They seem to know what's what.' He smiled briefly but kindly. 'Good luck.'

Hastening towards the group of men the policeman had pointed out, Sophie's hand slipped from Isla's as she squeezed her way in between the bystanders who were being regaled with the tale of how the ship came to be at the bottom of the ocean.

Interrupting the red-headed seaman who had come to visit Donny in hospital that time, Sophie asked the question at the forefront of her mind. 'Patrick! I'm lookin' for Donny . . .' She stopped speaking as she realised she hadn't a clue as to Donny's surname. She was turning to say as much to Isla and Peggy when Pat got to his feet.

'It's Sophie, isn't it?' She nodded, and he jerked his head in a forward motion. 'He was around here somewhere – I'll help you look.' But even as he spoke they both heard Donny's voice, as he hastened over. 'Sophie?'

'Donny!' Rushing forward, she remembered in time that they hadn't so much as gone out on a date as yet. Smiling from ear to ear nevertheless, she stopped in her tracks. 'I cannae tell you how relieved I am to see you! When I heard your ship had sunk, I thought . . .' She shook her head. 'I'm just glad you're all right.'

Donny smiled back, the whiteness of his teeth brilliant against the darkness of his beard. 'You don't get rid of me that easily . . .' His voice trailed off as he stared into the crowd.

Following his gaze, Sophie spoke apprehensively. 'Donny?'

Donny's gaze was fixed on just one person, and it wasn't Sophie. *'Isla?'*

Chapter Fifteen

Isla, who had been deep in conversation with Peggy, slowly turned her head. 'Dad?'

Weaving his way between the men who separated them, Donny looked as though he'd seen a ghost. 'I – I don't understand.'

Isla stared open-mouthed as her father came within feet of her. 'What don't you understand?' she said blankly. 'I realise you never expected to see me again, but—'

Donny hid his face in his hands. 'They told me you were dead.'

'Who?' she demanded urgently, her voice barely above a whisper. 'Who told you that?'

His hands balled into fists; he cursed softly beneath his breath. 'That bloody Harman woman, that's who!'

Isla swallowed. 'When was this, exactly?'

He held his head in his hands as he tried to remember. 'A couple of months after I . . . ' His voice trailed off as if he couldn't bear to say the words.

'Left me there,' Isla said for him.

He nodded ruefully. 'I knew I'd done the wrong

thing as soon as we set sail, but I was powerless to do anythin' about it. As soon as we came back to port I went straight to Coxhill, but when I got there Harman insisted you didn't want to see me. I demanded you tell me that for yourself, but she was adamant that you didn't want to know and that as far as you were concerned I'd burned my bridges the day I set sail. Of course I wasn't goin' to let that put me off, so I went back—'

'You came more than once?' Isla asked, as if she couldn't believe what he was saying.

He nodded fervently. 'I went back every time we docked in Clydebank.'

Still uncertain as to whether he was speaking the truth, she spoke her thoughts. 'So what made you give up?'

His features darkened. 'She said you'd been the victim of a dreadful accident whilst working in the laundry.'

She stared at Sophie before looking back at him. 'What sort of accident?'

'She said you'd slipped and banged your head on one of the drums.'

Sophie held a hand to her mouth. 'That's exactly what she said about Kayleigh!'

The tears trickled down his face as he spoke. 'It didn't occur to me for a minute that she might be lyin'. I mean, why would she? You'd think she'd be ashamed that somethin' like that had happened under her watch.' He shook his head. 'I reported her to the polis but they didn't want to know – they said that accidents happened all the time in places like that. I was beside myself with grief because I knew it was all my fault.'

Unable to bear hearing her father blame himself a moment longer, Isla rushed forward into his open arms. 'If only I'd known . . .' Speechless, she wept as she buried her face in the crook of his neck.

Donny's bottom lip trembled as he held his daughter tight. 'But why on earth did she lie? Surely she'd have been glad to see the back of me, as well as havin' one less mouth to feed?'

'I know why,' said Isla grimly. 'For starters, you might've asked for your donation back. Also, with one less mouth to feed she'd have one less inmate to claim for off the government. In other words, she'd have been down on money.'

'Down on money?' echoed her father. 'She's not runnin' some sort of business.'

'Only she was,' said Isla softly. 'That was the whole point.'

His tears seeping into the collar of his jacket, Donny continued to apologise. 'I should never have left you in the first place! It was a cowardly thing to have done and I'm thoroughly ashamed of myself for not havin' been the father you deserved.'

'Don't say that!' Isla wept. 'You did what you thought was right at the time.'

Donny was looking grim as he gazed down at her. 'That may be so, but it's still no excuse for my givin' you up. As for that Harman woman, I'll make sure she rues the day she ever lied to me.'

To his surprise, Isla brightened slightly. 'Believe you me, she already does. Cos had she let me go with you it's likely she'd not be doin' time right now.'

He raised a confused brow. 'Sorry?'

Isla went on to tell him how she had exposed Harman resulting in her incarceration along with the help of Meg and Sophie.

Donny's eyes were alight with admiration. 'I don't think I've ever been prouder of you than I am right now!'

Isla was about to reply when her eyes fell on Sophie for the first time, and the penny dropped. Stepping back, she looked from one to the other before her gaze finally settled on her father. 'Why did you tell Sophie that your name was Donny?'

He grimaced. 'After everythin' that had happened I wanted to leave Patrick Donahue far behind, and a good way of doin' that was to introduce myself to folk as Donny – short for Donahue. It didn't work, mind, because you cannae escape your past no matter how hard you try.' He turned to Sophie as his brain caught up with what Isla had told him. 'Isla said that you helped her to escape from Coxhill?'

'I did, aye,' admitted Sophie, before adding guiltily, 'Remember the feller that ran you over?'

'I could hardly forget. What of him?'

'He was in cahoots with Harman,' Sophie explained, 'and even though we didn't manage to put him behind bars he did lose his job, for which he blames me because I was the one who clocked him with the coal shovel.'

'So . . . you've known Isla all this time?' he asked incredulously.

'Aye. Ironic, when you think about it. Talk about so near and yet so far!'

Donny was eyeing her curiously. 'Forgive me, but I sort of assumed you were around the same age as myself. I'm forty-three.'

She smiled faintly. 'I'm thirty-two. Age is just a number when you're in a place like Coxhill. I know that Isla often forgets that I'm older than her.'

'You're my friend,' said Isla. 'Same as Peggy.'

Smiling, Peggy wagged a reproving finger. 'There's no need for you to be mentionin' my age, just so you know.'

'Aye, but our friendship proves that age really is just a number.' Isla looked to her father with affection. 'I cannae believe it's been three years since we lost Mammy.'

She saw his jaw quiver. 'There's not a day goes past when I don't think about her, but the pain is less than it was.' He glanced meaningfully at Sophie. 'Sophie helped to ease that pain. She even managed to make me smile.'

Isla nodded slowly. 'We all deserve to be happy, and if that's what Sophie makes you, then that's fine with me.'

He took his hand in hers. 'Most people would've crumbled if their father had left them at the poorhouse, but not you. You've come out stronger and wiser than ever you were, and your mammy would be proud.'

Isla smiled, but was too choked with emotion to reply.

'I see that you're in the WAAF?'

She glanced down at her neat uniform. 'Balloon operator.'

'You're your mother's daughter, all right,' said Donny. 'A woman to be admired!'

Aware that time was slipping away from them, Peggy spoke up. 'I don't know what your plans are, Donny, but this is mine and Isla's last night before we head back to Liverpool, so . . .' She left the sentence for him to finish.

'I won't be settin' foot on another ship for at least the next couple of days,' he told them.

Peggy nodded. 'Sophie and I will go for lunch, seein' as it's nigh on twelve o'clock.'

'Good idea!' said Sophie. 'That way the two of you can have some time alone together. How about we all meet up for dinner tonight at the Three Mariners?'

Isla nodded. 'That's fine with me. Thanks, both of you.'

Sophie wrinkled her brow. 'What for?'

'For bein' my pals!'

Many hours had passed by the time Isla had finished filling her father in on all that had transpired since he had left her at Coxhill. Racked with guilt, Donny had remained silent through most of the conversation, only interrupting to apologise repeatedly for his part in her journey.

Now, as Donny eyed his daughter with approval,

he asked the question that had been running through his mind the entire time she'd been talking. 'How the hell have you managed to come through all that with such a level head? Most people would've gone to pieces – myself included – if they'd had to face just half of what you have.'

'With the help of good friends, and ...' She hesitated.

'And what?'

She shook her head. 'You're goin' to think I'm bein' daft.'

He held his hands up in mock surrender. 'I would never think that of you.'

'They say that everythin' happens for a reason, and I agree, but even so, my whole life seems to have been one big coincidence after another since we parted ways, which makes me think that there's a stronger force at play here – and what's more, Sophie agrees. In fact she was the one who put the idea in my head.' She drew a deep breath. 'We think Mammy's been guidin' me.'

Rather than dismiss the notion, as she expected him to do, Donny was nodding slowly. 'I can see why you've come to that conclusion, and I have to say I'm rather inclined to agree with you, especially when you consider recent events.'

She was nodding. 'If you're referrin' to Dennis, then—'

But he was cutting across her. 'Not just Dennis. I'm talkin' about my ship sinkin'.'

Isla gasped. 'Mammy wouldn't sink your ship!'

'Normally I'd agree with you, but had we not sunk I wouldn't be here with you now – on top of which not one person lost their life when the *Apollo* went down, which is pretty rare to say the least. In fact, I even heard one of the fellers say something about lady luck bein' on our side!'

She eyed him levelly. 'If all that we're sayin' is true, and Mammy really has been orchestratin' our lives, then we have to believe that she also arranged matters so that you and Sophie came together.'

He shrugged. 'I did think it a pretty big coincidence that I just happened to be standing beside Madson at the exact time he decided to execute his plan.'

'It was. We even said how lucky it was for Sophie that you were watching Madson at the time. So with all that bein' said, I'm guessin' you don't think me silly?'

'Not in the slightest. She always was a shrewd one, your mammy.' He hesitated. 'How do you feel about my friendship with Sophie? I should imagine it might feel a tad . . .'

'Awkward? Dad, if I were to choose any woman for you it would be Sophie. She's a lovely, true-hearted woman who will never let you down. She's been there for me through thick and thin, and you'd be mad to let a woman like that slip through your fingers.'

He smiled. 'There's always the possibility that *she* might change her mind about *me*.'

Isla rolled her eyes. 'Why on earth would she do that? You're honest, loyal and fun to be with and whilst the idea of the two of you together might take a bit of gettin' used to, I'd rather that than see either of you on your own.' She paused. 'Out of curiosity, what made you decide to ask her out? Cos from what Sophie said, it wasn't lookin' likely when you were in hospital.'

'I knew that I couldn't expect a woman like Sophie to wait forever, and what's more it wasn't fair of me to ask her to. Women like Sophie are as rare as hen's teeth, and as you quite rightly said, I'd be mad to let her go.'

Isla opened her mouth to speak, but instead let out a small, practically inaudible gasp.

'What?'

'Sophie was the only one of us who got chosen for the Wrens! When we went to sign on the dotted line we all hoped we'd end up in the WAAF, but the queue was huge and Sophie got called to a different desk, which is why she was sent to the WRNS and we landed in the WAAF. We thought it bad luck at the time, but what if it was meant to be? After all, had Sophie not been in the Wrens she wouldn't have been posted to Plymouth, where she first saw you, and then Scarborough.' She stopped speaking as another thought struck her. 'Come to think, how did you end up in Scarborough? Bit of a long shot, don't you think, considerin' all the ports you could've been sent to?'

His lips parted slowly. 'My pal got us both a job on a bigger ship with better pay. It just so happened to be berthed in Scarborough.'

Isla assumed an air of smug satisfaction. 'I rest my case!'

He held his hands up in mock surrender. 'You'll hear no argument from me.' He glanced at her uniform. 'Peggy said you had to go back to Liverpool tomorrow, is that right?'

She pulled a rueful face. 'I'm afraid so.'

'Well, from now on I shall do my utmost to find a vessel that berths in Liverpool from time to time.'

'Oh, Dad, that would be wonderful! Do you really think you could?'

'I can but try,' said Donny. 'It shouldn't be too hard, what with Liverpool bein' such an important port – and it's not exactly the first time I'll have been berthed there.'

She stared at him. 'You've been to Liverpool before?'

He nodded. 'A fair few times.'

'In which case, there really is no doubt about it. Mammy didn't just want to bring you and me back together, but Sophie too.'

He glanced at the clock which hung behind the counter. 'Talkin' of Sophie, we did say we'd meet them for dinner.'

Isla swigged down the last mouthful of her tea and got to her feet. 'I didn't realise that we'd been in here so long.'

'We had a lot to talk about,' said Donny. 'What's more, I daresay we'll be chewin' the cud for most of the evenin' now, never mind the weeks and months to come.'

She linked her arm with his as they left the café. 'I cannae wait for you to meet Rory and Meg.'

'And I cannae wait to meet them – especially Rory.'

She grinned. 'Lookin' out for your little girl, eh?'

He patted her hand. 'A bit late for that, don't you think? Besides, you've managed just fine without my help. In fact, I'd go as far as to say you've done a grand job on your own!'

She rested her head against his shoulder. 'Maybe so, but I'll *always* need my daddy!'

Isla, Donny, Sophie and Peggy were on the platform discussing the previous evening as they waited for the train to arrive.

'I think I speak for us all when I say it's been a real whirlwind of a visit!' said Peggy. 'And whilst I shall miss bein' spoilt, it'll be good to get back to my own bed!'

'I cannae say I'm lookin' forward to bein' back in my bunk bed,' Isla said wryly. 'Although it will be nice to see Rory – he's not goin' to believe his ears when I tell him all that's gone on.'

'Someone will have to tell Meg, too,' said Sophie thoughtfully, 'although it might be wise to make sure she's sittin' down first!'

Isla began to laugh. 'Aye, especially as Meg thought that Dad might be battin' for the other side!'

Donny's eyes nearly fell out of his skull. 'She *what*? How on earth did she jump to that conclusion?'

Still chuckling, Isla explained. 'We were tryin' to

work out why you didn't appear to be interested in startin' a relationship with Sophie.'

Sophie choked. 'And that was Meg's answer? Although I suppose I shouldn't be surprised, because she's never been afraid to voice her thoughts.' She eyed Isla quizzically. 'I am curious as to why you didn't tell me sooner, though.'

'I didn't want to put ideas into your head,' said Isla. 'It was either that or he didn't fancy you – neither option was good.'

Donny winked at Sophie as he smiled. 'I can assure you that your friend Meg was wrong on both counts.'

Sophie's cheeks warmed. 'I'm glad to hear it!'

'I still can't believe we've found you, Donny,' said Peggy.

'I must admit, I had to pinch myself when I woke up this mornin',' he confessed. 'And I hate to be waving Isla off when we've only just been reunited, so as soon as her train leaves I'll be trawlin' the docks to see what work I can pick up. It might take a while, though, what with the whole crew lookin' for a berth.'

'I don't mind how long it takes as long as I don't lose you again!' Isla told him.

'That will never happen, trust me.'

'I do,' said Isla, adding. 'Completely.'

'When you come to Liverpool I shall cook my infamous Woolton pie by way of celebration,' said Peggy. 'It's my Clive's favourite!'

'One of mine too,' said Donny. 'That and scouse.'

'Peggy makes the best scouse in the whole of Liverpool,' said Sophie loyally.

Blushing, Peggy waved her hand airily. 'I don't know about the whole of Liverpool . . .'

'We do,' Isla told her, 'and yours is the best, bar none!'

Donny groaned as a train approached the station. 'I reckon this one must be yours,' he said glumly.

Isla felt her stomach fill with butterflies as the person on the tannoy announced their train's arrival. 'I'm afraid so,' she said. 'I cannae believe we're sayin' goodbye when we've really only just said hello!'

'Life certainly can be unfair at times, but just remember who's lookin' after you,' Donny told his daughter with a half-smile. 'Your mammy won't let the two of us be parted for any longer than absolutely necessary – not now she's managed to bring us back together again.'

'I hope you're right,' said Isla wistfully, 'cos I know that Rory's goin' to be mad keen to meet you. It was his idea that we put word out down the docks.'

'He sounds like a good feller,' said Donny, 'and he must be one heck of a man to have stolen my daughter's heart.'

She smiled. 'You know me. Only the best will do!' They watched as the arriving passengers filed from the train onto the platform. 'I wish you didn't have to go to sea. It's so dangerous out there. Why don't you get your old job back down the docks?'

Donny pulled a doubtful face. 'I think I'm safer on a merchant vessel than I am down the docks.'

Picturing the damage the Luftwaffe had inflicted on the Liverpool docks, Isla conceded. 'All right, but what about after the war? What then? Please don't tell me you're goin' to be married to the sea!'

His eyes rounded with alarm. 'No chance! As soon as the war's over I'll be straight back down the docks as a supervisor. Bein' at sea takes you away from the ones you love, and I've had enough of that lately.'

Peggy smiled as both Isla and Sophie gave visible sighs of relief. 'You've just made two young ladies very happy,' she observed, as the guard who had been pacing the platform stopped to call out: 'All aboard who's goin' aboard!'

Wrapping her arms around her father's waist, Isla did her best to prevent the tears from forming, but saying goodbye to him so soon was proving too much. 'Please look after yourself. You're too precious for me to lose.'

Nodding, he kissed her on the cheek, saying in the stilted tones of someone who's struggling to control their emotions, 'Don't you worry. I don't plan on losin' my not-so-little girl ever again!'

Taking Sophie in a warm embrace, Isla kissed her on the cheek. 'Look after him for me? I know he comes across as a roughty-toughty, but he's really just a big softy at heart.'

Crying for the pain her friend was going through, Sophie nodded through her tears. 'Of course I will! And Isla?'

'Yes?'

'Thanks for not makin' this awkward.'

Isla smiled affectionately as she pulled back from

their embrace. 'Only for you! I couldn't have done it for anyone else.'

'It means a lot to me to have your stamp of approval.'

Peggy tapped Isla on the shoulder. 'Sorry, Isla, but we really do have to get a move on.'

Nodding, Isla gave both Sophie and her father one last hug before picking up her bag and joining Peggy, who was already boarding the train. When the guard had closed the door to their carriage Isla pushed the window down and leaned out.

'Look out for each other – and make sure you keep me in the loop!'

Sophie was crying into her handkerchief as she leaned her head against Donny's shoulder. 'Will do! And first bit of leave I get I'll be straight to Liverpool!'

'You must all come to mine for a proper catchup,' Peggy called out behind Isla. 'I've plenty of room!'

The guard blew his whistle, and Isla and Sophie broke into fresh bouts of tears. 'I'll call Sophie's base to let you know that we got home safely,' Isla sobbed, adding as the train lurched into action, 'I love you . . .'

'To the moon and back,' Donny said, his voice choked by unspent tears.

Unable to say another word, Isla buried her face in the crook of Peggy's neck. She hadn't heard the age-old family cry since the day her father left her at the poorhouse, and to hear it now, although heartwarming, was more than she could bear. Allowing Peggy to guide her to a window seat, she sank down gratefully. 'I thought I'd cried all the tears I could ever cry,' she sniffed, as she blew her nose.

'You've been through more in the last few months than most of us face in a lifetime,' Peggy soothed her, 'and you've done your best to dam your emotions throughout that entire time for the sake of others. But you can't hold back the flood for ever.'

'I know. And whilst finding Dad was one of the happiest moments in my life, I want more than that – which I know is selfish – but—'

'Poppycock!' cried Peggy. 'It's not selfish, it's natural! Who wouldn't want to spend more time with their loved ones after bein' parted for so long? And when I think what the two of you have been through . . .'

Isla smiled weakly. 'Thanks, Peggy. I didn't want to come across as a selfish brat.'

'You're bein' too hard on yourself, as per usual,' said Peggy. 'It's goin' to take you and your father months to iron over the past; probably longer, considerin' your busy schedules.' She coddled Isla's hand in hers. 'But trust me, the time will come when you'll be together again. You just have to be patient.'

'Words of wisdom, as ever,' said Isla. 'I hope someone does that Hitler in so that we can get back to normal – whatever that may be!'

Chapter Sixteen

DECEMBER 1943

It had been four months since Isla had last seen her father, and she was currently in Peggy's kitchen with Rory, who had brought Tammy's latest epistle for them to read.

Dear Rory,

I hope this letter finds both you and Isla well. It's been a while since I wrote last, and a lot has happened in that time. I'm not sure whether you've already heard, but we received the news a couple of weeks ago that my father had let his temper get the better of him once again (no surprises there!) and thrown one punch too many, killing the man he'd been arguing with. I suppose we all suspected that this day would come, but quite frankly I thought it would be either me or Mammy who died at his hand. I expected the officer who broke the news to say that the argument was over money or cigarettes, so to hear that it was over a cup of tea absolutely floored me. I mean, who on earth gets so angry over something so trivial? According to the officer, the man he attacked was just as bad as my father for throwing his weight around, and they had long suspected that the two would butt heads at some stage or other. The guards did their best to keep them separated, but as you'd expect, my father found a way to get to the other man, and the rest, as they say, is history!

Anyhow, as I'm sure you've already guessed, there's only one outcome for someone who commits murder. Mammy cried when she first heard the news, I think more out of relief than anything else. After all, my father's had the luck of the devil when it comes to getting off the hook, and we were both worried he would be out of jail and seeking revenge before the year was out! So whilst I wouldn't actually have wished death on him, it is quite a relief to know that we won't have to spend the rest of our lives looking over our shoulders!

Having listened in silence as Isla read the most important part of the letter, Peggy made her thoughts known as she poured the tea into cups. 'May God forgive me for sayin' so, but I'd say that's the perfect ending for a horrible man. People like Dennis never learn from their mistakes, because they think they're in the right, and nothing would have convinced him otherwise. In my opinion it was only a matter of time before he actually murdered someone, and we should all be grateful that it wasn't Tammy or her mother.'

'The thought of two men dyin' over a cup of tea is sheer lunacy,' said Rory. 'Which just about sums Dennis up!'

'I know the whole business has been weighing

heavily on Meg's mind, because she played her part in sendin' him down, and she was afraid that he might seek revenge when he got out. It will come as quite a relief to her to hear that he's no longer a threat.' Peggy glanced at the clock on the mantel. 'Talkin' of Meg, what time does her train get in?'

Isla pushed the letter back into the envelope without looking at the clock which she'd been checking at regular intervals. 'About half an hour, so more than enough time to finish our cuppa.'

'And how about Sophie and your father?' Rory asked, leaning forward in his seat to take the cup of tea Peggy was holding out to him.

Isla laid a hand to her tummy, which was dancing with butterflies. 'Any time now. Sophie said she hoped to leave before ten, because—' She was interrupted as someone knocked a brief tattoo against the front door and pushed it wide open.

'Coo-ee,' called Sophie as she entered the house.

Her eyes dancing, Isla's chair scraped back across the kitchen floor as she called for them to: 'Come through – we're in the kitchen!'

They all heard the front door close, and Sophie and Donny appeared in the kitchen a few seconds later.

Enveloping Isla in his arms, Donny squeezed her tight. 'How's my one and only daughter?'

Isla beamed. 'Happy!'

'Good!' Releasing Isla from his grip, he pulled a chair out for Sophie, who was stifling a yawn beneath her hand. 'Sit yourself down, Sophie luv. It's been one hell of a journey.'

'Hasn't it just,' yawned Sophie from behind her hand. 'Sorry, folks, but I'm absolutely shattered!'

'Not surprising,' fussed Peggy. 'It's a fair old trek from Scarborough to Liverpool.'

Stifling another yawn, Sophie sank her head into her hands. 'I could murder a cuppa if there's one goin'?'

'Isn't there always?' soothed Peggy as she set about making two more cups of tea.

Rory stepped towards Donny, his hand held out. 'Pleasure to meet you, sir.'

Donny took his hand. 'Please, call me Donny, and it's good to meet you too, Rory. I wish it could've been sooner, but better late than never, as they say.'

'Here you go,' said Peggy, passing Sophie and Donny their cups of tea. 'Get on the outside of that!'

Thanking her, Sophie took a sip, whilst eyeing up the pie that was sitting on the sideboard. 'Is that a Woolton pie I spy?'

Peggy was positively beaming. 'It is indeed – I always said that I would do you a Woolton pie when you came to Liverpool, but this one isn't just for you lot, but my Clive as well!' She clapped her hands together excitedly. 'He's comin' home for Christmas! It'll be the first one we've spent together since the war broke out, which is why I'm beside myself with excitement!'

Sophie immediately looked round at the others. 'That's wonderful news, Peggy, but are you sure you want us here? Only—'

Peggy waved a dismissive hand. 'Of course I want

you here! You're part of the family now, I thought you knew that?'

'Well, yes,' said Sophie slowly, 'but you've not seen Clive in an age.'

Peggy smiled. 'It wouldn't be Christmas without a house full of love and laughter, and much as I love him, one Clive does not a party make!'

Isla pulled a rueful smile. 'It's a shame your boys couldn't be here.'

'God willin', I shall be seein' them in the New Year. So no long faces, please!'

'Message received and understood,' said Isla, pulling off a mock salute. 'Although I have to say I think that the services should let all members of the forces have at least one Christmas with their families.'

'Wouldn't be fair on those serving overseas though,' Rory pointed out.

'Talkin' of people bein' overseas, have you told Theo about your father?' Sophie asked as she warmed her hands on the teacup.

'I did indeed, and he was cock-a-hoop.'

'Did he mention his belle at all?' asked Peggy, who was surprised to find that she was absent-mindedly crossing her fingers in her apron pocket.

Isla cleared her throat. 'You mean his fiancée?'

Peggy nearly dropped the pie on her way to the pantry. 'No!'

Isla smiled. 'Yes, and even though I was a wee bit disappointed with him at first, he managed to convince me that he was doin' it for the right reasons this time.'

Sophie arched an eyebrow. 'Being?'

Isla coughed again. 'He thought it best to take her down the aisle before the baby arrived.'

Peggy emitted a shriek of laughter. 'Oh, my good God! That boy certainly doesn't do things by halves!'

Sophie was blushing to the roots of her hair. 'I must admit I didn't think Theo was that type of man.'

'Red-blooded, you mean?' chuckled Peggy, adding, 'I dare say the heat of the African sun will've come into play somewhere along the line.'

Isla was smiling at Peggy. 'Not in those words exactly, but he did say that the African lifestyle is far more relaxed than the British, and that things we might think shocking are more accepted out there.'

Rory laughed. 'It certainly sounds that way. What have his parents had to say on the matter?'

'That they're proud of him for doin' the right thing,' said Isla, 'though Theo was quick to assure them that he was marryin' his belle because he loved her. He said he wouldn't have found himself in such a position otherwise.'

'You know him better than us, Isla,' said Peggy. 'What do you think?'

Isla shrugged. 'I think I believe him – cos for one, you can practically hear him smiling when you read his letters.'

Peggy relaxed. 'In which case, I'm pleased for him. Question is, who'll be next?'

'To start a family?' squeaked Sophie.

'No!' Peggy filled the kettle with fresh water. 'To get married!'

Giggling, Isla was the first to reply. 'My money's on Kenny and Meg.'

'I'm surprised they're not wed already,' Peggy told her.

'Me too.'

'I wonder why they aren't?' said Sophie.

'Well, it's not for want of tryin' on Kenny's part. I think he'd have married Meg a long time ago given his way.'

'So Meg must be the one who's holdin' back.' Peggy pointed to the clock. 'Talkin' of Meg, hadn't you best get a wriggle on if you're to get to the station before she does?'

'We had that,' said Rory.

Getting to her feet, Isla looked to Sophie and Donny. 'I would ask if you fancied joinin' us, but I think poor old Sophie could do with a rest.'

Sophie smiled gratefully. 'You'd not be able to stop me normally, but I didn't just drive straight from Scarborough to Liverpool. I had to stop off just before Nottingham en route.'

Peggy wrinkled her brow. 'Nottingham? But that's not on the way! And how come you drove instead of catchin' the train like everyone else? Surely it would've been easier?'

Sophie nodded sleepily. 'It would, but I get an extra day's leave this way, plus none of the other girls wanted to drive all this way just to deliver a bunch of papers.'

'I'm surprised the Navy allowed you to carry a passenger,' Peggy commented.

Sophie pulled a guilty grimace. 'Strictly speakin' they didn't, which is why I picked Donny up a mile out of Scarborough. And then I was so nervous that someone might see us that I didn't stop again until just short of RAF Winthorpe.'

Isla blew out her cheeks. 'You took one heck of a risk, Soph! I know Theo and his pals took me in the back of the wagon that time, but at least I wasn't in plain sight!'

Donny quirked his brows. 'Neither was I when we came to towns or villages.'

Rory laughed. 'That's one heck of a long way to sit bent double.'

'Put it this way; I was extremely grateful to reach Liverpool,' said Donny. 'It was kind of excitin', though – a bit like bein' a young lad again.'

Sophie's eyes widened. 'I'm glad you enjoyed yourself! I, on the other hand, was a nervous wreck!' she said tartly.

Isla laughed, and headed over to the row of hooks that housed everyone's coats, hats and handbags. 'Much as I hate to rush off, I don't want to be late for Meg, and I don't like the idea of her arriving in Liverpool without a welcoming committee.'

'I always meet my Clive off his ship whenever he comes into dock,' said Peggy. 'It's not a proper welcome home otherwise!'

Isla slid her arms into the jacket Rory was holding out for her. 'Does anyone want anythin' whilst we're out?'

Peggy surveyed the table in front of her. 'No, thanks, I think I've got everythin' covered.'

Bidding them goodbye, Isla and Rory headed out into the bitter cold. 'Flippin' 'eck!' said Rory, his teeth chattering. He lifted his collar against the icy wind. 'It's brass monkeys out here!'

Isla hastily pulled up the cuffs of her mittens so that not a millimetre of skin was on display. 'Peggy's kitchen was so warm, I'd forgotten how cold it was outside,' she said. 'Still, a nice brisk walk will soon warm us up.'

'Never a truer word said,' agreed Rory. 'Those measly tortoise stoves they use to heat the huts are all but useless – in fact if it weren't for mornin' exercise I don't think we'd ever get warm!'

Isla's breath clouded the air as she laughed. 'Don't let them hear you say that, or they'll take the stoves away in favour of non-stop exercise!'

'Don't you worry, I'm savvier than that,' said Rory. 'The last time someone moaned about the lack of heat in our hut, they were told the cold would put hairs on our chests.'

Isla couldn't help but giggle. 'How on earth would ice put hairs on your chest?'

'I'm assumin' they think your body will sprout hairs in order to keep warm!' He gave her a playful nudge. 'You'd best wrap up. The last thing you want is a hairy chest!'

Isla's cheeks flushed. 'God forbid!'

'I suppose that's the only up side of bein' in Africa,' said Rory. 'Theo will never be cold!'

'I think he's got more to worry about than the weather,' said Isla, a half-smile creasing her cheek. 'The pitter-patter of tiny feet just bein' the start of his worries!'

'I wonder what his superiors said when he told them he was gettin' married?'

'I shouldn't have thought they'd be best pleased,' said Isla, 'and I very much doubt they know about the baby yet. When they do I reckon they'll go ballistic!'

'I'd wager you're right. What did you think when he first told you about the baby?'

She grimaced. 'I'll not deny that I was disappointed at first, because I thought he'd not learned anything from his past, but on the other hand, can they really take a young impressionable boy like that to somewhere like Africa and expect him not to dally in things he shouldn't? Cos when it comes down to it, we've all heard the rumours, so it's not like they don't know what goes on.'

He eyed her curiously. 'You weren't annoyed with him at all?'

'I was more annoyed with the RAF than I was with Theo. But at the end of the day there's no point in cryin' over spilt milk, and anyway, does any of it really matter as long as he's genuinely happy?' She shrugged. 'Not as far as I'm concerned. I admit I was down on wartime marriages for the longest time, but lookin' back I think I was more against marriages made in haste than marriage per se.'

Rory was looking at her hopefully. 'Does that mean you've changed your mind about marryin' durin' wartime?'

'I still don't agree with people gettin' married when they hardly know each other, because that's just askin' for trouble. Even if they make it to the end of the war, there's no guarantee they'll get along once they've had time to get to know each other properly. And God forbid they bring children into the mix!'

'I thought you were worried about them becomin' widows, like what happened to Theo?' said Rory as he held out a hand to catch one of the flakes of snow which had just started to fall.

'That too,' said Isla. 'But logically speakin' that could happen to any of us at any time, war or not!'

Rory nodded, but said nothing. He'd wanted to ask Isla to marry him for the longest time, but had held fire because of her thoughts on wartime marriage. If she was having a change of heart, it might be time to have a chat with Donny. On the other hand, what would be the point of asking her father's permission to marry her if Isla then turned him down? After all, he didn't just have her worry over being widowed by the Luftwaffe to contend with but also her fear of being let down by the men in her life. Had that changed at all since she learned that her father had in fact returned to Coxhill for her? And whilst Theo had kept quiet about his marriage he hadn't hidden his feelings for her, but would that make any difference to the way she felt now? Having said that, if she did turn him down, it wouldn't be because she didn't love him, but purely because it was the wrong time. So with that being the case when would be the right time? He'd just have to do as Jimmy advised and rely on his gut instincts.

Trotting up the steps of the station, Isla spoke to Rory over her shoulder. 'I've not been to greet Meg from off a train since all that business with Dennis.'

Jogging to keep up with her, Rory slipped his hand into hers. 'Is that why you wanted to come and meet Meg, because you were worried about what happened the last time you did?'

'I hadn't thought of it like that before now, but yes, I think I am, cos even though I know it was different with Dennis, I cannae get the image of a burly man followin' a defenceless woman from out of my mind.'

'Do you think Meg feels the same way?'

'I've no idea. She's not mentioned it if she does.' She stopped speaking as they arrived on the platform. 'I wish Kenny could've made it, but the RAF bloomin' well refused point blank to give him leave. I'm grateful Meg agreed to come because I know she'll miss spendin' Christmas with him, but I don't know the next time we'll all be back under the same roof.'

As the words left her lips a train pulled into the station, and she began to wave excitedly to Meg who was beaming at them through a carriage window.

'I've not seen her since we found my daddy,' Isla told Rory as they walked along the platform to meet her, quickening their pace as Meg exited the carriage, kitbag in hand, and hurried towards them.

'Have I got news for you!' she trilled.

'Don't tell me you got married without us bein' there?' Isla cried.

Meg tutted playfully. 'As if! I wouldn't dream of gettin' married without my besties by my side!'

'Then what?'

Meg opened her mouth to speak, then shut it again. Nibbling the inside of her bottom lip, she finally said, 'Perhaps I should wait until we're all together?'

Isla was shaking her head. 'For a start you look like you're about to burst, and secondly, you cannae possibly expect me to wait now that I know somethin's afoot.'

Meg pulled a rueful face, although she was still smiling. 'I shouldn't have said anythin'.'

'But you did, so it's too late,' said Isla, who was longing to hear her friend's news, and at last, unable to contain her excitement any longer, Meg gave an excited squeal and waggled her ring finger at Isla. Grabbing hold of her friend's hand to take a closer look, Isla squealed with excitement in her turn. 'Oh, Meg!'

'Congratulations,' said Rory, as he admired the small circle of silver on Meg's finger.

'Congratulations indeed!' cried Isla. 'But when did this happen, and why didn't you tell us sooner?'

'You know what Kenny's like; he's always bangin' on about marriage.' Meg stopped short as her friends' laughter drowned out her words.

'I thought that was meant to be the woman's role?' chortled Rory.

'Aye,' Isla agreed, 'most men run a mile at the mere mention of the word.'

Meg pulled a sidelong grimace. 'I'm afraid it was a bit vice-versa for me and Kenny – not because I didn't want to marry him, but . . .' she heaved a sigh, 'none of us know what's around the corner, do we? And I like to know where I'm headed.'

'You mean after the war?' said Isla.

'Aye. When Sophie said she might stay on in the Wrens, it led me to ask Kenny what his thoughts were.'

'Had you not talked about it before?' Rory asked.

'Aye, but not seriously,' said Meg. 'It was different this time.'

'And?' asked Isla, who was eager to get to the part where Kenny had popped the question.

'Kenny wants to open up his own bakery. It's somethin' he did before the war and he's good at it. I cannae bake for toffee, but we started talkin' about other things I could do and I began to fall in love with the idea.'

Unable to bear the suspense any longer, Isla posed the question again. 'So when did he propose?'

'This morning, on the platform whilst we were waitin' for the train.' Meg blushed. 'He did it in front of everyone! I swear for a minute I thought I was goin' to die from embarrassment.'

Rory blew out his cheeks. 'He was takin' a bit of a risk, wasn't he? What if you'd said no in front of all those people?'

'I asked him that,' said Meg, to the others' amusement.

'And what did he say?'

'He said he just knew the time was right,' said Meg.

Rory nodded to himself. There was something in this whole 'waiting until the time was right' business. He just hoped he'd know when his time came.

It was the day before Christmas Eve and the house was a flurry of activity as everyone got ready for Clive's arrival.

'None of us have ever met Clive,' Isla explained to Rory as she set about scrubbing the kitchen floor, 'so we're super keen to make a good impression.'

Sophie, who was washing the windows, concurred. 'We want him to know that Peggy made the right decision when she decided to take three strangers under her wing.'

'I'm sure he already knows that,' said Rory. 'After all, wasn't it Peggy who said both Clive and her sons had been pleased to hear that she had company?'

'Aye, but . . .' Isla sighed as she wiped her forehead with the back of her hand. 'The thing is, Peggy means so much to us that we're as keen to not let her down as we are to impress Clive.'

Donny wagged a reproving finger. 'Believe me, none of you could *ever* do that. I've chatted a lot to Peggy, and she practically clucks when she mentions any of your names. It seems to me that you *all* benefited from her neighbour Irene – Harvey's sister, I think she said? – joinin' up.'

'Peggy's a dear,' said Meg as she peeled the potatoes to go with the Woolton pie, which was already in the oven.

Donny stood back from the tree which they had picked up from the market the day before. Resting his chin on his hand, he tilted his head to one side. 'Does that look straight to you?'

Sophie walked over to give her opinion. 'I think it'd look better if you turned it so . . .' she was turning the tree so that the fuller branches were visible as she spoke. 'Ta-dah!'

He gave her a small round of applause. 'And that's why women are better at these things than men! They've got a good eye for detail.'

'Or, to put it another way, we care about what things look like,' Isla called out over her shoulder as she poured the dirty water down the drain by the back door. Coming back into the room, she picked up the box of decorations Peggy had given them before heading off to meet Clive. 'We have Christmas trees in the NAAFI, but it's not the same as decoratin' your own.'

Taking a couple of the glass baubles from Isla, Sophie began hanging them on the branches of the tree. 'I cannae believe we were all lucky enough to get Christmas off together!'

'Me neither,' said Meg, who was chopping the potatoes into chips. 'I should've known Kenny wouldn't manage to wangle the time off, though – that would've been expectin' too much!'

'Talkin' of Kenny, when do you suppose the two of you will get hitched?' Isla asked as she handed Sophie yet more baubles.

'Not until I can have all of you at my wedding,' said Meg firmly, 'and goodness only knows when that will be!'

'What a pity he couldn't have made it for Christmas. You could've tied the knot whilst you were here.'

Meg stopped chopping for a moment as the truth of Isla's words sank in. 'We could've, couldn't we? I never even thought of that – I'd wager Kenny didn't either, cos he knows how I feel about havin' us all together. Not that there's anythin' we could've done about it; you know what the RAF are like when it comes to leave.'

'No means no,' chorused, Rory, Isla and Sophie.

'Exactly!'

'Well, I for one believe the circumstances will present themselves when the time is right, so don't worry. There'll be other times when we're all together,' said Sophie.

'When you say the circumstances will present themselves, what do you mean by that exactly?' Rory asked, hoping to widen the conversation so that Isla might voice an opinion which would give him a clue as to her feelings on the matter.

Sophie tweaked the star she had just put on top of the tree into a more favourable position. 'I suppose that depends on what your requirements are. For example, some women will only marry in church, whilst others dream of the perfect dress.'

Isla tutted audibly. 'If the dress is more important than the weddin' itself, then the marriage is doomed before you've signed the register.'

'And are you only sayin' that because of the war?' mused Meg. 'After all, I should imagine most women would have chosen to marry in a church before the war broke out.'

'A sign of the times,' Sophie observed as she glanced into the decoration box. 'I'll hang the paper chains if someone holds the stool steady for me.'

Isla picked up one end of the chain as Sophie climbed onto the stool Meg was holding. 'I suppose you're right, but to me it's more than that. Gettin' married in a registry office without the dress shows that you're marryin' for love, and not the look of the fairytale ending. Do you see what I mean?'

'I do,' conceded Sophie, taking the end of the chain and a pin from her friend. 'But a lot of hasty marriages take place in a registry office, which makes it a marriage of convenience.'

'It's what's in your heart,' said Rory absently. 'Only you know whether you're marrying for the right reasons or not. Quite frankly, I don't think it matters where you tie the knot as long as you're in love.'

'Rory has it in a nutshell,' said Isla warmly. 'Marriage should be a sign of your love and commitment for each other, nothin' more, nothin' less.'

'And you shouldn't refrain from showin' your love just because you're scared of what the future holds,' continued Rory, 'because none of us can predict the future. Not wanting to sound morbid, but you could wait until after the war to marry, only to get run over by a bus as you leave the church.'

Meg shuddered as his words washed over her.

'Could you imagine how dreadful that would be? Waitin' until the perfect moment, wearin' the dress of your dreams, only to have the groom buy it on the way out?'

Isla choked on a chuckle. 'Why would it be the groom who bought it on the way out and not the bride?'

'And ruin her perfect dress?' said Meg, her brows rising, 'I should cocoa.'

Laughing softly at Meg's words, Rory was the first to voice his thoughts. 'It just goes to prove that there's no time like the present.'

'Amen to that!' agreed Isla, before crying out in alarm as Rory fell to the floor in front of her. 'Are you all right? What happened?'

Rory was smiling up at her. 'I came to my senses, that's what happened. I've been worrying about findin' the perfect time to ask you to marry me for absolutely ages. But I've just realised it's not the proposal that matters, but the reason behind it. I love you, Isla Donahue, and I have since the moment we first met. And I *know* you feel the same way about me! You're my soulmate, Isla, as I am yours. The last piece in each other's jigsaw. We make each other complete. So why hold back when we already know that we're goin' to spend the rest of our lives together?' He switched his attention to Donny.

'I meant to do this properly, to ask you first for your permission to marry your daughter, but my gut took over. Quite frankly, sir, wild horses couldn't stop me from marryin' the woman I love, so I hope I have your blessing.'

Hiding his smile beneath his hand, Donny lifted his thumb in the air.

Turning his gaze back to Isla, Rory smiled up at her. 'So what do you say Isla Donahue? Will you make me the happiest man on the planet by agreeing to be my wife?'

Tears slowly rolling down her cheeks, Isla nodded. 'Yes!'

Whooping with joy, Rory scooped his fiancée up in his arms as he rose from his knees. 'You do realise I mean to marry you before we go back to work?'

Isla gaped at him. 'You mean . . .'

He smiled round at the rest of them. 'Whilst all your friends and loved ones are here? I couldn't think of a better time, could you?'

'No,' she said, adding uncertainly, 'Can we do that?'

He shrugged. 'If they've got a vacant slot we could marry there and then.'

'Then what are we waitin' for?' cried Isla.

Meg was gaping at them. 'Shouldn't we at least wait for Peggy and Clive?'

Isla laughed. 'It's the day before Christmas Eve, Meg. There's no way they'd fit us in until after Christmas Day.'

'Which is why we should make haste,' said Rory, 'else all the slots during our leave will be taken.'

He had taken Isla's coat down from its peg, and was holding it up for her to put on when they heard the sound of the front door closing.

'Goin' somewhere?' said Peggy, entering the kitchen with Clive close behind.

'To see if we can book a date in the registry office,' said Rory. He held his hand out to Clive. 'Hello, Clive. I'm Rory.'

Squealing her congratulations, Peggy rushed over to hug Isla, whilst the others introduced themselves to Clive.

Shaking each of their hands in turn, Clive stood back, a broad smile on his face. 'Peggy said there was never a dull moment with you lot around, and I see you're already provin' her right!'

'When did all this happen?' Peggy asked as she pulled the scarf from her neck. 'I've not been gone more than an hour!'

'A few moments ago,' said Rory. 'We're off to the registry office now to see if we can book a slot before we go back to work.'

Peggy pulled a rueful grimace. 'I don't wish to dampen the mood, but you'll be ever so lucky if you do. I've a pal who works down Brougham Terrace and she reckons they're choc-a-bloc.'

Isla groaned, but said hopefully, 'Maybe someone will cancel?'

Peggy patted her shoulder in an optimistic spirit. 'Fingers crossed.'

Having donned his own jacket, Rory held out his hand, gesturing for Isla to go ahead. 'Let's get this weddin' on the go!'

Tutting her disappointment as the registrar shook her head, Isla asked the woman if she wouldn't mind double-checking.

'I can, but there's really no point,' said the woman, who was obviously sympathetic. 'We've a list as long as your arm for cancellations, so even if there were . . .'

Isla nodded miserably. 'I know. Thanks anyway.'

Rory put his arm round Isla's shoulders. 'If there were any other way I'd grab it like a shot, cos God only knows when we'll all be together again.'

The woman took the end of her pen from between her lips. 'You could always try a church.'

Isla looked at her in amazement. 'Do you think they would? Only I thought it would be easier to marry in the registry office than a church.'

She shrugged. 'I don't see why not, provided they're not in the same position as ourselves of course.'

Thanking the woman for her help, they hurried out of the building. 'We'll try the church by Peggy's,' said Rory, holding up a hand to hail a taxi and ushering Isla forward as one drew up next to them. 'Arkles Lane, please,' Rory instructed the taxi driver as he took his place next to Isla on the back seat.

'We haven't even got a ring,' said Isla, who was beginning to have her doubts.

'I'll buy one,' said Rory.

The journey, which would've taken them half an hour by foot, only took a few minutes by car, and it wasn't long before they were tumbling out of the taxi. Thrusting the fare into the cabby's hand, Rory told him to keep the change and closed the door quickly. Then, straightening his jacket, he held his arm out to

Isla. 'Best foot forward, and don't forget to cross your fingers!'

With the decorations complete, Sophie looked anxiously at the clock above the mantel. 'Where *are* they?' she asked the room in general for what felt like the hundredth time. 'They should've been back ages ago.'

'You don't think they got married without us, do you?' said Meg, who was equally worried.

'I sincerely hope not!' said Donny firmly. 'Part of a daddy's role is to walk his daughter down the aisle!'

Peggy, who was beginning to think that Meg might be right, spoke her thoughts. 'On the other hand, if a cancellation *had* come up, they might not have had a choice.'

Sophie was shaking her head decidedly. 'The whole point of them gettin' married sooner rather than later is because we're all here. There's no way Isla would do it without her besties by her side.' She stopped speaking as the front door opened, and Isla and Rory bundled into the kitchen, both wearing broad beams.

His eyes flashing to his daughter's ring finger, which was hidden beneath her mitten, Donny spoke hesitantly. 'You're not married already, are you?'

Pulling her left hand from her mitten Isla held up her hand and wriggled her ring-free finger at them. 'No. And if it were down to the registrar we wouldn't be getting married any time soon either.'

Peggy was eyeing them suspiciously. 'So why do the two of you look so pleased with yourselves?'

'Because we're gettin' married at the All Saints church,' Rory told them.

Donny sighed with relief. 'Thank goodness for that!' He looked lovingly at Isla. 'I've missed out on enough of your life as it is, without missin' out on your weddin' as well!'

'We'd *never* have got married without all of you by our sides,' said Isla.

'That's what I said,' Sophie remarked as she looked up from the sprig of holly she was preparing to hang above the fireplace. 'So when's the big day?'

Isla and Rory exchanged glances. 'We weren't exactly spoiled for choice when it came to dates,' Rory explained. 'Everyone's so busy, and . . .'

Peggy was grinning. 'You're gettin' married on Christmas Day, aren't you?'

'If we could have done it any other day we would, cos we really didn't want to mess up your first Christmas with Clive in a long time,' Isla said apologetically, but Peggy was waving a dismissive hand.

'Nonsense! I couldn't think of a better day to get wed! In fact it makes perfect sense. I've already made a Christmas cake, which can serve as your weddin' cake, and we've got a grand meal planned, so you needn't splash out on a venue to hold your weddin' breakfast.'

Isla took Peggy in an affectionate embrace. 'Thanks, Peggy. You really are the tops, I hope you know that!'

'It's my pleasure,' said Peggy, beaming.

'All you need now is a dress,' said Sophie, but Isla shook her head.

'My uniform's just fine.'

Peggy, however, was wagging her finger. 'Not on my watch! I've a perfectly good weddin' dress hangin' in my wardrobe, and quite frankly I'd be offended if you refused to wear it. It may not be the latest fashion, but I'm sure we can fix it to your likin'. With no daughters of my own, nothin' would give me greater pleasure than to see you walk down the aisle in it, so I won't be takin' no for an answer.' Standing back, she ran a critical eye over Isla's frame. 'I dare say it'll need takin' in here and there, but nothin' we can't sort!'

Isla blew out her cheeks. 'I feel like I'm Cinderella, and you're my fairy godmother, Peggy.'

Peggy waved an imaginary wand. 'Your wish is my command ... or was that the genie out of *Aladdin*?'

Laughing, Isla looked to Rory. 'All we need now is the ring.'

Rory pulled his sleeve back to look at his watch. 'I reckon we've time for a spot of lunch first.'

'And you don't have to worry about a ring,' said Donny. Stepping forward, he held his hand out, palm up, revealing a small gold circlet.

Isla stared at the ring, which she knew had been her mother's. 'Are you sure?'

Donny nodded. 'She'd have wanted you to have it, and so do I, and it makes better sense for you to wear it than for me to keep carryin' it round in my breast pocket as I've done these past three years.'

'But you'll have nothin' to remember her by.'

He chucked her under the chin. 'How can you possibly think that when I've got you standing in front of me? Same eyes, same hair, same gumption.'

Isla looked at Sophie. 'Gumption? That's what Sophie said when we first met.'

Sophie nodded slowly. 'Cos it was true, an' it still is.'

'She gets that from her mam,' said Donny.

Isla gently took the ring from his hand and tried it on for size. Holding it up to show the others, she wriggled her ring finger. 'It fits!'

'So that's the ring, the weddin' breakfast, the dress and the church sorted,' said Sophie. 'What else?'

'Flowers!' said Meg. 'Although I dare say we can find you a nice bouquet easily enough.'

'Old, new, borrowed, blue,' said Peggy. 'The dress is both old and borrowed, so we just need somethin' new and blue.'

Gasping, Isla pulled the locket out from under her shirt collar. 'Mammy's forget-me-not locket!'

Peggy held her thumb up. 'That's the blue bit sorted.'

'Could the flowers count as new?' Meg wondered.

But Rory suddenly clicked his fingers. 'Don't worry, I've got the new covered with my Christmas present to Isla.'

'Then that's everythin'!' said Peggy. 'Now, if you girls have got everythin' in hand, and it looks very much as though you have, I shall get the dress down and we can make a start. After all, we've got less than forty-eight hours to turn Cinders into Cinderella!'

Chapter Seventeen

It was the morning of Christmas Eve and Isla was reflecting on the events of the previous day whilst she lay in bed waiting for everyone else to wake up. True to her word, Peggy had spent the remainder of the day working tirelessly on her wedding dress in an effort to get it to fit, and with the final alterations complete Isla had admired her image in the mirror of Peggy's wardrobe.

'It's simply stunning,' she had sighed as she twisted round to look at the fine lace detail running down the back. 'You have excellent taste, Peggy.'

Peggy had smiled proudly. 'I'm glad you think so, but are you sure you don't want anything changing? I really don't mind . . .'

Isla shook her head. 'It's perfect just the way it is.'

Meg was staring down at Isla's feet. 'What about shoes?'

'Peggy's wedding shoes are too small for me; we've already tried them on for size,' Isla told her sadly, 'but Clive's gone to ask his sister whether she's got anything suitable.'

Rory had called up from the bottom of the stairs to announce his return. 'I had a word with the florist and she's going to bring your bouquet round first thing in the morning!'

Isla had called down her thanks as she stepped out of the dress. 'I know you keep reassurin' me that you don't mind, but I cannae help but feel guilty,' she confessed to her friends. 'I've completely taken over everybody's Christmas, and that truly wasn't my intention.'

'Stuff and nonsense!' cried Peggy. 'If anything you've made Christmas all the more special.'

'Peggy's right. Christmas is about family,' Sophie agreed, 'and that's what we are, one big happy family. And since this is the first Christmas we've been together since leavin' Coxhill, your gettin' married just makes it all the more special!'

Now, as she lay in her bed, Isla turned her head to see Meg's feet poking out from under the sheets. Mischievously running her finger along the arch of Meg's sole, she smiled as Meg jerked the foot out of Isla's reach before letting it relax back down. Pinching her nose to stop her giggles she repeated the action, only this time Meg hissed 'Oi!'

'Sorry!' Isla chuckled. 'I couldn't resist!'

Leaning up on her elbow, Meg wagged her finger from the bottom of the bed in which they were top and tailing. 'It's like sharin' a bed with a monkey!' Meg said humorously.

Isla – who had also sat up – grinned. 'I know, but I'm too excited to go back to sleep!'

'But you're not gettin' married until tomorrow,' groaned Meg. 'Have we got a whole day of this?'

Isla nodded her head fervently whilst giving an apologetic grin. 'I'm afraid so!'

Woken by the girls' chatter, Sophie pulled her bedcovers back, before padding over the bare floorboards to join her friends. 'Morning, ladies! Or should I say, happy early Christmas?'

'Ooo!' gasped Meg. 'I'd forgotten we'd agreed to celebrate Christmas a day early. Does that mean we're doin' pressies now, or—'

Isla didn't need asking twice. Grinning like the cat that got the cream, she scooped her gift out from under her bed whilst talking in excited tones. 'It feels naughty swappin' presents before the actual day itself, don't you think?'

'Who cares!' said Meg, causing her friends to laugh. Slipping out of her side of the bed, she rummaged around for the package she had hidden the previous evening, whilst continuing to speak. 'Besides, it's better to do it today when we've plenty of time rather than rush tomorrow!'

'Which is why we agreed to do it today in the first place,' Sophie pointed out as she headed back to her bed to retrieve her own present, only to be stopped in her tracks by someone knocking on the door of their bedroom.

'Coo-ee,' Peggy called from the other side of the door. 'Are you decent?'

'We are indeed,' Isla called back. 'Come in, Peggy.'

Peggy entered the room with a jug of water in her hands. 'Merry early Christmas, girls! I thought I'd bring you up a nice jug of warm water for your wash.'

'We were just about to exchange pressies,' Isla told the older woman.

Holding up a finger to indicate that she wouldn't be long, Peggy hurried off to fetch her own gifts before swiftly returning.

Even though this was their first Christmas together since leaving Clydebank, the girls had made sure they exchanged Christmas gifts every year. With money scarce they had followed the tradition of a sixpenny Christmas, where each of them would buy a gift costing no more than sixpence for one of the others, meaning that everybody received one gift. Now, as they positioned themselves in a circle, they each handed their gift to their allocated person.

'Everton mints!' said Isla as she opened Peggy's gift. 'Thanks, Peggy!'

Sophie pulled back the tissue from Isla's gift, revealing a bar of scented soap. 'Lavender,' she said as she lifted the bar of soap to her nose. 'My favourite!'

Meg was next, and she was equally pleased with her gift of a compact mirror from Sophie. 'I'll try not to break this one,' she said, 'the last thing I need is seven years bad luck!'

With Peggy being last, they watched in anticipation as she opened a large box of chocolates. Seeing the look of astonishment on Peggy's face, Isla hastily explained the extravagant gift.

'Please don't be cross with us,' she said. 'I know we

all agreed to do a sixpenny Christmas again this year, but you've been an absolute rock since we arrived on your doorstep and we wanted to show you how much we appreciate everything you've done for us. Seein' as we know how much you love chocolate, we thought this as good a way as any.'

Peggy's cheeks bloomed as she eyed each of them in turn. 'Thanks, girls, but I don't think I deserve more than any of you.'

Isla, however, begged to differ. 'You've looked out for us ever since we arrived in Liverpool. Quite frankly, no one would have blamed you if you'd turned us away, but you decided to take a punt, and we'll always be grateful that you did. But for you our lives could've and I think most likely would've turned out very differently. Every time the goin's got tough you've been there to help us through it, never judgin' and always kind, and you've always given the best advice – none more so than when you agreed to come to Scarborough with me! Honestly, Peggy, you're a saint!'

'It works both ways,' said Peggy, her cheeks growing ever warmer. 'I was dreadfully lonely after my boys went off to war, but you girls were like a ray of sunshine on an otherwise cloudy day, and I'll always be grateful that you knocked on my door.' She looked directly at Isla. 'And I've offered more than one prayer up to thank your mammy for the part she played, cos I've no doubt it was her guidance that brought us together.'

Isla was about to reply when a voice called up from the foot of the stairs. 'Anyone for porridge?' Wiping the tears from her cheeks, she gave Peggy a watery smile. 'Not a doubt in my mind either.' Fastening the belt of her dressing gown, she hurried into the hallway to see Rory smiling up at her from the bottom of the stairs. She gave him a small wave. 'Merry early Christmas!'

Grinning, he waved back. 'Merry early Christmas to you too! Now, who's for porridge?'

Isla looked back at the display of hands. 'All of us, please,' replied Isla before adding in surprised tones, 'Don't tell me you're the one makin' it?'

He shrugged in a confident manner. 'You seem to forget I lived on my own for years. Making porridge is just one of my many culinary skills.'

'Mind you don't burn my best pan!' cried Peggy as she hurried over to join Isla. Seeing that Rory was already holding the said pan, she pulled a worried smile. 'I'll be with you in two shakes of a lamb's tail. Don't do anything until I get there!'

Isla and Rory both laughed as Peggy hurried off to get dressed. Twirling the pan as though it were a baton, Rory gave a low whistle. 'Nice dressin' gown!' Realising that she wasn't yet dressed, Isla gave a small shriek before disappearing back into the bedroom.

'I wouldn't worry about him seein' you in your nightie,' chuckled Meg mischievously. 'He'll be seein' a lot more of you than that tomorrow night!'

Blushing to the roots of her hair, Isla chided Meg for making such a comment.

'It's true though,' objected Meg, who couldn't see anything wrong with the remark.

'I know!' said Isla as she headed to the wash stand. 'Which is why I barely slept a wink last night for thinkin' about it.' Seeing Meg wriggle her eyebrows in a suggestive manner, she tutted. 'I don't mean I'm excited about the prospect – just the opposite, in fact. I've been worried sick!'

Sophie grimaced as she hurried over to comfort her friend. 'I cannae say as I blame you. The very thought gives me the collywobbles, and I'm not even gettin' married yet!'

'I don't suppose either of you have a clue as to what to do?' Isla asked them shyly, but with both girls shaking their heads so violently Isla feared they might do themselves a mischief, she held up a hand. 'So that's a resoundin' no, then.'

'Not the foggiest,' confirmed Sophie.

'Me neither,' said Meg. 'But Peggy would know.'

Isla accidentally splashed some of the water over the floor as she turned to Meg with a look of horror. 'I am *not* askin' Peggy! I'd rather . . .' She fell silent as she searched for a suitable comparison, but failing to find one she finished lamely, 'I'd just rather not!'

'Then you're just goin' to have to hope that Rory knows what goes where,' said Meg as she took her turn at the bowl.

Resigned to the fact that Meg was probably right, Isla rubbed her face dry on the towel Peggy had provided. 'This certainly beats havin' a freezin' cold wash in the ablutions,' she said, in a bid to change the subject.

'Do you remember the baths we used to have in the poorhouse?' asked Meg. 'They were ruddy awful until Sophie had the idea of nickin' the water from the washroom.'

'I'll never understand how nobody else twigged,' Isla said happily. 'We were the cleanest ones there, which was a miracle seein' as we were always last in line.'

'It's sad to say that we bathed better in the poorhouse than we do in the services,' said Sophie, 'but that's all that was better about it.'

'Do you ever think about what our life would have been like if we hadn't met Harvey? Even though I'd like to think we'd have been able to do it on our own, it was Harvey who orchestrated our escape really,' Isla said as she changed out of her night things into the frock which Rory had bought for her as a birthday present.

'I thought about it a lot when we first got out,' admitted Sophie, taking over the towel. 'Quite frankly the very thought of us still bein' in that hellhole brings me out in goosebumps to this day.' She held up her arm as visible proof. 'But for Harvey it's more than likely that we'd still be there.' She shook her head in horror at the thought. 'And if that were the case I very much doubt I'd still be alive.'

Meg shuddered visibly. 'I used to wonder what would've happened had we not managed to get the ledgers,' she said as she began to dress. 'Harvey would've made sure we were all right, but the poor buggers that lived there wouldn't have been.'

'Perish the thought,' said Isla, fastening her stockings. 'Nothin' would've changed with Harman still at the helm – in fact it would probably have got worse once she realised we'd escaped.'

'Harman was totally the wrong person to run that place,' said Sophie, slipping into a frock she'd bought on her travels, 'but I cannae help but think the government had a part to play in that.'

'How so?' Isla asked curiously.

'The reason why they had to close Coxhill was because they couldn't find anyone else to run the place, not on the wages the government offered,' Sophie reminded her.

'Fat cats fillin' their pockets,' said Meg sadly. 'And it's people like us that suffer!'

'Well, not any more!' said Isla, adding in an effort to brighten the mood, 'If one good thing comes out of this war it'll be the end of the poorhouses and the like.'

'I do hope so,' said Meg, 'but I'll believe it when I see it.'

'Hitler's taken out half the courts, as well as goodness knows how many other buildings,' said Isla, 'so it only stands to reason that there'll be plenty of work to do to rebuild Britain, which means jobs and lots of them!'

'I hope you're right,' said Sophie. 'I'd hate to think that we'd gone through all this just to end up in a worse state than we were before.'

*

When the girls headed downstairs for breakfast, they found the kitchen a hive of activity.

'Here they are!' said Donny, coming forward to greet them. 'Merry early Christmas, ladies. Toast is under the grill for those who want it, and the porridge is more or less ready.'

Sophie hesitated, a small package in her hand. 'Before we go any further, are we exchanging presents now, or . . .'

Donny rubbed his hands together enthusiastically. 'Now's as good a time as any!'

Isla looked around her. 'Where's Rory? I thought he was makin' the porridge?'

Peggy pulled a guilty grimace. 'He was, and even though I'm sure he would have done a grand job I was worried he might get distracted what with one thing and another and burn the pan, so I sent him off to fetch the Marmite from the pantry.'

Isla headed to the pantry, where she found Rory searching the shelves for the Marmite which was practically under his nose. Picking up the jar, she handed it to him. 'Lookin' for this?'

Smiling, Rory nodded before reaching behind her and closing the pantry door. Enveloping her in his arms, he kissed her softly, murmuring, 'Who's gettin' married in the mornin'?' in between kisses.

Knowing that her father was on the other side of the door, Isla blushed as she replied 'Us', before adding, 'I must say, I rather like startin' the day this way.'

'Start as you mean to go on, that's what I say,' said

Rory. He fished around in his pocket and pulled out a brown paper bag, which he handed to her. 'I hope you like it.'

Peering into the bag, Isla smiled as she brought out a pocket diary. 'Somethin' new! And you don't get much newer than a diary, plus I'll be able to keep a record of our special day!' She took Rory's present from her skirt pocket and pressed it into his hand. 'Men are notoriously hard to buy for, so I hope I've got it right.'

He grinned as he took out a tin of boot polish and a polishing cloth. 'Perfect, because it's useful! You know me so well!'

She sagged with relief. 'I'm so glad, cos even though I know you like practical things I worried I might've gone too far cos I'm not sure I'd be as pleased if someone got me boot polish for Christmas.'

Rory laughed as he took her back in his arms. 'Not to worry – I wouldn't dream of it!'

Donny cleared his throat loudly on the other side of the pantry door. 'Have you found that Marmite, Rory, only there's some of us wantin' toast out here?'

Isla opened the door, her blush still evident on her cheeks. She handed her father the jar. 'We've been exchangin' presents.'

He gave his daughter a wry smile. 'So I see.'

The colour deepening on her cheeks, she followed him back into the kitchen. 'I know you said you'd rather I spent my money on myself, but there's no way on this earth that I wasn't goin' to buy you a present.'

Donny's shoulders sagged as he took the offered bag from her. 'You're a naughty girl, Isla Donahue!' Pulling the blue-and-red-striped neckerchief out, he tried it on. 'How does it look?'

'Very nice!' said Isla.

'Dashing,' Sophie agreed.

He took a small parcel from his pocket and handed it to Isla. 'I know you're goin' to object, but it's to make up for all the Christmases and birthdays that I've missed.'

Taking the package, Isla peeped inside, only to gasp, 'Oh, my word! It's beautiful! Thank you, Daddy.' Eager to see what Isla had been given, everyone shuffled forward as she carefully displayed a fine silver bracelet.

Clive gave a low whistle. 'I shouldn't imagine that was easy to come by, what with the war and all.'

'That's a point,' said Isla, as her father fastened the bracelet around her wrist. 'Where on earth did you get it from?'

'I bought it from a shipmate who'd not long come back from Africa,' Donny told her. 'He'd bought it for his belle, but she'd run off with an airman whilst he was at sea so I persuaded him to sell it to me.'

'What a rotten thing for her to do.'

But Clive was looking sceptical. 'I'm darned lucky to have a wife like Peggy,' he said. 'There's not many women that can put up with their spouses spendin' months on end at sea. She probably got lonely what with him bein' away all the time.'

'It's why I swapped the sea for the docks when I

met your mother,' said Donny, much to Isla's surprise.

'I didn't know you used to be a sailor!'

He was spreading Marmite over a round of toast. 'Now I come to think, we never really talked about it because it used to make your mammy uneasy. She thought talkin' about it might make me want to go back some day.'

'But you were never tempted?' said Isla, adding, 'Or not until . . . well, you know.'

'Not in the least bit,' said Donny. 'The work is hard and the days are long.'

'That's true,' Clive agreed. 'But once it gets into your blood there's no escapin' the call of the ocean.'

'The call of the ocean,' murmured Sophie. 'It sounds so romantic.'

Clive and Donny both laughed. 'Anything sounds romantic in the right context,' said Donny. 'When people talk of the wind in your hair it makes you think of freedom, but not when it's a force ten gale and you're strugglin' to stay on your feet with waves crashin' over the bow threatenin' to drag you down to Davy Jones' locker!'

Sophie grimaced. 'Not as nice as it sounds, then!'

Peggy called them to order. 'If you'd like to take your seats, I'll dish up,' she said firmly, and they each did as she asked while the conversation continued.

'You must get to go to some fascinatin' places, though,' Isla said.

'Aye, the Mediterranean bein' my favourite,' said Clive. He looked to Donny, who agreed.

'I'm not a fan of garlic, though,' Clive went on, 'and they tend to shove that stuff in everything.'

Meg wrinkled her brow. 'What's garlic? I don't think I've ever heard of it.'

'It's a bit like onion in that it makes your breath stink,' he told her bluntly.

Sophie wrinkled the side of her nose. 'That doesn't sound nice.'

'I do quite like the stuff,' Clive admitted, 'but it doesn't smell good on your breath the next day – especially when you're below deck in the confined quarters of a ship.'

'I'd love to go abroad,' said Isla in a dreamy voice. 'Visit foreign lands and experience their culture.'

'Who knows what the end of the war will bring,' said Rory, but Isla waved a dismissive hand.

'It makes a lovely dream, but it will never become reality.'

Rory shrugged. 'Not necessarily. Look at Theo. He could well stay in Africa.'

She looked doubtful. 'I know I've never been, so maybe I shouldn't judge, but I don't think I'd want to live in Africa after some of the things I've heard.'

Peggy laughed. 'I don't think gettin' in the family way out of wedlock is mandatory!'

'I should hope not!' cried Sophie. 'We've a lot of our boys over there!'

'I think our Sophie's worried there'll be a population explosion,' chortled Clive.

Sophie began to object before bursting into laughter. 'I hope I have more faith in our boys than that!'

'So what are we goin' to do with the rest of our day?' said Rory, scraping his bowl clean.

'More to the point, where are you goin' to spend the night?' said Isla. 'Cos it's bad luck to see the bride on the mornin' of the weddin', you know.'

'Do you really believe that?' Peggy asked.

'They wouldn't say it otherwise,' said Isla reasonably.

'Let me put it another way, Do you know *why* they say it's bad luck for the groom to meet the bride before the ceremony?'

Isla shook her head, as did Meg and Sophie, so Peggy decided to fill them in.

'Back in the day of arranged marriages, the bride and groom weren't allowed to meet or even see each other until they were at the altar. So let me ask you again, why do you think it might be considered bad luck for the bride and groom to meet before the ceremony?'

A slow smile split Isla's cheeks. 'Oh, my good God.'

'Exactly!' said Peggy.

'I'd wager many an arranged marriage met its doom because the bride or groom had caught a glimpse of what they were expected to marry!' sniggered Clive, much to his wife's disapproval.

'Looks shouldn't come into it,' she said firmly.

'But we all know they do,' said Clive. 'That's human nature.'

Meg shuddered. 'I cannae think of anythin' worse than an arranged weddin', especially if you weren't even allowed to meet them first. How on earth are you meant to know if you get on or not when you've not so much as been introduced? Hardly makes for a happy ever after!'

'Only in most cases it wasn't about their happiness,' Peggy pointed out. 'Marriages were arranged for the benefit of the couple's families, and more often than not it all boiled down to wealth and status.'

Clive cast his wife a cynical glance. 'And who said romance was dead? If you ask me it's more alive now than it was in the old days. At least we don't have arranged marriages any more.'

'So where does that leave us?' Isla asked, somewhat confused. 'Do we ignore a superstition born out of greed, or do we hedge our bets?'

'Put it this way, I shan't be takin' any chances when I get married,' said Meg fervently. 'Call me silly, but I don't believe in taking unnecessary risks.'

'I tend to agree with Meg,' said Sophie, 'I think you'd be daft to tempt fate, especially durin' the middle of a war.'

Peggy tilted her head from side to side as she weighed up the arguments. 'I suppose there can't be any harm in followin' an old superstition.'

Rory shrugged. 'Makes no odds to me. I'll go back to my base for the night.'

Isla eyed him gratefully. 'Are you sure you don't mind?'

He took his dish over to the sink. 'Not at all!'

Peggy smiled brightly. 'So now that we've got that sorted, what shall we do with our day? We've done presents already, and as we're not doing Christmas dinner till tomorrow there's not much to do by way of preparation yet, so the way I see it the day's ours to spend as we please.'

'How about we go for a walk through one of the parks?' Clive suggested. 'We can pick up a couple of boughs of holly whilst we're about it.'

'We could go to the cinema this afternoon,' Peggy suggested. 'There's always somethin' good showin' on Christmas Eve.'

It had been the best Christmas Eve Isla had ever experienced. After breakfast, they had started the day with a walk through Princes Park, where they collected several impressive boughs of holly, before going to Lyons for lunch, followed by a trip to the cinema to see *The Wizard of Oz*. As evening approached they had retired to the parlour to play blind man's buff, charades, and Meg's favourite, Pass the Slipper, which she was very good at.

'I swear that girl's got X-ray eyes,' Rory laughed as he stood on the threshold of Peggy's door, ready to go back to his base.

'I don't know how she does it,' Isla agreed. 'She really should have a go at the pools before she goes back to Portsmouth.'

Smoothing his fingers through her hair, he twinkled at her. 'This time tomorrow we'll be Mr and Mrs Dougal.'

'Isla Dougal,' she said experimentally. 'I'll still have the same initials!'

He kissed her softly before breaking off to gaze

lovingly at her. 'Good. I wouldn't want to change you too much.'

She wrapped her arms around his waist. 'I wish we could disappear to the land of Oz, where there's no war or poverty.'

'Just wicked witches!' chuckled Rory.

'Ah, but not any more! Not with Dorothy and Toto coming to the rescue.'

He winked at her. 'I'm proud of you for watching the whole thing through from beginnin' to end, what with the scary witch an' all.'

'*The Wizard of Oz* is nowhere near as scary as *The Hound of the Baskervilles*!' she cried.

He shook his head. 'I think I'd rather face a dog than a witch!'

Isla smiled, but said nothing. She had no intention of admitting how close she came to covering her eyes whenever the wicked witch of the west had appeared on screen. 'All jokin' aside, it would be lovely to get away for a bit, though,' she said. 'Like the time me and Peggy went to see Sophie in Scarborough.'

Rory coddled her in his arms. 'You're right. It would be wonderful to escape, even if just for a little while.' He kissed the top of her head. 'I wish I could take us somewhere on honeymoon, so that we could celebrate our wedding properly.'

She patted the lapel of his jacket as she gazed up into his eyes. 'There'll be plenty of time for things like honeymoons once the war's over, and whilst I know that we both think that won't be for some time yet, I get the sense that things are beginning to swing our way.'

He nodded. 'Me too.' Leaning down, he gave her one final kiss before whispering, 'I shall meet you at the altar tomorrow, soon-to-be Mrs Dougal!'

Chapter Eighteen

It was Christmas Day morning, and Isla was sitting in the bay window of the girls' bedroom whilst Sophie pinned her hair into place. Speaking through a mouthful of grips, Sophie glanced to the peaceful snow-paved streets outside.

'A white weddin' *and* a white Christmas. Who could ask for more?' she sighed happily.

'It certainly is beautiful,' agreed Isla. 'I just hope Rory doesn't face any problems gettin' to the church.'

'He'll have no bother,' said Sophie. 'They have to clear the runways and roads because, well . . .'

'. . . there's a war on,' all three girls chorused together.

'I hope Jerry keeps to the other side of the water,' said Isla. 'The last thing we need is the Luftwaffe turnin' up to ruin our big day.'

'He won't! Even the krauts give Christmas Day a miss,' said Meg, adding, 'Or at least they always have so far.'

'I hope you're right, cos Rory and I both feel that things are beginnin' to turn in our favour, and desperate people tend to do desperate things. What better way to break morale than a Christmas Day blitz?'

Meg lowered her gaze. 'I pray to God that you're wrong, because you're right that it would definitely go a long way to break morale.'

With the last of Isla's locks pinned into place, Sophie stood back to admire her work whilst Meg fetched the handheld mirror. 'I can see why you'd both think it a possibility,' Sophie told them, 'and of course anything's possible, but I think it works both ways. Whilst bombing innocent people can never be seen as acceptable, I think even the Nazis might find it a bitter pill to swallow if they were asked to do such a heinous thing on such a religious day. Don't forget, Hitler will be convincing his troops that the enemy are the devil incarnate, and he'll find that hard to do if he instructs his troops to bomb Britain on Christmas Day!'

Isla breathed a sigh of relief. 'I do hope you're right.'

'I *know* I am,' said Sophie with conviction. 'Now let's stop worryin' over things that might never happen and go downstairs for some brekker.'

Getting up from her seated position, Isla held a hand to her stomach. 'I don't know whether I'll be able to keep anythin' down. It feels as though my tummy's been invaded by butterflies!'

'You'll be fine!' said Meg, leading the way down the stairs. 'All brides get nervous before the wedding!'

'I bet the grooms do too,' said Sophie, walking into the kitchen.

'Probably more so,' chuckled Clive, as they saw Donny, Peggy and Clive already tucking into their porridge.

Getting to her feet, Peggy fetched three bowls from the dresser. 'I know you're probably not wantin' anythin' to eat, Isla, cos God only knows I wasn't exactly peckish on the mornin' of my weddin' either, but trust me on this, you'll feel a lot better for it.'

Agreeing reluctantly, Isla gazed down at the porridge which Peggy had put before her. 'What if he doesn't turn up?'

Her suggestion was immediately dismissed by everyone at the table. With Sophie voicing the thought on all their lips. 'That man would walk over hot coals for you, Isla Donahue, so you needn't worry about him not turnin' up!'

She made a guilty grimace. 'It might sound soft, but I don't like feelin' happy because I still expect things to go wrong if I am. And that's not because of anythin' you've done,' she added hastily, for her father's benefit, 'but solely because that's what happened the day Mammy went to hospital. We were so excited, concentratin' solely on when the baby would arrive and whether it would be a boy or a girl, it never occurred to any of us that somethin' might go wrong.'

Peggy laid a soothing hand on Isla's shoulder. 'But you can't go through life afraid of bein' happy for fear of what might happen.'

'I know, but it's sort of like a gut reaction.'

'It'll ease as time goes on,' said Donny, 'and today is just the start of that journey – trust me!'

Standing outside the entrance to the church, Isla looked to her father. A faint smile forming on her lips, she held out her hand to him. 'It's not the thought of gettin' married that's makin' me so nervous, but my bloomin' dream.'

Donny looked at her, his brow furrowing. 'What dream's this?'

'I had the most awful nightmare that you were goin' to give me away, but when I went inside the church Rory was marrying Mary because he thought she was Tammy, and you were engaged to my pal Kate who's the same age as me.'

He waved a dismissive hand. 'That's just pre-weddin' jitters. Quite normal, especially given everything that's happened over the past few months or so.'

But Isla was shaking her head. 'I didn't have the nightmare last night; it was nigh on two years ago.'

He stared at her, his jaw dropping slightly. 'You dreamed that I was engaged to one of your pals?'

She nodded. 'Funnily enough, Sophie and Meg were the first ones I told, and whilst they both dismissed my dream out of hand, look what's happened to you and Sophie.'

'Crikey! I don't suppose you ever have dreams about the pools, do you?'

Isla took a playful swipe at her father's arm. 'Dad! I'm bein' serious!'

'I know, luv, but even you must see that there's a deal of difference between your dream and reality. For a start, if your friend Kate's the same age as you then Sophie's at least eleven years older than her; second of all, Mary is no longer the enemy within; and third but foremost, you've met Tammy, who is happily married to another man, and even if she weren't Rory isn't interested in her. It's you he wants.'

'Thanks, Dad.'

'What for?'

'For makin' me see things as they truly are. You were always the joker of the family, but you've done a marvellous job of takin' over Mammy's role, because that's exactly the sort of thing Mammy would've told me. She'd have been so proud of you.'

He gave a short, doubtful laugh. 'I don't think so, somehow.'

'Oh, I know she would. She knew you'd change your mind, which is why she's been determined to help bring us back together. Plenty of people make poor choices and hasty decisions. I should know – I lived in a poorhouse full of them – but do you know what?'

He shook his head, too choked with emotion to speak.

'Not one of them had a father like you in their lives. You would *never* have turned me over for financial reasons, you'd have fought tooth and nail to put a roof over our heads, you only did what you did because you thought it was in my best interests, and after meetin' Theo I can see that you did the right thing at the time. And who knows what might've happened had you been successful in gettin' me out of there.'

'I'd like to think that we'd have lived happily ever after.'

'Maybe, but maybe not. After all, you'd have still been workin' down the docks when the Luftwaffe came. We know from Theo's Maggie that you only have to be in the wrong place at the wrong time for your whole life to change. Who's to say that wouldn't have happened to you, and that your goin' to sea was Mammy's way of keepin' you out of harm's way?'

'I'd not thought of that, but you're quite right. I worked night shifts as well as day, so it would've been the toss of a coin whether I'd be down the dock or not when the bomb fell.'

'Mammy knew what she was doin'.'

'She'd be so proud of the way you've turned out,' Donny told her, his eyes sparkling with love and affection. 'Her little girl all grown up and ready to become a mother herself one of these days.'

'I wish she was here to see me now.'

Donny looked up. 'How do you know she isn't?'

'I hope she is.' A faint smile twitched her lips. 'She was one in a million, wasn't she?'

'She always said that a mother's job was to protect her child from harm and keep the family together,' said Donny, 'and boy has she ever done that!'

The organist struck up the wedding march, indicating that it was time for them to enter the church.

Holding on to her father's hand tighter than ever before, she smiled up at him. 'I'm so glad you're here with me. It wouldn't be the same without you to give me away.'

He smiled back. 'I wouldn't have missed it for the world. Now let's get this show on the road!'

The wedding had been filled with love, tears and laughter, and Rory and Isla were currently in the middle of Peggy's kitchen dancing to a slow waltz being played on Clive's sister's record player.

'This has been the best day of my life,' sighed Isla as she rested her cheek against his chest.

'Mine too,' murmured Rory. 'And even though I wanted to marry you for the longest time, I'm glad we hung on until now because I think it really was the perfect wedding.'

Her eyes rested on the ring that now adorned her finger as they moved slowly around the small floor. 'Everythin' happens for a reason.'

'It definitely does. I used to think of life as bein' good or bad luck, but I don't think that way any more. I honestly believe that we have paths set out for us, and even though we're bound to deviate from those paths from time to time, we always end up back on the road that's right for us.'

'So what do you think that means for our future?'

'How do you mean?'

'Will we end up runnin' our own croft?'

He nodded. 'Do you know, I rather think we will, because I believe that life's what you make it!'

She drew a deep breath before letting it out slowly. 'It may have been a bumpy road gettin' here, but boy oh boy has it ever been worth the journey!'

'Definitely. Some folk take a lifetime to find the right lid for their pot, but we're the perfect fit.'

She smiled. 'The right lid for your pot, is that what I am?'

He grinned. 'You most certainly are.'

She chuckled softly. 'I guess I've been called worse.'

Leaning forward, his lips met hers, and she felt herself melt beneath his touch. 'I love you more than words can say, Isla Dougal, and for the record I'd go through it all again for you.'

'And I for you,' murmured Isla dreamily.

Epilogue

JULY 1950

Having spent the remainder of the war in Liverpool, Isla and Rory had chosen to remain in the city which had stolen their hearts and call it home. Rory had taken a job working as a mechanic in a garage, and Isla was doing dress alterations from their terraced house in Fazakerley.

Now, with the summer breeze bobbing the heads of the daisies, Isla thought back over all that had happened over the past five years, starting with the news that had shocked them all.

'She's runnin' a *what*?' Sophie had cried incredulously when Isla had relayed the information over a cup of tea.

'An orphanage,' said Isla, a smile wrinkling one side of her face.

Sophie had puffed her cheeks out. 'I know Mary's not the vile individual we thought her to be, but why is it that I keep gettin' visions of Harman?'

Isla had laughed softly. 'You're not the only one! But it's probably Harman who caused her to arrive at the decision she did. She wants to make sure that children have a safe place to come to, and by all accounts she's doin' a crackin' job!'

Isla's thoughts now turned to Meg and Kenny, who had married not long after Rory and herself. Having been amongst the first to be demobbed, they had decided to stay on in Portsmouth, where they had started their own family-run bakery.

'The premises are only small, but they're big enough for now,' Meg had told Isla over the telephone.

'And what role will you play?' Isla had asked her pal. 'Is Kenny goin' to teach you how to bake?'

Meg had laughed. 'He was eager to give it a go, but as we cannae afford to burn all our stock to a crisp I thought it better if I remained out front sellin' all his lovely buns, baps and cakes.'

Isla gave an envious groan. 'I'd love to work in a bakery, but I know I wouldn't be able to resist all those wonderful pastries!'

Meg had patted her tummy. 'It's tough goin', what with my being chief taster an' all.'

'Oh, hell on earth, I bet!'

'It is!' chuckled Meg. 'Cos unless I want to be bustin' out of my frocks I can only take a small bite, and sayin' no has never been a strong point of mine when it comes to food!'

'Well, Rory and I will insist on bein' your first customers,' said Isla loyally. 'You can use us as your guinea pigs.'

'Sophie and Donny have already volunteered!'

'I bet they have!' Isla had said with tongue-in-cheek cynicism. 'Dad's always been a devil when it comes to sweet treats! When do you think you'll be ready to open?'

'A couple of weeks yet, so plenty of time to get everythin' shipshape. Talkin' of ships, when was the last time you spoke to Sophie?'

'A couple of weeks ago,' said Isla, before quickly correcting herself. 'Actually, I spoke to my dad a couple of weeks ago, but he filled me in on what's what.'

'And?' said Meg. 'Are they any closer to knowin' when she's goin' to be demobbed?'

'The Wrens have asked her if she would like to stay on for another six months, and as Dad's at sea she's agreed. However, they have made some decisions about the future.'

Meg had been on tenterhooks. 'And?'

'They're goin' to set up home here in Liverpool, and Dad's makin' enquiries into what's required to start your own taxi firm—'

She was cut short as Meg squealed with excitement. 'I *knew* he'd make sure Sophie's talents didn't go to waste!'

'And not just Sophie's,' said Isla proudly. 'They're goin' to employ ex-service female drivers who'll be paid the same wages as the men! Which is especially good news for Tammy, who's already agreed to be one of their drivers what with her and Cecil also settin' up home in Liverpool.'

Meg had crowed with delight. 'Oh, don't I just hope others follow their example! Talk about puttin' up two fingers to the powers that be!'

'Aren't they just?' Isla agreed. 'But there again, so are you and Kenny, because I dare say he won't be payin' you a pittance?'

'No he will not!' said Meg forcibly. 'He wouldn't dream of it, and not just because of the earache but because he values my talents.'

'Is that what they're callin' them these days?'

'Don't be cheeky! You know full well that he was referrin' to my work ethics.' There came an audible pause before Meg continued, 'It's still early days, and I really shouldn't be sayin' anythin' yet, but—'

Isla gasped. 'You're havin' a baby!'

There was an appreciable pause before Meg spoke again. 'How on *earth* could you possibly have known that?'

'Because I know you!' said Isla. 'Congratulations, Meg, that's marvellous news. You're goin' to make a wonderful mother!'

'Thanks, Isla. I hope you're right.'

'I *know* I'm right.'

'I'm not quite three months yet, which is why we're still keepin' it hush-hush, but you can tell Rory, obviously, and Sophie and Peggy as well, of course.' She paused for a moment, and when she spoke again her tone was sombre. 'Talkin' of Peggy, how's she shapin' up?'

Isla rubbed her fingers across her forehead, before

letting out a broken sigh. 'Not good. Poor Clive's not much better.'

'I don't know why, but I always thought her sons would return unscathed,' said Meg. 'I certainly didn't imagine for one minute that any of them wouldn't come home at all.'

'Me neither,' said Isla. Having been with Peggy when she received the dreaded telegram, Isla fell silent as her mind replayed the awful moment. They'd been standing in the parlour, with Peggy running her fingers along the top of the telegram.

'It could be anything,' she had told Isla, although her tone was hollow.

Keen to reassure her friend, Isla had agreed. 'You're right, but you won't know unless you open it, and the longer you stand there the more torturous you're makin' it for yourself, especially if it's somethin' simple.' She had hesitated, trying to come up with an example. 'For all we know, they might be comin' home on the next wave.'

'But what if they're not,' Peggy had said, her eyes beginning to brim with tears.

Isla had stepped forward. 'Then waitin' won't change the outcome, but it will prolong the agony.'

She had crossed her fingers behind her back as Peggy slit the telegram open and read the short message inside. Half falling, half sitting into the kitchen chair, Peggy had wept inconsolably as Isla did her best to comfort her.

Now, as Isla banished the hateful memory from her mind, she cleared her throat. 'Gregory, Richard and

Robert will be comin' home over the next few months, which I know will be a great comfort to Peggy, but Ralph . . .'

'Did they ever . . .' Meg left the question hanging, unable to complete the sentence.

'Find his body? No. But they are certain that he was in the tank when it . . .' She too stopped speaking.

The information that had been given to Peggy hadn't said much other than that Ralph had been in a tank when it came under anti-tank fire from German troops just hours before peace had been declared. The fact that her son had come so close to making it out of the war along with his three brothers had only added to her grief.

As part of Peggy's family the girls felt the blow keenly, and did everything they could to console her. Clive had been a pillar of strength, because both Peggy and Isla knew that his urge was to return to the sea where he could lose himself in his grief, but he had stuck by Peggy, helping her through the pain until a time came when she could cope.

'I told him to go,' Peggy had told Isla when she had called by for her daily cuppa. 'I could see the sea was callin' him and it was unfair of me to keep him here when I knew he needed to be out there. He never fares well on dry land as it is.'

'What was his reaction?'

'Relief,' said Peggy simply. 'It practically engulfed him.' She took Isla by the hand. 'You and I both know that it's not a question of abandonment, but a need to clear the mind so that you can heal. I *wish* I had such an escape, but I'm tied to the land and to the house that saw Ralph into the world.'

'Why don't you get away for a bit?' Isla suggested. 'I could come with you if you liked?'

But Peggy had shaken her head. 'I need to be here, where I feel closest to him.' She shrugged. 'I suppose in truth I don't want to run away. I just want him back.'

'I understand,' murmured Isla. 'It was one of the worst parts about bein' in the poorhouse. Not only had I lost my family, but our home, which was filled to the rafters with precious memories. It would've given me some comfort had I been allowed to keep Mammy's locket, but even that was taken away from me, though I did get it back in the end.'

So deep in her thoughts was she that Isla didn't hear the car pull up outside the church. It was only the sound of car doors slamming that brought her back to the present. She smiled as Sophie approached, her arms open to take Isla in a warm embrace.

'You were lookin' very thoughtful just now,' she said. 'Is everything all right?'

Isla held up her hand to shade her eyes from the sun. 'Just reminiscin' over times gone by, the good and the bad.'

Sophie glanced towards the church. 'If you're worried that havin' the christenin' in the same church as Ralph's memorial might bring back bad memories for Peggy and Clive, then don't be. Peggy comes here every day, Isla.'

'It did cross my mind until I reminded myself that

Peggy comes here to feel closer to Ralph.' She looked up to see her father making his way over from the car. 'Hello, Dad.'

Donny greeted his daughter with a peck on the cheek. 'Hello, luv. Where's Agnes?'

Isla gestured towards Rory, who was deep in conversation with the vicar. 'With her father.'

'Ooo! Would you mind awfully if I pop over and say hello?' Sophie asked, 'I promise not to disturb her if she's sleepin'.'

Isla smiled. 'Go on then, although I'm sure she'll wake up at the most inappropriate moment no matter how careful we all are.'

Donny shrugged as Sophie set off. 'No point in worryin' about it. That's babies for you! And if she's anythin' like her mammy she'll smile and gurgle right up to the point when the vicar dips her head in the font, upon which she'll let the world know exactly how she feels!'

Isla giggled softly. 'Was I really that bad?'

'All babbies are,' said Donny, 'and who can blame them? I wouldn't want some bugger to pour icy cold water over my noggin' either.'

Isla looked across to Sophie, who was cooing over the baby. 'She would've made a brilliant mother.'

He dropped his gaze, before bringing it back up to meet Isla's. 'I know, but Dr Hillman said some women just aren't able to have children. I did bring up the subject of adoption, but she said she's happy as she is.'

Seeing the way Sophie continued to cuddle the

baby, Isla raised an uncertain brow. 'And do you believe that?'

'I think havin' Agnes to love and fuss over makes a lot of difference. Same goes for Meg and Kenny's two. I know she doesn't get to see them as often, but she adores spoilin' them rotten when she does.' Seeing a familiar car pull up, he waved a greeting. 'I bet you never thought you'd see the day you'd welcome Tammy to your daughter's christening.'

She blew out her cheeks. 'You're right there! I dreaded the thought of our paths even crossin' and yet here we are all these years later as close as sisters.'

'Circumstance,' said Donny. 'However, it does make we wonder if things would've been different had her father not tried to commit murder that night.'

She arched her eyebrows slowly. 'How do you mean?'

Seeing the startled look on his daughter's face, Donny laughed softly. 'I don't mean between her and Rory! I mean how you'd feel towards Tammy. After all, the circumstances that threw the two of you together creates a natural bond in itself. Had that not happened, your first meeting – if indeed you ever had met – would have been very different indeed and you'd most probably have had your guard up still.'

Isla fell into contemplation. If she'd met Tammy through the normal turn of events her father was right: she would have had her guard up. She'd certainly not have looked upon Tammy in a kindred or sympathetic spirit. 'Which convinces me more than ever that Mammy had a part to play in that too!' she said. 'After all, we only met because the trains were all to cock.'

By now Tammy, Cecil, Grace and Archie had exited the car along with Tammy and Cecil's son Alby, all of whom were beginning to make their way towards Isla and Donny. Being the first to embrace Isla, Tammy said a quick hello before asking, 'How's the lady of the hour?'

'Havin' cuddles,' said Isla, indicating Sophie, who was still coddling Agnes. 'I just hope she behaves herself durin' the ceremony.'

Grace waved a hand dismissively. 'She'll take it in her stride, just like her mammy, you wait and see.'

Cecil glanced up at the cloudless sky. 'You certainly picked a beautiful day for it.'

'A bit like it was on your weddin' day,' Isla said, looking at Grace.

'God was certainly smilin' on us that day,' said Archie, looping an arm over his wife's shoulders.

Seeing that Isla was still looking nervous, Grace laid a reassuring hand on her arm. 'Don't worry. Nothin' can go wrong with you at the helm.'

Isla gave a small, embarrassed smile. She knew that they still felt indebted to her for coming to Tammy's rescue, even though she had told them many times over the years that it wasn't necessary.

'Not necessary?' Grace had gasped as they chatted during the reception on her wedding day. 'But for you my daughter would be at the bottom of the Mersey, and I'd probably be with her.'

'She's right there,' Archie had agreed.

'And Dennis would be sittin' pretty knowin' he'd got away with two murders,' said Cecil.

'So I for one shan't stop showin' my gratitude until there's not a breath left in my body!' said Grace firmly.

'Me neither,' said Archie. He had glanced meaningfully at the wedding ring that encircled Grace's finger. 'None of this would be happenin' if it weren't for you.'

'Aye, and Cecil and I wouldn't be havin' a family,' said Tammy as she laid a hand on her bulbous belly.

'But you'd all have done the same in my position,' Isla had protested.

'Maybe so, but that doesn't change a thing. As far as we're concerned you're heaven sent.'

'She certainly has someone in heaven watchin' over her,' Rory had said as he slipped his arm around his wife's waist. 'There's no denyin' that.'

'Your mammy,' said Grace, her lip trembling a little.

Isla had blinked back the tears as she nodded in agreement. 'If there's anyone to thank it's her.'

Coming back to the present, she squeezed Tammy's hand. 'I hope Agnes takes a leaf out of Alby's book, cos he slept right through his christening!'

'Probably because he's a boy,' chuckled Grace. 'Too lazy to kick up a fuss.'

Donny grimaced. 'I wish I could argue to the contrary, but . . .'

'Nail on head,' Cecil agreed.

Isla smiled. 'I seem to remember Peggy sayin' somethin' similar about her sons' christenings.'

Donny jerked his head to Peggy and Clive, who were walking up through the church grounds. 'Talking of whom . . .' There was a general welcoming of the new arrivals before Tammy and the others excused themselves, leaving Peggy and Clive to chat with Isla and her father.

'Where's our special little girl?' asked Peggy, before spying Rory and the baby. 'Ahh! I see she's with her daddy.'

'I was worried my nerves might transfer to her,' confessed Isla, 'so Rory's takin' care of her until after the christenin'.'

'Good ole Rory,' said Peggy. She glanced around them. 'Any sign of Meg, Kenny and the kiddies?'

Isla checked her watch. 'Not yet, and I must say I'm beginnin' to worry, because they're cuttin' it a bit fine!'

'That's the problem with ownin' your own business,' Donny said knowledgeably, 'you cannae just take off whenever the fancy takes you.'

'And especially not when you run your own bakery,' said Isla. She held out a hand to Peggy. 'I take it you've been to Ralph's memorial?'

Peggy nodded solemnly, before breaking into a smile. 'I was tellin' him how good it is to have somethin' to celebrate for once.'

'Agnes's christening?'

'Of course! It's always lovely to welcome a new life into the world, but even more so now that the war's over. It signals the start of a new generation, who will hopefully live in a world without war.'

'I've never looked at it that way before, but you're right. It's the dawn of a new world.' Seeing Rory signal that they were ready to go in, Isla grimaced. 'We cannae go in. Meg's not here yet!'

'I'll go and see if I can delay things,' said Donny, but just then, to Isla's relief, Kenny and Meg's car pulled through the gated entrance of the church driveway. Barely waiting for Kenny to apply the brake, Meg was already apologising as she got out of the car. 'Come on, boys!' she cried, hurrying over to join the small group. 'I'm so sorry, Isla. We're not too late, are we?'

Isla hugged her friend. 'Just about to go in.'

Raising her eyes to the heavens, Meg offered up a small prayer of thanks before giving Isla a cynical look. 'Never again!' she said firmly. 'I've told Kenny we're to hire proper staff so that we can have some time off! We was bakin' through the night just so that we could be here on time, and quite frankly it's not much fun drivin' all that way with someone who can barely keep his eyes open! In future we'll come down the night before so that we don't have to dice with death in order to make it on time.'

Grinning apologetically, Kenny tried to assure everyone that Meg was exaggerating, but their boys' animated imitation of their mother squealing as their father swerved to avoid a line of parked cars proved her to be telling the truth.

'We work harder now than we did when we were in the services,' said Meg as she hooked her arm through Isla's, 'and that's sayin' something!'

'I feel guilty now,' said Isla. 'If I'd known . . .'

'Not your fault!' Meg scolded, before quickly adding 'Mind you, it's not exactly Kenny's fault either. Payin' someone else to help with the bakin' will really stretch our budget, but we have to do somethin', cos as it is he's as good as chained to the stove!'

Donny laughed out loud. 'Most women complain it's vice versa!'

Lowering their voices as they entered the church, Isla and Donny made their way to the front where Sophie and Rory were waiting for them. Smiling at his wife, Rory crossed his fingers as the vicar began.

The christening had gone without a hitch, and everyone had gathered in the Adelphi hotel for a spot of lunch.

'Peggy's pleased as punch to be godmother,' said Sophie, as she and Isla watched Peggy introducing the staff to her goddaughter.

'I wanted to ask if you'd be her godmother, but really you're more like a grandmother,' Isla said, looking over to see Donny who was in deep conversation with Clive.

'Good, cos as far as I'm concerned that's exactly what I am!' said Sophie. She cast a thoughtful eye around the room in general as Meg came over to join them.

'Penny for them?'

'Just thinkin' how far we've come,' said Sophie. 'I sometimes wish I could go back to the young girls who planned to escape Coxhill, just so that I could tell them everything was going to turn out all right.'

'Better than all right,' said Isla.

'But do you think that we'd have believed it?' mused Meg. 'I wanted to get out of that place more than anything in the world, but I never thought that I'd end up owning a business along with my husband!'

'I knew I'd get out,' said Isla, 'but not for one minute did I believe that Rory and I would end up married, never mind havin' a daughter of our own!'

Sophie jerked her head to Rory, who was making his way towards them. 'Talkin' of whom . . .'

Slipping his arm around Isla's shoulders, he beamed round at them. 'How do we think the christening went?'

'Wonderful,' said Sophie.

Meg agreed. 'She was a little angel, which is amazing considerin' the near miss we had.'

Isla knew that Meg was referring to the moment the vicar had sneezed, causing Agnes to practically jump out of Isla's arms.

'She's got the heart of a lion,' said Rory. 'Just like her mammy!'

'Not just her mammy, but her granny too,' said Isla, who was still smiling. 'That's why we named her Agnes, cos she has my mammy's spirit.'

'She has that,' agreed Meg. 'I nearly widdled meself, and I'm a woman grown!'

They all fell about laughing at Meg's honesty. 'Always there to say it as it is,' chuckled Sophie. She waved to Donny, who was encouraging her to join him in a bid to get away from the vicar. 'If you'll excuse me, it looks as though I'm needed.'

As Sophie went off to save Donny, Tammy and Cecil came over to say their goodbyes.

'So soon?' said Isla. 'We've hardly had a chance to speak.'

'I know, but Gina's invited us to theirs for the week, and seein' as Mam's agreed to have Alby, we thought we'd jump at the chance.'

Cecil stretched his arms above his head in an exaggerated fashion. 'Freedom!'

'I believe France is lovely at this time of year,' said Rory enviously.

'Accordin' to Gina, France is lovely at any time of year.'

'How did they end up overseas?' Isla asked. 'I thought he was an accountant or somethin' of that nature?'

'He was – is, even,' said Tammy. 'He got a job workin' for a British firm in France not long after the war, and as he's fluent in the language they thought it too good an opportunity to miss.'

Meg smiled as one of her boys approached, a posy of flowers clutched between his chubby fingers. 'For me?' she cooed. 'Where did you get these from?'

'Off a stone outside the church,' said her son proudly.

Meg's jaw dropped. 'You got these from somebody's *grave*?'

'Dunno . . .' he began, before being cut off by his

mother's shriek as she noticed her other son trying to poke his finger into the christening cake.

'Give me strength!' Meg cried, before quickly excusing herself so that she could put a stop to his antics.

'A week in France is just what's needed,' chuckled Cecil as he watched Grace grab hold of Alby's shoulder before he could join Meg's son in his cake-tasting efforts.

Tammy pulled a guilty grimace. 'I hate to rush off, but let's get out of here before Mam changes her mind!' Laughing, they made their goodbyes before hurrying away.

Rory smiled as he watched Meg expertly field her son away from the cake. 'Do you know, I don't think I've ever been so happy in my entire life.'

Isla smiled. 'Me neither. I hope Agnes has as much happiness in her life as we do.'

'She will,' he said with certainty. 'We'll make sure of it.'

She glanced up at the underside of her chin. 'I love you, Rory Dougal.'

Leaning in to kiss his wife, Rory smiled. 'To the moon and back?'

She let her lips meet his. 'Aye, to the moon and back!'

THE END

Read on for an extract from Katie Flynn's new novel, *The Mersey Queen* . . .

The Mersey Queen

Prologue

10ᵀᴴ APRIL 1919

Her cheeks wet from crying, Nell Tanner hooked her arm through her mother's as they watched the body of her father, Herbert, being lowered into the unmarked grave.

'Hardly befitting of a war hero,' she sniffled, dabbing her eyes with her handkerchief.

'And left to me he'd have had the grandest spot in the cemetery, but things like that cost money, which we don't have,' her mother, Martha, murmured quietly.

Nell's eyes darted towards the gravedigger, who was waiting for them to leave so that he could get on with the work at hand. Being local to their community, she had no doubt that he'd have been privy to the rumours that surrounded her father. 'They say as to how them that survived are the lucky ones, but those who say that know nothin', in my opinion.'

Martha saw the gravedigger's jaw twitch, acknowledgement that he had heard her daughter's words, yet he said nothing, a clear indication in Martha's mind that he disagreed with Nell's statement. Her eyes narrowing, she gave her daughter's arm a gentle squeeze. 'C'mon queen, it's time we were off.'

Nell cast a scathing glance towards the gravedigger, who was keeping his head lowered as if he was unaware of their presence. *It was folk like him that drove Dad to go to war in the first place*, she thought bitterly. *But for them my father would've stuck to his beliefs and he'd still be alive today.* She continued to glare at the gravedigger, who made the mistake of breathing a heavy sigh. She stiffened. How dare he act as though she were boring him? Taking a step towards him, she spoke through gritted teeth. 'They say you should walk a mile in another man's shoes before you judge him. Cos it's all too easy to cast aspersions when you're sat at home in front of the fire, with a warm cup of cocoa and a copy of the *Echo*.' She was pleased to see that the gravedigger's cheeks whiten as her words washed over him, but leaning up from the handle of his shovel he looked her square in the eye.

'I may've been too old to do me bit this time, but that never stopped me in the past!'

'Then you of all people should know the effect that war has on folk,' said Nell grimly. 'Especially men like my father,' she added, and watched his eyes glaze over, suggesting that her thoughts were no longer of any interest to him.

'Don't waste your breath, queen,' murmured Martha, taking her arm to walk her away.

'You'd think I'd have learned by now,' said Nell bitterly.

'Learned?'

'That there's none so blind as those who will not see. He knows I'm right, he just doesn't want to admit it.'

'Or mebbe he wants to leave his head in the sand, and if he can manage to get through each day by doin' that then more power to him. It's better than the alternative – nobody wants that.'

The gravedigger watched the two women until they were out of sight before ramming his spade into the loose earth. Why didn't people just leave the past where it belonged, that's what he'd like to know. *It never does no one any good rakin' over what's dead and buried*, he thought bitterly as he proceeded to shovel the earth over the hemp-wrapped body of Herbert Tanner. *Relivin' the past is unhealthy. It's . . .* Before he could stop himself, he found his thoughts wandering back to the war of 1888 and the horrors he had witnessed. Doubling his efforts to turn his thoughts back to the present, he whistled a tuneless melody in an attempt to drown out the screams that still echoed in his ears.

Dear Reader,

When I started writing *The Winter Bride*, I had no idea of the ending. It was only when Tammy and Isla finally met one another that I started to envisage how this trilogy would end. Writing *The Winter Bride* has been an emotional experience, to say the least. Saying goodbye to characters I have grown so fond of is never easy. But I'm delighted with where Tammy, Cecil, Isla and Rory have ended up and, even though it's sad to bid them all farewell, it's time for me to move on to pastures new.

The Mersey Queen is the first book in my next series, and for the first time I've decided to travel back to 1914, when the world was a far darker place. I love this period, and the people in it, and without giving away too many spoilers, you know that your story has got legs when it opens with a young girl and her mother being evicted from their family home on the day of her father's funeral. I cannot wait for you all to meet Nell and Martha Tanner, and to watch them tackle the many trials that came with living in the early twentieth century.

Before I sign off, I want to wish you all a very Merry Christmas for when it comes. I can't quite believe it is that time of year again, but we are starting to gear up for the festive season already in our house and I, for one, am looking forward to some cosy evenings by the fireside with lots of good food and even better company.

Until next time!

Much love,
Holly Flynn xx

THE FIRST IN A BRAND NEW TRILOGY...

DISCOVER THE ROSE QUEEN SERIES

FROM THE UK'S NO. 1 BESTSELLING WWII SAGA AUTHOR

Katie Flynn

LOVED BY 4 MILLION READERS

DISCOVER THE WHITE CHRISTMAS SERIES

FROM THE UK'S NO. 1 BESTSELLING WWII SAGA AUTHOR

Katie Flynn

LOVED BY 4 MILLION READERS

DISCOVER THE LIVERPOOL SISTERS SERIES

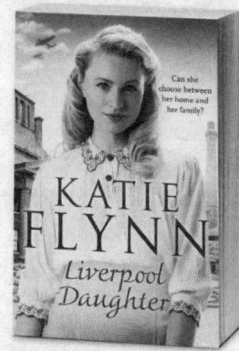  

FROM THE UK'S NO. 1 BESTSELLING WWII SAGA AUTHOR

Katie Flynn

Katie Flynn

If you want to continue to hear from the
Flynn family, and to receive the latest news about
new Katie Flynn books and competitions,
sign up to the Katie Flynn newsletter.

Join today by visiting
www.penguin.co.uk/katieflynnnewsletter

Find Katie Flynn on Facebook
www.facebook.com/katieflynn458

SIGN UP TO OUR SAGA NEWSLETTER

Penny Street

The home of heart-warming reads

Welcome to **Penny Street**, your number **one stop for emotional and heartfelt historical reads**. Meet casts of characters you'll never forget, memories you'll treasure as your own, and places that will forever stay with you long after the last page.

Join our online **community** bringing you the latest book deals, competitions and new saga series releases.

You can also find extra content, talk to your favourite authors and share your discoveries with other saga fans on Facebook.

Join today by visiting
www.penguin.co.uk/pennystreet

Follow us on Facebook
www.facebook.com/welcometopennystreet/

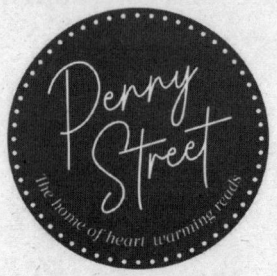